The
Glasnost Conspiracy

The
Glasnost Conspiracy

B. Jay Reich

THE GLASNOST CONSPIRACY

This book is written to provide information and motivation to readers. Its purpose is not to render any type of psychological, legal, or professional advice of any kind. The content is the sole opinion and expression of the author, and not necessarily that of the publisher.

Printed in the United States of America.

ISBN   978-1-953150-20-2   (Paperback)
ISBN   978-1-953150-21-9   (Digital)

Lettra Press books may be ordered through booksellers or by contacting:

Lettra Press LLC
30 N Gould St. Suite 4753
Sheridan, WY 82801, USA
1 303-586-1431 | info@lettrapress.com
www.lettrapress.com

Dear reader:

This story was crafted between 1992 and 1994. Unfortunately, from my standpoint (although fine for world peace), the cold war was over and we and Russia and its newly freed republics were engaged in a love affair known as "glasnost". For years, I grew up with the belief that the Soviet Union was not to be trusted. I could never quite shake this attitude, even as those more optimistic than I proclaimed that Russia was no longer a threat. However, that was not the time to introduce a "cold war" novel. Who would have published it—or read it? My sense is that now, with Putin's strong-arm tactics reminiscent of earlier days of Soviet aggression, the timing is right for my long overdue manuscript. I hope that you agree.

Sincerely,
B. J. Reich

Chapter 1

Arnie Rosen pushed aside a thick stack of highlighted National Security Agency transcripts, tipping a silver-framed picture near his phone. As he replaced it, he paused to study the three sparkling faces so crinkly with delight. He could almost hear yesterday's laughter as there were burgers spitting on the Weber and flies diving at the potato salad. A college buddy, Mark Hickey, down on business from New York, loosening up after a couple of beers and nostalgic laughter over Dottie Benedict and her major: screwing every Pi Lambda Phi on campus. Jonathon—a five-year-old in seventh heaven—getting tossed shrieking into the pool, only to come back for "just one more." Eleanor, a terribly precocious nine-year-old, squealing, "Oh, Daddy, shut up!" when he suggested that she and "the Hicker" made a cute couple. Barbara's rich body stretched on the warm concrete, her eyelids fluttering between watchfulness of Jonathon and midafternoon dozing …

How would what he was about to do change the lives of his family?

Rosen blew out a gust of air, forcing back apprehension regarding tomorrow's meeting with Hollings. Then he reached down to unlock the large bottom drawer of his desk.

Holy Christ—it was gone! Rosen scattered loose transcripts, directories of local and European KGB embassy staffers, and packets of double-rubber-banded satellite printouts, searching for the plain manila file. He always kept it locked in here. He dug into the other drawers, knowing it was pointless yet unwilling to concede. Perspiration, chilled by the highly efficient air-conditioning, trickled under his collar as he plowed through years of material accumulated as an analyst for the CIA. A few frantic moments more and he gave up. It just wasn't there!

Exhaling raggedly, Arnie Rosen squeaked back in his thin-armed swivel chair, staring vacantly at acres of car-splotched parking lot ringed by lushly foliated trees, Langley's shield against the world's curious eyes.

Nearby, grass steamed in relentless August heat. The view, normally pleasing, gave him no reassurance.

There was no getting around it, no other explanation. Someone had stolen the list of calls made last Tuesday from a public phone at Langley Exxon, a mile away. It was evidence to have been added to his main file documenting the actions of Charles Van Damme over the past two years—evidence categorically proving that the lean, aristocratic Van Damme compromised a cell of Czechoslovakian nationals helping dissidents escape into Austria and, worse yet, would soon hand over specifications for the United States' most advanced spy satellite to the KGB. Now, only a day away from presenting his evidence to counterintelligence, after checking every source at his disposal to satisfy himself that Van Damme's influence didn't reach that high, Rosen had lost some of his proof. A small part, granted, but how much did you need when you accused the chief of the European Division of espionage?

Rosen leaned forward, elbows on desk, raking long fingers through curly dirty blond hair, working his fingertips into the nape of his neck, releasing a warm rush of blood into the cramped muscles. Suddenly, his head snapped upward, face agape. Grabbing for the phone, he punched in his home number. He heard a cheerful voice: "You have reached a number that is inoperative or no longer in service. Please hang up and—" He quickly disconnected and aimed more carefully at the elusive buttons. "God!" The strongbox with the master file: travel itineraries, pictures, expense vouchers—the hard evidence against Van Damme—was in the den. It was hidden in the closet, past neatly tied stacks of *National Geographic* and beneath a host of Eleanor's discarded pandas, monkeys, and Raggedy Annes.

How could anyone know what Rosen's innocuous little file contained? He even brought whatever he'd collected in it home every night, just to be safe. Leaving the list of calls was his first mistake. *You miserable, stupid ...* He *had* to get hold of Barbara! My God, did Van Damme suspect? The receiver rattled maddeningly as his home phone rang seven miles to the east.

*   *   *

Just before the phone rang at 3016 Foxhall Road—a relatively modest home by DC's exclusive Wesley Heights standards but sharing the deep-set privacy of its more costly neighbors—the front doorbell chimed, quite a dilemma for Jonathon Rosen. He had been warned *never* to answer the front door alone, but Mom was showering and Eleanor had told him to stay out of her room or she would kill him; on top of that, he was anxious to get back to the TV to see if Wile E. Coyote's mail-order traps would finally snag Road Runner. Then the hall phone started ringing. Overwhelmed, Jonathon opted for the door. After all, that was *real* people, not just voices coming out of a plastic thing.

Two large men stood in front of him. Nothing unusual; to Jonathon, all men were large. But it was unusual that they were playing with guns, slipping them from their jackets and pointing them as they wedged their big shoulders through the door. From off to his right, he heard a reassuring "beep, beep." Road Runner had outsmarted old Wile E. again. Jonathon's tiny body catapulted across the room from the *fffft* of a .38-caliber bullet driving into his throat.

The two men closed the front door soundlessly, moving farther into the foyer. The shooter, six-three with dull gray eyes and a pointed jaw, nudged the little sprawl of arms and legs with the toe of his shoe, staring indifferently as Jonathon flopped over.

Shrill ringing continued. The phone on a black table to the right was a chrome and plastic replica of the long-necked models of the thirties. Both men stared intently at the instrument. A sudden interruption of the insistent bells could mean that someone had lifted a receiver in another room. It clattered on. Turning to his shorter, stockier companion, the shooter jerked his head toward the living room.

Carefully avoiding the blood pooling across the tiled floor, they flattened themselves on opposite sides of the arched entry and peered inside, silenced weapons at shoulder height. Satisfied that the room was empty, they repeated the procedure for the rest of the downstairs, ending back in the foyer.

Stepping over the spreading red puddle was becoming difficult, but they managed, deftly leaping to the stairs behind. They tiptoed upward, Stocky leading.

*　　*　　*

Although still early, afternoon commuters already clogged lanes as Rosen jockeyed his Camaro in and out of traffic along George Washington Memorial Parkway. He was oblivious to the cacophony of honks and to fists thrusting from open windows. The entrance to Route 123 was coming up fast. Buffeted by a nonstop chorus of horns, Rosen finessed the Camaro across the right lane, barely catching the curved ramp at the expense of a frantically lurching maroon Cadillac; skidding up the shoulder in a spray of grass and gravel; straightening the fishtailing vehicle in time to run the yield sign at the top.

His frenzy increased. At this point, 123 was no more than a single-lane country road whose sudden curves looped precariously through dense underbrush and the unforgiving trunks of massive trees. An unbroken double yellow line tracked its entire length. Unheeding, Rosen passed a semi bearing the logo friendly movers; cut tightly back into the truck's lane, eliciting a monstrous honk from the not-so-friendly driver; slid out past a cocoa Mercedes occupied by an attractive black couple who simultaneously flashed him manicured fingers; accelerated around a beaten-up Ford wagon overflowing with hair-pulling, punching kids whose mother flailed at them with her free hand; cutting back seconds before three terrified faces in a blue VW van hurtled by. The van driver's hand remained frozen to his horn long after.

*   *   *

Eleanor sprawled in a tangle of heart-decorated sheets and pillows. Her lanky legs rose and fell in time to Def Leppard pounding through her Walkman. The door, sporting a full-length glossy of Johnny Depp, crept open. Yanking out the earphones, Eleanor leapt off her bed, itching to trash Jonathon for violating her sanctuary. Stocky's hand shot through the opening choking off her tirade. Powerful fingers crushed her throat, shaking her viciously until her thin neck snapped, before flinging her back into the room like discarded newspaper.

*   *   *

The Potomac, limply slipping around the huge rust rocks that pierced its surface as if by saving its energy it could survive the ferocious afternoon heat, flashed beneath Chain Bridge. Soon a broad swatch of rhythmically swaying treetops and a symmetrical bright ribbon of water replaced it. Rosen jabbed his brakes for the sharp right onto Canal Road.

*   *   *

Barbara's not-so-bad rendition of "Evergreen" scaled up to a scream as they yanked open the shower curtain. Both men watched mirthlessly as her eyes darted for a way out. Her fingers quivered like insect antennas. They took a moment to appreciate—after all, she was a beautiful woman—and then shot her three times, slamming her against the wet tile. Dribbling blood, like wine from a cracked bottle, blended with falling water and spiraled into the tub. Her body slid downward, wet flesh squeaking against porcelain, buttocks blocking the drain, forcing the reddening solution to swirl between her thighs and eventually up against her breasts.

*　　*　　*

How could things change so fast? You went along years and years with a fairly stable existence—boring sometimes but predictable—and then *wham!* In one day you were screaming back through a fire wall of traffic to save it all! It seemed impossible.

The sound of that monotonous ringing echoed repeatedly in Rosen's ears. They were supposed to be home. Tonight they were all going to Cousin Barry's birthday celebration, and the kids would be up late. They were supposed to be resting this afternoon. How long he had waited, hoping someone would pick up so he could yell, "Get out of the house! Run! Go to your mother's, to your cousin's … anywhere!" He'd never gotten the chance. All he had gotten was that maddening ringing.

*　　*　　*

Within ten minutes, they found the flimsy metal box—no problem for professionals like Stevenson and Craig—and removed the file. They slipped it into a zippered plastic folder that Craig, the taller of the two, had brought. Passing through the foyer, they sidestepped Jonathon for the last time, opened the door, and strode casually toward the street.

Inside, television cartoons and splattering water competed in what was otherwise stillness.

*　　*　　*

"Oh God!" He was talking out loud now, praying as he swung left onto Foxhall, nearly clipping Ralph Mordanski's silver Volvo. "Please let them be all right! Please let them be away shopping, or playing in the park, or even at the emergency room because little John fell and split his lip. *Anything.* Let them laugh at me because I look so worried. Let them tell me how ridiculous I've been. *Please.*"

Roaring into the driveway, Rosen fixated on the front door. Barbara's runt geranium, a bedraggled plant that came back each season with fewer leaves and barely enough petals for identification, sprawled against their wrought iron railing. The house—longtime friend at the end of not-so-good days—looked cold and forbidding, not like *his* house at all. He no longer felt a part of it, nor it of him. His stomach churned as he flung open the Camaro's door and sprinted for the steps.

Rosen scraped the key back and forth but kept missing the lock. He steadied his hand with the other hand when the door slid a few inches on its own. His stomach convulsed, forcing sour bile into his throat. Barbara *never* left the door unlocked, even before those child-kidnapping stories had filled the airwaves. And the kids knew better.

For an instant, Rosen froze, unable to cross the same doorway he'd joyously entered thousands of times before. Suddenly, he burst through, his already strained features contorted beyond recognition. With an animal moan, Rosen rushed toward the little pile at the far side of the foyer, skidding on the semidry ooze, crashing into the banister. He lay there gulping air. Blood from a gash on his forehead blinded him. He snarled, pushed off the floor, doggedly whipping his head from side to side. Digging the heels of his palms into his eyes, he swiped away enough blood to crawl toward his boy. Arnie Rosen gently lifted Jonathon's blond head. He gaped in disbelief at the mushy hole flowering beneath the perfect little face. As blood rushed back into his eyes, Rosen brought the tiny cheek up to his own, rocking silently.

*　　*　　*

He sat behind his desk, snapping bullets into the Glock 9 mm semiautomatic. Until now, the gun had merely been a comforting but unused defense against prowlers, kept in Barbara's night table. Rosen was good with guns and not only because of his training in the service. He had also spent many hours on the Langley small arms range perfecting his pattern shooting, and he could cluster a tight grouping of shots into the target's head or torso at a eighty feet. He was solid in his weighting, steady as he extended his weapon in the efficient Weaver stance.

Rosen couldn't recall how long he'd held Jonathon or how long he'd wandered through the nightmare upstairs. So much of him was dead.

His bloody sleeves stuck to his forearms. Whose blood? He wasn't sure; probably a mixture. There was so much everywhere. His eyes smarted, painfully dry: no more tears left. He rubbed at them, only increasing the burning. The insides of his shoes were wet and uncomfortable; his trouser legs were soaked. He remembered a small lake pouring over the bathroom jamb, sopping into the hall rug so that he sloshed as he moved hollow-eyed toward what he knew he'd find inside. Knowing hadn't helped. Hadn't stopped him from clutching, grabbing, and trying to hug life back into Barbara's dear, wet body.

All three were together now upstairs, lying in each others' arms on his and Barbara's bed. Rosen remembered other times when he came home late to find them asleep in the master bedroom: TV humming, peaceful, the children waiting for Dad to kiss them, lift them, and shuffle them to their beds. Then the joy of coming back to Barbara, her sleepy arms wrapping around his neck—all silly words and mumbles—warm breasts pressed against him, a smooth thigh flung over his leg. Except for her soft breath, there was only contented silence.

He'd done his best to re-create one of those better times. He'd even tucked the pale blue spread, light and fluffy, seeming to be mostly air, up under their chins. They looked as if they'd watched one of their favorite scary movies, only there were differences this time. They couldn't be scared anymore, and they were *never* waking up.

Rosen sat across from them in his rocking chair. It was a gift from his fraternity brothers for a successful stint as rush chairman. "Best pledge class ever," they'd said. It was a high-backed version, painted white, with thanks, arnie and, below, pi lambda phi, cornell, 1977 in bold red letters. Barbara had periodically begged him to store it, saying it didn't fit the beige-and-blue room, and he had periodically agreed, but he never did. He'd rocked and watched them, rocked and cried, until the tears dried up and he would no longer look at them.

Then Rosen had stopped rocking, walked to the table next to the bed, and lifted the gun and box of shells from beneath his *TIME* and Barbara's latest William Goldman paperback (she read avidly, in spurts, and this had been Goldman's turn), scattering golf tees, pencils, and coins. Leaving the ravaged drawer ajar, he had wandered out of the room and down the stairs.

Sometime during the process of loading, Arnie Rosen's brain clicked on. There at his desk, across from the open closet, Ellie's stuffed animals heaped just inside, the methodical act of installing each bullet revived him. The snap of each cartridge jerked him closer to conscious reality. By the seventh, Rosen could barely force himself to continue. He ached to rush out and finish Van Damme now.

He finally understood—too late. Van Damme couldn't be stopped by exposure—not within the agency anyway. He was far too powerful, had too many people to protect him; too many to lie for him; too many to *kill* for him.

The loaded gun slipped from his hands, landing upon the desk with a *thunk*.

Rosen clawed at his face. What a fool! He thought that he could stop the division chief through channels, hand over his pitiful little file and be done with it. The magnitude of his misjudgment smashed him like a fist. Suppose someone in counterintelligence alerted Van Damme, maybe the head of counterintelligence himself? He'd checked, sure, but how could he know what debts were owed, what favors needed repaying? In those circles, morality was only a cape cloaking ruthless pragmatism. He'd been kidding himself, playing at detective. Taking time to do things right. Building a case. And what had it gotten him? Rosen's eyes traveled upward toward the master bedroom.

A sob—the last he presumed he had—forced its way through his taut lips. What a pompous fool, thinking that he could beat Charles Van Damme. There was just one way: kill the bastard!

Rosen lifted the automatic, tugged out the short-sleeved shirt that he had traded for his blood-soaked Van Heusen, and slipped the weapon between his belt and the small of his back so that his shirt fell loosely over his fresh slacks. He scooped the additional cartridges, sent them clinking into his pants pocket, rose, smoothed his matted hair, and strode toward the door, yanking a tan windbreaker from the arm of a nearby chair.

As he passed the staircase, Rosen paused, looking upward as if awaiting something. He heard nothing, only the TV in the living room.

Rosen stood there a long time …

Finally, he set his sloping shoulders and turned toward the rear of the house. He *would* kill Van Damme. But first he needed to make one stop. He would kill Van Damme *after* he showed him the duplicate file. Rosen wanted to watch Charles Van Damme's face—so sharp and arrogant—as he realized that he would be exposed as a traitor and murderer after all. *That* would be Rosen's revenge: watching Van Damme's monumental ego disintegrate before he died. Maybe the chief of the European Division could face death, but one thing Arnie Rosen was sure of: people like Charles Van Damme could not face disgrace—even if it was posthumous.

Rosen's face compressed with determination. He decided to use the back door, just in case.

Rosen scanned the leaf-dappled lawn, seeking unfamiliar motion in the jagged shadows of oaks and azaleas. He was so engrossed that he failed to notice the barbecue. It hit the concrete patio with a ringing crash. Its rounded top rolled back and forth, accentuating the clamor. Rosen crouched, eyes darting furiously, but only the sparrows responded with frenetic twittering. He rose slowly, unconsciously righting the barbecue. He stopped midway, transfixed by its charcoal remnants. Yesterday flooded in, playing itself out before he could fight it back. A wonderful warm, beery, good-friended, great-familied afternoon. How could it all be so clear yet so irretrievably gone?

Through Rosen's tears, the powdery charcoal appeared laced with diamonds. He gently rested the barbecue upon its spindly legs and then dashed down the grass-choked, slate path to his car.

CHAPTER 2

Washington's Union Station, created in classic proportions by renowned architect Daniel Burnham and recently infused with new life by the redevelopment corporation, pinked in the waning sunlight.

Tentative evening shadows blurred its ornate columns and deep arches.

Rosen stared dismally at lines of cars queuing along the east parking ramp like insects entering a nest. Not for him. He wasn't about to wait once he had the case. He gunned the Camaro up North Capitol, across H, down Second Street. Just what he wanted: a practically empty construction lot where F dead-ended. He swung through the open wire gates, kicking up dry dust as he skidded in at an angle and cut the ignition.

Irregular sections of high plywood fence blocked the lot from Second Street traffic, leaving one entire end in deep shadow. Rosen scurried across dust and gravel, sending larger stones clinking against the gate as he dashed by.

He tramped through the main hall with a hundred others whose footsteps and voices multiplied as they rebounded off the vaulted ceiling's golden octagons. The marble floors glowed coldly, except where they had been profaned by candy wrappers and mangled Styrofoam cups. Rosen's unwelcome companions dwindled as upscale eateries and high-fashion shops seduced them. He was alone by the time he reached the mezzanine.

Rosen exhaled gratefully in the relative peace of the locker area. The shouts and laughter of expectant tourists antagonized him. Smiling faces were an enigma. How could they be preoccupied with such trivialities—where to have dinner or what store to explore next—when his world had evaporated?

He punched in the combination to his locker, slapping in the extra coins that its computerized screen demanded, clicked the small dial, opened the metal door, and removed a leather attaché case. The locker slammed shut with a tinny *clunk*.

Rosen rested his case upon the rounded top of a high-tech blue wastebasket. He snapped it open and shuffled through the papers inside, fearful that everything would be there except what he wanted most. The file was intact, containing flight numbers, cities, dates, and surveillance logs, all organized in neatly handwritten rows. There were even pictures. It was an exact duplicate of the one taken from his strongbox. Relieved, he closed the case and hurried back through the bright phantasmagoria of shops and restaurants.

There was a bank of phones near the main entrance. He rushed past, jerked to a stop, squeezed his eyes shut, drew a monster breath, and turned back. It couldn't wait any longer. They were dead. Period. He had to tell the police. He raised the receiver, hoping that the phone would be trashed the way they always were when you needed them. No such luck. The dial tone was clear and strong. Rosen pushed the receiver halfway back, clicking it against the cradle, staring at it, and finally drawing it toward him as if it were an armed grenade. He punched 911 quickly, not giving himself time to think. It would be so permanent after this. Up to now, it had been their secret—his, Barbara's, the kids'. Once it was told, though, there would be no untelling it. Once it was told, they would be dead to the entire world, not-coming-back dead.

Rosen listened with the greatest sadness that he had ever known as a crisp female voice inquired as to how she might help. Tears—it seemed he still had more after all—traced his cheekbones and lips as he answered. At the end, she kept asking where he was, her voice more urgent with each request. After the fourth time, he hung up.

*   *   *

It was not quite dark but almost, with no life on the construction site where he'd parked, except for the brief flash of headlights between gaps in the walls bordering Second Street.

Rosen was just about at the Camaro when they separated from the shadows. "C'mon," he heard. "Now, man. Get him." They wrenched him from the door handle, grabbing arms and hair, yanking his head back, propelling him, toes scuffing the uneven dirt, toward the shadowy end of the lot, past the putrid odor of day-old garbage roasting in summer heat. They slammed his chest against an uncluttered section of wall, driving his breath out with a *whoosh*. Thudding blows to his kidneys forced out ragged gasps from him. Jagged splinters tore at Rosen's clothing as he tumbled toward the chalky dust.

They yanked Rosen onto his back. He sprawled, head jammed against the wall, staring up at three teenaged black kids. They hunched forward, weight on the balls of their feet, eyes wild even in the dim light. Rosen didn't move.

"Le's clean 'im, man. Le's clean 'im an' stick 'im." It was the one on the left—big, scarred, bouncing from one foot to the other, like a dancer feeling out a new routine, flipping a six-inch blade from hand to hand, lowering his body with each toss until the flashing point was inches from Rosen's face.

Rosen fought back the pain, concentrating on the big one's groin. One more pass with that knife and he might as well go for it. He tensed his right knee, ready to snap the foot up and out. His hands flattened against the ground, which was warm from the day's heat. Loose gravel gouged his palms.

"Cool it, man," the thin kid in the middle hissed, backhanding the other's hand with the blade. His eyes were the clearest of the three. "Le's be nahce. No need ta hu't the man if he he'ps us out. Raht?" He crouched, staring into Rosen's eyes. His own eyes were very white in the growing shadows. "Raht?" His tone was insistent.

"Right—of course," Rosen croaked.

"Ya see, we kin' a sho't." The kid smiled. He had two upper teeth gone, one lower. Rosen was reminded of a skinny jack-o'-lantern. "You ga' money, you okay. You don', you daid." The kid said it matter-of-factly, as if either option would be all right.

"I *have* money. Can I show you?" Rosen got a nod. Turning on his right side, he reached back with his left hand and pulled out his wallet.

The big one's eyes kept darting toward it and then rolling away. Spittle dribbled off his slack lower lip. His knife slowly inched back toward Rosen.

Rosen held the wallet out. There was a touch of warm flesh as the middle kid grabbed it.

The third, tall and wearing a brown raincoat with sleeves way too short for his gangling arms, peered intently over the middle one's shoulder.

Rosen pushed up on his hands, easing away from the wall. The back of his head flashed hot where its coarse ridges had pressed in.

They dug anxious fingers into Rosen's wallet, bulging it open. Pictures, credit cards, and IDs flapped to the ground. They pried at slots and pockets, finally pitching it across the alley as they counted, recounted, shaking their heads, anger whitening their eyes.

"Not 'nough, man," the middle one pronounced.

Rosen tensed.

The big one yelled, "Yeah!" He then tipped the blade downward. His eyes, snapping into focus at the prospect of violence, were hard and bright, his tongue flicking, his body lowering for a straight thrust as Rosen, raging from the afternoon's pent-up hatred, kicked out at the bending knee, straightening it, pushing through until there was a satisfying *crack*. The big one cartwheeled back. His mouth slammed shut mid-shriek as he flattened against a tall stack of two-by-fours. His blade sailed high, reflecting splashes of light, clattering, plastic handle splintering as it bounded off a cement-crusted wheelbarrow.

Silence except for the big one's soft moans and the startled breathing of the others.

Rosen pivoted on his left hand. He was forty-five degrees from the ground, bracing his legs to thrust up at them, when a kick caught him on the left side of the jaw, jamming his head back. He fought to clear his mind as he continued rolling to give himself maneuvering room. They lunged after him, sneakers clomping hollowly on the dirt. Rosen banged into a garbage can. It rocked forward, spilling its contents onto his head and face. Ripe melon seeped under his shirt, the seeds sticking to his chest. He swiped sticky substances from his eyes as he lurched to his feet, his hand lodging deeply in the can's soggy contents as he fought for balance.

They came wide at him, one from each side. Raincoat Man was clutching a previously hidden baseball bat, while the one who had grabbed his wallet wielded a Jim Bowie Special big enough to intimidate a grizzly.

Rosen crossed his hands, palms down, elbows out, trying to anticipate the direction of the first swipe. That kick had really gotten his jaw. It was killing him. Nerve endings up his cheek and even into his gums pulsed raw heat. Christ, it had been years since he had served on the Special Forces. He wasn't a damned two-handed killing machine anymore. He was in okay shape, but three guys at once? Well, two now. He *had* to take care of this. No punks were keeping him from Van Damme. Rosen crouched, weighting his feet evenly.

They did the smart thing: they both came at once. Rosen threw up his left arm. The bat skittered along it and off his shoulder, smacking into the plywood wall with a vibrating *wonk*. The monster knife darted back as its owner easily danced out of range of Rosen's kick to the head. Frustrated, Rosen bared his teeth. *My damned legs aren't limber enough to stretch that high anymore or I would have had him.*

Rosen never found out if he could take them. Footsteps thumped in from the street. Wallet Taker and Raincoat Man looked at each other and then at their buddy still heaped across the woodpile; then pounded off through the shadows toward one of the multiple openings in the wall.

Rosen spun, hands tensed.

Two men dressed in neat suits and fashionably wide ties trotted up to him.

Rosen released his breath, dropped his hands, settled back on his heels.

The taller one spoke. "You all right? We heard noises from our car."

There was a moan. Rosen peered through the shadows at the downed mugger. His eyes were open now, glazed, his right shin angling forward at the knee.

"What the hell happened?" The taller one gawked at the kid. "He try to rob you?"

"He and two others."

The men's eyes darted in both directions.

"They're gone. Ran away when they heard you." Rosen dabbed his jaw gently with his fingertips, then repeated the gesture along its length, grimacing at the contact yet perversely unable to stop until he had tested the entire area.

"They got you there?" The tall one peered closely. "It's turning colors." He stared over Rosen's shoulder, intent on the shadows behind. "We'd better get out of here. They may have friends." At this, the second man also squinted nervously into the dusk. "You have a car?" the first one asked.

Rosen nodded.

"We'll walk you, if it's close. Otherwise, we'll drive you."

The shorter one tried to take Rosen's arm, but Rosen shook him off. "I'm okay. It's right over there. Thanks for the help … and the escort," he added quickly in order to avoid offending. Rosen stooped by the garbage can whose contents he'd scattered. He was relieved to find his attaché case still wedged between it and a second can. He yanked it out by the handle, using the side of his hand to skim melon rinds from its surface. The expensive leather was badly scuffed.

"No problem," said the tall one. The two flanked Rosen like bodyguards, glancing toward him every few feet as if they expected him to keel over. "We'd better call the cops about that kid. He looked in pretty rough shape," the tall one called across to his friend. "Whatever you did to him, you did pretty good."

Rosen tuned out the man's chatter. It was meant to comfort him, but it only succeeded in increasing his anxiety. All that he could think of was getting his hands around the wheel and speeding off. Just about dark now. Rosen's Bulova—the only unmarked part of him—said 8:21. Good. Langley would have cleared out hours ago. Only the moles in their glass-lined computer rooms—the weird people who worked all night and who, Rosen always imagined, came to their front doors blinking like owls if visited during daylight—would be there, along with the skeleton night staff, communicating with operatives in embassies on the other side of the world. And security, of course. There was always lots of that at Langley. But it didn't matter. Rosen wasn't going to try to escape. He'd probably call security himself after he'd finished. Sit there and wait for them. Maybe in Van Damme's chair, behind his goddamned antique desk. That desk cost sixty times what standard issue desks used by flunkies like Rosen cost. Van Damme's whole goddamned office was like that. Vases, Impressionist paintings, Louis XIV chairs ... all out of his pocket. Actually, Van Damme's society wife's pocket, according to rumor. Van Damme's office was fancier than the director's was, for God's sake. And nobody knew that for all his fancy furniture and society connections, he was a goddamned traitor! At least grunts like Rosen, with their crappy government-issue metal desks and metal chairs and metal bookcases, were loyal to their country. Some joke!

They were finally alongside his car.

"Want me to hold that while you open the door?" the tall one asked, nodding toward Rosen's attaché case.

"No thanks." Rosen slipped the case under his arm while he fished for his keys.

"You sure you're all right? You want us to get you to a hospital?"

"You c-could have a c-concussion. Never hurts to h-have it ch-checked."

It was the first time the shorter one spoke. In addition to the stutter, his voice sounded gravelly, pained, as if his throat had been damaged. And Rosen hadn't seen too many crew cuts like he had except on old-timers in the military, yet this guy couldn't be more than thirty-five. Interesting, but all Rosen wanted was for the two to leave. He knew they were only trying to help, but their hanging around was driving him crazy.

"Thanks. Really. I'm okay. If anything bothers me later, I'll get it checked out." Rosen half smiled, leaving the keys dangling from the Camaro's door as he raised his right hand in a mock oath.

"All right," laughed the tall one. "You proved you can take care of yourself."

Rosen slid in, grimacing as he bent to navigate the low seat.

The tall one's face went stone cold as he surveyed the entrance to the construction area. Satisfied, he nodded to Crew Cut, who stepped between him and Rosen, cocked his elbow, mashed its point into the back of Rosen's neck.

"Nice shot, Stevenson." Ted Craig helped Stevenson manhandle the limp body into the backseat. "That's going to leave a helluva mark, if you didn't already kill him."

"So f-fuckin' what?" rasped Stevenson. "The shape this g-guy's gonna be in when we're done, no one's g-gonna notice a few extra bruises. Pull that seat down so I can g-get him all the way back."

*　*　*

Twenty minutes later, they were on the Baltimore-Washington Parkway, driving leisurely toward I-495, Stevenson in the agency Taurus, Craig behind the wheel of Rosen's Camaro. Craig switched on WXTRA. Oldies. Beat the hell out of the crap that passed for music now—fuckin' screaming freaks with words you couldn't make out and wouldn't want to if you could. Give him the Bee Gees or Dylan any day. Cat Stevens was good before he went nuts and became some kind of Muslim. None of the assholes today could hold a candle to any of them. And that fuckin' rapping! Craig made a face.

He glanced at Rosen's attaché case. Its leather handle swung with every swerve of the car. Van Damme had been right: there was a second file. All they had had to do was play it cool. Rosen had gone right for it, like a dog after a bone. Hadn't even waited for the cops, assuming Rosen even called them. Damned if Van Damme wasn't always right. Craig pounded the wheel in time to "Yellow Submarine" as Maryland's exits popped in and out of his headlight beams. Not much farther. Boy, those Beatles could sing. Not like the assholes today.

CHAPTER 3

Craig glanced back at Rosen. The guy was still out. Good. Not that Craig couldn't clock him again if he had to, but this made things easier. He felt bad about Rosen's kid. Cute little guy but you couldn't leave loose ends; they always came back to bite you in the ass. Craig checked the rearview mirror for Stevenson. The Taurus was thirty yards behind, holding even, its headlights haloing wisps of Rosen's hair through the rear window.

Craig studied the slumped figure. He looked like a regular enough guy, but why would anybody be crazy enough to steal an "Eyes Only" file? Usually for money. Maybe an expensive honey stashed in some fancy apartment? Rosen's wife sure had been some damn fine piece of ass, but to some guys, strange stuff always looked better. Whatever. This fucker was dead meat now.

Craig slowed, signaled, and slid the Camaro over in time to catch a long, climbing exit ramp. By the time he reached the top, four or five other sets of headlights were snaking their way up, splashing random sections of foliage with imperfect circles of light. Good. Just enough traffic to do the job.

The area to his right was woodsy, another plush little Maryland suburb with lots of space and plenty of trees between homes and road. He pulled deep onto the shoulder, cut the ignition, and waited for the Taurus.

* * *

Charles Van Damme fiddled with a reproduction of a Fabergé egg, one of the few non-authentic art objects in his large office. Of course, he had the original at home, but that was in a solid oak case with hidden wires connecting its glass top to a twenty-four-hour security service. Leaving the pearl and jeweled object on his desk overnight would have been a stiff test even for the handpicked Langley maintenance crew. For the thousandth time, Van Damme marveled at the minuscule village set in the confines of its gold shell, exactly the size of an egg, before gently clicking it shut. He leaned back and then swiveled to view his latest acquisition, a small Seraut for which he had outbid a corporate president, a Persian businessman, and a well-known television personality at private auction. He stared intently at the profusion of dots blending into the silhouettes of delicate strollers in a sunny Paris park.

Charles—he tolerated "Charlie," or other such overly familiar abbreviations, only from those with sufficient influence to justify such distasteful liberties—was tall, over six-four, and rail thin, his Savile Row suits hand-tailored to accentuate what little shoulders he had, the pants tapered to avoid bagginess around his meager thighs. He clasped pale hands behind his overly large head, intertwining the long fingers for support. His hair and pencil mustache were jet black, any traces of gray obliterated by daily applications of tint; his sallow skin was indicative of one who considers the outdoors a means of getting from one indoor location to the next. His eyes, surprisingly soft for his sharp, narrow features, alternated from blue to gray, depending on the reflection from the Tiffany lamp to the left of a massive leather-trimmed blotter that dominated the desk's center.

Van Damme swiveled 180 degrees toward the sprawling window behind his desk. Flecked by the lights lining Langley's extensive lawns and the occasional wavering beams of late hour parking lot entrants, the black glass mirrored his office. He moved closer so that his own features reflected back. An involuntary smile grew as his upper lip rose like a stage curtain over a perfect row of large white teeth. He stretched his long arms high above his head and resettled them across his narrow chest.

Everything was going smoothly. Craig had called his private number five minutes ago saying, "The party we were to meet, *and* his luggage, is being escorted to his embarkation point." Even if the cryptic message could be tapped—an eventuality made virtually impossible by both the company car phone and Van Damme's own electronic scrambler—it would be meaningless to an outsider.

Of course, there was a second file. He had been positive there would be—Rosen's pitiful attempt to protect himself, maybe a bargaining chip to save his life. Van Damme shook his head. That this nobody ... this bug ... this *analyst* should try to stop him was actually laughable.

Even if this Rosen had stayed home; hadn't panicked and led them right to the file; had called the police instead, the outcome would have been the same. A nearby van would have intercepted his call with Ted Craig and his contract help, Stevenson, Van Damme thought–although he didn't care to know anything about contract people—appearing as plainclothes police minutes later. True, they might have had to work on Rosen a bit, but either way, they would have gotten the second file. As usual, he had covered all his contingencies.

Suddenly, Van Damme frowned back at his reflection, thin eyebrows squatting upon his sharp nose. How had this nobody from analysis—the most useless group in all of Langley—gotten so close? That question had bothered him from the beginning. Was it intercepted communiqués from his KGB contact? Impossible. The system of European drops was foolproof. Maybe a breach in the transmissions back to Moscow? Dangerous, if that.

Van Damme first discovered Rosen's intrusions when it came to his attention that someone was meddling with his travel vouchers. He hadn't known that it was Rosen, only that someone was pulling up records of his trips over the past two years. Very cautiously, granted, with decent enough covers: requests for airline receipts, supposedly to be used for costs study by the travel coordination people, and rechecks of totals by the accounting people. Rosen's efforts had been clever individually but excruciatingly obvious once a pattern had emerged. Van Damme had identified Rosen within a week.

That hadn't been enough, though. He had had to know what other evidence Rosen had so that no one else would be able to follow his trail. Part of Van Damme's rage, although he always made a point of keeping his emotions under control, was at himself for having slipped up.

It had been hard to refrain from killing the meddler immediately, but Van Damme had forced himself to wait. Instead, he had ordered the little bastard watched. His justification was that Rosen's questionable psychological profile—easy enough to change Rosen's personnel records to show signs of instability—made him a security risk. Three weeks later to the day, Rosen, now under surveillance, was caught sneaking the list of phone calls from that miserable gas station (the damned odor from those smelly pumps always gave Van Damme a headache) into his desk.

A file hidden in Rosen's lower drawer. Imagine! It was so obvious that Van Damme's people hadn't looked there initially, concluding that not even an analyst could be *that* stupid. And if the rest of Rosen's evidence wasn't in his desk, then where else would someone with so little imagination keep it but at home? All Rosen's goodies for his meeting with tight-ass Hollings on Tuesday (good thing Van Damme had contacts in counterintelligence who owed him *big*) in a nice tidy little metal box in his closet. Of course, Rosen would have had to die before tomorrow's meeting regardless, but it was so much simpler using him to locate the second file first.

Not that there was much time left for anyone else to pick up where Rosen had left off. Still … Van Damme never took chances. Nothing—*nothing*—must stop the Indigo II transfer. It was the culmination of two years' planning. First, wooing Kharkov, an influential hard-liner and the KGB's highest army liaison. Next, compromising low-level Czechoslovakian assets to establish good faith (when you played poker with the KGB, you had to ante up.) Even accelerating his agenda as the improbable dream of glasnost gained momentum.

Now arrangements were nearly complete. In less than three weeks, Gruhaber would have the optical data. Then Van Damme could offer the revolutionary satellite—capable not only of the most minuscule high-resolution imagery but also of pinpointing missile strikes within its three-dimensional quadrants—to the other side.

He pondered his years of frustration as press hungry politicians interfered, leaking information, destroying morale. The snooping dilettantes didn't understand or care about national security unless they were undermining it to enhance their worthless careers. Impotence—that was what they caused. Impotent leaders. Impotent missions. The agency had become one limp dick! Well, not anymore—not for him anyway. *Power* was necessary to protect and nurture a system. Without the power to protect itself, no political system survived. The Communists understood power and had used it magnificently, once you got past their glasnost and perestroika nonsense. And Indigo was the price of his admission into that world and into power: the power to act fully and decisively to protect. He *had* to have it. And when he soon got his opportunity, Charles Van Damme would make the most of it, by God!

The division chief stared at the window. His wolf's smile reflected back. He spun toward his desk. Craig would bring the files soon. Then he would figure out how Rosen had known and close the book on it for good. He ran a slender fingertip along his moustache as he lifted a report on yet another of the new wave of ex-Communist presidential candidates, this time in Rumania.

*   *   *

"Don' wan' no more," Rosen sputtered as Craig tipped the half-empty fifth of Cutty Sark toward his lips.

"Wider," growled Craig.

Stevenson pressed stubby fingers into the hinge of Rosen's jaw, forcing his mouth open to another flood of burning liquid.

Rosen's throat constricted as he gagged, sending the scotch streaming over his chin, down his neck, and onto his soaked shirt. The rest flowed along his tilted face, some into his nose—hot, suffocating—some into his right eye, the stinging of his nose minor compared to that burning agony. Rosen couldn't move. His ankles were tied to his wrists. His back arched painfully in the Camaro's tiny rear seat. Stevenson, squeezed in next to him, pressed his jaw open on Craig's command. Stevenson's breath was sickeningly sweet, as if he had just swallowed a whole roll of breath mints. The Camaro reeked of spilled booze. Was this the first or second bottle? Rosen couldn't remember; he couldn't remember much since they slapped him awake who knew how long ago? It could have been ten minutes or an hour.

More fire slid into Rosen's raw throat, cascading all the way down. His mind faded in and out. He should fight, but he couldn't concentrate. He was amazed to hear himself giggle. Why the hell was he doing that? This wasn't funny. *Nothing* was funny. His goddamn life was over because of … Van Damme. How the hell could he have trouble remembering that bastard's name? More scotch sloshed over his face; he breathed some in. God, it stung! More giggles. *What the fuck are you doing, Rosen, you stupid bastard? You want them to think you're having fun?* He blinked open a burning right eye, glanced up at Stevenson. The guy *did* look funny, his nostrils huge like a pig's snout. He was a fuckin' pig with a goddamn crew cut! The giggles welled up, bubbling past the incoming liquid. Rosen gagged, gasping and giggling. He couldn't stop. The giggles escalated into hooting laughter that swelled in the car's tiny confines, causing him to laugh even louder.

*   *   *

"He's ready." Craig was all business, Rosen's helpless laughter unamusing. Whether the guy laughed or cried—Craig had seen both, ludes and booze being accepted tools of his trade—it didn't matter. The guy had stolen secrets. He was dead. It was just business.

"Untie him." Craig scanned the road, easing the darkened Camaro along the deep shadows of the shoulder, turning it around toward the exit. "Got the note?"

Stevenson slipped over, flopping into the passenger seat. "Yeah, in his f-front pocket." The strained voice always sounded irritated, so Craig couldn't be sure if Stevenson was bothered by the question.

"You torch the brake cable?"

"Yeah. I did."

"My gun?"

"Yeah, C-Craig, your gun is all s-set—like we talked about ten t-times already!

Ted Craig smiled to himself. This time Stevenson was definitely pissed. Well, the job had to have *some* perks. They had removed Rosen's gun from the glove compartment and substituted Craig's, replete with Rosen's fingerprints. "Okay, Ernie, okay." Stevenson hated being called that. "Just checking." Craig stopped fifteen feet from the ramp. Dense shadows hid them from exiting vehicles. "Let's get him in the front." There was no humor in his voice now. The taunting smile was also gone.

They got out, lugged Rosen from the back, and propped him up in the driver's seat. He laughed, sprawling across the gearshift. They righted him, slamming his head against the steering wheel to daze him, twining his arms through the wheel's spokes until he stayed put. Stevenson checked traffic. There was a lull. They rolled the Camaro to the ramp's edge. Four pairs of headlights shown at the bottom of the long climb. Craig nodded. They pushed the idling car onto the ramp as Craig reached in to straighten the wheel.

The Camaro started slowly, holding to its course. It veered right as its front wheels caught the ramp's outer curb and spun forty-five degrees; then it hurtled the curb and rocketed down the grassy slope toward I-495.

Craig watched, fascinated. This was even better. Instead of plowing into four or five exiting cars, Rosen would hit the oncoming traffic full speed. It would be spectacular! He wanted to watch, but the climbing headlights were only about two hundred yards away. Reluctantly, he sprinted after Stevenson toward the Taurus.

*　　*　　*

Rosen revived, laughing, although blood trickled steadily down his face from where the tall one had slammed him against the wheel. He was still giggling even as the Camaro jumped the curb and began bouncing down this crazy slope, jarring his jammed arms until he just knew that one more good jolt would snap both elbows. Rosen's hilarity finally dissipated as his head cracked into the dash for the third time, rattling his teeth and swelling the bridge of his nose as the Camaro creaked and tottered toward oblivion.

Pressing his cheek hard against the madly vibrating wheel, shooting spasms of pain into his injured jaw, Rosen wriggled his right arm free, scraping his forearm painfully in the process. The car hit a depression, driving his funny bone into the door as he fought to unwedge his left arm. His fingers numbed instantly. Rosen clawed at the dash, snapping the headlights on to reveal a broad wash of low-cut grass receding like an intermediate ski slope. Suddenly, the beams dipped sharply, carving into a stretch of blackness that ended in a silent river of northbound headlights.

It should have been terrifying, careening toward that ribbon of metal that zipped by faster and faster as the distance narrowed, but it wasn't. It was more like a scary movie; it couldn't actually hurt you.

Through the blood and pain, Rosen's giggles returned. He knew he shouldn't, but he couldn't help it. Whatever those guys had given him was more than booze. No booze could keep him laughing as a hundred thousand cars were waiting to squash him flat in less than two seconds! *That* was what he had to remember. He didn't really want to get squashed flat. It was just that whatever they gave him had made him stupid. He wouldn't feel this way if this was happening tomorrow morning. Tomorrow morning he'd be scared shitless! Well, if he'd be scared shitless tomorrow, he should be scared shitless *right this minute*!

The lights were very close now. He could hear the traffic whooshing by like the ocean. Cars veered from the right lane, wheels screeching, horns keening, making way for him. "Thanks," he intoned to their anonymous drivers. His headlights bounded up against a passing car. The shocked faces of little children zipped by, mouths wide, noses pressed against the windows …

Gone.

They were replaced by a white-haired passenger, hands frozen into claws to fend off the Camaro. Of course, she couldn't do it. Rosen yanked the wheel hard right, skidding the rear end forward, crunching the terrified woman's rear door before sending her and her driver veering up the slope that he had just vacated. Brakes screeched behind him. He tensed, awaiting the inevitable smash like a curious spectator at a deadly intersection. The noise of impact lasted interminably before translating into a jarring motion. It flung his head backward as the Camaro's rear was thrown into the next lane.

More frantic horns and metallic thuds, the Camaro bouncing one way and then the other like a pinball. A mighty *whang* on the far door heaved it up. Another thump shot Rosen toward the roof as the Camaro flipped onto its back with a wail of tearing metal.

The sound reverberated through every chamber in Rosen's head. Then his perception went from dim to black to silence.

Chapter 4

osen awoke to the screaming of a siren. He lay on his back, rocking wildly as his ambulance dodged traffic. He couldn't move. Panicked, he arched his neck painfully up and found that he was strapped to a stretcher. An IV bottle swayed perilously above his head. He wondered if he was dying. He strained against the powerful straps, twisting his shoulders, fighting death. He couldn't die. It would be too unfair.

A lightning bolt of jagged electricity vibrated through his brain. He screamed. A white-uniformed attendant flew from his jump seat. He was a young black man, and he looked terrified. *First day on the job,* thought Rosen. The youth's eyes repeatedly darted from the IV to Rosen's face and back again. His hands rose, pink-palmed, and then fluttered back to his sides. He stood there above Rosen, swaying with the ambulance, frozen with indecision.

"Give him another ten ccs or he'll crack our damn eardrums," a voice bellowed from the front of the van.

The attendant produced a syringe; inserted a clear fluid from a tiny glass bottle; tested a small squirt; aimed toward Rosen's arm. Just then, the vehicle lurched right. The young man spun off, slapping into the padded wall. He recovered as the vehicle righted, gripping the edge of Rosen's stretcher as he prepared for a second thrust. He stopped halfway down. The needle was bent like a fishhook.

A big hand appeared on the youth's shoulder, jerking him back out of Rosen's line of sight. In his place stood a large fat man with tufts of red hair shooting from his scalp like antennae. His beefy hands disappeared above an overflowing belly, returning almost immediately with a fresh syringe. "Rookies," the man muttered as the needle grazed Rosen's arm in surprisingly delicate fashion. "I should let this asshole scream his guts out." The man glared at Rosen. He leaned closer, wrinkling his bulbous red nose as wisps of red hair peeked from his nostrils. "This guy smells like a damn distillery. Bet he's responsible for that mess back there."

His young assistant reappeared, wider-eyed than ever, watching Rosen as if he were a poisonous snake ready to strike.

"An' he don't even look that bad. Ain't that the way? Ten or twelve people, mindin' their own business, get killed out there an' this prick's so loose he only gets a couple of scrapes. They should kill a few of these bastards, make an example. Then maybe the other drunks would stay off the road." The redheaded man's watery eyes blazed as Rosen's fluttered shut.

*　　*　　*

Barbara, Jonathon, and Eleanor looked *so* great. They were all excited, ready for Cousin Barry's birthday: Jonathon in his new navy blue blazer, a silly extravagance that the little guy would outgrow in two months but one that Rosen and Barbara couldn't resist; Ellie, pretty in a crinoline-skirted peach party dress that she complained was "uncool" and made her "look like a six-year old"; Barbara, dazzling in black velvet that showcased her blue eyes and knockout tan. They stood just inside his front door, beckoning and imploring Rosen to hurry. He lengthened his strides, but his front walk elongated each time that he narrowed the gap. They called louder. He broke into a trot, but he couldn't gain on the walk. They were begging now, their faces dripping terror. Rosen dropped his briefcase and sprinted, but he just couldn't reach them. His heart thumped ferociously, his body clenched with effort. They kept calling his name.

Someone *was* calling his name. Rosen's eyelids wavered and then opened. The ceiling was bright with multiple fluorescents, their light rebounding off the walls and his sheets as well as the uniform of the serious young man in gold-rimmed glasses who stood next to his bed. The dazzle hurt Rosen's eyes. He blinked repeatedly.

As realization hit, emptiness poured into Rosen, filling every cranny as if he were hollow. He would never see them again—except in occasional dreams. They were so real to him now, but would he forget little pieces of them over time? Jonathon's cowlick? Ellie's exasperated skyward eye-roll? Even Barbara's "Your hands are cold" giggle? It seemed impossible, but life happened that way. He wanted it all to stop now, right now before their memories started dimming. But first he wanted Van Damme. After that, it didn't really matter.

"You'll adjust in a minute." The young man's voice was brisk, businesslike. "You were sedated while we examined you, but it looked a lot worse than it was."

"How bad is it?" Rosen cringed inwardly. Doctors always told you it could have been worse. He didn't feel that bad but they'd probably gotten him so doped up that he wouldn't know if his legs were missing.

"Actually you only have bruises and a few sprains. Plus a couple of stitches in your forehead. You were damn lucky." The man didn't sound overjoyed.

Rosen exhaled deeply. There was nothing wrong. How incredibly lucky! He could be out of here today. Right now. The hell with "bruises and sprains." He couldn't believe it. "I want to leave now. I need my clothes."

"I'm *Dr.* Atkinson," the young man said pointedly, "and under no conditions will *I* allow you to leave."

Hell of a bedside manner, thought Rosen. "I'm going." He lifted himself off his pillows, gasped, dropped back.

"You see." Atkinson actually seemed gratified by Rosen's discomfort. "I didn't say you wouldn't feel *anything*. You're pretty beat up. You just didn't do any serious damage. Worst part was that jaw—a minor crack. Not enough for us to wire but it'll hurt for a while. Try to chew on the opposite side and eat soft foods for a few weeks." Atkinson jutted his pointy jaw, pursing his thin lips at the end of each remark as if daring Rosen to even reply, much less disagree. "Any questions?" Atkinson was already stuffing Rosen's records back into the sheath at the foot of the bed. It seemed like questions were the last thing that he wanted.

Rosen might have waited a few hours, rested a bit. But the doctor's arrogance tapped a rage pooling beneath his nerves. He was as shocked as Atkinson clearly was when it poured out like indigestible food. "Listen, you high and mighty son of a bitch, I'll fucking leave when *I* say so. And I say I'm leaving *now*—so get my goddamn clothes and don't give me any more of your bullshit!" Jaw throbbing, neck aching, Rosen lifted himself off the bed for a second time, propping on an elbow, chest heaving, holding the pain at bay with his anger.

Atkinson's eyes squinted nearly closed behind the glasses. He drew his thick lips back over gapped teeth as he cocked his head in disbelief. Next his skin went beet red, starting above the prongs of his stethoscope, working up his narrow oval face to the crown of his freckled forehead.

Rosen would have bet that the top of the doctor's scalp would be fiery red beneath gaps in his thinning dark hair if the man in white had chosen that moment to bend over. He didn't.

Quite suddenly, Atkinson's mouth relaxed into a wicked smile. "Fine, Mr. Rosen. As far as I'm concerned, you can do what you want, but the *police* may have other ideas. I was going to give you a chance to rest, but since you're feeling so energetic, why don't I tell them you're ready?" Atkinson paused to savor his adversary's discomfort. Apparently satisfied, he strode out, white coat billowing like a reversed spinnaker.

Rosen swiped the loose sleeve of his hospital gown across his forehead. Of course the police would want to talk to him. What was he thinking, that they'd just let him walk out, tell him to forget about a little possibly twenty-plus car accident? "No problem, Mr. Rosen. Happens every day. We're only going after shoplifters this week so you just run along now."

And now he'd antagonized Atkinson, the only one who could keep them off his back until he could come up with a decent story. Rosen licked dry lips, rubbed his hands over his eyes, across his temples, to the back of his neck, kneading the taught muscles of his shoulders, trying to get blood—and ideas—flowing. He wouldn't tell them about Van Damme. *He* wanted to take care of that. But what about the accident? He was still mentally scrambling—without appreciable results—when they walked in. There was a tall, beefy white one and a short, skinny black one, like a salt-and-pepper Laurel and Hardy—the shorter meticulous, the taller sloppy. Only there was nothing humorous about their cold eyes.

"I'm detective Amos," said the short one in an incongruously deep voice for a hundred and fifty pounder. "This is detective Francis." The other nodded briefly. "How are you feeling, Mr. Rosen? That was quite an accident." His voice was soft, sincere.

Should he smile back, look as if he were in agony? *What?* He ended up with something in between, helping himself not at all. "They say I'm okay."

"Good. You were very lucky." Amos smiled, his angular face softening as it spread, sending creases outward from the corners of his lips and eyes, clearly a man who liked to smile. "Mind if we sit down for a few minutes?" He and Francis pulled over two metal chairs before Rosen could answer. "We need to ask some questions. You understand. The doctor said it would be all right."

He seemed nice enough, and the other one looked bored to tears. Rosen took a deep breath, which hurt his ribs. He replaced a pillow that had slipped from under his neck to between his shoulder blades and rolled toward them, wincing more than necessary for their benefit. He couldn't believe it—*yet*—but maybe this was only going to be routine. Maybe in the dark and confusion, no one had identified him as the cause of the accident. Maybe they hadn't tied him in with Barbara and the children. It hadn't been long, so *maybe* if he handled this right, he'd be out before they made the connection. That's all he wanted. Just time to kill Van Damme. "I guess so. Sure."

Amos leaned forward, the amiable smile broadening his features again. Rosen detected a wisp of light nostril hair. "Would you mind telling us what happened on the interstate?"

Francis sagged back, tipping the little chair precariously. He appeared more interested in picking at a callous on the side of his thumb.

"There was a big accident. I'm not sure how it started. It all happened before I knew it."

"Where were you when it started, Mr. Rosen? Can you tell us that?" The deep voice oozed encouragement.

"I was coming out from the city, doing about sixty … second lane, I think." Rosen's fingers clenched and unclenched beneath the sheet. His stomach felt like a dribbled basketball, but his voice held.

Francis stopped picking, looked toward Rosen with mild interest for the first time. The room was well air-conditioned, but Rosen noticed a ring of perspiration beneath the heavy man's hairline.

"Are you pretty sure?" Amos's soft voice brought Rosen's eyes back to his.

"Reasonably so."

Francis's chair slammed forward, front legs screeching on the bare floor. "You're full of shit, you drunken bastard! You came down off the goddamn grass and killed *four* helpless people before they even knew what hit them!" His beefy jaw thrust forward. Flecks of saliva sprayed out. Rosen lurched back against the bed's metal side bar as the large detective towered above him. Perspiration flowed freely down Francis's puffy nose and cheeks.

Amos's thin hand shot out, grabbing Francis's baggy sleeve. His eyes never left Rosen's. "Come on, Marty, take it easy. Let's give Mr. Rosen a chance." His smile had vanished, but the voice was still soft and inviting. "Marty lost a son to a drunk driver, Mr. Rosen, so he's not very understanding when it comes to this subject. Why don't you just tell us what *really* happened?"

Rosen edged up so his back wedged against the bunched pillows. They were coming down heavy: Amos the soft one and Francis the one who would tear his head off. It was the old "bad guy/good guy" routine, played to the hilt. He'd seen it before, done it himself more than once. Only problem was, they weren't about to let him go just because he'd figured out their game plan. That was an off-the-wall pipe dream. "Look," Rosen began, drawing a hand along his cheek, finishing with a rub of the bristle lining his chin. He avoided Francis's stare by focusing hard on Amos. "I was kidnapped by two guys. They loaded me with booze, and whatever else they had, and sent me down that hill. They thought I'd be killed."

Amos's lips thinned derisively.

Rosen couldn't blame him; it did sound ridiculous.

Francis voiced Rosen's thought. "That is the *biggest* load of load of shit I've heard in twenty-five years of listening to shit!" The words hissed out through stiff, white lips as Francis fought for control. It made him even more frightening. He thrust forward, throwing his bulk against the bed; jarring it backward; leaning on hamlike fists; lowering his huge red face into Rosen's. "I don't care if we are in a hospital, you miserable bastard. If I have to hear any more bullshit like that, you're going out the goddamn window!" Francis's collar was darkening with perspiration; his breath was sour, like spoiled milk.

"C'mon, Marty. Sit down."

"I just want to crack this bastard one, just *one.*"

"Marty, come *on.* Let's give him a chance."

The big detective backed toward his chair, his smoldering eyes locked on Rosen.

"What about your family? Want to tell us about them?"

Rosen's head flopped back on the pillows. What the hell was the point? They knew everything and were probably doing the "Colombo" number to get a confession. He'd been kidding himself. Again. "They're dead," he mumbled toward the ceiling, closing his eyes. "I called to tell the police."

"Why'd you kill them?" Amos's tone was conversational. He could have been asking about the weather.

"What?" Rosen pushed up from the bed, the muscles along his ribs flashing fire. He gaped at the little man, who stared back, unblinking. "What the goddamn *hell* are you talking about, you son of a bitch?"

Francis growled deep in his throat and started to rise, but Amos stopped him. "Sit down, Marty." His eyes chilly, his voice cold. "I'm talking about a woman and two children: all dead and set up like they're posing for a family portrait. In your bedroom. *That's* what I'm talking about."

Blood flashed in front of Rosen's eyes. His breath would not clear his throat; it kept catching on the tightness down there. He lurched from his bed, intent on the little man, hands groping. Francis's huge body loomed, forcing him back, pinning him to the covers. The policeman's acrid perspiration blanketed Rosen, stifling his breath … and rage. He lay exposed, helpless, like a defeated dog offering its throat to the victor. Francis pushed off Rosen, watching and ready.

"That's quite a temper you have." Amos sounded the same, as detached from Rosen's violence as if he hadn't been its object but only an observer. "Is that what your family did? Make you mad?"

The man's dogged obstinacy sent new tremors of rage down Rosen's spine. He rose again to confront Amos. Francis tensed, ready to move in. "You think *I* killed my family?" The voice wasn't his; it was too high, too uncontrolled, the inflections out of sync with the words. *Definitely* not his voice. "I love"—he could not express his feelings in the past tense— "them more than my life. I would die for them if I could. What's the matter with you? Would you kill *your* family—"

"We're not talking about me. We're talking about *you!*" Amos shifted in the chair, crossing his right leg over the left, fastidiously smoothing the knee to protect his crease. "We found the gun that killed your son and wife in the front seat of your car." He laid his hands on his lap, interlocking his delicate fingers and making a steeple of the thumbs.

"It belonged to the men who took me. Obviously." Rosen snorted, throwing up his hands. "Come *on!*"

"What about your confession?" Amos's thumbs worked back and forth, back and forth.

"*What are you talking about?*" Rosen shrieked. It was like the old football shit drills in high school: they put you in the middle of a circle and came at you from all sides. He was losing it, had to get a handle on things.

The thumbs stopped as Amos leaned forward. He stared intently at Rosen. "You don't understand 'gun' or 'confession'? Which?"

No reaction from Rosen.

"Never mind. I'll tell you about both. We found an unregistered Colt .38-caliber revolver in your car. In the passenger seat. Your fingerprints were on the grip … the barrel … everywhere. We also found a typed note in your pocket, with your signature, saying that you … Here, would you rather read a copy? Since you don't seem to remember." Amos dug inside his jacket, pulled out a folded letter-sized paper, reached it toward Rosen.

Rosen watched it flutter in the air-conditioning, his eyes not quite focusing. Realizing that they were both staring, he grabbed at it. It was typed on the bum Selectric that stood on the empty secretarial pool desk near the water cooler. He could tell from the lopsided *g*'s. It had been a joke, a throwback to pre-computer times used by the analysts as a prop to emphasize the agency's notorious penuriousness. His eyes skipped to the only handwritten part, the bottom. His signature. No question. He scanned the text, went back, and read more slowly.

I can't take it anymore. This place is filled with spies. The whole organization is corrupt. I can't trust anyone; even Barbara is one of them. She has been acting strange, hanging up the phone when I come into the room, taking trips that she says are for shopping. I know better. She is dealing with the division chief, telling him what I've found out about his lousy deals with the Communists. Selling me out. I've been so clever, pretending not to care. Just do my job, not make waves. But I've been watching. Now they know I know, thanks to my jezebel wife. Tonight I'll straighten that out. They're after me, but I'm leaving copies of this everywhere so even if I die, everyone will know what they're up to.

Rosen gaped at the small detective. "You really believe I wrote this drivel? It's like a goddamn soap opera. Use your head, man."

Amos took a deep breath, nodding. "We thought so too. Until we reviewed your files at Langley … A Mr. Leo Walter, head of your analysis section, accessed them for us. They were going to recommend a medical leave for you. Require you to take therapy. They felt that you were showing signs of massive paranoia … You were classified as a major security risk, Mr. Rosen—"

"That's—" Rosen stopped, fists clenching, saliva working out of his mouth as the words flew. "That's bullshit! That is *absolute* bullshit! There's nothing wrong with me. They've got nothing like that on *my* records. You're trying to get me." Rosen bit his lower lip, imagining how he must look.

"Excuse me. Everything all right?" A heavy woman in white appeared in the doorway. She carried her bulk erectly, a no-nonsense look of authority in the intense eyes behind her black-rimmed glasses. "Mr. Rosen cannot be excited. He needs rest. I believe that Dr. Atkinson told you that." She glared accusingly at Francis.

"We'll only be a few minutes longer." Amos shot her his face-widening smile. "We just got a little carried away." He nodded to Rosen for confirmation and got it.

The nurse looked like a suspicious schoolteacher who knew there was mischief but couldn't get the guilty parties to confess. She backed out the door, lips pinched, spreading furrows through her lower face. "All right. But let's not hear *any more noise*."

Rosen lowered his voice, keeping one eye on the doorway. "It's *not true*! His jaw tensed, the words streaming in a sibilant whisper. "There is nothing wrong with me. They *couldn't* have said that." He stared at the little detective. "They put that crap in there to set me up. Don't you see? Van Damme could easily plug that stuff into the computer. Did you ask Walter or the other people I work with? His voice was rising. He fought to steady it. "Harvey Kilgore ... Randy Moroski ... Dave Doyle? They'd tell you I was okay. *Did you ask them?*" Rosen thought there was a sadness in the little man, as if the victory that the detective had anticipated had turned sour.

Francis's eyes, on the other hand, bore into him malevolently. "We talked to Kilgore and Doyle. They backed it up all the way." He scrutinized Rosen like a kid dissecting a bug.

"That's crazy! They couldn't! They must all be in on it—" Rosen clamped his mouth shut, but it was too late. Their eyes told him. "I wouldn't kill my family." His voice sounded weak and unconvincing, even to him. It was too much. Too much, too fast. He had to think—but he was tired. Every thought led to a dead end, like the deadness behind the detectives' pupils. "I called. Why would I call the police if I ... killed them?"

Amos looked at him, the sadness clearer now. "Guilt. That's common. Your realized what you'd done." He shrugged his slight shoulders. "I'm not saying that this is premeditated. Far from it. It might have been something you just couldn't help. That's for others to decide."

A volt of tension twitched Rosen's right eyelid. *This isn't working. I need their help. The note and the records ... Van Damme didn't miss a trick.* He settled back against the pillows. *Everything aches. My jaw feels as if it's grown a bigger jaw around itself.* He blew air through partially closed lips and tried to relax as he rubbed a palm over his hair, surprised that it felt reasonably well groomed except where perspiration had clumped it to his forehead. Its smooth texture soothed him. *What the hell—I'd better level. At least I'll see Van Damme in jail. Maybe even figure out how to kill the bastard somewhere along the way. The only one I'm hurting now is myself.*

Amos leaned his small frame forward neatly at the waist. "You all right? We can get back to this after you rest awhile. Don't want to complicate things."

Rosen was touched by the look on the little man's face until it dawned on him that the detective didn't want anything delaying his case. A relapse would screw up his plans. Rosen almost laughed, but the impulse died deep in his chest. Somehow he didn't feel like laughing. He shrugged off Amos's suggestion. "We have a division chief at the agency. Charles Van Damme. He heads up European operations. I'm in research. I review intercepts from NSA—the National Security Agency—which runs all the electronic surveillance equipment. They penetrate enemy embassies, phone lines, and things like that. Our guys physically install the bugs. Anyway, I sort out the relevant stuff and feed it to our operations people."

Francis kicked at one shoe with the other. Amos's eyes began to glaze over.

Rosen spoke faster. "About four months ago, I got an intercept from the Russian Embassy in Bonne. The local KGB operative—theirs are stationed in the embassies just like ours—was talking on what he thought was a secure line to Moscow. Something involving a first installment of plans to be dead-dropped two weeks later at the usual location in West Berlin. Someone referred to as Mr. Benheim was bringing them. Everyone in espionage has code names. Anyway, he must have been a big deal because the transmission went on to say that Kharkov should leave a message at the drop about where they'd meet after the plans were authenticated."

Amos wore a polite but "Where is this going?" look; Francis appeared to have mentally taken off for parts unknown.

Rosen increased his volume. "Nikolai Kharkov." Francis's head snapped back, ready for trouble. "Colonel Nikolai Kharkov is a political officer, a military liaison of the KGB and a very close confidant of General Yermakov's. General Alexi Yermakov is an old -line Communist who advocates overthrowing the governments of the republics in favor of a unified Soviet Union." Rosen's back and neck throbbed, but he didn't want to distract them by moving. "He is rabidly anti-West, and unfortunately his message plays very well to the military, the KGB, and to many of the starving population who are beginning to think of communism as the good old days. A man like Kharkov wouldn't even walk to Gorky Park unless it was damned important, let alone travel to Berlin. Don't you see what I'm getting at?"

Their looks told Rosen that they saw nothing but a ranting madman. He rushed on, panicky now. "He had to be meeting someone really *big*! Benheim was a heavyweight—a major player—*turned* by the Russians—"

"Mr. Rosen—"

"No, no, *wait*! Forty-nine people traveled to Berlin that week, but only *four* were of station chief status or above. You see, the pecking order is DI, who heads up the agency; DDI, his assistant, the deputy director; the deputy director of operations; the division chiefs, with responsibility for various areas of the world; and station chiefs, who supervise operations at our embassies. I couldn't see Kharkov responding to anyone lower than that."

Amos rose abruptly. "This is all extremely interesting, Mr. Rosen, but I don't think it's helping us solve *our* problem." He rested his palms on the bed, eyes level with Rosen. "Let's get to the point. You're going to tell us that some higher-up in the CIA was meeting with the Russians to sell secrets, right?"

Rosen nodded rapidly. Yes, that's right. I narrowed it down over the next few months to the one man who—"

"Do you have any proof?" Amos interrupted, voice raspy, impatient now. "No. I did, but the men who killed … Whoever was at my house took it. And they got my second file when they grabbed me at Union Station.

But Van Damme put them up to it. *He's* the one I narrowed it down to. The European Division chief. I had the proof. Made an appointment with counterintelligence to report him. Van Damme must have found out so he had to—"

"Had to, my ass!" Francis walked to the bed, planting his ham hock fists next to Amos's tiny ones. "I told you we'd get nothing out of this wacko, Reggie. He's just as nutty as they said." He glared at Rosen, brown eyes veiny in the strong fluorescent light, talking to Amos out of the corner of his mouth as if Rosen weren't worth including in the conversation.

"Wacko!" Rosen thrust his face into the big man's. "I'm telling you what happened—all of it—and you call me a 'wack'—"

"Yeah. That's right." Francis shoved Rosen back like a sack of laundry and leaned over, sour breath cascading over Rosen's face. "Wacko. Ya hear me? *Wacko*! That's what your goddamn file said … and that's what you are!" His voice became a low growl. "Only problem is, no one knew how far gone you were." Francis backed away, looking at Rosen as if he were something stuck to the bottom of his huge shoe. The big policeman flung out a heavy paw in disgust. "Bastard'll probably get off 'cause he's nuts. They all do nowadays," he muttered as he shambled out.

Rosen could take Francis's hatred, but the pity in Amos was too much to bear—too final. He stared at the wrinkles in his sheet, white waves crashing off the bed. He heard shuffling but didn't look up until the little detective called from the doorway.

"We'll see you, Mr. Rosen. You will be formally charged for the murders of your wife, son, and daughter … and for those on the interstate. Your rights will be read to you at that time. I extended you the courtesy of not doing that now because you seem like the kind of man who'll do the right thing once you have a chance to think about our conversation. There *will* be a policeman outside your door until then." He looked at Rosen, started to say something more, stopped, made an ineffectual little gesture with his hands, turned, and left.

Rosen stared at the doorway long after he was gone.

Chapter 5

Rosen was released from DC General three days later, in the custody of two unsmiling patrol officers who took him directly to DC Superior Court. There, a blue-uniformed marshal fingerprinted him with bored efficiency and then released him to a second, who walked him past eight video screens highlighting different angles of the jail's interior and through a green-barred door that buzzed loudly at their approach. Inside was a yellow-tiled corridor. Grizzly sounds emanated from the cages on either side. They stopped. An unyielding bar smacked Rosen's shoulder as he was shoved into a crowded holding cell. Inside, the faint aroma of antiseptic was succumbing rapidly to the combination of sweat, urine, and vomit. The agitated energy of too many men in too little space vibrated through him. He sought refuge. Sidestepping as one of the hunched figures staggered up, gargled deep in its throat, and lurched off in glazed-eyed oblivion, Rosen darted toward the man's vacated spot. He slipped down the smooth tile, hugging his knees when he reached the floor. Rosen closed his eyes as if the act itself were sufficient to obliterate the cell. It wasn't. The sounds and smells assailed his other senses.

Only two things varied the routine: the "openings" and the "scuffles." The clanging openings of the heavy cell door evoked sudden silence. The prisoners whose names were called, except for those too far gone to recognize their names, rushed out as if they were being freed rather than facing the tedious presentment procedure before a packed court. Rosen soon realized that that was because in comparison, anything outside of the cell was freedom. He didn't mind the openings.

The scuffles, though, were the worst: sudden grunts followed by pleas, then thuds, then whimpers, then back to the usual sounds—until the next scuffle. Rosen's imagination supplied the combatants. The instigator was a monster, with low-slung forehead and brutish pink-rimmed eyes, working his hulking way closer and closer toward Rosen. As much as he fought it, a perverse part of Rosen's mind insisted on tracking the beast's progress. The most recent blows were definitely nearby. Any moment now ...

It never happened. The fifth "opening" was for Rosen. A nasally voice called out a name. He didn't connect it with himself until a second more irritated call got his attention. A heavyset marshal, beer belly overlapping the standard black cartridge belt, glared from across the cell. He obviously had no problem picking Rosen out from the sixty-odd other inmates. Rosen scanned the packed room for the first time. The guard was not prescient. Rosen's hospital-clean appearance stood out, along with his clothes. He rose, wondering why the monster who had instigated the "scuffles" hadn't singled him out earlier, but as Rosen looked around, he couldn't decide who was the monster. Still wondering, he negotiated his way toward the marshal, stepping over sprawled arms and legs, avoiding hunched bodies, ecstatic to be leaving.

They moved along the clean corridor, reflected light from the bland yellow tile jabbing at Rosen's eyes, the marshal's beefy hand on his elbow. Their pace was brisk. His guard obviously had more charges than just Rosen to worry about. His fleshy cheeks jiggled as they hurried along. The gold department of justice insignia on his big-breasted chest jutted toward the ceiling rather than outward as his massive body swayed beneath the taught uniform like a badly listing eighteen-wheeler. Rosen speculated as to whether they would attempt to clear the small doorway at the corridor's end simultaneously. If so, he would be pulped against the steel jamb. At the last moment, the guard dropped back, shoving Rosen through as the mechanical locking device rasped open.

They were in an area lined with small doors. The walls were the same lifeless yellow as the previous corridor. Two sobbing women, one young and one old, followed a nattily dressed man with a handlebar mustache and a lawyer's briefcase through a door to the right. A tall youth wearing a faded Redskins jacket slouched out of a similar door to the left, pursued by another lawyer type, who buzzed at him insistently.

"Arnie." The sound of his name, called in a friendly tone, shocked Rosen as much as anything that had transpired in the past hellish hours. Larry Topper, his undergraduate roommate, strode regally toward him. He was a small man, not more than five feet six inches. His thin neck was almost totally hidden behind a monstrous yellow bow tie with red-polka-dots—bow ties were Topper's trademark—and his three-piece herringbone was meticulously tailored to his diminutive proportions. A brightly burnished walking stick with a large silver handle in the shape of an open-mouthed bulldog's head tapped along at his side.

Topper had affected his flamboyant image shortly after law school, when he passed up lucrative offers with large corporate firms to open a one-man criminal office. It set him apart. Made him noticeable. That, together with his skills and the fortuitous representation and acquittal of the youngest murder suspect in the district's history during his fourth month in practice assured Topper of a consistent string of six-figure years. Although Rosen had had no need for Topper's services until today, the two lunched at least once a month.

Topper's confidence was infectious. Despite his friend's foppish appearance, Rosen marveled at how completely at home Topper appeared in this degenerate environment. For the first time since Detective Amos and his gorilla partner's visit, Rosen allowed himself a small hope.

"Quite sorry about the holding cell, Arn. All that I could accomplish was to get you out a trifle faster than most." Topper's language, a combination of reformed Brooklynese and Cambridge English, had amused the hell out of Rosen years ago during its evolutionary stage. By now, it was just Topper, as much a part of his concept of his friend as the outlandish apparel.

"Let's chat for a few moments." Topper waved him toward a nearby door. Inside was a small room divided nearly in half by a strong wire screen. "You may wait out here," Topper instructed Rosen's guard. They moved to a small wooden table gouged with hundreds of initials, some nonsymmetrical hearts, and a couple of swastikas. Two gray metal chairs sat neatly underneath.

Topper indicated that Rosen take one. He delicately perched on the other, hands resting on the walking stick thrust between his legs, like an eighteenth-century aristocrat attending the opera. His eyes, behind the gold wire-rimmed glasses, were bright and concerned. "Normally they bring you in through there." Topper gestured toward a door on the opposite side of the screen. "But it seems that I have a certain amount of clout. Those cells are disgusting. Are you okay?"

"Okay" was one of Topper's involuntary concessions to his past.

"Yeah. I had a couple of bad moments, but I minded my own business and it worked out." An icy thought pierced his bravado. "I won't have to go back, will I?" He thought back to the scuffle initiator who was still stalking somewhere in the bleakness of the holding cell—or his imagination.

"No. I don't know if we can get you out, but you'll at least have a semiprivate cell or …" Topper paused and held up a tiny hand, palm outward. "Look. Allow me to start at the beginning. Just because you're a friend does not mean that I should behave like a boor." Topper's eyes wandered somewhere up and behind Rosen. "First I want to say how terribly sorry I am about Barbara, Eleanore, and Jonathon." After a long moment, Topper returned his gaze to Rosen's face. The cloudy emotion in his hazel eyes dissipated as his lawyer self took charge. "My team and I took the liberty of interviewing your coworkers. Somebody must have intimidated them. They all adhered to their evaluations of you as being unstable. Sorry. We simply could not shake them." He leaned the walking stick farther forward and patted his friend's extended arm. "*Yet!*" He winked …

Rosen hardly heard. He was overcome by memories. Seeing Topper, who frequently had dinner at the Rosens' home, especially after his divorce from the air-headed but sexy blond who wormed her way into his office as an uncommitted receptionist, then into his home as an uncommitted wife, gave Rosen the feeling that they were all together again in this drab little room.

Rosen forced himself back as the impact of Topper's words sunk in: there would be no quick fix. Rosen was thankful that he'd bridled his hope. At this point, he couldn't handle another disappointment. At least he'd seen this one coming. Rosen pondered Topper's information halfheartedly. "They're all tough guys. I really only knew Kilgore—but not that well. Everybody did their work and left. No real palling around at lunch or drinks after work. That's more for the operations guys with lots of war stories." He had to get mad, he decided, and fight his overwhelmed feeling. He couldn't expect Topper to take care of everything, make it go away like some wizard. It was up to you. When it came down to it, it was always up to you: school … the military … now. Rosen breathed deeply, squeezing his fingers into his palms to get the adrenaline flowing. Even if they weren't the best of buddies, those guys at work should have done the right thing—told the truth. "It's a tight group as far as the outside world is concerned. If someone gave them the word on me, they'd figure it's their patriotic duty to stick by it."

The anger *was* back. Rosen savored it; let it sweep through him. It would save him. Get Van Damme for him. Fuck Kilgore's and the others' warped sense of duty. They were selling him out! For whom? For lousy Van Damme, a goddamn snob who hung around with his good ol' operations buddies substituting "analysts" for "Polacks" in put-down jokes! "You oughta be able to crack them. They basically hate people like Van Damme." Topper took off his glasses and rubbed his eyes. "I'm sure I can break them on cross-examination, but that is not until trial. I just don't have much opportunity before then." He looked at Rosen, half smiling, sandy eyebrows arched. His voice was tentative.

Rosen assumed that was for effect. Topper was anything but tentative. From past experience, Rosen knew he was about to be asked to do something he didn't want to do.

"Arn, I believe our best chance is to request a psychiatric evaluation."

Rosen's chair flipped over as he shot up, gouging his hands into pockets while stalking toward the far corner of the tiny room, distancing himself as much as possible from Topper. "I am *not* crazy!" He pivoted, jabbing his index finger at the lawyer. "Van Damme wants it to look that way … but it's *not* true! Are you telling me that you think I am? If you are, you can just get the hell outta here *right now*!"

Topper's gaze held the half smile still in place. "Come on, Arn. You don't think that I believe you killed your family, do you … *Do you?*" His tone was calm, but Topper wasn't going to let this go until he got an answer.

Rosen glared at his friend, hands practically pushing through his pockets, face tense. After a long moment, he answered no.

Topper's smile widened, although his voice remained soft. He never pressed an advantage unnecessarily, one reason that he was such an exceptional negotiator. "Please listen. I need time to have my people investigate. As you are no doubt aware, your agency is a formidable opponent. It will require availing myself of all my not insubstantial recourses, but that requires time. I can delay your presentment and keep you out of a cell … if you allow me to. I will accomplish this by going along with the evidence, which your detractors have so conveniently provided, i.e., that you are mentally unstable. Make your opponent's efforts work for you. A wise principal in martial arts as well as the judicial process."

Rosen righted his chair and raised his hands, palms outward, in surrender. "Okay, Brain." He used Topper's college nickname, a comforting reminder of their closeness. "Whatever you say."

*　*　*

The commissioner of the court, an appointed attorney who preferred to refer to himself as "Judge," although this was technically incorrect, was a balding black man with a frizzy halo of white hair. The judge was not in a good mood. He never was by 3 p.m., with at least two more hours staring him in the face. "I used to think that when I made the bench, the shit would be over," he often told his wife. She doused him with proper amounts of sympathy but would have seen him dead rather than relinquish his post, which put her on equal footing with her uppity sister and plastic surgeon brother-in-law. "But I still do all the dirty work for the white dudes." He referred to the interminable string of presentments—first stop in the judicial assembly line of criminal processing— while the elected judges were always home, drinks in hand by four thirty.

The judge stared sourly at the packed courtroom. More were waiting to come up from the cells below when these were done. He'd be lucky if he didn't run past five. He rolled weary eyes toward his bailiff. The infuriating civil servant lounged against the glass divider that separated the officers of the court from the rows of fidgeting observers. Appointees like himself got the lousiest staff. "Next," droned the bailiff's bored voice, as if the judge had imposed upon him.

Lawrence Topper strode forward, Rosen and the heavy guard following. *Oh boy,* thought the judge, *the perfect end to a perfect day.* Topper was a heavyweight, maybe the heaviest. There would be no quick wrap-up of this one, no intimidating Topper as he could the younger lawyers. No "Say what you have to say and shut up" routine would cow Topper. Topper was a showman, and the judge knew that he was in for the full performance.

The fresh-out-of-school district attorney gaped at Topper like a high school basket baller watching Michael Jordan come out to shoot a few. *No help there,* thought the judge, glancing toward the implacable second hand of the huge clock over the rear doors. Sighing, he settled in as Topper began, too weary to remind Topper that the awestruck kid DA should review the charges first. God, was it going to be an un-fucking-believable long afternoon …

Within a couple of minutes, the judge felt so much better that he almost laughed, barely stopping himself in time. This big shot Jew lawyer was going to make his life easy. *Very* easy. That was because he knew something Topper didn't know, and did that make the judge feel oh so good. What he knew that the high-and-mighty-Mr.-Lawrence-Topper-Jew lawyer didn't know was that the psychiatric commitment Topper was working up a head of steam to get for his client was *exactly* what the judge was going to give him. That was at least since about 12:15 this afternoon, when a cold voice called his chambers to "suggest" it. The outraged judge had acquiesced without a whisper after his caller played a taped excerpt of the judge's past Thursday night escapade at the Ramada. The contralto "Oh, yes, Daddy, oh, *yes!*" of his amorous—and expensive—companion had been unmistakably clear.

*   *   *

Things went as smoothly as Topper predicted that they would. The assistant district attorney didn't get in a word. Then the judge waved Topper off, practically before the dapper lawyer had even begun, remanding Rosen for psychiatric evaluation in less time than it took to go through a McDonald's drive-in. Rosen ran the scene over and over in his mind on the ride to Fair Oaks Medical Center, clinging to it, taking strength from it, believing with everything he could muster that Topper's competence would unravel the maze that Charles Van Damme had erected around him.

A white-coated orderly drove. Rosen's heavy guard had turned him over to another heavy guard at the jail's side entrance. The man sat glowering across from Rosen, hand never far from his holstered revolver—with the safety strap off— like an old Western gunslinger daring Rosen to draw. Rosen ignored him, staring out instead at occasional passing cars, late-lit hillside houses, and his own frustrated reflection in the night-black window.

What was Van Damme doing right now? Laughing to himself? Celebrating how easily he had smashed a nobody analyst who tried to interfere—tried to apply rules to a life that was above rules—as he sipped an especially good sherry from wafer-thin crystal? Yes, that was exactly what the arrogant murdering traitor was doing, having a late drink with the old boys at the club, discussing the scandal, showing appropriate shock and embarrassment that such a thing could have taken place. No doubt being consoled by the others. "How can you keep track of every little analyst?" they would say. "I suppose you're right," he'd agree, eyes down, playing on their sympathy, laughing his ass off inside. It was unbearable.

For a single moment, Rosen tensed, ready to take the guard up on his challenge; he wanted Van Damme that much. The man's hand slid perceptibly closer to his weapon, fleshy fingers undulating in anticipation of the deadly scenario. Had the guard really sensed Rosen's intent or was it only the effect of the stress upon his imagination? Rosen couldn't chance it. He'd have his shot when the odds were more in his favor. Or Topper might get him out without his having to take any foolish risks. Rosen settled firmly back against the hard vinyl seat to diffuse any potential confrontation.

How easy it must have been for Van Damme to change his personnel records. What about getting Kilgore, Moroski, and Doyle to lie? Had Van Damme appealed to their patriotism—the agency was full of patriots. Something like: "I'm worried about Rosen. He could compromise our operations people in his present state." Everyone would bend over backward to help the division chief. No one wanted a loose cannon endangering field agents' lives. They'd be glad to help him clean the matter up neatly with no outside interference.

Since Carter, the agency was paranoid about outside interference. Do anything to avoid it. Outside was the enemy: congressional oversight committees, the press, the courts. The only ones you could trust were your brothers in the agency. Rosen himself had believed it. Not as much as some, but sort of. Until now …

His records could have been changed weeks ago. Then Van Damme set his operations guerillas on him until they got what they wanted. Rosen's head dropped. He sniffed through moist nostrils. Van Damme's ops people wouldn't even look at the contents of the file for which they killed his family. Not when Van Damme told them, as the clever bastard would, that it was classified "Eyes Only".

Face it. After the last three days, why shouldn't the guys he worked with back up the agency and agree he was wacko? After all of the allegations against him, they'd have to be crazy not to believe it. Hell, wouldn't he if the situation were reversed?

Depressed, Rosen slouched down even more, vinyl squeaking where his butt scraped along the seat. He stared at himself staring back from the window.

*　　*　　*

The van swung into a tight left, jerking Rosen away from the window and then throwing him back. A shadowy guard stepped from a small booth with a peaked roof. Behind was a large wrought iron gate, the fantastic curves and angles of its flower-shaped scrollwork accentuated by the headlights. Except for the guard's failure to wear a grenadier's red uniform and tall black hat, they could have been before the entrance to Buckingham Palace. Maybe the queen would greet him, Rosen mused, moonlighting as a shrink in white robes and stethoscope. The guard shined his light at the driver and then tiptoed back to flash it around the van's interior. Its beam caught Rosen square in the eyes. Apparently satisfied, the guard withdrew to his little house.

The gate swung inward, its massive sections moving quietly through the heavy air permeating the driver's open window. They lurched forward, gears whining as the van climbed a gradual but steady incline. Silhouettes of large trees flashed by. The van swayed as the road curved sharply past a row of parked cars, slowing in front of wide white stairs.

Rosen's beefy guard rose, knees creaking, and yanked at the doors before the driver had quite stopped. He dropped heavily to the ground, grunting at Rosen to follow. Together they trudged upward toward an elaborately carved stone fence, backlit by a low row of halogens that highlighted its eerie contours.

Beyond the fence was an enormous patio. Harsh moonlight lit intertwined geometric designs in its tile surface. It had a hypnotic effect on Rosen as he and his guard traversed toward the long castle-like building. A thousand crickets harmonized with the echoes of their footsteps.

The castle's large wooden door swung open before Rosen's guard reached the bronze dragon head knocker. Someone inside was already waiting. Rosen glanced toward the carved stone archway but was unable to locate the surveillance camera. A snarling gargoyle perched at its peak, another at each of its corners, their grotesque features further distorted by the scanty light from two lantern-shaped fixtures flanking the doorway. Cameras could easily be hidden in the gaping mouths or deeply hollowed eyes.

Rosen's speculation was interrupted by a jovial voice. "Good to see you again, Hansen. Please come inside. Yes. Yes, do come in." A nervous little man, hands fluttering like restless moths in the light, dressed in a tweed sport coat, beckoned anxiously. Flanking him were two large men in white uniforms. Their biceps stretched the cotton material of their jackets to near ripping. Rosen's guard, Hansen, lumbered over the jamb, yanking Rosen along by the handcuffs.

Observing Hansen's rough maneuver, the little man tsk-tsked. "There is no need for those in here. Kindly remove them." He stared reproachfully at the guard, but Hansen's moon-faced scowl remained firmly in place.

All eyes remained fixed upon Hansen for the better part of a minute before he reluctantly dug a beefy hand into his pants pocket. It was already stretched taught by his huge thighs. Rosen waited for the pocket to rip, spewing condoms, coins, Lifesavers, and whatever else guards possessed, but it held as Hansen dug around—pushing his luck—until, after many tugs, the hand reemerged with a large key ring. Hansen bounced it up and down in his palm, sending a raucous jangle echoing back from the hall's domed ceiling. Once more, Hansen's tiny black eyes dared Rosen to bolt for freedom. Rosen ignored him. Hansen's scowl deepened until his cheeks buried his eyes. He jammed his key into the cuffs and clicked them open, scraping Rosen's skin as he yanked them off. Stuffing them into his rumpled jacket, Hansen dug out a dog-eared sheet of pink paper and handed it to the little man, who signed and handed it back. Hansen turned with a grunt, leaving the door ajar as he exited.

The little man shook his head as Hansen lumbered across the patio. "Someday I suspect someone will be delivering *him* here." He smiled conspiratorially at Rosen, darting a quick hand out as one of the uniformed men swung the heavy door shut. It closed with a well-oiled click.

"I'm Dr. René Gorgone, assistant director of Fair Oaks. You certainly were fortunate to be placed here for testing." Gorgone nodded his Leprechaun-like head in support of his assertion.

Rosen noticed large freckles beneath thinning red hair, more peeking from behind monstrous brown horn-rims.

"You definitely must have some pull. Most of them are sent to that Bedlam of a state hospital. If they're not mentally disturbed when they arrive, they certainly are after a few days there." Gorgone's laughter tinkled like wind chimes, his eyes crinkling in appreciation of his own humor.

Rosen felt almost *comfortable*. A gusher of loss instantaneously immersed Rosen's momentary respite.

Gorgone must have sensed it. His lenses magnified the compassion in his eyes as he softly introduced the others. "Mr. Rosen, this is Leonard." Gorgone nodded toward the large black man on his right. "And that's Eddie," indicating the equally large white one who had closed the door. Both remained immobile, arms locked behind backs in "at ease" position, impassive as concrete columns. "They will help you during your stay. Feel free to ask them for anything you might need—anything except the key to the front door, that is." Again the tinkling laugh. Rosen detected no malice in the joke.

The little man glanced over Rosen's shoulder. Rosen followed his gaze to a massive grandfather clock guarding the base of a wide marble staircase that spiraled up to the next landing. Its mahogany case was burnished to a degree, rivaling the sheen of the stairway's curving bronze banister. A smiling man in the moon peeped through a cutout at the base of the clock's face. Rosen presumed that an equivalently jovial sun replaced it during daylight hours.

"It's terribly late, and I'm sure that you are tired after your ordeal. Eddie will show you to your room. Good night, Mr. Rosen. See you tomorrow." Gorgone's "tomorrow" had an upward lilt. With a perky smile and farewell flutter of his small hands, Gorgone turned and, followed by the hulking Leonard, scurried toward a lighted corridor to the left.

Eddie grunted for Rosen to follow him up the stairs. One-by-three notches were cut into the plaster every few feet. In each was a brightly colored vase, backlit from above. Solid Plexiglas sheets, screwed tightly into the wall, protected them from stairway traffic.

The second floor was carpeted in lush pile. They walked along a corridor paneled in rich mahogany to shoulder height, finished off in light yellow to the ceiling. There were no sounds from the regularly spaced heavy doors they passed. Eddie stopped him at the fourth one on the right and dug out a monster batch of keys from inside his shirt. He squinted at them in the dim light, cursing under his breath, finally grasping one, clicking it into the lock, and shoving the solid door open.

Eddie gestured for Rosen to enter, and then he followed. "Dat's da baath." He pointed a bulky arm toward a door at the left. "Plenty a towels. Closet's next 'a it. Ring da bell near da bed if ya need anyting."

Eddie sounded bored, like a bellhop who'd given the same spiel a thousand times. His broken nose was too far left, as if an amateur had reset it. His right ear curled inward, a classic "cauliflower." Although he only looked to be in his late twenties, the man had done some hard living, Rosen believed.

"Robe 'n pajamas inna closet. Since it's so late, we'll let ya sleep in tomorra. Sombody'ul comfaya aroun' ten."

Despite his size, Eddy was light on his feet. Speech over, he was at the door and out before Rosen turned back from his inspection of the room. The heavy lock snapped decisively into place.

White tile gleamed in the bathroom. It was fully stocked with a fresh tube of Crest, toothbrush still in its box, razor, shaving cream. There was everything he needed, but Rosen was too tired to do anything but splash water on his face and use the modern replica of an old pull chain toilet. The lush towels nearly matched the yellow of the corridor. He remembered reading that certain colors were considered soothing. He assumed that yellow was high on the list.

Rosen staggered toward the bed. His jaw still hurt if he ground it around, so naturally he kept testing it. Why did he do that? He was too tired to analyze his action. Plenty of time tomorrow. Or the next day … He stripped off his clothes, dropping them near the bed. Heck with the pajamas. He was too tired to walk to the closet. He flopped down, sliding under the light yellow—what else?—quilt. His king-size bed was nice and firm, the sheets cool and smooth. Yeah, plenty of time to think tomorrow.

His eyelids fluttered down, jolted up, floated down again. Topper was right. This *definitely* beat jail. Good ol' Topper. Topper'd help him beat this so he could kill Van Damme. Thank God for Topper, not that Rosen was too high on God right now. Well, he'd also work on that one tomorrow … or the next day. He had time, lots of time to work everything out, even how to escape if Topper couldn't help. It would be easier getting away from here than a prison. He'd figure it all out tomorrow or the next day. Plenty of time.

Rosen was wrong, dead wrong!

Chapter 6

Lawrence J. Topper was ecstatic. He felt so good that after he parked his Mercedes convertible in the underground garage of his Connecticut Avenue high-rise, he strolled out the side exit instead of taking the elevator to his one-entire-floor penthouse.

He was too wired to sleep, although it was pushing 1:00 a.m. Court always excited him. The jitters of his first day and his first misdemeanor motion—just a rookie; nervous in front of the old pros with their shiny suits, worn briefcases, and chewed cigars; praying he didn't screw things up for his pitiful junkie client in a borrowed jacket—were long gone, but the thrill was the same. Even after … God, was it ten-plus years? And this was the best yet, defending a good friend instead of the usual sleazes. Sure, they were richer sleazes than in the old days. His clothes and his accent—boy, had they paid off! Along with his damn sharp lawyering, of course. But sleazes nevertheless. Now here he was with a *real* client, a good guy who was actually the screwee instead of the screwer, like most of the garbage he represented.

Topper still couldn't get it through his head: Barbara and the kids. He'd just been at their house for dinner two weeks ago, playing the old pull-the-coin-out-of-the-ear trick with Jonathon, the little guy giggling every time, as if Topper hadn't been pulling quarters out of Jonathon's same ear since the youngster first started walking. Kidding Eleanor, "Lanie," as Topper called her—although at nine she considered that undignified and told him so every time—also about her latest TV heartthrob. Envying Arnie, Barbara, who truly did get better, not older.

No good to think about that. He had to think about helping Arnie. No way he could have done that unspeakable thing. Arnie had been set up, and *that* was the added thrill! Topper couldn't help it; he knew he shouldn't feel good about any of the atrocious things that had happened, but damn if he wasn't jazzed about taking on those bastards at the CIA, just like the old activist days of Nam. In the government's face! Back then, it was general: a wrong against the American people. Now it was personal, making the challenge even sweeter. The government had destroyed those dear to him, closer by far than his brother's two brats and nasal scarecrow of a wife. He couldn't wait for tomorrow. Topper checked the luminous dial on his watch. No, today. With some real probing, he would get the bastards. He could not wait.

Topper looked up, startled, not realizing how far he'd walked. Too busy concentrating on his thoughts. He scanned a row of super-expensive, squeezed-together Georgetown houses, most of the lights out by this hour. Everything painted and clean. Beamers in the garages, no doubt. Different way of life from the folks with whom he spent most of his time. Even his "better" clients lived in gaudy splendor, unable to recognize tasteful elegance if it bit their behinds.

He fondled the walking stick's handle, comforted by the metallic feel of the dog's face. He became a little lonely in places that were the antithesis of his own life style. Kids up in those dark bedrooms. Golden retrievers and fat black cats sleeping in the kitchens. Matching eighteen-speed bikes in the garages next to the Beamers. Stability. People bound to each other. The concept simultaneously scared and intrigued him.

Suddenly, Topper felt very lonely. He'd lost three of the only four people that he really loved, whom, he liked to think, had loved him in return. Topper shivered, although the sticky air was residually hot. He turned for home.

Hurrying across the street in a futile effort to outdistance his thoughts, Lawrence J. Topper never saw the car coming until much too late. The Chevy Lumina roared from a dead stop to forty bone-crushing miles per hour in ample time to intercept Topper before he reached the curb. The impact shot him straight up, his cape spreading on his descent, like a midget Batman wannabe. He crunched back onto the hood before bounding off into a row of neatly trimmed shrubs. After a teetering moment, Topper's body flopped into the street.

The Chevy accelerated off, its screaming engine barely audible as the first lights in the sleeping rows of bedrooms snapped on.

* * *

Rosen had not enjoyed the day. Maybe if he'd been able to relax first, get himself mentally prepared. Oh, everyone had been nice enough—no problem with that—but the interviewers, a procession of psychiatrists, psychologists, therapists, and everyone but the plumber, started getting to him about midafternoon. Everyone listened politely as he explained what happened, and then they went back to the same questions—about work pressures, family relationships, outside stresses—proving that they hadn't heard a word he said. The doctors were only there to do their jobs: determine if he was too crazy to stand trial. They didn't care that he hadn't killed his family. Didn't even seem to consider the possibility.

Rosen's frustration had escalated minute by minute. By the time the orderlies brought him back along yellow corridors to his yellow room, Rosen was in knots. Dropping his shirt and pants at the bathroom door, he shuffled to the shower, slid back the glass panel above the tub, yanked the handle toward *H*, tested the temperature with a raised left palm, peeled off socks and underwear, and stepped onto the tub's smooth surface. Little no-slip butterflies, green instead of yellow—thank God—gave him a secure grip. He adjusted the shower massage to high letting the fierce pulsations gouge his back and neck muscles until they released. Next he worked his scalp and then let blasts of water pound off his chest and stomach. The contraption did its magic. Twenty minutes later, Rosen no longer minded the room's hateful yellow. Naked, he yanked the quilt back and slapped face-first onto the sheets.

Knocking awoke him two hours later. Eddie was outside to take him to dinner.

The dining room came complete with white tablecloths, high-backed chairs, beige drapes held away from slim two-story windows by flowing tassels, and gray-uniformed servers scurrying between large round tables.

The plastic utensils were the only giveaway, except, of course, for the diners themselves. Perplexed women and dull-eyed men stared at their meals without recognition, while white-uniformed orderlies coaxed chicken and vegetables through their slack lips. Wildly gesturing manics, bright eyes flitting from food to private visions high above, jabbered nonstop to themselves. Most, however, appeared perfectly normal, eating and maintaining quiet conversations with tablemates, stopping with disapproving looks as the din rose, continuing when it subsided.

Eddie walked Rosen to an empty table toward the rear. A server was there almost at once with soup. Eddie sat, heavy shoulders hunched forward, staring at Rosen's food.

"Want some?" Rosen ventured.

Eddie's bushy blond eyebrows descended, as if he was surprised that Rosen could talk. "Nah." The big shoulders shrugged. "We et befaw." He went back to staring.

So much for sarcasm, thought Rosen. He spooned his soup. Split pea. Not his favorite, but it beat Eddie's conversation. He was halfway into his chicken Kiev when Gorgone fluttered over.

"May I join you, Mr. Rosen?"

Rosen nodded toward a chair. The little man, this time in tweed with leather sleeve patches, settled lightly down. "Hello, Eddie." He beamed toward the big man. "Everything okay?"

"Fine, Dr. Gorgone." The orderly's face lit up like a kid trying to sell his teacher on an A.

Eddie must be going for orderly of the month, thought Rosen.

After rewarding Eddie with another smile, Gorgone turned his attention toward Rosen. "How about you, Mr. Rosen? I hope that you've had no trouble finding your way around. Fair Oaks can be a little intimidating at the beginning."

"No problems with Eddie helping me." Rosen smiled.

Plainly embarrassed, Gorgone *ahem-ed.* "Yes. Quite. Quite. Well, we do have to make sure you are all right. It would not be fair to the other guests if we were to allow you to harm them, would it?" The magnified brown eyes behind the glasses radiated sincere regret. The man was truly sympathetic. In spite of his general hostility toward Fair Oaks and its staff, Rosen was drawn to Gorgone, just as he had been the night before. The little doctor actually seemed concerned, not dutifully polite like the others. But would Gorgone help? Rosen wasn't sure. Nor was he sure that he was emotionally up to telling his story, just to risk getting shot down again.

Gorgone smiled at the big man again. "Eddie, would you be so kind as to excuse us for a few minutes?"

"Shaw, Doc." Eddie rose, flexed, and moved to a nearby empty table, still only three large strides from Rosen.

The small man's smile turned sad. He leaned closer to Rosen. There was the faintest aroma of alcohol on Gorgone's breath. "We haven't had much luck with you so far. Frankly, Drs. Carey and Morganstern are baffled. They both feel that you have erected a rather impenetrable barrier, an illusion, if you will. Of course, we have all the time that we need, but I wish that you would give some thought to something. Would you?" The Leprechaun face was open, hopeful.

Rosen waited.

"Tomorrow would you try—just try—to consider the possibility that there might have been other reasons for what happened … other than your superior's machinations?" Gorgone's little hands fluttered up, blocking Rosen's angry response. "I know what you believe … and I'm not drawing any conclusions yet. I'm only asking you to help me by allowing us to explore some other possibilities. Just to get a clear fix on the entire picture." His voice was soft and friendly. "That's not an unreasonable request, is it?"

"Dr. Gorgone." Rosen found his voice quavering as his hands knotted beneath the table. "Everything I have told those doctors … and the police before them—*and* my lawyer *and* the judge, *and* everyone else who has been after me ever since I woke up in that hospital room—is absolutely true! There *is* no alternative interpretation. Can you try to understand that? *Please*."

The little doctor leaned even closer, a good friend sharing secrets in the school cafeteria. "I do. Really. I *do*. But, Arnie … may I call you that? Arnie, if you could just *try* tomorrow. Just for argument's sake. I believe you, but things would be so much easier if we could approach the situation from a different angle. Please just say you'll try."

Rosen did try. He tried very hard, in fact. But his right hand came out from beneath the table, anyway. Gorgone was no different from the others, only phonier. He watched the hand as if it belonged to someone else. It was too much. Everything was too much! Rosen watched his hand edge toward his shallow dish of Jell-O as if the appendage belonged to someone else. He felt the springy substance squish through his fingers as they clamped the smooth, cool surface. Gorgone sat there, face close to Rosen's, looking confident and probably thinking that he had made a reasonable request so of course Rosen would agree. Gorgone's cockiness was the last straw.

Rosen knew he shouldn't do it, but Gorgone had betrayed him. Gorgone, of everyone with the exception of Topper, should have comprehended that Arnie Rosen was a victim: someone who lost everything because he tried to do what was right. He *was* right. *Van Damme* was wrong. He'd been so sure that the assistant director would understand. Gorgone had seemed so empathetic. But Gorgone was just acting: a bedside manner for the crazies. Gorgone didn't care about the truth.

Rosen's despair bubbled into frustration, which overflowed into anger. The hand came up, filled with Jell-O. Gorgone—the betrayer—didn't have a chance. The red stuff flew, sticking to his face, hair, and glasses— dripping toward the tweed jacket even as Eddie's chair screeched behind

Rosen, splatting and spreading into the woven fabric as Eddie bear-hugged Rosen's arms to his sides.

Gorgone was a good sport; he kept a faint smile on his face while wiping Jell-O from his glasses, jacket—just about everywhere—but there was a smoldering glow in his eyes as he quietly suggested that Eddie escort Rosen upstairs. Rosen glanced back as they hurried from the room. The assistant director delicately flicked a piece of red goo out of his white-tufted ear, to the astonishment of the fifteen or so diners sufficiently in touch with reality to comprehend the event's momentousness.

As if Eddie weren't enough to handle Rosen, Leonard joined them at the stairs, squeezing Rosen's other arm in his vice-like hands. Rosen's toes barely grazed the ground as they hoisted him toward the second floor.

"You not only crazy—you stupid," was Leonard's assessment during the brief trip to Rosen's room. Once inside, they sprawled him on the large bed, hard enough to make it rattle. Eddie shook his head as he took a last long look. The powerful orderly pursed his thick lips as if contemplating Rosen's unspeakable fate, and then drew the door nearly closed.

"Dawc was roit not tell'n 'im dat 'is lawya's dead." Eddie's gravelly voice, directed down the corridor at Leonard, filtered through the crack in Rosen's door. "He's nuts anough awready." The door clicked shut.

Rosen stared long at the ceiling, watching the shadows of tree branches sway across the etched glass light fixture. The fragile black lines dimmed and blurred as the afternoon light waned. Rosen continually blinked to keep the fading silhouettes in focus.

Now Topper was gone. They'd taken everyone! There was nothing more to lose, no one left. Fine. The part of Rosen that was half-dead died all the way. It sort of made things easier.

Eventually, all but a few outside lights switched off and his shadow branches evaporated. Outside, "good nights" were exchanged as locks clicked up and down his corridor. It was not easy to detect sounds through his thickly paneled door, but if he kept very still, he could, just a little. The creak in front of his room a couple of hours later did not surprise Rosen one bit.

*　*　*

Stevenson didn't talk much because of his lousy lisp, but he sure thought plenty. Right now, Stevenson was thinking about how he was really getting tired of this Rosen. First the bastard got out of a damn car crash that should have killed Superman, so Craig got his ass chewed until two in the morning. *So then I have to take fuckin' Craig's bullshit until four 'cause fuckin' College Boy Craig is agency, while I'm just an independent contractor—no benefits, no future, no protection—'cause I didn't have the money to go to college.*

Then I have to drive around in that damn Chevy on the hottest night of the whole fuckin' year with no fuckin' air-conditioning-'cause the asshole who left it in the supermarket parking lot with the keys sticking out of the trunk forgot to have the coolant checked—tailing Rosen's lawyer in his stupid Halloween outfit until I get to splatter him all over the street.

Now I have to kill another night finishing this Rosen asshole off. And all for the same original price 'cause the agency says I screwed up! And Craig, the agency pet. Craig, who fucked up just as bad as I did. Craig gets to screw some hot little bimbo from secretarial while I sweat my ass off finishing our job.

Stevenson reached the second-floor landing. At least getting into this damn nuthouse was a piece of cake. That goof-off at the front gate wouldn't see a six-hundred-pound gorilla slip over the fence. Too busy watching some 1930s rerun on a goddamn little TV instead of doing his job. And getting in the main building was no harder.

Place is supposed to be wired in case the nuts try to escape, so I bring current sensors, jacks, the works, but they leave the damn windows open back of the kitchen. What a laugh. Probably some spic dishwasher. That's the trouble with this country—too many lowlifes screwing it up. And the surveillance. Sheez, my grandma could have dodged those old cameras sticking out of the walls—unless the whole thing was a setup! Yeah, it was too damn easy! It'd be just like that bastard Craig, bustin' my hump when I probably could'uv walked in the front door. Son of a bitch! Maybe Craig already had someone on the inside. Whoever the guy is, he better keep out of my damn way.

No one around, although that big mother of a clock was loud enough to wake dead Uncle Shamus when it hit three. Three! Another fuckin' night shot to hell! Thanks, Craig, you ...

Stevenson moved softly down the corridor. A green exit sign at the far end threw off enough light to make out the doors, but Stevenson needed his penlight for the keyhole. He shifted weight in order to slip the thin chrome cylinder from his black windbreaker. The damn coat was too heavy, but it made him less visible, as did his black sweatpants. Couldn't use blackface, although he would have preferred it, because how did you explain *that* if you got caught?

The weight shift did it, damn it! A floorboard gave under the carpet. *Why the hell don't I just yell, "Here I am, come to kill you!"* Stevenson thought in disgust. His short-sleeved cotton shirt was soaking under the windbreaker. *The cheap fuckers who ran the place must cut the air-conditioning when everyone was asleep. Probably charge a fortune too, judging from the fancy vases and shit.* Stevenson stood for a full two minutes, shoulders hunched forward, weight on the balls of his feet, breathing deeply, ready to move fast if a door opened …

Nothing.

Two more steps and he was at the fourth room on the right. He crouched, gripping the penlight with his teeth. The tiny beam speared the keyhole. Stephenson inserted a thin metal pick. The lock flipped open in less than a second. A lot quieter than a key, if you knew what you were doing. He dropped the pick and light into his pocket; patted the other for his hypodermic, although he knew it was there; nudged Rosen's door open just a crack.

Listened. Nothing.

Nudged it a little more …

Still nothing.

Slid through, crouching …

There wasn't much light, just a patch on the ceiling from the window. Good enough. Eyes darting, ears tuned, Stevenson rose slowly, hating the way his sticky shirt tugged against his skin. All because of this asshole. Stevenson couldn't wait to finish it. A pillow over the face to slow him down and then a little prick of tabun to finish it. Clichéd but effective. Causing instant nerve paralysis. Untraceable. One of the few truly natural causes of death.

Stevenson was halfway out of his crouch when he realized that something was wrong: no breathing from the bed. Sleeping people don't hold their breath. They breathe loudly, relaxed.

The contract killer crouched back down, hands spread, fingers stiff. Silhouettes materialized as his eyes became accustomed to the feeble light. A high dresser, two armchairs by the window, one hell of a huge bed with the quilt thrown back—*empty!*

Stevenson spun, but he was too late. He couldn't believe the bastard had fucked him up. Again.

* * *

Rosen slipped from the space between the dresser and wall, easing carefully past the partially opened door. The crouching man had not even looked in his direction; he couldn't have seen him in the shadows anyway. But the guy's instincts were good. Half spinning, he caught the descending onyx tiger paperweight, the heaviest thing that Rosen could find on short notice, on his shoulder instead of his head. There was a soft grunt as the tiger's base cracked the man's clavicle. The sound filled Rosen with satisfaction. Dim light from the window haloed his attacker's head. The man had a crew cut. This was one of the two who had boozed him up and tried to kill him. CIA? Maybe he could bash Crew Cut enough to find out.

Crew Cut was tough. He spun back and up, circling, keeping his damaged left shoulder away from Rosen, his right hand forward at waist level. Rosen noticed from the man's hand movements that he wielded a blade. A momentary glint of light confirmed it. Whatever deadly little accident Crew Cut had planned for Rosen was forgotten. Now Crew Cut was desperate, prepared to kill Rosen in any way he could and worry about the cover-up later.

The bed rammed the back of Rosen's knees as he maneuvered away from the knife. There was no room to move. He tried to reverse his direction, but Crew Cut was on him. With his bad arm, Crew Cut pummeled Rosen's face, distracting Rosen's attention from the slashing blade as he forced Rosen onto the bed, crowding him as he pressed his weapon closer. The blade darted out, but instead of lunging backward to avoid it, Rosen pushed forward, chest slamming inside the other's left elbow, blocking the swiping knife arm. Crew Cut was strong. His forearm and biceps bulged, forcing the knife hand around Rosen's cocked elbow and toward Rosen's back. Crew Cut's breath rasped loudly in Rosen's ear. The stench of perspiration poured from his half-open windbreaker. Rosen could not stop the arm because one of Crew Cut's feet was planted firmly upon the floor, while Rosen was bent over the bed, giving the shorter man superior traction. Rosen began bending farther backward. Crew Cut's knife arm closed in like a vice. Rosen tensed, anticipating the point's contact. Shifting his chin away from the pressing head, Rosen dropped it hard on the injured shoulder, gouging by tensing his neck and jaw muscles. Crew Cut groaned. Rosen dug deeper. Crew Cut cried out, tried to back away, relaxing his knife arm as he disengaged. Rosen hung on, digging all the more, feeling the cracked clavicle give, hearing it snap. He locked his fingers around Crew Cut's wrist as he backed the whimpering man off the bed and toward the wall.

Crew Cut's head shattered a picture. Rosen drove his right knee upward, missing the groin but coming close enough to hurt. Crew Cut was going down, gasping through clenched teeth. Suddenly, Crew Cut's perspiring wrist jerked free. Rosen grabbed for it with both hands as he pivoted his shoulder into his crumbling opponent. He had the wrist again, but Crew Cut's blade was already whipping toward Rosen's stomach. The passing blade tore at his waist, yet he yanked Crew Cut's arm through, taking a worse cut as he used the shorter man's momentum to accelerate the blade back toward his assailant's chest. Warm liquid dripped over Rosen's wrists as Crew Cut's breath whistled out in a long, low sigh. The body, limp and heavy upon Rosen's shoulder, sagged to the carpet, forcing Rosen down with it.

Rosen slid all the way down, too exhausted to fight free. Crew Cut's chest rested upon his shoulder, soaking his stomach and lap in hot blood as Rosen gulped for air. When his breath returned, Rosen felt for the carotid artery. Crew Cut was dead.

Rosen shrugged Crew Cut's body off, propped it against a wall, and hunched over. Crew Cut's blood soaked deeper into Rosen's pajamas, warm, sticky, bonding him with this stranger who had ravaged his future. He studied Crew Cut. The face was open and peaceful in the gray light. Crew Cut looked as if he would cooperate if he could, clarify his role in the horrors of the past five days—even testify on Rosen's behalf. If only Rosen hadn't killed him. Rosen peered more closely. Crew Cut's slack jaw was square, his face wide and strong, the close-cropped hair disciplined. This man wouldn't give away ice in a blizzard; he would take a prison sentence in silence. Typical agency macho. Suddenly, Rosen was glad that Crew Cut was dead and that *he* had he killed him. He was only sorry that he didn't know if Crew Cut was Barbara's killer. His insides told him yes—but he would find out for sure. He *definitely* would.

*　*　*

Five minutes later, washed and back in his clothes, the painful but not deep cut from Crew Cut taped with adhesive from his well-stocked medicine cabinet, Rosen slipped out the open door. *Too bad the window is barred*, he thought with a last look.

Rosen spotted the first camera halfway down the hall and waited for it to turn away before sprinting under it. Silence, except for his soft breath. The thick carpet helped. The camera hummed overhead on its return swing. He darted forward, stopping at the corridor's mouth, flattening against the wall, wood molding pressing against his chest. The next camera was halfway down the circular stairs, between two of the highly protected vases—a longer distance than his previous dash. He leaped, slipping on the top stair, catching the banister, pushing off toward the wall, spinning under the panning camera by a hair. This time he hadn't been so quiet. He waited, fighting the urge to take a good deep breath.

There was no sound but the powerful ticks of the clock. Rosen tiptoed toward the banister. Another big white-coated orderly—one he hadn't seen before—sat slouched over the security desk. Earphones were clamped over his bushy brown hair, and he was tapping out rhythm with two pencils held like drumsticks. His head was bobbing, no doubt in time to the music, but he looked demented in the utter silence. A bank of TV screens glowed in front of him.

Rosen backed under the camera. No way out, that way. How had the agency guy gotten in? He remembered an article about Fair Oaks, some star coming here to detox or something, in one of the scandal rags Rosen enjoyed leafing through while killing time at the supermarket checkout counter. Fair Oaks was the kind of place where socialites went for fashionable breakdowns. It couldn't be agency controlled, so how the hell did Crew Cut get in? Certainly not through the front door.

When the camera swung away with a *whirr* of tiny gears, Rosen padded back to the entrance of his corridor, crouched low, futilely trying to peer across the bright hall into the dim arch on the opposite side. The only exit on his side was a fire door, complete with alarm, so whatever entry Crew Cut found had to be in that other wing.

There was fifty feet of glaring hall between Rosen and the other corridor. Risky, but the guy at the desk didn't look all that interested and might easily miss him. It was worth the chance because there was no future for him here, waiting for Van Damme to take another crack at him. The camera's tubular lens pointed downstairs. Rosen sucked in breath, whipped the air out through puckered lips, ducked across the open area. The camera panned back while he still had twenty feet to go. He pitched forward, skidding on the hallway's marble floor, his perspiration-wet palms squeaking as they stuck to its sleek surface, squeezing his face against the cold floor. The instrument's whirring went on forever, louder by the second. Rosen held his breath.

A chair scraped below. Rosen closed his eyes, considering his options if the orderly mounted the stairs. Maybe the man was already ringing for help. How did they do that? Did they have silent alarms like a bank? No point waiting. He tensed, preparing to dive down the corridor, and then a long sigh floated up the staircase. Rosen relaxed. That was not the sound of a man in pursuit of anything except a nap.

Keeping his eye on the camera, Rosen slid the rest of the way toward the far corridor's comforting darkness. A small red light halfway down indicated a camera placed similarly to the one in his corridor. He sprinted toward it, squatting beneath, while his eyes accustomed to the dim light. Another green-lit exit sign at the far end, similar to the one on his side. Rows of doors, same as his. What the hell was going on? Was he wrong? Was there no escape along this side either? Was this whole thing a company setup after all? If it was, he was only prolonging his own death. They could take him anytime they wanted. Chills of hopelessness skittered down Rosen's back.

It couldn't be true. The agency couldn't be this powerful! This was pure paranoia. *Never make your enemy more than he is, Arnie,* he thought as he struggled to calm himself.

But even if the agency didn't control Fair Oaks, Van Damme knew he was here and *that* was bad enough. He wouldn't live out the week. The *week*? How about the *day*? Crew Cut probably had a backup who was looking for him right now. He had to get away. Look hard, damn it …

There it was! A dark recess on the opposite side, halfway down the hall. Yes. It had to be! As the camera swung away, Rosen sprinted toward the black space in the wall, ducked in, located the handle of a small door, high-fiving to heaven as it gave. He stood blinking into a string of fluorescents illuminating a narrow wooden stairway that spiraled downward, like that of a lighthouse he'd seen in Nantucket. Servants' stairs leading down to the kitchen or pantry. Rosen tried to minimize the creaks, but the ancient steps wouldn't cooperate.

Rosen stepped into a little room lined with drawers and a massive sink, its porcelain yellowed but remarkably unchipped. He pushed open a swinging door between two glass-enclosed cupboards.

It was a monstrous kitchen, permeated by nostril-stinging antiseptic. Commercial-sized steel stoves occupied one wall, banks of refrigerators and freezers the other. The center was an obstacle course of butcher blocks on sturdy wooden legs, with knife handles protruding at odd angles from their flat surfaces. Rosen checked the upper walls for cameras. He saw none. High above a row of glistening stainless steel sinks at the far end was a bank of windows. The entire room was as immaculate, as if it had been steam cleaned.

Rosen stared up at the windows again. Thick wire-mesh grates were locked into place on all except the one on the far right. It hung open, resting on the grate beneath. Beyond was comforting night blackness. He rushed toward it, skidding on the slick tile, catching the sink underneath's edge for balance, clambering into it and up, then leveraging onto the window jamb as he slid his knees around and out. He dug his toes into the crevices of the rough stone exterior wall and lowered himself into the honeysuckle-heavy air. At the bottom, Rosen crunched onto a bed of moist flowers, imbedding his shoes deeply in the soggy soil beneath. His intrusion initiated a crescendo of cricket chirps as he sprinted off.

*　*　*

Eddie walked across the lobby from staff quarters. "You're up early," Stans said, keeping time to the music in his earphones as Eddie approached.

"Yeah. I couldn' sleep. Fuckin' Molla's snawrin'."

Stans rocked his head back, mouthing a silent laugh. His eyes rolled toward the ceiling as the music took over again.

Eddie saluted and lumbered up the stairs. He was agile when he had to be, like his sophomore year at Erasmus, in Brooklyn, when they were talking all-league football honors for him next year. But "next year" turned out different than everyone figured, with two busts for auto theft and one for breaking and entering, which he beat because the old couple was too scared to testify. No more football after that. No more school either. Most of the time, though, he walked like an elephant, clomping along in his size fourteens because it took less effort than picking his feet up.

Now he was going to clomp down the corridor to the new guy's room—find the corpse, tidy up if needed, and then notify Gorgone. Eddie already had it worked out. He'd say he wanted to check because what's-his-name—*Rosen*—seemed pretty agitated when he locked him in last night. Then tomorrow he'd collect the other five hundred to go with the five that preppie guy, Craig, laid on him this morning.

Funny, that Craig guy sure new everything about him: arrests, convictions, even the stuff Eddie thought no one knew, like that hooker in Atlantic City he worked over because she wouldn't throw in some freebie head after he came too fast for the two hundred he'd paid her. One thing Eddie did know: when a guy knew that much about you, he was better connected than you so you'd better play ball—especially if the money was good.

Something was wrong! Eddie could tell even before he saw the crumpled figure against the wall. It wasn't the right guy. Great! Instead of Rosen in bed with a heart attack, he had some Green Beret-looking schmuck bleeding all over the carpet. Shit, nothing was easy! Now he'd have to clean up the damn mess, get rid of the body, get the hell out of the room, and play dumb about what happened to Rosen.

For just a second, Eddie thought about taking off, but Craig said that if he was in, he was in, no matter what, and something told Eddie that Craig wasn't the kind of guy you wanted to piss off. Besides, now that this dead fuckup in the room was out of the picture, maybe Craig could use Eddie on a regular basis. *He* sure as hell wouldn't have screwed up, killing a weenie like Rosen. And he'd sure as shit would rather kill people than empty their fucking bedpans, anyway. And the money was probably a thousand times better!

Eddie turned on the bathroom light and yanked some thick bath towels off the shower door to wrap around the dead guy. Now that he thought about it, this could be a hell of a opportunity.

Chapter 7

Otto Manfred Gruhaber hunched over the Macintosh screen as if shielding its contents from his coworkers, which in fact he was. The frantically blinking red diagonal line would have alerted any but the most unsophisticated employees at Sklar Industries to the fact that classified material was being brought up by someone without clearance. Although Gruhaber had been a key member of the Indigo team since its inception four years before, the computer was right: he was totally without authority to screen the satellite's imaging system.

The late Henry Sklar, founder of the highly successful Silicon Valley technological firm whose major clients were the military and intelligence communities, had long ago instituted a sophisticated need-to-know security system, augmented by the latest enhanced user authentication devices. Henry had died at eighty-seven believing that his projects were inviolate.

Henry was wrong. It had taken Otto less than two hours to bypass the first two codes, which were known only to those working on Indigo's imaging system and changed daily. The third, which altered itself on a random schedule, took him a little longer, nearly four hours. It was all so simple that Otto could have laughed, if he were given to laughing, which he wasn't. Oh, maybe once or twice a year. Otto couldn't remember the last time, exactly, but he was certain he must have laughed at least a few times in the past twelve months. Anyway, he was much too busy to worry about it now. Otto's chubby fingers skipped along the keys.

Beating the system really had been easy, but then, anything involving computers was a snap for Otto. All he'd done was reduce the possible code components to computer-generated language and then … Well, anyway, nothing to it.

Of course, the computer knew that something was wrong. It franticly flashed its red warning, just like some little grade school tattletale. But aside from this futile ploy, the machine was helpless.

Sure, Otto had had to work late so that no one would see the spiteful system's warning, but since he always worked later than everyone, it was no inconvenience. No great price to pay for stopping those communist animals.

Otto thought back to the horrible stories—the ones he had heard as a frightened child. They were so frightening that the visions still haunted him.

His father's baby sister was raped repeatedly by a band of drooling Russian soldiers sweeping through his family's small town on their murderous rush toward Berlin. The poor girl's screams. Her sanity dribbling away as the clutching beasts mounted her again and again. Two months later, her mangled body was found sprawled on the vicious rocks below the village's steep entry road, a road that had been more-than-adequate protection from generations of aggressors on foot or horseback, but not from Russian half-tracks. The unfortunate child's broken fingers still cradled the two-foot crucifix that she carried like a favorite doll since her rape.

Of course, Otto had never actually known his aunt. He was born in Chicago, where his father, Heinrich, a ranking German physicist, had been spirited away by US Intelligence, as much to deprive the Russians of his brilliant rocketry know-how as for the United State's own use. But Otto occasionally saw her face in that of Heinrich Gruhaber, usually when too many Heinekens tipped over the barricades around his dear father's nightmares.

And who had killed her, not only her but also so many other helpless residents of the beaten fatherland? The Russians! Communists or noncommunists, it didn't matter. They were all Russians, all sharing the guilt. Now Otto had the chance to get back. The CIA needed his help in an operation to trap the Russian murderers in the middle of their double-dealing and a chance to be accepted.

Otto had had an awful cross to bear: his unmistakable, undeniable German accent. It was the result of his early exclusive contact with parents who were mistrustful and suspicious of the country into which they had practically been kidnapped.

Until school, other children were curiosities, startling Otto when they passed on the street or popped out from behind an aisle in the market where he shopped with Mama. And by then, it was too late. Otto was already different from the others. He was shy, pudgy, and worst of all, he "talked funny," and in school different was not admirable. It was a crime, punishable by teasing, hitting, and even exclusion.

Loneliness: that was real pain. Deep pain. And it had never left him, all through high school. All through brilliant accomplishments at college and during graduate studies, it *never* left the pit of his soul. No awards were sufficient to erase it or the doubts that it left in its wake, which shadowed him like muggers stalking a victim. Doubts that he would never, ever be accepted as a real American.

Now everything had changed. Otto had a chance. A glorious opportunity afforded him by "Blue." That was the only name by which Otto knew his mysterious benefactor. He had a chance to help America destroy the maggots who still infested the corpse of his old enemy, Russia.

Oh, they couldn't fool Otto with glasnost. Or with the breakup of the Soviet Union. Russians were Russians. They always would be. Trust them and you paid the price. But *he* would help Blue expose them for the deceivers they were. And by helping, he, Otto Manfred Gruhaber, would become a hero. And heroes were always accepted—even loved.

Otto felt a strange sensation around his lips as he saw his own bright future reflected on the flashing computer screen. It was a grin, or at least the start of one. Otto knew it. He knew that he smiled occasionally.

*   *   *

Van Damme used the safe phone in the den at the far end of the upstairs hall. It was 2:00 a.m. The staff of the fourteen-room Georgetown mansion were long asleep, as was his wife. She'd barely stirred as he eased from between the satin sheets of their extra large four-poster bed. Felicia Pelt Van Damme was not only accustomed to her husband's nocturnal intrigues; she was totally disinterested since he refused to discuss them with her.

Mortimer, their fat old tabby, brushed against the bare skin between Van Damme's slippers and pajama bottoms. It felt good. With a gentle shove, Van Damme directed the cat away from his desk. Mortimer looked back reproachfully, and then, ears stiffening at sounds that only cats can hear, stalked out.

The other side picked up immediately. "Yesss?" a heavily accented voice answered.

"It's Blue." Although the instrument was tap-proof and no records of the call would ever show at the phone company, Van Damme insisted on code names. "How is the project?"

"I ahm reviewing the updated receifing technology. I should haf a complete presentation ready zoon. Ven do ve need it?"

Van Damme stifled his impulse to laugh at the "we." He responded in his most earnest voice. "Do you think we can have it in three weeks, Gray?" He'd humored Gruhaber by assigning him a code name too. The little man had been positively thrilled.

"Yesss. Yesss, I definitely cahn haf efreything in three veeks. Yesss."

"You're sure? We can't have delays once the meeting is set. You understand that."

"Yesss, Blue. I understand. I vill haf efreything ready. You cahn depend on me."

Van Damme leaned back with a smile. The man was so damn happy to please; it was as if *he* were doing Gruhaber the favor. In retrospect, Van Damme supposed that he was, if one considered Gruhaber's psychological profile. "Very good, Gray. Be sure to apply for some personal leave time."

"I already haf." Gruhaber's voice practically beamed through the receiver.

"Very impressive, Gray. I'll talk to you again."

"Again" meant the same time next week. Gruhaber had loved that.

"Yess. *Again!*"

Van Damme almost burst out a second time as he broke the connection.

CHAPTER 8

Rosen squinted into the rising North Carolina sun. He'd made good time once he had squelched his crazy notion of taking a crack at Van Damme. Since the division chief had attempted to kill him at Fair Oaks, he knew that Rosen had escaped and would be expecting him. Not that Rosen cared about dying if he had a chance of taking that son of a bitch out, but what was the point of making things easy for Van Damme? He was not going to be another easy-to-eliminate loose end like his family had been. Rosen's knuckles whitened on the wheel.

The rental car, a white Plymouth four-door sedan—not sporty enough for Rosen's taste— was surprisingly powerful. He zipped by muddy pickups with nervous hounds pacing their littered rear beds as if they were standing still, which wasn't far from the truth. He supposed that they would be replaced by faster traffic later, but right now, the wide flat concrete belonged to him and the slow-driving farmers.

The dashboard digital clock said 7:53. Damn good time. He could be in Key West by tomorrow evening. Might even make it sooner, depending on how tired he was.

Splotched dairy cows eyed him from behind uniform white fences. They chewed calmly, unperturbed by his speed. He wanted to honk—see if he could unsettle those bland faces—and decided that the experiment wasn't worth the attention it might attract.

A steady gush of morning air laced with the odors of hay and manure poured through his open window. Good things: solid and obvious. Not like the treacherous subtleties of his world.

Fast-flowing air whipped tears back across Rosen's face. He couldn't help it. He never knew when tears were coming until they were already there. He supposed that things would be that way for quite a while.

*　　*　　*

Rosen pulled out of a Howard Johnson's parking lot somewhere in South Carolina at 1:44 p.m. The clam chowder had hit the spot. It was the chain's specialty. So had the fried clams. HoJo's wasn't actually a seafood place, but Rosen had always liked the combination. The kids loved their double-decker burgers, loaded with dressing, lettuce, cheese, and a bunch of other stuff.

This time Rosen's memories didn't make him cry. Instead, he lurched out from behind a slow moving station wagon planted firmly in the passing lane, cutting back in front of it with only inches to spare. *Real bright,* Rosen thought. *Get yourself killed.* That'll solve Van Damme's problems. He turned on the radio, only to hear farm reports and mournful ballads.

*   *   *

Rosen finally called Fred from Georgia. In retrospect, he didn't know why he'd procrastinated, considering that Fred Marquand was his reason for coming to Florida.

Freddie was his old boss. Well, not his boss, exactly. An operations man, actually. Freddie had been the Eastern European/Soviet division boss for years, but his career was already winding down when they had met. Eastern European had already become its own division—part of the Carter administration's pointless shake-ups—before Marquand retired. Although operations people normally treated analysts like shit, something had clicked between them. Maybe it had been Rosen's enthusiasm. Those had been the days when he really believed.

Rosen thought about that. He supposed that he'd continued to believe until recently. But his cynicism had festered over time, tainting the purity of his belief, like wine to vinegar. Rosen had always been glad that Freddie had retired before Rosen's idealism had completely eroded, because Fred Marquand had never stopped believing in the agency concept, regardless of its misapplications, and Rosen's metamorphosis would have pained him deeply.

Freddie—or "Papa," as he was known around the agency, not so much for his vague physical resemblance to the legendary author as his obsessive emotional affinity for Hemingway's lifestyle—was big, solid, with a large head, piercing eyes, and a propensity for flannel shirts with no jacket on drizzly Washington nights. And beneath it all, he was the purest man that Rosen ever knew. Papa was truly one in a million.

Rosen hadn't said much; he didn't have to. Marquand invited him to stay, without hesitation, when Rosen told his mentor that he was on his way down.

Although Rosen only realized it when it happened, he desperately needed Marquand's offer. The knowledge that someone who was important to him still cared eased the deep void within. Someone alive. He *needed* that. He thought that he had killed the need. But there it was, back again, like a ragged stray that couldn't be abandoned far enough away not to be able to find its way home.

The need had always been there. Ever since Rosen could remember, he had needed people, first his parents and later other kids. After that, there was always a woman in his life. Not necessarily the same one, but always a woman. Rosen needed closeness. He supposed that it was a weakness—this need—but he had never been totally sure of that because it had been responsible for the best moments of his life. Could that be wrong? It was the reason for his agony now—gnawing emptiness, in fact—but what about the years of richness? It had given him that, too.

Marquand's concern had salved this impossibly persistent need. As he pondered it over the dragging miles, Rosen concluded that somewhere in the need—the causer of the pain—was also the cure. Sometime after Van Damme, maybe there could be hope.

He took a deep breath and shoved his hair back with flared fingers, blinking to soothe the tension in his eyelids as the brightening sun engulfed his windshield. It ringed flattened bugs with glowing halos. The moment passed, and his glistening windshield transformed into the fires of hell. Rosen's mind's eye placed Van Damme in its center as his hands sought a stranglehold on the steering wheel. The Plymouth jolted forward to seventy, sucking after it a swirl of dry Georgia road dust.

*　*　*

Rosen drove straight through, nodding off more than once along the moon-glowing causeway, which shot like a ray through the black Atlantic from one Florida Key to the next. He hit Key West around 3:00 a.m.; pulled onto North Roosevelt at Seventh; parked along the water next to a darkened Winnebago; and flipped back the seat. He didn't remember anything until four brightly clad fishermen, complete with rods and six-packs, shouldered by his window at sunrise. Rosen slouched down, hoping to slip beneath the vibrations of their grating laughter. He failed but fought for sleep for another fifteen restless minutes before grudgingly opening his eyes.

First sunlight spread over the calm ocean like golden syrup over pancakes. Despite his weariness, Rosen was compelled to savor the gentle morning. He pulled off his shoes, rolled up the legs of his badly wrinkled slacks, yanked off his sticky cotton shirt, and sprang from the Plymouth, slamming the door shut as he barreled toward the glowing sand.

His toes dug in, and his knees compressed as he propelled himself toward the lightly slapping waves fifty yards ahead. The clinging pants bothered him. Shit, it was too early to worry about modesty. He fumbled with his belt, hopping leg to leg, still moving forward while he kicked them off.

Rosen didn't actually plan to go in. He just wanted to run alongside, skimming the water, maybe kicking up some spray, but when he got close, he kept going. Surprised to find himself there, he waded farther out, eventually plunging through a three-footer, arching up on the far side, pumping his arms toward the next one, digging under again, pulling up, treading water with churning knees, surprised that for all his effort, he could still touch bottom.

Salty water trickled into his mouth. Rosen didn't bother spitting it out. He was too enamored with the big fresh ocean. He wanted all of it. He needed it. Water had always restored him.

Rosen was a strong swimmer. He surged out toward the horizon, alternating strokes, rolling front to back, blinking up at the pinking sky, snorting as warm waves washed over his face. After a few minutes, he rolled back onto his stomach and, turning to parallel the shore, sprinted forward in a loose, powerful crawl. His mind went on automatic, losing itself in the rhythm of his pounding arms and legs. Eventually, he stopped, checking his progress against the shore, then turned, retracing his route in a slow, relaxed breaststroke.

Twenty feet onto the beach, Rosen dropped to the cool sand. He sprawled. White particles clung to him everywhere that his body touched the sand, like sugar sticking to warm dough. His chest heaved, sending beads of ocean water trickling along his ribs. Rosen lay still, comforted by warming air, hugged gently by the sand, soothed by the surf's soft *hiss*.

* * *

Marquand lived, as Rosen would have expected, in the island's historic old town, two blocks from Hemmingway's multi-veranda home and even less than that from Sloppy Joe's, where the author purportedly spent long nights drinking.

Marquand had a small white Victorian trimmed in light blue gingerbread. Its wide, comfortable veranda rested on a lawn of perfectly manicured Bermuda grass delicately lined with pink, white, and purple pansies.

Papa answered on the second ring of the brass twist doorbell, set below a glorious stained glass replication of fisherman and marlin locked in mortal combat.

"Arnold, my boy, welcome. Papa's precise tenor had not changed. Neither had his intelligent dark eyes, set below bushy white brows that fluttered with emphasis when he was enthusiastic about a topic—which was almost always. A well-known workaholic, Marquand had always seemed rather pale to Rosen, with transparent skin that revealed blue close-to-the-surface veins. Now Marquand's deep tan made him look years younger and slightly more like the real Hemingway.

Marquand read Rosen's surprise. "Yes. The sun may be harmful according to recent studies, but it certainly makes old men look younger. Come on, Arnie." He chuckled at Rosen's embarrassment. It came out like the snigger of a kid in class trying to hold in his laughter as the teacher glared. Rosen had always gotten a kick out of that laugh; he wished he could now. "We always told each other the truth, didn't we?" Marquand's eyes twinkled.

"Sure, Fred," Rosen smiled back. Like many older people, Marquand spotlighted his memories in soft favorable light. The truth was that Rosen, as a green subordinate, had willingly done most of the listening. He couldn't honestly recall that many heart-to-hearts with Marquand, but he would have died rather than say so. "We always did." Rosen gripped the broad but hunching shoulders and smiled into the bright eyes. "I was just amazed at how good you look."

"Right." Marquand grinned back. "But underneath, it's the same old machinery." Rosen wasn't sure. Was there a momentary darkening in the pupils? Before he could nail it down, the eyes glowed anew, accompanied by the famous Marquand smile: a room brightener, exposing the whitest set of teeth this side of a toothpaste commercial. "What a miserable host I am standing around talking about my good looks when you're probably exhausted. Let's get you inside. Where's the luggage?" Marquand chuckled as Rosen shrugged. "Travelling light, huh? What'd you do, Arnie, steal NATO's contingency plans for a Warsaw Pact attack on Berlin?" Marquand laughed at his own question. "Boy, does that date me." He threw a solid arm over Rosen's shoulder and ushered him in, but his dark eyes remained intensely curious.

*   *   *

"In conclusion, I want to make it very clear that this supposed breakup of the Soviet Union has not eliminated the KGB as a political threat in the slightest. Behind the closed doors of their newly painted headquarters, with its daily tourist show, they are still watching out for their own interests. For example, they have contributed over three million dollars to nine prominent hard-line candidates since the attempted coup. Gentlemen, the KGB constitutes one hell of a political action committee, if you want to look at it that way. Imagine how potent their financial war chest is in a currency-starved environment like Russia. And their darling is General Alexi Yermakov, the man who makes Stalin look like a revisionist. In fact, the KGB is becoming so confident that they have actually stepped up attempts to recruit high-ranking nationals in Austria and Germany within the last three months. Does that remind any of you of the good old Cold War days?"

Van Damme paused, placing his knuckles on the polished wood surface of the director's conference table, stooping toward the five seated men to emphasize his point. In addition to Agency Director Richard Savin were Deputy Director of Intelligence Martin Alstead, Secretary of Defense P. T. Botwell, National Security Advisor Stuart Korn, and Chairman of the Joint Cheifs of Staff, Admiral Luca Barnum. D. I. Savin initiated the monthly briefings three years before in an attempt to convert interagency competition into cooperation. Although the rivalries persisted, everyone agreed that the increased exchange of information was mutually beneficial.

"Come awn, Chahlie. Aren't you overreacting? What'er you doing, goin' for a bigger budget allocation next yeah?" Barnum, a large man with a bulbous red-veined nose, was a W. C. Fields look-alike. He was known as the "Circus Clown" behind his back, in honor of his famous namesake, but beneath his grating exterior was the superb mind of the only noncom ever to be awarded the rank of admiral.

Van Damme hated "Charlie", which he was sure Barnum knew. He ignored the man. Barnum half chortled and half-coughed, clearly delighted with himself. Van Damme paused, benignly smiling down at Barnum. "When the admiral is finished …" The others turned toward Barnum, who shrugged and waved for Van Damme to continue.

"During the same three-month period, assignment of known KGB personnel to embassies in France, England, and Spain is up ten percent, with a five percent increase in Germany and Finland. We consider these to be significant."

"What conclusions are we supposed to draw from this information? Russia, or whatever you want to call that hodgepodge of feuding republics, is scaling down troops and reducing nuclear capacity. They've got no money, or desire, to assist their little pals like Castro, and most of the others in their support group, like Vietnam and North Korea, are cozying up to us because *they* know the game is up."

Richard Korn, President Clendon's recent appointment, reeked of academia. *Logical,* Van Damme thought, *considering that his only experience was as a tenured professor of political science on the isolated, albeit lovely, Princeton campus.* Van Damme disliked the man's ivory tower perspective of the world, untempered, as was the case with most academics, by reality as Van Damme knew it. The fact that Korn was a die-hard liberal, appointed by Clendon to appease that wing of the party, did not improve Van Damme's opinion of the man. The fact that he was Jewish helped even less. Korn placed an index finger against his temple and squinted. "How can they be giving such different signals?"

"Obviously because there are at least two different forces at work: the hard-liners and the reformers, each vying for power. That should be reasonably apparent. Then there is the long-term threat—"

"Spare me your bogeyman theories, Van Damme. Is this a cute little lead-in for that 'glasnost gang' crap again?" Korn removed wire glasses, holding them delicately between thumb and forefinger as if they were a demitasse. His posture was so rigid that he could have been starched into his machine-washable navy suit. He sucked in pale lips, shaking his head in mock recrimination.

Van Damme smiled. He had developed fierce self-control years ago, a legacy from parents who considered excess emotion a demeaning indulgence of the nonaristocratic masses who toiled and propagated outside the high gates surrounding their hidden Long Island pocket of gentility.

His voice displayed no change in volume or tone. "I call it the 'Glasnost Conspiracy,' Professor Korn. A very clever group of powerful men in the Communist Party who realized that they could never dominate the world without a first rate economy. If you look at it logically, it wasn't we who beat communism. To be perfectly truthful, they had us on the ropes. It was their run-down, outmoded economic system that couldn't sustain them. Give them Western or Japanese efficiency and with their natural resources and dedication to education, we wouldn't have a prayer. And they don't need the Sandonistas or Cubans to get at Europe. That's where the action is: the EEOC. It's the biggest economic force since the Pacific Rim. Russia can't go head-to-head with the Japanese and Chinese. But they have a historical affinity with Europe. Look at Greece."

"Greece!" Deputy Director Martin Alstead squeaked. He was a chubby five-footer with large freckles on his perfectly smooth head and a voice that shattered glass. Easily the most detested person at the agency, Van Damme could name at least forty veterans who would have waylaid Alstead after work if they knew that they could have gotten away with it. Savin had appointed Alstead for his unswerving loyalty. There was no other reason. Personally, Van Damme never thought of loyalty as sufficient reason for anything, because fear or manipulation could always duplicate what loyalty accomplished. The little geek was so damned paranoid that he sought to review every report and proposal before their submission to Savin. Since Van Damme would sooner be run over than clear anything with Alstead, he certainly could not expect any support from the twerp.

"Greece," Alstead repeated, as if anyone could miss his piercing voice the first time. "A rather poor example, wouldn't you say, Charles?" He pronounced it "Churls," his mouth screwing up like a mouse nibbling cheese. "Their Socialist government is just about out after the recent scandals. They're going to have a backlash there that sweeps in an ultraconservative coalition government according to conventional wisdom. How on earth are the Russians going to make progress there?" Removing a used-looking handkerchief from his crumpled jacket, Alstead dabbed the top of his head while rolling his eyes for the benefit of those at the table.

Van Damme jumped at the opening. "An excellent observation, Martin." Alstead nodded graciously. "One which, on the surface, would appear completely valid." He emphasized "on the surface," turning Alstead's victorious smirk wary. But the actual truth is that the KGB and GRU have at least fourteen hundred known operatives there, not to mention those nationals whom they have turned, or are in the process of turning, or"—his gaze fell on Alstead, whose shoulders sagged under its weight—"the ones they *will* turn in the future."

Van Damme walked toward one of the wide tinted windows lining the director's spacious corner office, staring at the distant curtain of trees insulating Langley from the surrounding highways. He paused, considering briefly the thousands of people who sped by each hour straining for a glimpse as they vainly tried to imagine what transpired inside the streamlined glass structure. Van Damme was aware that the window's light outlined his fine profile, and he let it do so for almost a full minute, accentuating the effect of his next statement. He turned at just the right moment, knowing that the backlighting broadened his stature.

"And that is exactly how the Glasnost conspirators plan to dominate Europe within the next ten to fifteen years!"

Korn exclaimed, "Ridiculous!"

"He's right, he's right." Barnum's harsh growl pierced through his own fit of coughing laughter. "These crazy republics are maw dangerous now than they was befaw as a unified countray. Ah agree. An' when they reduce their army futha, they'll be a bigga threat than eva."

Pointing a delicate index finger directly at the admiral, Van Damme inclined his head. "The KGB numbers over four hundred thousand members plus many more controlled nationals. The entire intelligence communities of all other nations can't even come close to that figure. And effective operatives of disbanded Eastern Bloc services will surely be invited to join, swelling its ranks further. They are totally dedicated to the old ways. In the hands of the Glasnost group, with its calculated ten-year plan, they are ideal plants in embassies, trade missions, and UN facilities. Aeroflot and other Russian businesses are crawling with them. Think of all the nations into which those businesses will expand as trade increases."

Without awaiting a reply, Van Damme walked slowly back toward the table. His eyes were intent on Savin and Botwell. "It will be, hands down, the most formidable force in our peacetime world. Its techniques are tested, and its members are experienced. By two thousand twelve, the KGB will have subverted key decision makers in every government in Europe. Members of its former Fifth Directorate will kill—I said *kill*—those who can't be won over or threatened. They do it without a trace: we have records of over eighteen hundred suspected but unproven political assassinations outside of the Soviet Union—*after* Stalin!"

"Who says that this mighty KGB of yours will still be around?" shrilled Alstead. "As far as I can see, they've already been whittled away, and with the economic crunch over there, Russia won't be able to afford them and maintain its army at the same time."

"I agree, Martin." Nothing made Alstead more miserable than Van Damme's agreement. Van Damme savored the way that Alstead's fat face pinched in as the little man cringed in anticipation of hearing how he had unwittingly helped his enemy prove yet another point. "Whether or not the KGB stays a viable political force—or even continues to exist, for that matter—is irrelevant to these people. Consider that the Glasnost conspirators have been systematically stealing from the Russian people for over seventy years. Have you any idea what vast wealth they have at their disposal? If the KGB continues to exist, they can appeal to its many members who are still fiercely loyal to communism. Others can be easily bribed. If the KGB is eliminated, they will recruit former members into a secret organization, which will serve them just as effectively. They could bankroll such an organization for a century, if necessary." Alstead receded back into his pudgy shell.

"For now, the conspirators are programming the KGB and others to infiltrate the Russian republics during this period of mass confusion," said Van Damme. "You are probably aware that the KGB successfully planted a number of sleepers here in the United States during the past twenty years. These are people who have no idea that they are being used as secret agents until they receive some sort of psychic wake-up call. Well, I believe that they are currently placing untold numbers of sleepers in every republic. Within the next ten years, Russia and the other republics will get their economies back on track. Due to massive shifts in production from military to consumer items, coupled with extensive Western aid and investment and, most of all, their massive oil supply and other natural resources. And ironically, we good-natured Americans are *helping them develop all this*. Once their economic goals have been attained, the conspirators will take over with the aid of their sleepers and plants, their KGB nucleus, and the many remnants of the army and Soviet society who still dream the Communist dream.

"Gentlemen," Van Damme's eyes searched their faces, "do you realize how many Communist bureaucrats are entrenched in high-level positions throughout the republics? How many bigwigs who ran the former military/ industrial complex still have their fingers on the pulse of production and distribution? Why do you think Yeltsin is having so much difficulty implementing his economic reforms? It's because these people are fighting him every step of the way. Well, my friends, most of these Communist bureaucrats are still going to be around in ten years, just waiting to promote the new revolution, and this time it will succeed without a shot being fired!"

Van Damme reached for a glass of water. He tipped it upward, controlling the gulping sound as the cool substance slid down. Van Damme used the pause to scrutinize the group from behind his glass. What were they thinking? Was he getting through? Hard to tell. The ones who counted—Savin and Botwell—were good poker players. Their faces showed only polite interest. Nothing more. Van Damme replaced his glass.

"What was the first thing that the populations of those republics did when the communist foot came off their necks? Did they get down on their knees and thank God? No. The very *first* thing that they did was to start their age-old fighting and squabbling again. Croats against Serbs, etcetera, etcetera. They will never be able to unify against the Communists. Just like the Poles in World War II watched the Germans devastate their country rather than supply the Jews of the Warsaw Ghetto with weapons to fight, the insane hatred within these republics render them impotent to withstand a determined aggressor, not only now but in the foreseeable future." Van Damme lifted an upturned right palm toward the table. "And who knows how many of Russia's one-point-five-million-man army will still be stationed in the other republics at that time? Right now, Yeltsin can't bring them home because there are no jobs or housing, but it plays into the conspirators' hands to have them stay there indefinitely. Why? Because what republic could withstand such an occupation force?

"The conspirators have created an infallible network for takeover when the time is right. Once they have consolidated their power in the republics, they will be welcomed into subverted regimes all over Europe. By that time, it may be much too late for us to stop them."

"'Scuse me. Ha' does that go again, Chahlie?" Barnum's forehead curled down toward the bridge of his nose.

"They will also have a massive system of illegals in place: Soviet citizens, KGB, subverted nationals, and sleepers who completely integrate the host society. They can be used for demonstrations and rallies to create the illusion that there has been a shift in public opinion—you've seen how the press loves to make a few screaming idiots look like the majority.

In extreme cases, these same elements might even sabotage key facilities, disrupting the host country's ability to resist."

"Oh, yeah." Barnum smirked. "Well ha' 'bout all them happy Russian folks whose standud a livin' has been goin' up an' up ovuh this ten years a yours? Why they gonna wanna go back ta the Commies agin?"

"Because, Admiral, the price that Russia will pay for a market economy and capital investment for industry will be to sink many of its people as low as the worst economic days of World War Two. Foreign aid alone can never do more than make a small dent in the vast cost of revitalizing their economy. The real sacrifice will come from them. Especially when they watch their best products being exported to build up foreign exchange and worldwide markets, while they have to make do with obsolete junk at home. And do you know who will suffer the most? The rural masses—the very heart and soul of the original revolution."

Van Damme stared from face to face, unblinking, lowering his voice to something above a whisper. "The Communists will come back stronger than ever, able to accomplish what they never have in the last seventy years: create an efficient economy that utilizes their inexhaustible natural recourses so that no one can outproduce them. And after that … I'll leave you to guess what their next step might be." Van Damme looked from face to face again. "Do any of you gentlemen seriously believe that fanatical Communists will have forgotten their desire to spread their system across the world a mere ten years from now? I don't."

The room was quiet. Even Barnum fingered a thick lower lip, contemplating. After a moment, Alstead straightened to speak, but a look from Savin silenced him, forcing his chubby body back into its customary slouch.

The director turned toward Botwell. "What do you think, PT?"

Phineus Throckmorton Botwell made it clear to everyone who knew him that he greatly preferred PT. As Clendon's oldest friend, everyone in politics obliged him.

"More important, Rick, what do you think?" The secretary of defense, a veteran politician of thirty years, never voiced an opinion before everyone else had—and sometimes not even then.

Savin smiled, looking not in the least surprised to have the ball back. He leaned forward, pulled a stained meerschaum from a pipe rack. It was carved in the form of a kneeling elephant and perpetually lay on a bookcase to his left when not in use. Savin took three matches and well over a minute to light it. He held the flame steady, despite the plethora of liver spots that ringed his hands. At seventy-two, Richard Savin should have retired and was fully expected to after Clendon's inauguration. He stayed on only after the president's personal appeal, which was highly unusual considering that Savin was a registered member of the Opposition Party. He was *that* good. Savin blew a gust of smoke toward the ceiling while running his right hand through lustrous white hair.

"The KGB and its military wing, the GRU, are certainly the most formidable espionage force ever assembled." Savin puffed again, curling the smoke out around a cupped tongue. The aroma was old apples and crushed almonds. "We assumed that it would be reduced along with other Soviet forces, but there have been no direct discussions in this regard. Still, I find it hard to believe the Russians would dismantle everything else and leave the KGB intact, especially their citizens' innate hostility toward it." Savin pointed the meerschaum's chewed mouthpiece at Van Damme. "Have you any hard evidence of this, Charles?"

"The increase of known agents into their consulates and embassies, sir. I alluded to that before."

Barnum's grin was back. It wasn't that he loved the Russians—far from it. It was just that he considered the CIA politically inept and largely responsible for the military's public disfavor. "Bunch a little sissies hiding behind corners taking pitchas a each otha peein'," had been his most recent characterization of the agency at a colleague's retirement dinner.

"How can we tell at this point what they plan to do? Isn't this rather speculative?" Personally, Savin did not like Van Damme; he was a bit too secretive for his tastes. The European Division chief ran his operation like an agency within the agency, demanding (and receiving) the kind of loyalty that made Savin feel like an outsider. Yet Savin did respect Van Damme's ability. He was quite sure, in fact, that Van Damme was brilliant. Not nearly so sure, however, that Van Damme's loyalties transcended Van Damme himself. Nevertheless, Savin was fiercely protective of his people. He knew that the country was in no mood to disbelieve 'Glasnost' and the breakup of the Soviet Union. Nor was the world, for that matter. Savin also knew that Botwell felt similarly, but rather than have an outsider pick one of his own apart, he had preferred to do it.

"Sir." Perspiration trickled from Van Damme's scalp toward his eye, tickling. He fought the urge to sweep it away, hating his body for betraying him. "We can't prove anything conclusively at this point. Our budget cuts over the past ten years have reduced our ability to recruit high-level informants, and the Eastern Bloc breakup has eliminated defections, another previous source of information. But I have been in this business for many years; successfully, I might add. And I know how these high Communists think. They always seek the advantage. Their commitment to destroy us is just as great today, only their methods are changing to conform to the economic realities. We *cannot* underestimate them. That would be fatal."

"Charles, we all get your point … and your knowledge of Russian activities is unquestioned." Savin sucked at the meerschaum; he pulled it from his lips and frowned at the dead ashes in its yellowed bowl as he placed it atop Van Damme's red-bordered briefing file.

Van Damme saw the brush-off coming.

"But times are changing rapidly. More so than at any time in the past forty years. Maybe more than in all of modern history. We have to be open to new opportunities regardless of how long the status quo before Gorbachev … and evidence of massive change is undeniable." He looked around the table. There were nods of confirmation from all but Barnum, who stared at the ceiling.

"Congress, the country, everyone wants to believe that the Communists are through for good. Smashed. Yesterday's news. The president"—Savin nodded toward Botwell—"as Clendon's proxy, cannot take an opposing position without risking public disfavor and he *certainly* cannot hope for additional intelligence appropriations from Congress. Hell, it'll be a miracle if we keep what we have. Unless"—Savin's voice rasped from the lengthy speech, but his intense blue eyes locked firmly on Van Damme's— "we have hard evidence." His eyes remained fixed on Van Damme for a long moment. The challenge and the opening were given. Intelligence loyalties ran high, and Savin had shown Van Damme the mark of respect to which all members of the agency were entitled: a willingness to explore any theory if corroborated by hard facts.

Like most agency insiders, Van Damme distrusted directors of intelligence—he had seen four to date—as politically appointed dilettantes who would have preferred cabinet positions if they had been higher in the presidential pecking order. This one was different. While he would never like the man, Savin had learned to honor the code, and Van Damme respected him for that. The DI's courtesy, despite the council's unfavorable reaction to his report, impressed Van Damme, softening him—for a moment.

Then the rage hit him. He studied the faces of his persecutors and saw their attention shifting, dismissing him, fingers fidgeting; anticipating the next item on the agenda. Only Alstead's slight smirk indicated that he, at least, was still cognizant of Van Damme.

His insides burned. His stomach threatened to erupt. Bile burned deep in his throat. He fought to focus on Savin. The man was saying something to Botwell. "Do you have anything to add to this, Mr. Secretary?"

Botwell shook his head, already sliding the next file over Van Damme's. Van Damme betrayed nothing, concentrating his attention on Savin, despite the rage, despite the fantasy of riddling each of them with a steady flow of bullets. … Bullets and more bullets, pouring into their bodies from the clacking muzzle of the automatic weapon in his hands. Watching their smirky know-it-all faces splatter all over that shiny mahogany conference table.

"Thank you, Charles."

Charles Van Damme smiled, nodded, and walked toward the door with measured steps. They didn't know that they were all dead—so far, he'd killed them only in his mind. He heard the drone of renewed conversation. They had already forgotten him. Soon they would know better.

*   *   *

As the door closed behind Van Damme, Botwell carefully looked up over his thick-rimmed bifocals, making sure that the thin man was gone. Clearly satisfied, he turned toward Savin.

"He's a little panicky for an intelligence guy, isn't he?" His non-accent was Ohio, the same as the president's.

Barnum's coughing laugh erupted down the table. As the DI and secretary both glared at the admiral, his mouth snapped closed, but he continued shaking his close-cropped head in silent amusement.

Savin fingered emerging stubble on his chin. "PT, he is one of the best. If he thinks the proliferation of Russian intelligence activities poses a future threat, it cannot be discounted. You can be sure that if proof is developed, I'm going to yell like hell about it to the president. And every damn congressman too! The problem is that we just don't know, and won't for quite a while. Right now, we can only go on what we see, and that looks like better times ahead. I know that we can't pull the rug out from under the peace process unless we have one heck of a good reason, but that doesn't mean that I would be surprised if Charles turns out right down the road."

Botwell nodded. His jowls shook with each head movement, and broken capillaries in his corneas gave his eyes a permanently red hue. People who didn't know Botwell attributed his appearance to heavy drinking, but the man had not touched alcohol for over seventeen years. The commencement date of his abstinence was May 3, 1977, pursuant to a vow in a hospital waiting room as his oldest son, Brian, fought for breath in a respirator. Four jagged ribs, crushed by the steering wheel of his overturned MG, had shredded the All-Conference halfback's lungs, causing any oxygen collected there to bubble away long before it got to the arteries. The police report had revealed a staggering quantity of blood alcohol, the result of Brian's unlimited access to his father's overstocked liquor cabinet while the Botwells enjoyed a long Bermuda weekend with then-senator and Mrs. Clendon. Brian had lost the battle, but Botwell stuck to his vow anyway.

His look was actually due to a hereditary glandular condition, but its attribution to alcohol persisted. Botwell no longer cared. He had gone as far as he was going politically.

"Yeah, I agree. I'd rather see 'em eliminate their nukes. We'll worry about the other stuff later." He tossed up a dismissive hand. "Assuming it ever becomes necessary."

"About his nervousness," Savin continued, reaching for the next folder to bracket the conversation. "He had a ghastly experience recently. One of our analysts, fellow by the name of Rosen, was showing extreme symptoms of stress according to our computer profiles. Unfortunately, we didn't pick up on it soon enough. Rosen massacred his family a few days ago and then blamed it on Charles. He claimed that Charles was involved in some sort of plot to sell secrets to the Russians. Said that Charles killed his family in the process of stealing his evidence against Charles. Crazy, obviously. Terrible tragedy! I believe that the man is institutionalized now, but you can imagine the strain on poor Van Damme."

Botwell stilfled a yawn. "I certainly see. That is very tragic."

Savin noted that the secretary's eyes were glazing over. So much for the human condition. "Well, gentlemen, we have a lot more to cover. Please refer to the next report from South America. It seems that the Shining Path is kicking up its heels over in Peru again."

* * *

Acid rage flooded up from Van Damme's chest, yet he was able to return greetings, even remember names, while walking the long corridor back to his office, because his brain never gave way to emotion. It acknowledged it, even experienced its force. But emotion never penetrated. It was like a powerful storm whistling past doors and the chimney of a well-insulated cabin without affecting the warmth of the inhabitants.

So they needed proof. So it wasn't the *right* political climate. So they really didn't *want* to know anything about the Communists and wished he'd go away. They'd actually had the damn gall to dismiss him like some flunky. They'd pay for that. Yes, they would. His suggestions weren't in vogue currently but he knew damn well that he was right. He wouldn't be surprised if some of the others had considered the same possibilities, but not one of them had the guts to buck the current love affair with the Communists. Naive dupes!

The Russian system had beat hell out of ours because it always focused on its enemies and its goal, no matter what cosmetic changes it might have undergone. But these so-called experts were too stupid to see that. No wonder Van Damme preferred dealing with Kharkov and the others. They were pragmatists, not wishers and dreamers. How could fools like this run the National Security Agency? Liberal intellectuals, political hacks, and over-the-hill military. It was tragic!

Van Damme nearly overshot his office. That miserable meeting had gotten to him more than he had thought. He didn't like that. His slowed his breath, allowing his facial muscles to relax. He paused outside his door, releasing all the tension, letting calm fill its place.

What difference did it make? They didn't like his ideas; they ignored him. Fine. Soon they'd see how right he was. But by then, it would be too late. They were history—they just didn't know it yet. The thought warmed Van Damme as he nodded pleasantly to his secretary.

"Mr. Craig is waiting for you, sir." Points of light reflected from her glistening teeth. *Pretty young thing,* Van Damme thought for the fortieth time since she had arrived from secretarial. His previous girl, Maxine, had left for family life in the suburbs, and this new one, Shelley, represented a big improvement as far as looks. Van Damme felt disloyal. Maxine had been with him seven years, always cheerful, and he couldn't recall more than three mistakes. *That* should be worth something. And this one's hair was gold on top with little snatches of dark beneath, indicating that she might not have been born quite so Nordic. However, for Shelley, mild fraud was forgivable when one considered those definitely real breasts and certainly real calves that tapered perfectly into delicate little ankles. And her solid body had just the slight roundness that he loved. As he entered his office, Van Damme speculated briefly on what it would be like to touch Shelley all over.

Seeing Craig sitting primly on his favorite Chippendale changed Van Damme's mood fast. Fantasies of Shelley drained away like tainted motor oil. Craig usually sprawled infuriatingly over the irreplaceable piece. One look at Craig's face confirmed Van Damme's fears. Something was definitely wrong.

CHAPTER 9

Fred Marquand sat in an overstuffed chair that Rosen remembered from Marquand's office at the agency. It had occupied a corner near his desk from long before Rosen's time. The once shiny beige velour had been rubbed down to a few scraggly patches; wear marks on the armrests exposed swatches of yellowed under material; its cushion had compressed to wafer-thinness. Still, they seemed comfortable with each other: Marquand and the chair.

Actually, Marquand, the chair, *and* the room. There was a magazine- and paper-littered desk with more of the same oozing from its half-opened drawers. Bookcases with horizontal rows of paperbacks—impossibly compressed between vertical hardcovers and covering every topic from *Art Nouveau* to *The Upcoming Stock Market Crash of 1990*—covered two walls. More paperbacks rested against a large stone fireplace—Marquand explained that although a fireplace in Florida was as necessary as "tits on a bull," it gave the room a cozy touch—on the far wall.

Alone on the mantel—indicative of its importance to Marquand in a room where space was at a premium—was a plastic laminated letter from Reagan for distinguished service.

Two spindly lamp tables flanked a sleeper couch. It was covered in Floridian blues and greens on a white background and was to double as Rosen's bed in Marquand's one-bedroom cottage.

Marquand's slippered feet, white cotton socks sticking through the toe holes, rested on a maroon footrest with legs carved in the shape of poised cobras. The piece reminded Rosen of cheap Chinese import shops along Grant Avenue in San Francisco.

Marquand sipped Courvoisier from a glass that looked like a tiny rose vase, while Rosen slouched over a reversed straight-backed chair, hugging a Coors.

"We've talked plenty of small talk, Arnie, but I get the feeling you've got more to tell me. Am I right?" Papa's voice was soft, soothing—the kind of voice that you wanted to confide in. His open face, lined from laughter, enhanced the effect. One eyelid dangled a bit, not quite clearing the upper edge of the iris, the only souvenir of a recent stroke, Marquand had explained laughingly when he caught Rosen staring at his eye for the third time. His casualness eased Rosen's embarrassment. Marquand was good at that kind of thing.

Rosen gulped the rest of the beer and crushed the puny aluminum can, hardly aware he was doing it. "Remember when it took a strong guy to do this?" he laughingly said. His humor sounded hollow.

Marquand waited.

"I escaped from a mental facility yesterday. They were evaluating me for trial." He looked from the Coors to Marquand's feet—anything but the other's face. Finally, he looked up.

Marquand's eyes were calm: no judgment there.

Rosen pushed it. "They say I killed my family last week."

No change in the calm eyes.

"Aren't you going to say anything?"

"I already knew. I'm still in touch with some of the lads."

Rosen stiffened. "Why didn't you say something? Why make me go through this?"

"I knew you'd tell me when you were ready." Marquand's voice was calm, soothing. "You needed a little time to think of other things—or nothing."

Rosen's stomach clenched. He knew that he shouldn't ask, but he had to. "Did you tell anyone?" he blurted through a tight jaw. He regretted the question immediately.

The hurt in Marquand's eyes answered before the words. "Do you think I did?"

"No." Rosen slumped down on the chair back. He wiped foam from the top of the ruined can and then laid it near his foot. "I didn't kill them," he said to his own dusty loafer.

"I had no doubt of that."

"Why?" Rosen's eyes traced scuffs and cracks in his shoe's smooth tan leather. It had taken a beating the last few days. Come to think of it … what part of him hadn't?

"I think I know you pretty well. You would have killed yourself first."

"They tried to make it look like I did. After …" Rosen's words increased in intensity.

"Who is 'they'?"

"Didn't your sources tell you?"

"They only told me that the word was that you'd gone off the deep end. Operations records showed you were being recommended for psycho evaluation."

"Funny. They never mentioned anything to me."

Marquand raised his slipper-clad feet and rose; he walked to the lower shelf of a bookcase that doubled as his bar. "I've got another beer in the kitchen."

"I'm okay." Rosen considered his choice of words, amused—but not really. He said it out of sheer habit. He was definitely *not* "okay."

Marquand tipped the cut-glass decanter. Thick amber liquid rolled into the delicate glass. "That's not procedure. You're always given an advance consultation with your supervisor. More than one, usually. *Long* before an actual psych eval goes on your record. They give you a chance to take some time off, talk things over with your own doctor, or whatever. None of that happened?"

"Nope."

"You sure? Nothing?" Marquand slipped back into his chair. It accepted him with a resigned groan. The calm of his face metamorphosed into perplexity. Violation of procedure was an enigma to Marquand.

Rosen stared.

Marquand settled back. "Then why? Why is all this happening to you? Sorry, but now let's cut to the chase. Things like this just don't happen. You're a bright lad, unless you've been lobotomized since you called last Christmas. Chanukah. Sorry. I feel terrible about what happened to Barbara and the children—Good Lord, you *know* that—but I can't help if you don't tell me everything." Marquand reached up to scratch his white mane. "That's assuming that you want help and that I *can* help."

Rosen was amazed by his own reluctance. Only Larry Topper had believed him about Van Damme. By now, he supposed, he had been conditioned to incredulity from others. Could he expect more from Marquand? They were friends, but Marquand's love for the agency was as strong as the day he was recruited, forty-some-odd years before. Papa had no wife because the agency was his woman. Rosen's belief that Marquand would help had sustained him through his empty hours on the road.

Now that he was face-to-face with his mentor, Rosen's confidence evaporated. Would Papa's love for the agency override his desire to help the man who sat before him accusing his lover of corruption?

Rosen studied the older man, trying to fathom the depth of their relationship in Marquand's calm brown eyes. He saw nothing to help him decide. Only patient watchfulness. Was he kidding himself? Was this man really his friend at all? Was anyone a friend if the stakes got too high?

Too late to stop now. "Van Damme set me up. Had his operations guys kill Barbara, Eleanor, and Jonathon and then tried to have them take me out in a phony drunken car crash. When that didn't work, they sent someone to get me at the psychiatric center, except I got him first and escaped and …" Rosen stopped, listening to himself in disbelief. He sounded like he was raving paranoid, rattling on nonsensically. He'd planned to tell the story nice and slow and logically, but instead it sounded like the run-on ravings of a bona fide weirdo! It was just that his pain was stuck inside of him—stewing, festering—wanting to spew out all at once, like stored-up vomit.

Rosen shook his head at Marquand, raising his palms outward in a halting motion. Then he dropped his hands back into his lap, shoving them along the inside of his thighs to rest on his knees.

"Look, let me go over it again, a little more coherently this time." Rosen snorted out a little laugh, shaking his head while puffing out air past his partially closed lips. "About six months ago, I came upon some expense vouchers of Van Damme's that showed he was in Berlin the previous May. It only caught my eye because we had just had a big hoopla about reducing the travel budget and there was nothing going on over there that I knew about. I don't know why I did it. Maybe I was just bored. I don't know."

Marquand leaned forward, eyes curious. "You are talking about *Charles Van Damme*, chief of European ops?"

"Yeah. That's the one. Anyway, I dug up some old satellite intercepts from the same time period, and the only significant thing was that Nikolai Kharkov, former deputy chief of Directorate Five, now floating between the KGB and GRU, was in East Berlin at approximately the same time."

"I know who Kharkov is." Marquand's voice was sharper, his eyes narrowing. "So what if they were there at the same time? Coincidences can happen."

Rosen looked up, surprised by the change in Marquand. Had he alienated his friend that much already? He'd thought that he'd at least get a hearing. Had Marquand already written him off? Disappointment and frustration colored his own tone. "You always told me there *were* no 'coincidences' in our work."

Marquand nodded. "Touché. I did, didn't I?"

"I back checked for the previous two years. It's easy enough to do. All operatives going in or near sensitive areas have to leave destinations and emergency numbers in case they get grabbed by the opposition." Rosen smiled and shrugged apologetically. Marquand probably initiated the damn system.

Marquand dismissed it with a wave of stumpy fingers.

"He made four trips that included Berlin. Kharkov was in East Berlin at the same time at least twice. More, for all I know, but I could only come up with two definites. More coincidence?"

Marquand tipped the delicate glass high, drained the brown liquid, but made no move to refill. "Go on."

Rosen was heartened. Papa was definitely listening. He gripped the back of the chair, leaning farther toward Marquand. "I decided to follow him once in a while."

A frown from Marquand.

"Nothing crazy, you know. Just occasionally after work, when he left earlier than his usual ten at night. Anyway, nothing much happened: dry cleaners, theater, stuff like that. Until about a month ago, when he drives up to Baltimore; goes to a pretty bad part of town; parks the Mercedes; walks two blocks to a beat-up old brick wall between two condemned buildings; slides something into a crack down near the base; and walks back the way he came. A goddamn drop. He's made a goddamn drop!"

Rosen's eyebrows thrust upward wrinkling his forehead. "So I went for it. I'm not great with technical drawings, but I've seen enough NSA stuff to know my way around. This was half a page of satellite plans. Cut right down the middle, like an installment! It doesn't say, of course, but NSA has been going crazy waiting for the Indigo upgrade—greatest satellite in history, control the skies and all that—and I'd bet anything this was it! So I put it back and hung out across the street in the basement entrance of some ratty old apartment house, piss stench coming up from everywhere. Soon a big guy in a trench coat—that's right, a *trench coat*—came out of nowhere, pulled the envelope out and took off."

"Anything else?"

Rosen couldn't tell if Marquand was still interested or not. "Yeah, I checked pictures of personnel stationed at the Russian Embassy. The guy was Boris Gribov. Official title: assistant cultural attaché. Real title: lieutenant of the KGB. Gribov also has a degree in physics from the Moscow Aeronautical Institute." Rosen searched the older man's face for reaction.

Marquand pushed his lower lip up over the top one, held it there a moment, let it slip back. "That it?

Rosen frowned. "Isn't that enough?"

"Anything else?" Marquand repeated patiently.

"Yeah, there's something else. About two years ago, Van Damme escorted a group of Midwest industrialists up to Amtorg in New York. You know, that phony trading front the Soviet's had on Third Avenue. The one that's never made a significant deal in over twenty years? He got sent as part of our big PR push—show the country that the CIA can do more than just start coups; the CIA is good for business too! Anyway, according to a letter of complaint from one of our Midwest friends, Mr. Van Damme got lost for a while, which didn't fit in with their concept of hosting. Later, Van Damme explained that it was only twenty minutes in the john, some kind of food poisoning. I think it was to tip off the Czech Intelligence Service. An STB officer was there at the same time, supposedly displaying a line of wooden toys for a Prague manufacturer."

Marquand chewed at his thick lower lip. "Why couldn't that be true?"

"'Cause three weeks later, a very effective cell that had successfully herded hundreds of dissidents out of Czechoslovakia into Austria over the past seven years was suddenly rounded up by the STB."

"Pretty flimsy tie-in."

"Three days before he set me up, Van Damme went to a particularly dirty little gas station to use the pay phone. The exact time he was there, a call was made to the Russian Embassy. That do anything for you?"

"That all of it?" Marquand rubbed a thumb along his brandy glass's rim, making it ring tremulously.

"No, that's not all of it." Rosen's voice rose. "You want all of it— here's *all* of it: That file, the file I put together on all this ..." He shut his eyes, willing himself to slow down, but it poured and poured, faster and faster. He'd stop at some of the bad parts, staring at nothing in particular, catching himself, continuing, in a voice without focus.

Toward the end, Rosen lurched upward, his chair tipping precariously, righting itself at the last second, its front legs thumping back to polished hardwood floor. "Van Damme sent his people to get the file. I had him, and he *knew* it." Rosen loomed over Marquand. "They followed me to the train station. That's where I had a backup. In a locker. They knew I'd make a second copy. That's when they trashed me, after they got the second file. It was all so Van Damme could get my files. They killed my ... for that goddamn … that *goddamn file*! Who the hell else would want it but Van Damme?" Rosen thrust his face close to the older man's, smelling the musky brandy; spotting white stubble that Marquand's razor had missed; daring Marquand to defy his logic.

Unintimidated, Marquand looked up calmly. "Did anyone else see these files?"

"*No!*" Rosen yelled down into the emotionless face. He realized it and shook his head, backing away. "No," I told you that I was going with them to Hollings the next day."

"Did anyone know what you were doing? Before all this happened?"

"No, damn it. *No!* You don't run around advertising that a head of Ops is really a Russian Spy. *You* know that. What the hell is this? And what about the computer, huh? What about rigging it so I look like *a fucking nut case*?" He was screaming, Goddammit. Screaming at Papa!

Marquand just stared—a long, sad stare.

Rosen licked his lips, walked toward the bright couch, flopped down, wedged his hands between his knees, and stared at the floating gauze of a spider web anchored between the top of the bookcase and the ceiling. A loud ticking came from the kitchen.

"That's the point, Arnie. He *is* head of European ops, a very important man." There was a pause.

Rosen turned.

Marquand's eyes were hard even in the backlighting from the window. "A very *dedicated* man." Papa's voice went cold. "A man whom I knew for years, who worked harder, longer, *and* brighter than I ever could! Do you understand what I'm saying?"

"What? That he didn't do it?" Rosen mumbled as he gnawed his lip.

"No." Papa waited.

Finally, Rosen looked up.

"That you have to be *damn sure* before accusing a man like that. Listen, Arnie …" Marquand cut off Rosen's nearly begun retort. "Dealings with the KGB by our side are not unheard of, especially by a man like Charlie …"

Rosen resented the familiarity. Marquand seemed to notice.

"A man as highly placed as Van Damme.… They exchange information whenever it suits their purposes, but that doesn't mean they're turning. My God, I've exchanged information with them when I needed to. Does that make *me* a traitor?"

"He went after the file! Had my family killed." The rage had filtered out of Rosen's voice, supplanted by bitterness.

"But the files are *gone*. You can't prove there ever were any." Silence.

"And you never saw your original health evaluation on the computer, did you? So you don't know who put the new information in … or when."

"Right." Rosen felt it slipping away. It was as if he were in a dream where truth was a balloon that he wanted to drop in Marquand's lap. Only every time he grabbed for it, the air from his swinging arms pushed it farther away. Rosen shoved up from the soft cushions, hunched forward, rose wearily. "I thought you'd believe me." He pressed his lips into a weak smile. "See ya, Papa." He was down the hall, the open front door dousing him with blinding sunlight, when Marquand's voice caught up with him.

"Rosen, get *back* here!"

Conditioned by years of respect for authority, Rosen followed the command automatically, forgetting that neither of them were agency anymore. He stood in the entrance to the living room, staring across the room at Marquand.

"What?"

"I didn't say I wouldn't help."

"But you don't believe me." Rosen saw the answer in Marquand's eyes.

Both stared away uncomfortably.

After a moment, Marquand rose, knees creaking. He walked over. His hand went to Rosen's shoulder. "I'm not sure. Put yourself in my place, Arnie. I respect this man … but I also care about you and the terrible things that have happened. Try to understand. It's a lot to hit me with all at once."

"It wasn't too slow for me either."

"I know, Arnie." The voice was quiet.

Rosen's head came up quickly. Marquand looked older and more tired than he had an hour ago at the front door. Rosen felt a touch of guilt. Was it fair to lay this on Marquand? Papa had already paid his dues. He was entitled to a rest.

Marquand read his mind. "Don't give it a second thought, pal. I *mean* it. I'll check some sources. Then we'll see." His voice was strong and full again, the eyes brighter. This was "Papa."

"How long?"

"Not long." Marquand dropped his hand from Rosen's shoulder, eyes flashing the warning: *No more pushing.*

"Okay."

"If it's him, I'll do everything I can to help."

Rosen smiled, a real smile this time. "I can't lose."

Marquand nodded toward the kitchen. "Get some sleep. You look like I will in fifteen years. Use my bed ... past the kitchen. Towels in the bath.

I could have some answers by evening."

Rosen nodded, proceeding into the bright kitchen, shuffling his feet along alternating white-and-yellow squares of linoleum. He toyed with the idea of using the open bathroom before the neatly made double bed caught his eye. Forgetting the bathroom, Rosen flopped down, fumbling off shoes and slacks, lurching up only to yank the blue bedspread out from under his butt before pitching forward until his cheek furrowed into the cool pillow ...

*　*　*

"Well?" Van Damme fiddled with an intricately carved walrus tusk letter opener: his prize acquisition as one of the first tourists ever to go to Antarctica. Craig returned his stare without volunteering anything for the past minute. Score one for Craig.

"We had a little problem at that sanatorium last night."

Van Damme waited. Nothing more from the other. It was maddening. The infernal man was going to make him work for every bit of information. "Sanatorium?"

"Fair Oaks." The lips closed. Craig was back in his shell.

"What *kind* of trouble, Craig?" Van Damme's thin lips formed a tight smile. "Do you think you could elaborate without taking this through lunch?"

"We lost him."

Again that obstinate silence, like a child afraid of being spanked. Only Craig was no child and, in Van Damme's experience, the man feared nothing except admitting failure, a flaw that Van Damme used to great advantage. With proper manipulation, Craig could perform the impossible. Van Damme kept his voice relaxed.

"Craig, please give me the whole story. *Now.*"

A floodgate opened, confession leading to hoped-for, but not expected, absolution. The tall, muscular man leaned forward to describe Eddie's recruitment, the painstaking plans for Stevenson's entry, the care, the timing, the failure, and Rosen's escape. Craig stopped, peering sidewise at Van Damme, waiting for what he hated most: his superior's acknowledgement of his failure.

Van Damme thought a moment about how to play it. Should he come down hard? Make Craig suffer? He wanted to. He wanted to make the miserable bastard suffer! What the hell did it take to close the book on this Rosen? He wanted to bury the damn walrus tusk in screwup Craig's throat … but wouldn't it be better to use Craig's fear of failure?

Van Damme decided to leave Craig's guilt up to Craig. In the end, that would grate excruciatingly, hounding Craig until he would rather die than fail again. He lowered the ivory opener, pursing his lips, staring toward the far end of the room. "Needless to say, I'm disappointed."

"So am I, Sir. More than you can know."

Van Damme looked at Craig. He *was* suffering. Good. He'd definitely chosen the right tack. "How can we correct things, Ted?"

Craig's face was so solemn, so sincere, that Van Damme could have laughed if their problem weren't so serious. "Rosen doesn't have many places left. His lawyer was his best friend. He's got a mother, seventy, in New York. Father deceased. No brothers or sisters. Only child." Craig was plainly too involved to notice his redundancy. "I've got Crowley watching the mother's place. Another guy is parked outside his wife's cousin's place in Wesley Heights, but I doubt we'll get much out of that."

He shrugged, confirming Van Damme's own analysis that the mother and cousin would be a waste of time. Rosen had lost enough family. "Any *other* ideas?" Van Damme punched the word with an arch of thin eyebrows.

"We're checking his records for outside contacts …friends. Also in the agency …active or retired …" Craig's voice trailed off, head dropping so that he had to look at Van Damme through the extreme top of his eyes. He was tapped out.

Van Damme opted for a new tack. He didn't want to break Craig, just motivate him.

"Tell me, Ted, do you recall that this man was armed when you caught up with him at Union Station? What do you think he intended to do with that gun?"

Craig took a long moment. His Adam's apple rippled as he answered. "Kill you."

"I couldn't agree more. Now, when did he escape from this Fair Oaks?"

"Sometime after three in the morning."

"And was it possible that he would continue with his plan to kill me when he escaped?"

Craig's head snapped up. His eyes regained their usual confidence. He was on safer ground now. "I thought he'd be more apt to get the hell out. Regroup, so to speak."

"And you were so certain of your analysis of Rosen's mental state that you were willing to risk my life by not even *warning* me for over eight hours?" Van Damme's chair lurched forward with a shrill squeak, his eyes blazing as he thrust the tusk out at Craig's face.

Craig smiled his slow heavy-lidded smile. His annoying cockiness was back intact.

First undermine him and then rebuild his confidence. Van Damme experienced warm satisfaction. It always worked.

"No problem, boss. I didn't want to have to wake you up, so I put a bunch of contract guys on your house. They followed you to work. A couple of our guys took over once you were there. He couldn't have gotten you with a bazooka." Craig rocked back in the Chippendale.

Van Damme cringed as the chair's delicate rear legs absorbed the strain, but he controlled his urge to lambaste Craig. On his way home last night, he had easily picked out the yellow GTO that followed him. Only an amateur wouldn't have noticed it as it frantically swerved in and out of rush hour traffic, maintaining the requisite three car lengths behind Van Damme in textbook surveillance fashion. But let Craig have his victory.

Van Damme paused to register the proper amount of surprise. His eyelids arched over delighted wide eyes. "Excellent, Ted. Excellent thinking. I appreciate the consideration." He rose.

Craig, looking like the cat that swallowed the canary, followed suit.

"However, Ted, I give you permission to call me at any time, day or night, if someone wants to kill me again." Van Damme said it with a thin smile.

Craig snorted out a cocky laugh, causing Van Damme to visualize burying the walrus tusk letter opener in him for the second time. "Now get out of here and find him—for *good*! I don't want to have to think about Rosen ever again." He winked at Craig.

Craig gave him a thumbs-up.

Winks were such a powerful tool for bonding. Van Damme's eyebrows, cheeks, and chin melded into a smirk as the frosted glass door to his office closed behind Craig.

*　*　*

Van Damme drove out the wide Langley drive, past the third and last security post, at 1:15. Accelerating his gray Mercedes 650SL up the southbound ramp, he jockeyed his way into one of I-495's center lanes, heading deeper into Virginia.

Normally he would have swung all the way left, passing traffic with a smooth purr, barely feeling seventy-plus in the powerful vehicle, his pleasure interrupted only by the occasional road hog who refused to be intimidated by his bumper hugging and flashing high beams. But Aronovsky wouldn't be back at the embassy until 2:00, and he needed time to think.

Van Damme adjusted the air-conditioning to medium. Although it barely whispered across his face, the car was suddenly cool. He pressed back into the pliant leather, willing his mind to enter each muscle of his body—one at a time—making him heavy and warm. Within two minutes, he was completely relaxed.

Rosen had followed him to the drop in Maryland. Rosen's file said it. That had been a real slip, and Van Damme was not pleased with himself. He was always so careful: doubling back an inordinate number of times; repeatedly switching his methods of transportation; entering crowded public places, then leaving immediately through side exits. All standard procedures for which he would hang a subordinate by the balls for failing to follow. But he had been running late, and the pickup was at 3:00 p.m. sharp; it was imperative that Kharkov have the cut-in-half plans by the following day because Van Damme had wanted the Russian to get cracking on *his* end of the bargain.

Van Damme did not tolerate failure in others, or himself, and instant tremors of self-disgust disintegrated his relaxation. He concentrated on heavy and warm arms and legs for five minutes before he was relaxed again.

The lush countryside was startlingly green, despite weeks of record-breaking heat. Only upon closer inspection did drooping clumps of tall grass and flagging leaves betray the hot summer's toll.

Van Damme swung over, up an exit ramp, emerging onto a shadow-dappled road winding around grassy outcroppings with ancient oaks, streamers of ivy looping their trunks and branches. He barely felt the heat-cracked asphalt's depressions and ridges as he guided the heavy vehicle toward open wooden gates in a bougainvillea-draped wall.

The parking lot was one-third filled, largely with other expensive vehicles. Van Damme parked next to a forest-green Jaguar, overlapping into the adjoining space to leave the Jag's driver plenty of room. Locking the

Mercedes, he strode toward another gate in the high wall, walking onto an uneven brick path set between rows of azalea. Bees hovered about shoulder-high hollyhocks, competing with blurred hummingbirds for their succulent centers. The jasmine and honeysuckle that proliferated along the rough wall surrounding the garden lent an oppressive sweetness to the heavy afternoon air. Cricket chirps contrasted with the low hum of bees, while the harsh calls of crows and jays descended from the overhanging oaks.

La Petite Auberge, Van Damme's private sanctuary, stood before him, its white-trimmed French doors beckoning him away from the world of chaos and responsibility like a timely oasis. The interior was dim and cool.

Maurice, the diminutive owner, dressed in a tuxedo—the only way that Van Damme had ever seen him in over fifteen years of lunches and, less frequent, dinners— popped out of the darkness so suddenly that Van Damme would have jumped had he not been accustomed to the routine. With a somber greeting, Maurice, who took everything about La Petit seriously—resulting in a three-week waiting list for all but his favored customers—inquired about Mrs. Van Damme's health while leading Van Damme to his favorite corner table.

It occurred to Van Damme that despite knowing each other for so long, he and Maurice never discussed anything more personal than health and the weather. He speculated briefly upon whose fault it was, but he lost interest as he reviewed the tasseled cloth menu.

He loved reading descriptions of exquisite delicacies, allowing his expectations to build to orgiastic heights. He never touched the tempting warm rolls or ordered a drink. He wanted his palate clear for that glorious first bite.

The meal—creamy vichyssoise, then endive salad, setting the stage for glorious salmon quiche, capped by delicate orange sherbet and La Petit's robust filter coffee—provided Van Damme with the perfect escape.

Only one brief incident marred his superb experience. While taking his last bite of salad, Van Damme had a horrible premonition that Rosen, disguised as a busboy, approached his table. Before he could react, Rosen pointed the gaping barrel of an Uzi and blasted away, scattering rolls, exploding the delicate cut-glass flower vase and water goblet, depriving him forever of his eagerly anticipated main course.

His hand snaked reflexively under his jacket and was already fumbling with the safety strap on his underarm holster before he got control. Chiding himself under his breath, Van Damme slipped his hand back out, reaching for his salad fork instead. He peered through the tops of his eyes to see if anyone had noticed. Apparently not. Soon he was in seventh heaven, scooping up the last drops of creamy dressing.

Rosen. The man couldn't get near him! Craig's contract people were guarding him and Felecia. Not only that—since this morning, he'd also put his own agency people on the job. No way Mr. Rosen could get to him.

Rosen! As he squeezed the wafer-thin lemon slice against the tiny demitasse spoon, Van Damme had to hand it to him. The man had gone from a total nonentity to someone about whom Van Damme had become grudgingly aware. My God, he had actually taken the time to study Rosen's file earlier today.

Arnold Frederick Rosen: thirty-seven, Cornell undergrad. Joined the agency at twenty-five; attended law school at night until twenty-nine; passed up unsolicited offers from two respected Washington firms after graduating number two in his class. Strange for a Jewish boy to be so patriotic, but Van Damme had no doubts that that was exactly Rosen's reason for failing to seize more lucrative opportunities. Another strange thing: Rosen hadn't avoided the service although his grades entitled him to a grad school deferment. On the contrary, Rosen went in straight out of college. The Special Forces, no less. Strange for a smart little Yid. And a hand-to-hand combat champion, to boot. Very strange!

No doubt Rosen was coming after him when he was intercepted at the railroad station. No other reason for Rosen to be carrying a gun. Still, hero or not, Rosen knew by now that he didn't have a prayer of driving over to Langley and blowing him away. Things were never as easy as they seemed, eh, Arnie? Van lifted the demitasse in mock salute. Enough! The man was nowhere around and anyway, wherever he was, he was already dead—he just didn't know it yet.

Patting his lips with a large napkin, Van Damme signaled for the check. Once he paid, he made his way toward the restrooms, pushing into one of the two full-sized phone booths that separated "messieurs" from "mademoiselles." Yanking the creaky accordion door closed, he dialed the old-fashioned rotary phone. *God Bless Maurice for his good taste in a tasteless world,* thought Van Damme.

"Embassy of the Russian Republic. How may I help you?" A female voice repeated the query in Russian and English without inflection or accent.

"Cultural attaché, please." Van Damme smiled at the euphemism. Everyone at the embassy had such impressive titles: "chief economic officer,

United Nations liaison officer" … The list was endless. But it all boiled down to the same thing: KGB or GRU. Armonovsky was a captain.

"Cultural attaché's office." This voice was almost an exact duplicate of the first woman's.

"Mr. Armonovsky, please."

"Whom shall I say is calling?"

"Mr. Benheim."

"One moment, Sir."

Van Damme toyed with the door, squeaking it open a slit, closing it again, repeating the process.

"Mr. Benheim, it is good to hear from you." Armonovsky's voice was deep and smooth. Unlike the women, his accent was soft but noticeable. "It" sounded more like "eeeet" and "good" was more like "goooot."

"My collection will be complete in two weeks. I trust that your principal will also have his works catalogued and ready by that time."

"I vill tell him. In regard to your question, it is my understanding that his material is already available for your inspection."

"Excellent. Thank you. I'll be in touch." Van Damme broke the connection and strode into the bathroom.

He stopped before a mirror lighted by a row of etched glass globes. He checked his teeth for food remnants; rinsed his mouth, just in case; brushed back a strand of … *graying sideburns*! He would have to do something about that.

Van Damme had no doubt that one or more of the intricate and ever-improving NSA electronic devices trained on the embassy had monitored his call. It did not concern him in the least. The sheer volume of such receptions left a three-to-five-week backlog before they could be reviewed.

Besides, the obscure conversation wouldn't mean a thing, in any event. He wondered briefly about Armonovsky. Did the KGB captain, himself, have the slightest idea as to the nature of the information exchange for which he was a go-between? Van Damme rinsed his hands under Maurice's golden faucet. More than likely not. Kharkov would certainly not entrust the captain—that would needlessly increase Kharkov's own exposure—and Armonovsky would not dare stick his nose into the business of a high-ranking superior like Kharkov.

With a final frown at the gray, Van Damme turned and walked out.

Chapter 10

Rosen woke midafternoon. He wandered through the kitchen, stubbing his toe on an obvious table leg, cursing his way into the den and out to the living room. The house was empty. He staggered back to the bath and splashed cold water on his face, rubbing it vigorously to counteract the grogginess.

Digging into Marquand's top-of-the-line GE—a modern beige refrigerator in contrast to the dated avocado stove and dishwasher—he grabbed two slices of whole wheat bread, Swiss cheese, salami, ham, and tomatoes; slapped on some Grey Poupon; and went to town, washing it down with a Diet Sprite.

Borrowing a towel, Tom Wolfe's *Bonfire of the Vanities*, and one of Papa's baggy bathing suits, Rosen reached for a spare key from a neat row of pegs over the sink, locked up, and drove to the beach.

When he got back at 6:15, Marquand was in his armchair. He looked up quickly, removing his half-lensed reading glasses.

"Describe the men who kidnapped you." Rosen frowned.

"Go on." Marquand stared sharply, his face giving away nothing. "One was about six-two, a little taller than me, thin but strong....

Uh … dark hair … longish nose, kinda longish face. You know … kinda horse-faced. He ran the show. The other guy was about five-ten … solid. Had a crew cut. Blond. Stuttered like you wouldn't believe. He was the one with the knife in my room."

Marquand relaxed visibly. His shoulders dropped, and his face softened. "What?" Rosen's frown deepened. "What, Goddammit?"

"The men you described. Craig, the tall one, handles 'terminations.' Works for Van Damme's division. This has to be really special for Van Damme to violate the mandate against local operations. The other, Stevenson, is non-agency, a contract guy, paid by the assignment. You know how it works. Anyway, Craig used him a lot. Rumor was that

Stevenson wanted to be agency but the education wasn't there. Stuttering would have kept him out, in any event." Marquand's bushy eyebrows arched. "I guess he'll never make agency now."

Marquand gave Rosen time to absorb his words and then rose. He walked toward the younger man, placing a hand on his shoulder. "Arnie, it looks as if the bastard *did* try to nail you." Marquand's voice softened as he instantly regretted the glib characterization. "And had Barbara ... Anyway, I apologize for questioning you."

Rosen shrugged. "Hey, who can blame you? It would sound pretty wild to me if I hadn't ... lived it."

"Of course I'll help." Marquand's dark eyes crinkled above the pushed-down reading glasses riding the bony bridge of his nose. "I'll call in a few favors, try to find out what the hell he's up to. Then we can figure out how to get him."

"Not 'we,' Papa. Only *me*." Rosen's voice stung the air.

Marquand gave him a long look. "Sure, Arnie. Only you." His craggy face wrinkled into a smile. "Now let me make you the best chicken cacciatore this side of Italy. Followed by key lime pie, made as only we old Key folk can. How's 'at sound? Go shower. I'll call you when it's ready." With a wink, Marquand lumbered toward the kitchen.

*　*　*

Dinner was delicious. Rosen pushed his third helping of key lime away, leaving the creamy meringue in chunks, like a shattered snowman. Fingering the hefty mug of Marquand's "special brew" decaf, he smiled over at the big man.

Marquand thrust out his substantial stomach, patting it with beefy hands as he sighed hugely to indicate the scope of his contentment.

Rosen had to laugh, his first laugh since he could remember. For a moment, he was actually peaceful, safe with an old friend. It didn't last. As if in response to his momentary relief, a wave of guilt surged through him, leaving the old rage in its wake. "I do need your help desperately. There's no one else."

Marquand picked up fast on the change. Yanking in on his stomach, he sat upright. "Give me a few days. I can get enough to back you with the FBI. Once they go to work, it should all come out. But it may take a while. Company guys don't crack easily."

Rosen could have sworn that the last was said with a touch of pride—forty years with the agency did not disappear overnight.

"No FBI. No cops—no one but me!"

Marquand shook his white mane, pursing thick lips in a tolerant half smile: a teacher explaining the rules to a stubborn child "Arnie, you can't take him on—"

"They'd never believe me over him. Van Damme's got it stacked. It'd take forever to reconstruct my proof, and they might not give me the chance. I don't have a soul to corroborate me. And what the hell happens when I hit jail? I'm dead! Van Damme arranges a nice little accident for me. Christ, with his contacts, it's a piece of cake! A fall, a knifing, a fire … He knows where I am, and he's got all the time in the world to do me." Rosen slapped the mug down, rattling a nearby fork. "Am I wrong?"

Marquand stared into his coffee as if looking for an answer beneath its murky surface.

"*Am* I wrong?"

Marquand slowly looked up from his coffee. "You can't take him. Damn it, Arnie, he's always protected. More so now that he knows you're still around. He'll have an army around him." Marquand's bright tenor lowered, softly and sadly. "And another horde looking for you. You've got no choice."

Rosen's eyes went icy blue. "I'll find a way … because you're right: I've got no choice."

Marquand chewed on that, making funny shapes with his lips, staring vacantly at everything in the room but Rosen. He finally peered up from beneath bushy eyebrows. "What can I do?"

"Get me everything you can on him. Where he's been; who he's called; where he's going. Hell, you know the routine better than I do. You taught me."

"Yeah, I did." Marquand was surprised at how little pleasure he took from the compliment. His gradual disillusionment with his former life had come as a shock to Marquand because, for months after retirement, he had spent most of his waking hours fantasizing about returning to action.

Why had it happened? he used to ask himself once he realized that his disenchantment was irreversible. Had those glorious cellophane-dorsaled Marlin seduced him, the rolling green waters softened him, the monster moons changed him? Had the years Marquand so cherished caught up with him, turned on him? Was it the circles within circles that he'd set into motion, where the whole was always more important than any single part?

Now the lost "parts"—dedicated young men whom Marquand had trained and sent out and often lost, either literally or because the field ultimately killed their souls if not their bodies—seared Marquand's memory, while his all-important "wholes" had withered into obscurity.

The intra- and inter-agency politics, which Marquand had accepted as necessary, had been corrupted. Political carryovers from prior administrations did their best to sabotage a current administration from a different party. Leaks to politically sympathetic news outlets— something no one in the agency would have dared consider before— were commonplace now. The old-fashioned phrase "For the good of the country" was a cynical platitude at the agency. It was all just cheap political war by now, conducted by hacks whose loyalty stopped at the voting booth.

The process of offsetting his disillusionment, once acknowledged, with the good he had accomplished, had been long and painful, but he had finally succeeded. Now this.

Marquand fought to rekindle the fire—it had to be in there somewhere. You didn't let a friend down. You never did that! He smiled, hoping that his misgivings didn't show through. "I've still got some pretty good sources. Guys owe me favors. We'll get the dirt."

"And how about Germany? I think that's key."

Marquand was heartened by the energy in Rosen. The kid looked as if he was snapping back a little—the enthusiastic kid Marquand had liked so well, even back when the little so-and-so hadn't known his ass from a hole in the ground. Hell, Marquand wasn't about to let him down. Arnie Rosen had had enough letdowns for a lifetime. "Yep, I think you're right. We'll try to find out, okay?"

"How long?

Boy, Rosen was really cooking, thought Marquand. *Well, good. He needed something to hold on to.* "Soon as I can, pal. Soon as I can. Promise."

Rosen looked at Marquand, dead serious. "I know you will, Papa. I appreciate it. I'm sorry to be pushing, but—"

"I know, kid. Meantime, let's get you ready."

"What do you mean?"

Marquand clucked. "Do I have to teach you everything? God, I thought my work was over, but I can see it's just beginning." He shook his head in mock frustration—true as hell on the inside, though. "Survival, my little neophyte. Survival is what I'm talking about."

"Okay. Thanks for the grand plan. Now could you get a little more specific for the poor 'neophyte'?"

"Your credit cards. How are you planning to finance yourself? You can't use them or draw on your bank, 'cause Van Damme wouldn't be worth a crap if he wasn't already tapped into their computers. You use 'em, he'll find you."

Rosen slid off the thin-legged chair; grabbed his white-mounded pie plate, fork, and mug; and shuffled toward the sink, barely making it before his tottering fork plummeted into the haphazard accumulation of dishes with a tinny *clank*. "I've been using cash up to now. But that, for sure, is running out."

"I'll cover you. I'll get to my bank tomorrow. Just don't touch your credit cards or checks. Matter of fact, leave them here so you won't be tempted."

"Yes, Mom." Rosen poured hot decaf from Marquand's Mr. Coffee and reseated himself. He jammed a thumb into the too-wide elastic waistband of Marquand's slacks. "I may not be able to pay you back for a while—"

"Forget it. I got plenty, and this ain't exactly the Plaza." Marquand roved the room with his eyes.

"What else, Teach?"

"Passport. You might need a passport, right? At least, last I heard, Germany was still requiring them."

Rosen couldn't help it; he had to laugh. Marquand's sarcasm brought back old memories of learning the ropes, ever mindful of Marquand's caustic slashes, never meant to hurt, only instruct. Nobody who knew him ever resented Freddie Marquand.

"Riiight, Papa," Rosen repeated dutifully. But inside, he was thrilled. Marquand was responsible for more successful covert operations than anyone in modern company history.

"You can't use yours, obviously. I'll arrange for a local to create a substitute. He's got a better selection than Macy's has ties. He'll photo you with your disguise—which we'll work on later. And of course, you'll need some fake credit cards and IDs." Marquand struggled up for a third coffee refill. "The guy isn't cheap, but he's good. Better than good." Marquand sloshed too much milk into the coffee, muttering as he poured it into the sink and tried again. "He's over from Cuba, not too long ago. I don't think anyone at the company will recognize his work."

Satisfied with the color of his coffee, Marquand shuffled back to his chair, his leather slippers scuffling along the glistening linoleum. He settled heavily with an enormous sigh. "You sure you don't want to take this on like a civilian? You're going to need a hell of a lot of luck the other way."

"I need a hell of a lot of luck either way." Rosen looked straight at the older man. "I'll do it. Coming to you was a good start, wasn't it?"

Marquand tipped back, his old kitchen chair creaking under his bulk. "Touché." Marquand grinned. "Maybe you can, Neophyte. Maybe you can." His eyes looked anything but sure.

Chapter 11

Van Damme watched her dress. He loved to watch her dress. In fact, as he thought about it, the simple truth was that he loved to watch her do anything. She, his wife, Felicia Pelt-Van Damme. She refused to give up her ultra-rich, socially prominent maiden name. In fact, Van Damme considered it no small victory that she had deigned to let his be included. It certainly did nothing to enhance his sense of possession—did some men actually possess their wives? *Nothing* about Felicia did.

She was always, to him, a beautiful piece of art on loan to a museum—he being the "museum"—ready to be reclaimed by its rightful owner on short notice—the "owner" being her father, the eighty-two-year-old patriarch of the Pelt clan, Richardson Pelt IV. While the situation did not enhance Van Damme's sense of self-worth, it did make Felicia the most desirable woman in the world in his eyes, even after eighteen years of marriage.

Van Damme simply adored her—in his own way. Which was not to fawn or make a fool of himself. That was definitely *not* his way. But Van Damme would watch her, as now, the brush crackling through her soft wheat-blond hair; the healthily tanned skin toned with good muscle from a lifetime of sports. She had recently undertaken weight training to "keep in shape now that I'm forty." The huge almond-shaped hazel eyes with gold flecks, which were glancing up at him from the vanity mirror, were amused (perhaps flattered?) by his staring. Embarrassed, Van Damme pretended to fiddle with the already-made bow tie under the rigid collar of his ruffled shirt.

Of course, Van Damme was too late and too slow. He was never able to deceive her. Felicia knew how Van Damme felt, and it gave her power. And no matter how much he loved her, Van Damme did not particularly like that. He did not like anyone having power over him. It made him feel helpless and vulnerable, also rendering his feelings for Felicia Pelt-Van Damme, the one true ambiguity in his life.

"Darling, you're very quiet." Were her eyes taunting or just concerned? Van Damme could never be sure, damn it! "Hardly the kind of mood for our famous annual Milk the Rich for Charity Ball."

One thing about Felicia: if she taunted him occasionally, she also laughed at herself (another reason why he loved her, damn it!).

Their annual cancer ball, held the second weekend after Labor Day, attracted two hundred of the absolutely and irrefutably prominent. It took months to plan and required a retinue of forty servers, chefs, car parkers, and security people, and it was reviewed by not only the society columns but a hundred jealous biddies planning their own affairs. Yet here was Felicia, calm, beautiful, and laughing at the whole thing.

"I met with those national security idiots today," Van Damme muttered.

"Can't hear you, Charles." Her throaty voice bounded off the vanity mirror.

He glared across the space between his dresser and her vanity. Their monster bed was like a lime-colored oasis on a desert of gold carpet. Night tables, chairs, and lamps were reduced to diminutive proportions by the room's sheer size. Not that Van Damme didn't enjoy his lifestyle. Despite what that old son of a bitch Richardson Pelt thought, he came from luxury too. But it did have its inconveniences. "I *said*"—Van Damme disliked raising his voice. Having to do it *also* made him feel out of control—"I had a bad time with those national security idiots today."

"What happened, darling?" Felicia did not miss a brushstroke. "They dismissed my ideas. Treated me like some damn moron when I know more about the Russians than any of those political hacks ever will." He moved toward her in order to use his quiet voice again.

The brush came down, and the lipstick went up. "Darling, why don't you simply leave? You'd be worth much more on the outside. And you wouldn't have to put up with these awful people."

Van Damme felt his face flush. He confirmed it by glaring into her mirror. "*Felicia!*" he was close enough now, but his voice seemed to be rising once again. He fought it. "Felicia," Van Damme said evenly, "I *believe* in what I do. It is important that somebody protect this poor naive country."

This time she did focus on him, lipstick poised midway, like a painter interrupted mid-stroke. Smoldering contempt flashed up at him from her mirror. It was a topic that they had been over many times, one of the few, aside from her father, that disrupted an otherwise civil relationship.

"Then do what Daddy would do. Get to the top so you make policy!" There they were, both touchy topics at once. Two for the price of one.

This time Van Damme lost the battle with his temper. The bitch could really push his buttons. "I am *not* your 'Daddy'! I have never *been* your 'Daddy'! I never *want* to be your 'Daddy'! I pity anyone who *would* want to be your 'Daddy'! Are we clear about my feelings about your *'Daddy'*?"

"Yes, Charles." Felicia was back at her lipstick, unfazed. She enjoyed shaking his calm.

What an idiot he was. He could maintain control while shuffling legions of agents around like pawns on a chessboard, but let Felicia decide to needle him and he was off like a pinwheel. Van Damme had to laugh despite himself.

"It's not that easy, love. The top spots are political. The President and his Cabinet cronies appoint the director of intelligence. I'm high, but I don't run in those circles. And there's no time to build relationships with them. Christ, the players change so often now that you can't even count on two terms from the same president. Especially the Democrats. Not that they'd be falling over themselves to appoint someone with my background, anyway."

"Nothing is easy."

Interesting, coming from a kid who was born with a platinum spoon in her mouth. But Van Damme had to admit, she hadn't stopped there. Felicia did whatever she set out to do, even if what that was didn't exactly keep the world turning.

"I have faith in you."

It was a nice thought, but it might have meant more to Van Damme if Felicia hadn't been hunched against the mirror perfecting the red arches of her upper lip.

"Besides"—it came out "bissssidz" during the delicate lipstick operation—"we have plenty of friends who agree with you. Senator Culcane will be here with that frumpy Lucy." This time Felicia turned, animated by one of her favorite topics: other people. "You know, the one who moans about the simple life in Augusta, where 'neighbahs still stop ovah with Christmas gifts rathah than have big phonah pahties wheah no one reallah cahs.' Anyway, he certainly agrees that those Russians aren't the good guys everyone's making out. And he's powerful, Charles. He's head of … the defense committee something—"

"Second on foreign relations—"

"Whatever. He could certainly help. And there are plenty of others, I'll bet. You just have to take the bull by the horns."

"Maybe you're right." Van Damme smiled down at the unblemished tan back, wanting to stroke it, knowing that she'd tell him not to while she was trying to finish. He was unwilling to risk her rejection. Felicia hardly ever rejected him later at night, although lately.... Well, he didn't want to think about that now. He was just starting to feel good.

Anyhow, Felicia was right. She didn't know how right. It *was* time for some changes. Time for him to get his due—one way or the other. Soon they would all know who Charles Van Damme was.

Van Damme was tempted to tell her; he wondered how she'd handle it when she realized—*once and for all*—that he had more nerve in his pinkie than her miserable father had in his whole cadaverous varicose-vein-filled body. Of course, he couldn't tell Felicia, but the thought of doing it radiated delightful tingles of satisfaction along his spine. Reluctantly, Van Damme forced the tempting words back, replacing them with, "Felicia, maybe you're right," but his precious secret continued to titillate his innards.

Felicia studied his reflection in her mirror, pleased with his mood change. The ball would be a success. Charles would, at least, be civilized, maybe even mildly charming. Everything would go beautifully, just as she planned. "Wonderful, darling. I know it will all work out. Now would you zip me, please? We'd better get down there and make sure our guests leave their wallets at the door."

*   *   *

Oh, dahlings and *Fabulouses* and *Wait till I tell yous* and *She didn't reallys* in the higher registers and *Damn Liberals* and *Damn Conservatives* and *horses asses* in deeper tones swirled around Van Damme as he pushed his way through the massive vaulted area that he and Felicia laughingly called their "family room."

It was their multilevel joke, inspired by an extra round of late night Kahlua. Level one: no way in hell was this two-hundred-plus-capacity cavern, complete with stage, sound system, and sliding glass roof—for the few nights a year when the weather was neither too hot nor too cold—going to be confused with a family room. Level two: no way in hell were he and Felicia going to be mistaken for a "family." Their decision to postpone children, based upon Felicia's unwillingness to give up her Pelt "Go where you want, when you want" lifestyle and his "Work comes first" approach, crystallized into permanence when society gynecologist I. Richard Fornam determined that, whatever their desires, Felicia's uterus was better adapted for sports and parties than childbearing. Van Damme could no longer remember if he had regretted the news or not, since he and Felicia had been childless for years by the time that Dr. Fornam made his pronouncement. He thought he might have felt badly long ago, but …

There was Culcane. Van Damme slid and sidestepped between wide matronly gowns and sculptured youthful gowns. Laser flashes from broaches, necklaces, and earrings stabbed his eyes as he returned hellos and tossed light compliments, never taking his eyes off his target: Senator Jim Culcane.

Van Damme was always put off by the appellation: "Jim." It seemed to him that a true Southern senator, returned to office for the seventh time, should have the decency to be called Lucius Thaddeus or Harlan C. Or, at the very least, "Big Jim." Just "Jim" made the man seem like an imposter appointed to complete the term of the real Southern senator. Of course, it wasn't true. Plain old Jim Culcane was a power. He would chair foreign relations when the ancient senator from Rhode Island stepped down, reputedly within the month.

Culcane held court against the bar. More precisely, the long fold-up table draped in laundry-service white, provided by Artistic Caterers at an exorbitant price, that served as the bar. The senator's fat rump rested on the edge, causing the bottles behind him to teeter precariously as he laughed often and hard. The young bartender/student behind the table watched in horrified fascination, probably worried that the bottles couldn't possibly recover. Somehow they did.

Surrounding the senator were two junior members of the house of representatives, one federal judge, a lobbyist for the dairy or cattle industry—Van Damme could never remember—and two unknowns. All acted as if they were front row at a Bob Hope benefit rather than listening to the warmed-over tales of an aging politico. Such was Washington. Van Damme worked his way closer, catching Culcane's eye during a lapse in the hysteria.

With barely a good-bye, Culcane pushed through his fawning audience and waddled toward Van Damme. "Waddle" was the operative word for a man five feet six inches and 219 pounds. His suit was, at the same time, too loose at the chest and too tight at the waist, no custom tailor being skilled enough to reconcile the disparity. His smile was so practiced that it actually appeared genuine, and in Van Damme's case, that may have actually been true. Culcane *did* like him. At least as much as anyone, who devoted his life to being everyone's friend, could.

"Wondaful pahty, Chahlie. Wondaful pahty." The senator's pudgy hand pumped Van Damme's. Van Damme pumped back in return. Culcane used nicknames as a way of establishing quick, insubstantial intimacy. Van Damme hated that. He was not a "Charlie." Never had been; never would be. But try to tell that to Culcane, who even had a nickname for the president!

"Glad you are enjoying yourself, Senator." For all of his informality with others, Culcane didn't at all mind being called senator.

"Heck, ah always enjoy mahself. Yuh know that." Culcane was one of those people who would have prided himself in making the most of the Titanic cruise. For an instant, steel glinted behind the senator's puffy eyes. "Come, take a walk with me, Son. I wantta smoke." Culcane placed a pudgy hand on Van Damme's elbow, propelling the tall man toward the open French doors without awaiting a reply.

They emerged onto a broad flagstone terrace that fronted an acre of meticulously tended garden, complete with fountains, Greek-replica statues, and sculptured rose bushes. The garden was semi-visible in the diminishing dusk. Rose sweetness caressed Van Damme's nostrils for a delicious moment. Then a match erupted and the delicate aroma dissolved in billows of pungent smoke. Culcane puffed delightedly on an obscenely huge Cuban cigar, oblivious to Van Damme's misery.

"Son, ah'm worried."

More smoke blasted by Van Damme, who did his best to stare intently through the smelly fog.

"Owa fahn Pres'dent, bless him, is intent ahn kissin' Yeltsin's ass. 'Fraid a whattle happen if the hahd-lahners git back inta powah. Cain't say that ah blame him, but ah gotta diffunt concern."

Another massive puff hit Van Damme. It didn't matter now; Culcane had Van Damme's full attention.

"Ah ain't as sure as owa Pres'dent that Yeltsin has given up on the ol' game plan. Yuh know: bury us. Mehbbe he onla put his plans ahn hold for a whal. An' even if *he's* not play'n games, how 'bout them otha communists that are fuh sure? What's ta keep 'em from dumpin' Yeltsin latuh, afta we pump a fo'tchun inta their damn economy?"

"I couldn't agree—"

"Ah read yo' repote, Son." Culcane dismissed Van Damme's interjection with a flick of ashes over the terrace railing. "You are raht ahn, ta use the modahn vahnaculah. Unlike that dog food makah tha's headin' up thaings now."

Van Damme smiled at the reference to Savin. The DI had been the head of a massive pet food empire before his appointment.

"Anaway …" A young couple shuffled near, elbows entwined upon the railing, blissfully squinting into the darkening garden.

Culcane pointed his diminishing cigar toward a secluded spot farther down. Van Damme followed. He was positively dying to hear what came next.

Culcane slouched over the rail, beckoning Van Damme to do the same. The Senator's voice dropped low. "Anaway, a buncha us, an' I mean a *bunch*"—his chubby fist pounded Van Damme's forearm—"would like ta see a change. See a mo' suspicious sote in the job. One who's mo' apt ta keep an eye on the Rooskies. Ya get ma drift?"

Beyond the darkness, Van Damme was sure that the Senator's eyes were flashing steel again. Van Damme played his cue. "Yes, Sir, I do."

"Now, ya know we cain't jus say, 'Mistuh Pres'dent, we want yuh ta fo'ce this man Savin, who yuh liked enough ta keep ovah from th' opposition regime, ta make some changes in his intell'gence pro-ceedures. How 'bout it?'" Culcane giggled. "It don' work that way. Nossir. Owah Pres'dents ridin' high nah. Evathing looks peaceful an seerene." Culcane's glowing cigar stub flashed dangerously close to Van Damme's nose. "But you jess wait. Those damn Rooskies gonna get caught with theh hainds in the cookah jah. Then mebbe we'll see some changes, huh, son? Yuh keep up the good wook, mebbe you gonna be one a those 'changes.'"

Van Damme leaned close. "I'm flattered, Senator. Flattered, that is, if I'm not being presumptuous. You *are* suggesting that I might be considered for deputy director of operations for the agency? Assuming certain circumstances? At least insofar as you and your colleagues are concerned?"

"If tha's longhand way a askin' if we would trah ta get yuh in, the ansuh's hell yes. Yuh intrusted?"

Van Damme said with perfect and utter seriousness, "Why, yes, Senator. I am."

"We bettuh git back in. Yuh know how faist rumahs spread in this town if'n anabody talks ta anabody fuh too long."

Culcane's glowing butt arched high over the railing. Van Damme prayed that the blasted thing didn't land on one of his prize rose bushes. He followed the almost square man back into the music and chatter. In contrast to the subdued terrace, the noise in the room had reached an intolerable crescendo, but this time Van Damme scarcely noticed.

*　　*　　*

Van Damme was circulating again—waving; talking golf, of which he cared little; or polo, about which he couldn't care less—surreptitiously eyeing the young ones with their tight clingy gowns. He even tried his hand at flirty repartee once or twice, the results of which were inconclusive at best. From time to time, Van Damme would catch glimpses of Felicia, always surrounded and loving it.

What little interest he had been able to muster in his party dribbled away as the interminable night dragged on. Van Damme couldn't help it. He didn't like parties. He was good enough at them. He practiced plenty during the busy Washington social year, not to mention agency-related diplomatic functions. But damn it, he just didn't like them. He would rather read—there was never enough time to read everything that he wanted to—or think, or plan, or do any number of other things that he cared for more than ridiculous parties.

He was actually relieved when Hodges, the retainer foisted upon him by Pelt IV (probably to spy on him for the old geezer), announced in his tubular tones, "A Mr. Craig is waiting in the den, Sir. I told him that you were engaged, Sir, but he insisted that it was urgent. Shall I ask him to leave, Sir?"

Van Damme never liked Hodges's "Sir." He couldn't prove it, but to him it always came across sarcastically, as if Van Damme might have been many things to Hodges but a "Sir" was definitely not one of them.

"I'll see him." Van Damme did his best to react as if Hodges had just eaten three cloves of raw garlic.

"Very good, *Sir.*"

Ugh. There it was again. Van Damme hurried up the stairs and down the corridor. What in God's name was wrong now?

Van Damme's first glimpse at Craig convinced him that nothing was wrong. Unlike the other day, when Craig had sat ramrod straight in Van Damme's office, Craig slouched and fiddled with a jade elephant paperweight on Van Damme's desk. No, things definitely had to be looking up for Craig to have the unmitigated gall to touch his things. "*Yes.*" Van Damme hit the word hard, hoping to undermine Craig's cockiness.

Craig merely swung part way around, continuing to balance the valuable piece carelessly in his left hand. "I think we found him." The casual opening, without respectful pause or salutation, first, meant that Craig was quite sure of himself. "Or at least the guy who's helping him." Van Damme liked subordinates better when they were insecure. They were easier to control. "That sounds like a lot of nothing to me." Van Damme used his best put-down voice, which was very good. He walked toward the door, making sure no guests had wandered upstairs into the corridor, and then swung it shut. He strode back toward Craig, planted his feet wide, his hands on his hips. "I told you to kill him. *Period!* I didn't ask where he was or who he was with, did I?"

"Okay." Craig rose, thrusting his long legs up under himself as he set Van Damme's elephant back onto the desk. He pushed himself up and ambled toward the door.

"Since you're already here, tell me about it."

Craig released the knob and turned back with that same cocky-ass smile on his face. He was definitely not going to be beaten down *this* night.

Van Damme gave up. He poured a brandy from a cut-glass decanter on the long table behind his desk and slipped into his swivel chair, nodding for Craig to return to his seat. "Brandy?" His voice was party cordial again.

"Sure … thanks." Craig knew better than to push his luck; he kept the triumph out of his voice. It didn't pay to rub it in with Van Damme. Van Damme always won in the end, so you took your small victories gracefully, knowing that they were only temporary. Craig sipped deeply—Remy Martin he believed—letting it sit sweetly on his tongue for a moment and then flow down, coating his throat with warmth. Craig would have prolonged the process, but Van Damme's eyes told him that he had better get on with it.

"I had a trace put on Kelsey's home phone." Craig was referring to Brian Kelsey, the grandfather of all analysts, a jovial fatherly type who would have been put out to pasture years ago if Van Damme had had anything to say. He hadn't, so Kelsey and his deadwood buddies lived out their declining years at the expense of agency efficiency. "He doesn't have class one priority, so any calls that are made to him at the company would already be monitored. But not his home phone—"

"I know that." Despite his good intentions, Van Damme felt his level of irritation rising again. "Kindly stop informing me of facts that I know far better than you and get on with the essence of what you interrupted my very important charity party to tell me. Can you do that for me before the guests leave?"

Craig's horse face lengthened further. He gulped a second sip of brandy, getting the burn but none of the flavor. "Okay. Sorry. Anyway, I figured Kelsey keeps in touch with a lot of the pensioners, the old guys who used to work at the agency—"

"I know to whom you're referring. Go on, *please!*"

"Anyway, I figured maybe Rosen put the touch on one of them. You know, someone Rosen was close to … Sure enough, Kelsey gets a call yesterday from Fred Marquand. The guy they called 'Hemmingway' or something—"

"I know who Fred Marquand is. Everyone knows who Fred Marquand is."

"Yeah, so Marquand calls him last night asking about you and any trips you're planning, mentions Germany in particular. Wants him to find out about Stevenson and me too." This time Craig took a real sip, throwing back his head as he eyed Van Damme through half-closed lids. "Whaddaya think?"

"Marquand used to be close to a lot of recruits. Fancied himself a mentor, I suppose." Now Van Damme picked up the paperweight elephant, rubbing its cold smoothness, thinking. "He used to eat lunch with them." Van Damme's thin face puckered at the revolting image of a division chief lunching with wet-nosed beginners. "Rosen could have been part of that group—who knows?"

"Call came from Key West. I checked. Marquand lives there now. Hemingway lived there too. Funny."

Van Damme's eyes told Craig that there was nothing funny, or interesting, about the coincidence.

Craig sped on before another put-down issued from the tight lips across the huge desk. "I'm heading down tomorrow with Eddie."

Van Damme frowned.

"Eddie is the guy who cleaned up after Stevenson. He worked at Fair Oaks. Big guy. Strong. Wants more than being an orderly. He got rid of

Stevenson fast. No trace. Did a real good job. I offered him a contract deal. I needed someone to replace Stevenson, and I think he'll work out—"

"That's your department. If you think he'll work out, I'm sure he will. As long as they are 'outside' help, I don't care if you employ the Hunchback of Notre Dame." Van Damme rose. The session was over.

Craig set his snifter on a magazine. You never put things down on Van Damme's furniture. That was made abundantly clear the first time that he laid a Coke on Van Damme's office desk. Craig turned at the door. "Why is Rosen so important? We've trashed him. His credibility is zilch. I mean, I don't mind taking the asshole—'scuse me … the *guy*—out. 'Specially after what he did to Stevenson and making me look bad and all that. But why? Why not just tip off the cops?"

Van Damme's face was close to Craig's. Very close. His voice like a smooth sheet of ice. "For two reasons, Craig. First, because *I told* you to. *That* is reason enough, right? *Right?*"

Craig backed up a step, flattening against the door. "Right."

"Second—and I only tell you this because I choose to—because the names and information on four deep cover Russian civilians were in the files you reclaimed from Rosen. These assets were painstakingly recruited. Countless hours were invested in setting up communication channels to them. And I want to keep them secret, Glasnost, or independent republics, or whatever other way that mess over there turns out." Van Damme relaxed his voice, reaching a hand toward Craig's shoulder, his strangely soft eyes drawing Craig into his confidence. "The man is certainly deranged by now. We need damage control, Ted."

Craig's eyebrows rose involuntarily at this rare sharing of confidences.

"Otherwise, Ted, this Rosen could bring down those nationals, as well as our people who run them. We can't afford that. We'd never get any locals to trust us again, and our men in the field would have to come home. Or get reassigned. Do we want that? All for one traitor who stole classified information?"

Craig's shoulders squared. "No way. We'll get the bastard. Night, Boss. Sorry to interrupt the party." He pulled the door open and stepped through.

"No problem." Van Damme gave Craig's departing back a final pat. "Thanks for the good work." He paused in the doorway, smiling. Great fun: looking someone like Craig straight in the eye and telling him anything that worked. He loved it.

Craig would never have looked at the file because Van Damme had said it was "Eyes Only." No agency man worth his salt would, and Craig was that, despite his annoying ways.

Van Damme punched his open left palm with his right fist. Damned if this little meeting hadn't turned out to be the high point of his evening! Along with Culcane's endorsement, of course. All things considered, tonight had not been nearly as great a waste of time as he had feared. In fact, it had turned out quite excellently. Now his only concern was that those pieces of fluff downstairs would wander about eating his food, blurting inanities, and spilling crap on his rugs for at least another two hours.

Oh well. Van Damme stared wistfully back into his peaceful den and then closed the door with a sigh. His insubstantial shoulders hunched as he approached the stairway. Lord, was it his imagination or had the din downstairs increased?

CHAPTER 12

Otto Manfred Gruhaber was nervous. Not "I hope I didn't lock myself out of my car" nervous but stomach-turning, full-sweat scared-as-hell nervous.

His chubby fingers struck at the Mack's keyboard repeatedly, but the answer was always the same: someone had accessed his machine. Someone knew that he had copied key elements of the Sklar 3 Laser Image Recovery System last night!

And anyone who could enter his system was someone who would know that Otto had no right to any information about the laser system. Otto's scalp moistened with perspiration. Next, his neck, chest, palms … *everywhere.* Soon he was sopping wet.

Otto swiveled, hoping to catch a pair of eyes on his back or a giveaway lurch from one of the other eight heads bent over their own Macs. No one paid the slightest attention to him.

Otto erased the laser specifications directly from their file without using his screen. Bringing them up would have triggered the red stripe— that wildly flashing alert that must have given him away. It had finally won. Last night someone must have seen it from the outside corridor. Someone who had stayed late.

And damn if Otto hadn't left the classified material in his computer for the first time. Every other night over the past months, he had carefully deleted it after taking notes. He never even made copies to prevent the meters on the copiers from raising suspicions. He had done everything so right—until last night.

It wasn't fair! Only on one night had Otto broken his own rules and left the material in his computer. Only for a few hours. He hadn't left until 12:30 a.m., knowing that he'd return by 6:00 a.m. He would have been late for *Rear Window* if he had taken time to delete both the material and his access request codes, missing the beginning of one of his top ten movies. He certainly would not have had time to make a tuna fish sandwich on that nice fresh pumpernickel that he'd bought.

Otto loved *Rear Window*—Jimmy Stewart and Grace Kelley dancing to Hitchcock's magic—and he loved tuna on nice fresh pumpernickel, and he loved the two together, Hitchcock and tuna, better than anything.

So why was he being punished like this? He had worked hard—harder than anyone—and he never took time for himself except one night. One miserable night. And now this.

What was he going to do? Call Blue? Otto was scared. What would Blue say in that cold, smooth voice? Otto couldn't imagine the voice yelling, but maybe it would. Or maybe it would just tell him that he wasn't needed, that they would look for someone more responsible. Maybe it would say, "Don't ever contact us again."

Oh God, he couldn't stand that. He hated failing. His hand thumped the keyboard hard. Three or four heads popped up. He tried to smile, shaking his head, shrugging. The heads popped back down.

No, Otto *had* to stay on the team. He'd waited so long to finally *be* on a team. He had to prove to Blue that he still belonged. He had to do his job now, but later he would figure things out. Better to wait until he had figured things out before calling Blue. Yes, that was it: wait until later. That was it.

*   *   *

Lunchtime. The employee cafeteria's pale pink walls were calculated to create an environment of relaxation and well-being. Another legacy of S. K. Sklar, their founder and the originator of that awful red line alarm that had gotten Otto into trouble. Today pink had the just opposite effect on Otto.

He sat alone at his usual spot in the far corner, watching the Mexicans stack trays laden with squashed milk containers, used napkins, partly melted pads of butter, and littered plates on a tarnished metal cart jammed between his seat and the wall.

The walls, the noisy conversation, and regular eruptions of laughter— pink walls obviously had their desired effect on other Sklar employees— also depressed Otto. He gulped down whatever was left on his tray and studied the room rather than scurrying out and back to the safety of his computer. Even at the best of times, Otto generally snuck out before lunch hour was officially over. He just never seemed to be able to mingle with the happy groups who hooted and whooped and strung the lunch break out to the very last, as if nothing in life could be sweeter than five more minutes with their compadres. Sure, sometimes Ferdie Steerforth or Andy Bushoff, not exactly members of the Sklar in crowd either, stopped to gossip about who had screwed up a program or what new computer virus was making the rounds. But usually Otto ate alone and depressed.

Today was worse. Today Otto was alone and depressed and *frightened*. He watched Sklar employees queue along the aisle past cheerfully displayed fruit plates bulging with cottage cheese, sparkling green salads, and glistening Jell-O molds. They glanced here and picked there, apparently with nothing more on their minds than what to have for lunch. Which of them knew what he had done? Otto scrutinized the line, all the way up to where they milled around the register waiting for the unflappable cashier to ring them up.

He spotted familiar faces. There were at least six or seven other researchers in the food line. Plus how many already seated? Another twenty? Plus how many people he didn't recognize? Plus how many others who ate at the later shift? Plus how many who were eating their sandwiches from home at their desks? Were there over one hundred?

Otto let out a loud sigh, causing two table clearers jabbering away in Spanish near the trays to frown in his direction before renewing their staccato dialogue.

It was useless. There were just too many candidates. He'd hoped to get a lead down here. Catch a look, a smile, some clue. Otto got up. One of the clearers darted over and grabbed Otto's tray, brushing its edge along his trousers. Otto looked down. A line of milk residue spread along his thigh. He glared at the clearer, who was already reengaged in conversation. With another sigh, Otto slunk through the nearby wide doorway.

*   *   *

The afternoon was hell. Otto kept waiting for the heavy hand of a snarling security guard to clamp his shoulder, yanking him up until only the tips of his shiny black lace-ups touched the ground; dragging him down the long corridor to the Chief of Security's tiny, sweaty office. Otto had been there once, eight years before, when his tape deck was stolen from the employee parking lot.

Back at his desk, a hand actually did land on his shoulder—but lightly. A female coworker requesting statistics on fuel percentages. Otto lurched up so violently that he smacked escape, wiping out a half hour of calculations. The poor girl, a bespectacled thirty-five-year-old with a poorly corrected harelip, was so thoroughly terrified that she forget her question. She returned later, approaching Otto as if he were a zoo lion whose cage door just swung open.

Should he call Blue? The thought bracketed every one of Otto's other thoughts, like the refrain to an unpleasant but persistent song.

Otto kept postponing the inevitable, hoping for something concrete. His odds diminished with each waning hour. Soon he definitely would have to call. Blue *had* to know. Soon he would call. *Soon.*

"Soon" became 6:00 …

"Soon" became 7:00 …

At 7:18, Otto decided that he couldn't wait any longer. It would be late back East. He didn't need to have Blue mad at him for that too. Otto rose slowly, rolled his head around, loosening some but not all of the tension that froze his muscles. He blinked his aching eyes for a moment, turned, and stared into the grinning face of Ralph Jackson! Bubbles of despair escaped from his thumping heart.

Otto Manfred Gruhaber hated many things, of that there was no question. But none—except for the Russians—*more* than Ralph Jackson! Before the horrid mouth opened, before the Binaca-sweet breath assaulted him from behind an array of perfectly shaped teeth, Otto knew who had been at his computer. The worst person imaginable if he had ever hoped to get out of this mess. Who else? He had to be an idiot not to suspect before. His worst, worst enemy in all of Sklar—all of the United States, for that matter—stood before him, possessing the complete and total ability to ruin his life.

Ralph Jackson: upward mobile, handsome, smart, and very, very ambitious. Dressed in a fresh-looking blue blazer, while everyone else's jackets were as fatigued as their owners by this late hour; slacks with a crease that could draw blood; bow tie (old man Sklar reputedly wore one); wire-rimmed glasses, although Otto was unconvinced that anyone as young and healthy as Jackson really needed them. And on top of all that, Jackson was black. The perfect man for the perfect opportunity, now that Sklar had firmly embraced Affirmative Action.

Otto had always stereotyped blacks as run-down, seedy-looking, and dangerous. He avoided them on streets and stayed clear of their neighborhoods. But the man before him was new to Otto and even more frightening, for Ralph Jackson represented a black man who could not be geographically or educationally avoided.

Otto held his breath, trying to appear calm, picking at his left thumbnail despite himself.

"Hello, Otto." Jackson's smile broadened. It hardly seemed possible to Otto that anything so big and so wide could increase in size, but sure enough, it did.

Otto tried a smile. Maybe he could bluff it out.

"Let's not beat around the bush."

Otto gave his best innocent look, his face as forthright as a chubby peach.

"I know that you had the laser plans, and from the way you've been skulking around all day, you *know* I know."

Otto gave his best confused look, his face approximating a wrinkled chubby peach.

A cloud crossed Jackson's perfect features. "Would you rather we take this up with security?"

So much for the bluff. Anyway, had he heard right? Was this hope? "You haf not discussed dis yet?" Could it be that this awfulness would work out after all? Otto wished that his question hadn't sounded so grateful.

Jackson's smile blossomed anew. He rolled a nearby secretarial chair over, settled his body loosely around it, reaching his long legs nearly to where Otto stood. "Sit down, Gruhaber. Ree-laax." Jackson spread the word out like sweet, flowing syrup. "We better do some talking before anyone else finds out." Jackson stretched his long arms, locking his hands behind his conservative Afro.

Otto scurried to his chair. "Okay," was the best he could do.

"Good. Now I'm sure you were just looking at laser imaging out of curiosity, just to see how the whole system works. Right? I mean, I really can't blame you. You work on a project this long, you want to see how it all fits together. Right?"

"Yess. Yess. Exactly—"

"But everyone is not going to see it that way, Gruhaber. At best, you flagrantly breached company policy. At worst..." Jackson shook his large head, chuckling, "They could think you're a spy. They could ..." The head shaking and chuckling increased.

"Ya. Ya." Otto joined in, head shaking and chuckling along with Jackson. He was really getting into it, but suddenly he didn't hear Jackson laughing anymore. He looked up.

The man's face was rigid. "I want section head."

Otto stopped. It was easy. He hadn't really felt like laughing anyway. Just going along. "Vot?" Although Otto already knew exactly what Ralph Jackson meant. Just like he knew that this whole horrible day never would come out right.

"You know perfectly well what I mean. Clancy retires in two months, and I want propulsion section head. I might get it anyway, but why take chances—considering the little plum life just dropped in my lap." Jackson winked a tapered eyelash. "You are ASH right now." Everyone shortened things at Sklar. Jackson referred to Otto's being propulsion's second in command: assistant section head. "If you decline the SH slot, let's say due to fatigue, or health, or something—we'll work it out—then I'm in."

Jackson inched the chair up by crab walking his long legs. There were flecks of yellow in his irises. "But don't worry; I won't keep it for long. I got my eye on bigger things. This boy don't intend to be no damn researcher his whole life." Again the explosive smile. "Sheet. I'll even recommend you for SH when I go up to four."

"Four" was Sklar's executive floor. Otto had been there only twice. He still remembered his quick glimpse of the dining room on his way back to the elevator. Thick burgundy carpet, white tablecloths, exquisite oils suspended over wood paneling, silver tea services poised for use. Paradise. Otto envisaged Ralph Jackson, legs sprawled under a graceful circular tables, young Henry Sklar III on one side, middle-aged Henry Sklar II on the other, both pandering to Jackson's arrogance rather than suffering the effects of minority political pressure on Sklar's defense contracts.

"Now isn't that fair?" Jackson laughed. Otto was lost somewhere, unappreciative. Frowning, Jackson unfolded as he scooted his chair back. "Do we have a deal or not ... now or never?"

Otto didn't look up at the other's face. Instead, he talked to the incredibly sharp creases in Jackson's slacks. "Yess, ve haf a deal."

"I'll expect your recommendation of me after you decline, if that's the way it shapes up." The creases became the backs of Jackson's slacks. Soon the backs of Jackson's slacks disappeared behind a row of computers. "Why didn't you ask how I could prove that you had the material?" Jackson's voice echoed from far off to Otto's right.

God, Otto had to shut the braggart up before someone outside heard. "You backed up to main through my unit and reqvested rezeipt confeermation," he whispered back as loudly as he dared.

"Yeah. Right." Jackson sounded disappointed. His footsteps soon disappeared.

Otto sat. His pulse throbbed in his throat. Eventually, he chewed his lip, then popped from his chair. Now it *was* time to call Blue.

Chapter 13

The bullshit is as thick in here as Lauder's cheap cigar smoke, thought Amos as he tugged a pant leg to keep the knee from bagging.

He sat facing Chief of Detectives Eric Lauder. The litter on Lauder's desk created such a formidable barrier that the diminutive Amos literally had to arch his neck to see his boss. More than once, Amos wondered why he had bothered. Lauder was not a pretty sight. His massive jowls hung from his face like slabs of meat, dragging his lower eyelids down with them, giving Lauder the look of a pale basset hound. Even Lauder's voice came out like a woeful moan.

As if that wasn't bad enough, Lauder apparently planned to take all the nonsmokers in the department with him when he kept his inevitable rendezvous with the cancer ward. Another mammoth gob of smoke blasted through the Styrofoam coffee cups, take-out plates, and milkshake containers that inundated Lauder's desk. Amos would have bet that Lauder could reconstruct all of his meals for the past week from the strewn remnants. Since Lauder's divorce, the Chief of Detectives did not spend much time out of his office.

"I would really like to know what the hell is happening at Fair Oaks, Chief." Lauder liked being called chief, hated being called Eric. Amos used this knowledge to his best advantage. "I couldn't get a thing out of them yesterday. Flashed the badge—the whole schmear. Nothing. No entry. No info. *Nothing.* 'Mr. Rosen is still under evaluation, Officer Amos' … Blah, blah, blah. What they're really saying is, 'We're doctors; you're just a cop so don't bother us until we're ready to tell you whether Rosen does time or stays as our guest indefinitely.'"

"So?"

"Please don't go overboard, Chief. It isn't seemly for the men to see you so emotional about my problem."

"Cut the shitty sarcasm, Amos. I want humor; I'll catch Rickles." Lauder's lower lids drooped another quarter inch, revealing pink flesh.

Those lids go down any farther, I'm going to barf on his desk. Amos thought. "Chief, Francis and I got a great collar. Things have been slow. We need the credit. Plus, I hate seeing guys that wipe out their five-year-olds get a cushy stay in a plush nuthouse instead of doing hard time. So what's wrong with those reasons, huh?"

Lauder leaned over the desk. His big hands burrowed through sprawling Styrofoam and papers like two knobby moles. He leaned on his elbows, black hair curling out from beneath his partially rolled-up sleeves. "Look, the guy's only been there four days or so, right? So what is the big fuckin' deal if they still don't know if he's psycho or not? Hey, the better the job they do, the more chance the conviction holds up when some shyster lawyer tries to get him off on temporary insanity. Right? So what's the beef? Go help Frieberg and Mando on that decapitated body at the airport if you're so damn bored."

"Some Mafia goombah. Who cares?"

"Very nice. Maybe we'll make that the department motto." Lauder spread his coarse white hands above his desk, framing imaginary letters. "'Who cares.' I love it!"

"Yeah, yeah." Lauder was the ace of all hypocrites. When the Caputo mob from South Jersey looked like it was going head on head with the local Farios a few years back, threatening untold mayhem for DC and surrounding areas, Lauder's pep talk to the team had ended with something like, "May the bastards massacre each other before we get there."

Amos rose, smoothing his already perfect slacks, adjusting his already perfect jacket. "Something smells. I don't know what … but something. Those docs better come across soon." He turned, seeking the doorway through tearing eyes. That damn smoke. Nobody visited Lauder very long. "See ya, Eric."

Lauder's saggy eyes drew up into a squint as he yanked his cigar out. "Listen, Amos, I ain't in no mood for your bull—" He slapped his mouth shut, jowls flapping. No point yelling at a closed door.

*　　*　　*

Ralph Jackson was delighted. Couldn't be happier.

He kicked off the fluffy slippers, wriggled his toes on the soft ridges of his bath mat, and tested the tub water. Perfect. Hot enough to be just bearable after the settling-in process. He dipped his feet and ankles, waited, crouched over, while the heat numbed them a bit, crouched some more, letting his butt and balls dangle above the heat, slowly lowered, hands against both sides of the tub. Jackson gasped as the steamy water made contact. Next he wriggled down, savoring the blood rush as his body adjusted. A nice tingly, numbing sensation until he was sprawled flat, only his neck and head above water. Jackson waited until his brow was wet with perspiration before using his big toe to turn on a trickle of cold water.

Yessir. Ralph Jackson was *definitely* delighted with himself. And why not? He was on his way, wasn't he? That little Nazi Gruhaber had folded like a tent. Shit, so what if Gruhaber copped a peek at some laser crap. Big deal. But sure as shit, tight-ass Murray at security would raise hell, and tighter-ass old Clancy, the section head, would fire Gruhaber on the spot. Nobody screwed around with old man Sklar's rules.

Anyway, what did Ralph care? It sure had worked out fine for him. Old Clancy had been so surprised when Gruhaber came to his two-by-four office yesterday afternoon with his sad story declining the job as Clancy's replacement. Like most Irish, Clancy didn't like blacks, but what could he do? The old man's announcement of his successor was due today, and Clancy had no other choice with Gruhaber out of the running. Besides, the fourth floor had been pressuring Clancy to promote Jackson in the first place. Clancy was stuck. Let's hear it for minority mobility! Jackson broke the water with a fingers-forward clenched fist and then yanked it back under to keep the heat buildup going.

Ralph Jackson was on his way. That ghetto bullshit was over for him. *Forever.* No more smells, noises, screams, late night fights. He had never belonged there. Always knew it. Funny, even though he'd actually been away from his grimy birthplace for over eight years, he could still feel its nightmare-like quality if he closed his eyes and concentrated. Too bad he'd never have kids. His kids would have grown up free of the ghetto stench.

Ralph flashed on Larry and got an immediate erection. Larry Seivers: short as Ralph was tall; weak as Ralph was strong; white as Ralph was tan. Opposites sure did attract, at least in this case. The past six months had been sheer romantic delight. Everything, but *everything*, was comin' up right for big Ralph.

Ralph had just burst into his own fabulous rendition of "Respect"— usually reserved for baths or after great sex (he'd been singing it a lot lately)—when something whizzed over his nearly submerged head. It was his bedroom—if you could believe it—radio, blasting away, drowning out the last of "Respect" and the first of his screams as it arched neatly down into the water between his knees. In that crackling, ear-smoking, brain-burning moment, Ralph Jackson realized, sorrowfully, that nothing, but *nothing*, would ever come up right for him again.

"Piece of cake." Kreider spoke to his hazy reflection in the steamy bathroom mirror after checking Ralph Jackson's twitching body. Kreider would never think "nigger" or "coon," like some of the other guys. He didn't have a prejudiced bone in him; he was damn proud of it. It was how he'd been raised.

Tracing the extension cord into the bedroom, Kreider unplugged it, followed it back to the bathroom, yanked the radio plug out, and curled the extension into his jacket pocket. Next Kreider dragged the radio by its cord toward the near end of the tub and re-plugged it into the outlet over the sink. It was close, but the cord stretched just far enough for the radio to dangle in the bath water. You had to make things look right if you were going to get ahead.

Satisfied, Kreider checked around the room, then the body. Kreider had never electrocuted anyone before, and frankly, he was somewhat curious. Eyes a little dried out; tongue somewhat black; maybe a little burning near the nails on that right hand, which now looked more like a claw. Kreider sniffed the steamy air. Was that a slightly sweet smell? Kreider wasn't sure. He would have been able to tell better if the guy hadn't been under water because water probably stifled whatever odor came from a fried body. Well, he'd certainly seen enough to hold his own with the more experienced guys, if they ever got to bragging about electrocutions.

Kreider made a last check of the bedroom and then pulled the extension cord from his pocket and reattached it to the arc-shaped halogen in Jackson's living room. He noted the gold-framed picture of Martin Luther King above the blue velvet sofa. Some of the guys would have laughed. Not Kreider. He just wasn't prejudiced. After a moment of silent respect for Reverend King, he left.

*   *   *

"Not a damn thing about me in the papers. Nothing on the news." Rosen left the *Miami Herald* fanned on the couch, rose, and paced in front of Marquand's chair. Four days of sun and Rosen's partial tan had gone bronze; his brown hair blonder; his usually light eyebrows almost invisible.

"Naturally." Marquand rested Walt Whitman on his broad lap and scratched both sides of his trim beard simultaneously. "Wait'll you see your passport picture after we redecorate you just enough so no one can recognize that glamorous face of yours." He beamed. "You'll see. This cobbler is a true artist." Marquand used the CIA vernacular for a passport forger.

Rosen half smiled. He had to admit that he was getting a little better at smiling. During his first two days here, there had been practically no smiles; the next, a quarter of a smile; now, here he was up to half a smile. Of course, Rosen still didn't feel like smiling, but Marquand was trying so hard that he felt he owed Marquand the effort. "It's very nice."

"Please—enough effusiveness. You're embarrassing me. Keep it up and I'll never do you another favor."

This time Rosen's smile was sincere. "Really, I do appreciate it. With a little touching up, I'll be almost unrecognizable. Amazing what a mustache, a little tint, and some glasses can do, plus those terrific pads of yours to puff out my cheeks."

"Unsolicited enthusiasm. I love it." Marquand went back to Walt Whitman.

"Why, Goddammit? Why, Papa?" Rosen directed his question toward the fireplace. "Why aren't I a hot news flash?" He spun toward Marquand, framing imaginary copy with spread fingers and thumbs. "'Mad Dog Family Killer Murders to Escape Asylum.'"

Walt Whitman went down again. Marquand stared at his friend, obviously noting the tension in Rosen's shoulders, neck, arms. He spoke softly, reluctantly: "Fair Oaks never reported your escape."

Rosen dropped his arms. They swung limply at his sides. "The bastard has that much clout?"

"If it's not a company front, and I don't think it is, at least they play ball pretty well. Van Damme has probably asked them to cool it for national security reasons. He probably promised them he'd send you back when they caught you. By keeping the whole thing quiet, Van Damme can avoid jurisdictional questions when he goes after you. And Fair Oaks keeps its reputation of not losing dangerous patients so that rich ladies, with conflicts about whether to screw their tennis or golf instructors, will keep coming. A 'win, win situation,' I believe they call it."

"Yeah, but if I come back to them dead?"

"Not ideal, but there is always suicide. That's easier for Fair Oaks to explain than losing you."

"Goddamn. Shit. But how'd the judge—"

"A fix, Arnie. The fix was in—"

"That powerful? That goddamn powerful?"

"You weren't in ops, son. You just don't know how powerful." Marquand rose, walked toward the smaller man, and rested a large hand on his shoulder.

Rosen shrugged it off, pulled away. "So if I'm brought back dead, Fair Oaks covers it up, huh? That easy?"

"Or if Van Damme's people take you back alive and you never get out. Hell, Arnie, they can turn you into a catatonic with a couple of shots."

Rosen's right fist smacked his left palm. His eyes squinted shut, lips drawing far back from his teeth. "And Larry Topper thought he saved me. He actually thought he had pulled off a great legal coup to save his best friend." Rosen's voice broke. His head followed, lolling around on his neck as if his spine had snapped. His clenched fist plummeted to his side like lead.

Marquand moved forward, fearing that his friend would drop, thought better of it, and stopped halfway.

"A setup. He was a great lawyer and his last case was a fucking setup! They made a joke out of him, then …"

Marquand waited.

Waited some more.

"They killed him."

Marquand still waited.

"Not 'they.' Not *they*. Van Damme. Van … *Damme*!" Arnie Rosen shook. Then harder. Marquand wanted to help but didn't. Rosen shook some more, clenching and unclenching his fists, squinting his eyes tighter until the colors and shapes behind his lids swam through his brain until his pupils hurt, until his taught lips ached, until he wanted to scream and scream but didn't; until his eyes opened; until his fists unclenched; until his lips loosened; until his voice was very soft and very controlled. "I don't care *how* powerful; I don't care *how* important."

Marquand walked to his bookcase/bar. He grabbed the Courvoisier and two glasses and motioned for Rosen to join him at the kitchen table, shoving salt, pepper, and a green frog-faced napkin holder away to make room. Rosen hesitated, then followed, setting his chair away from the table and leaning back, uncomfortable about being too close to Marquand. Marquand understood. He had not often seen a completely exposed and wounded soul, even during his operations days. He didn't believe that he wanted to ever again.

"I will get him," Rosen said, staring into his brandy. "I promise you I will."

"Of course you will, Arnie—"

"Don't patronize me." Rosen's head snapped up, arm following, the brandy slopping dangerously side to side.

Marquand's voice went very soft. "I'm not. I know you will. That's why I've been doing some checking …"

"And?"

"And he has been seen with Kharkov in East Berlin, when it *was* East Berlin, on at least two occasions."

"I know that. I told you that—"

"Calm down, son," Marquand interrupted. "In light of your recent odyssey, a little confirmation would not be considered totally out of line."

Rosen swirled the red-brown liqueur. Watched the light jiggle through it. Inhaled its sweet burning fumes. He let it slip past his lips, surround his tongue with its warmth, and slide hot down his throat. "He's pulling something, Papa. I swear it."

"Doesn't prove it, Arnie. Opposite sides often meet. You should know that."

Rosen dispensed with protocol, tipping the rest of the brandy straight down. "I know he is."

"I agree. I just can't help playing the devil's advocate. Too many years in the business, I guess." Marquand winked one of his dark-eyed winks, then was serious again. "I'll try to find out."

"What do you think it is, selling secrets?"

"Who knows?" Marquand lowered his glass while watching Rosen. It *thunked* the frog napkin holder. He looked down, frowning, reset the glass on a clear space. "Sure can't be for the money. He and that society wife have more than the Russians."

Rosen stared at the table, thinking, absentmindedly moving the saltshaker with a finger so that it clinked against the pepper. His head rose. The pepper fell over unnoticed. "I'll take him in Berlin."

Marquand's thick eyebrows pulled together. "You don't have a chance! It's all *his* game there. He and Kharkov make the rules. For God's sake, at least try for him before." He gripped Rosen's arm. "Yes, go for him before he gets to Europe. He'll have less security here than there, believe me. And if you try to take him in Europe, do it *before* he gets to Berlin. At least then he won't have the whole KGB to protect him. I don't care what anybody says—Berlin's still crawling with 'em."

"No. I can ruin him in Berlin." Rosen stood and strode toward the window, checking the night sky through the reflection of his shadow on the glass.

"*Ruin* him? What in God's name is the point?"

Rosen turned. "A crucial point," Rosen stated. "First I intend to take his reputation. I'm going to catch him at whatever dirty scheme he's involved in and let him know he's been made. Then, after he chews on that, I'll kill him."

"Dead is dead, Arnie! That's a hell of a lot more risk for a little pre-death shame."

Rosen's lips pulled back, eyes glowing. Consumed. He rushed toward the table and hovered over Marquand, squeezing his friend's forearm. "No, that's not right. For some people, it's right, but not Van Damme. *Not* Van Damme. With Van Damme, dead with shame is worse. Dead with shame is like double death. He's a walking ego. Knowing that his reputation will be destroyed, that he will be remembered as a miserable spy forever ... Yes. Yes, that's the way—"

"Okay son. I should have some more news tomorrow." Marquand pulled away. Rosen's eyes were unnerving. Marquand could swear that he saw layers of normality peeling away, revealing a venomous core. Marquand wanted the old Rosen back; he hadn't realized how much had changed beneath Rosen's surface. He stood, hoping sudden movement might break the spell. It did. The smoldering behind Rosen's eyes cooled slightly.

"Thanks, Papa. I'm going to need all I can get on the Berlin scenario." Rosen peered into Marquand's wide face. "I'm okay." A deep sigh escaped. "I'm *okay*, Papa." He gave a halfhearted wink. "Guess I just need a little sleep. See ya in the morning."

With inexpressible sadness, Marquand watched his friend disappear into the living room. Marquand continued staring at the startled furry face on the cat calendar on his kitchen wall for a long time after.

CHAPTER 14

Breakfast was quiet. Maybe not quiet like old couples in restaurants, who have absolutely nothing left to say, but quiet enough. There were a few pointless Marquand comments like, "Looks like it's going to be another hot one" or "Seems like there are more damn tourists all the time." But for the most part, Rosen schemed, Marquand watched Rosen surreptitiously, and Rosen felt him watching. Rosen knew that he should have eased Marquand's mind by feigning lightheartedness, but that would have diluted the energy that he so desperately needed to fuel his resolve. Marquand would have to work it out himself; Rosen couldn't help him.

So they ate mostly in silence.

"You'll see what you can find out, huh, Papa?" Rosen said at the door. Marquand was off to his boat, his errands, then to massage his contacts for more information about Van Damme. Rosen was off to get the passport, cash Marquand's generous check, and catch a last workout at the beach. Later they would meet and head for Marquand's favorite oyster and crab place, the Crab Barn. It was a weathered archive of business cards, initials, and memorabilia dating back to the thirties, the most famous of which was a keg that the original "Papa" supposedly drained single-handedly to celebrate an advance on his new novel.

The morning heat sucked at Rosen as he stepped out of the comfortable house. Marquand filled the doorway, putting on a brave smile, like a father watching his only son go off to enlist. He waved self-consciously. In that moment, Rosen loved the man. He had come close to loving Marquand at the agency during his rookie years, when Marquand had figuratively picked him up, blown his nose, and sent him back into the fray, but this time he really *loved* Marquand.

Sunlight glistened in Rosen's eyes as he waved back. He walked quickly down the slate walk, avoiding the overflowing pink and white petunias.

Rosen made a sharp angle onto the sidewalk, forcing his eyes straight ahead, unwilling to invest any additional emotion by looking back.

*   *   *

The heat increased, slapping Rosen like a moist towel each time that he left the air-conditioned stops along his route. Only when he stepped out of the passport maker's, a skinny Cuban with squinty eyes and brown crooked teeth, did he appreciate the stifling air. It was refreshing by comparison to the cigarette smoke and cat box stench of the man's apartment. The thought of going back later revolted him, but according to the forger, one Armando Gutierrez, it was "a streekly cosh een odvance deeel."

Rosen's morning, even prior to Armando's, had not been good. The cheerleader type at the one-hour eyeglass place had wrinkled her perky nose when he eschewed an eye exam, wanting only frames with clear glass, while the clerk at Marquand's bank smiled through his annoyance when Rosen requested that the sizable amount be broken into smaller bills.

Sick of human contact, Rosen sped toward the beach. He was just about on schedule. At 2:30, he kicked off his Birkenstocks, dropped the Disneyland beach towel in a heap with the smaller dry-off towel on top of it, plunked his lotion-stained polo on top of all of it, and padded off toward the surf. He dug heels, then toes, into the wave-soaked sand, his calves burning as he picked up the pace. Sea spray cooled him on his side facing the ocean. Rosen forced his ribs out so that he breathed evenly long after his body fought to gulp air. The trick enabled him to race one lifeguard chair farther than his previous best before turning back. He sprinted his last hundred yards and then crashed into the tepid foam until it sucked at his waist. Then he plunged away from the sun and into the salty darkness beneath the surface. Rosen came up snorting, falling backward, squinting upward at rolling Florida clouds through salt-stung eyes. They were puffy and golden but not sufficiently dense to block the sun. He spun away from the feeble peaks of small waves, facing toward shore as they *whooshed* jetlike over his head. Something stringy ringed his arm. Fearing an errant man-of-war—blue-pink balloons whose trailing tentacles produce fiery welts—Rosen recoiled and then laughed as he unwrapped an innocuous length of dripping seaweed from his biceps.

Finally, he emerged. Hot sand clung to his feet and ankles. Blinking against the white glare, Rosen sought his towels from among the multiple bright mounds of other bathers that littered the beach. When he located them, he trotted directly over. Spreading the Disney towel against the light breeze, Rosen dropped down, knees gouging Goofy and Mickey deeply into the sand as he flopped onto his stomach. Rosen dozed to the accompaniment of ocean and one mercifully distant portable radio, thinking that, at least for the moment, things could be worse.

They were worse!

* * *

Marquand's day was lousy. For the first time since he could remember, he did not enjoy working on his pride and joy, the *Louisa May*, a forty-foot Stevens built in the thirties, when, as Marquand frequently joked, "They really knew how to build 'em." Rubbing down her heavy brass fittings failed to give Marquand the proud tingle that he usually got from watching newer fiberglass-hulled models with their cheap chrome trims cruise by. Even breathing in the rich aroma of *Louisa May*'s fresh-polished mahogany just didn't make it this morning. He even procrastinated about installing the Marantz depth finder, a task that he had gleefully anticipated since trading with old Rickard, three berths over, for a Zodiac raft and motor, whose novelty had worn thin. At that point, Marquand decided that he might as well give up. With an apologetic glance at *Louisa May*, Marquand shoved his hands into his denim deck shorts and trudged up the long dock.

His shopping didn't go much better. After grabbing a quart of milk, forgetting to check if it was low fat until he had reached the checkout and had to go back, three Lean Cuisines, and a loaf of multigrain bread, he lost interest in this project too.

He was just so damn worried about Rosen. That was it. It was hard to love your boat and shop and pick up shoes and do other stuff when you were worried about whether the kid that you were most fond of—of all the legions of helpless bright-eyed hopefuls that you'd been fond of in over forty years with the company—was going off the deep end. Real hard. Impossible, if the truth be known. It had been that look in the kid's eyes last night. Maybe his voice too.

Marquand could understand killing Van Damme. Hell, *he* was helping Arnie find the bastard, so obviously he could understand that. But this killing him at the right time stuff, this humiliating him first stuff, that was what had Marquand worried. You didn't wait for the right time to kill a powerhouse like Van Damme. You just took him when you got the chance and considered yourself damn lucky if you succeeded. Forget about the moon being in the right phase or Jupiter aligning with Mars. And goddamn, why pick the toughest turf and the worst time just so you could—could you believe it?—humiliate him first?

Marquand wandered disinterestedly through the rest of his errands before returning home at 3:15. The red light was on that confounded answering machine. Marquand had bought it last Christmas, after yielding to intense pressure from his perpetually convalescing mother, who insisted on being able to leave messages "like my friends can with their sons." He had finally installed it two weeks ago, after an exceptionally heated dispute with the dear woman.

He rewound and played. Kelsey's voice sounded shaky, and not just because Marquand's machine was a low-end model. His longtime pal and best source of agency wheelings and dealings was definitely frightened. "The Hotel Kempinski, Berlin, September twenty-sixth. Kharkov's usual meets are at Kuhlstrasse forty-four, off Oranienburger Strasse. Got to go."

That was *it*. Not the usual who did what to whom or who was promoted over whom that pissed off whom. Just that. Marquand replayed, jotting down dates and addresses, then snapped off the machine and went for a beer.

Thirty seconds later, he was on the phone to Langley. "Mr. Kelsey left early today. May I refer you to someone else?" the polite agency receptionist inquired. Marquand didn't know her, but he was sure that she was a clone of all the others he had known: straight-backed, healthy-looking, and shorthaired.

"No, thanks," he muttered.

"May I take a message for Mr. Kelsey?" Agency receptionists did not give up easily.

"No *thank* you." Marquand hung up before she could take another crack at him. Next he tried Kelsey's home phone. It rang monotonously. He redialed just to make sure. It rang and rang some more.

He brought the beer over to his chair and sat, rubbing the can's cold metal against his perspiring upper lip. Because he always turned the air-conditioning too far down when he left, the house was always too hot when he got back. He supposed that he was turning into an old penny-pincher like the rest of the local retirees, who would rather save ten cents on toilet bowl cleaner than have sex.

Fred Marquand sipped and worried. He couldn't say why, but his nerve endings were getting raw. Over the years, Marquand had developed a firm belief in his instincts. He chugged the Bud and walked back to the phone.

After his call, he showered. It didn't help. The cool spray usually calmed him. This one hadn't. Wrapping a towel around his—he hated to admit it—growing paunch, he tried Kelsey's home a third time, with no better luck than before.

Marquand grabbed cotton slacks and an old Lacoste alligator shirt from the closet. He checked his alarm on the dresser as he unwrapped the towel. It was 5:40. Better hurry.

The scraping at his back door set him worrying more than ever. The snap of its lock sent his pulse through the ceiling …

*　　*　　*

Beams from the lowering sun slipped beneath Rosen's closed lids. He jerked up. The beach had thinned out, now down to only a few die-hards. Rosen dug into his tightly wrapped shirt until he felt his watch. It was 5:27. Shit! He was supposed to be at the passport guy Armando's at 5:30. Should he call or just go, hoping that the Cuban didn't have any big plans for the evening? From the looks of him, the high point of Armando's evening would be a Miller and wrestling.

Rosen couldn't see a phone. He grabbed the towels, shirt, and sandals, shaking off the sand as he trotted toward his car.

It was 5:47 when he parked. After slipping on the Birkenstocks and shimmying his good shirt down his salt-sticky skin, Rosen peered up at Armando's second-floor apartment. The shades were drawn. Did that mean that the Cuban was out? Rosen left on his bathing suit, not wanting to take the time to put on his pants. He was sorry now that he hadn't called.

Rosen walked through a doorway adjoining a late-hour liquor store; up a creaky stairway covered with frayed rubber runners, within whose crevices crumbs, cigarette tobacco, and substances that he didn't even want to speculate upon had collected; down toward the front end of the insect-littered hallway. Initials and burn marks scored a once-regal wood banister on his left. He knocked on number 2 but got no response. For the tenth time, Rosen cursed himself for not calling. He wanted to wrap this up tonight and never have to see Armando or his disgusting apartment again.

Rosen knocked louder and longer. Muffled muttering came from inside. It gradually got louder: "Hol' yer waatah, man. Sheeeet, I'm coming!"

Rosen was almost happy to see the ugly little man. Then the smell hit him. Was it more putrid than before or was it just all that fresh air that he'd been breathing since his last visit?

Armando nodded him in. Rosen's prayer that their transaction could be completed at the door was apparently going unanswered. The mildly humorous thought cost him. He paused to estimate how many of his prayers had gone unanswered in the past week. Badly depressed, Rosen walked in. He didn't care about the smells anymore.

"Hey, man, you'ah late. I ga stuff ta do." Armando gestured toward the rear with a half-smoked cigarette. The end of its long ash plummeted to the molting shag carpet.

Rosen did not apologize.

Armando shrugged. No one ever apologized to him. Not even the old guy Korean at the liquor store, who gave him change for a ten the other night when Armando handed him a twenty, until Armando mentioned it nicely enough. If that son of a bitch Fidel ever got kicked out on his ass, Armando would go back home the next day and say, "Fuck thees United fucking States of America." Anyway, forget it. "Eet came out reel good, huh?" Armando asked as he handed over the passport.

The goddamn blond bastard just stared at it.

Could you fuckin' believe that? thought Armando. *I hand him a goddamn masterpiece, somethin' he can go all the hell over the fuckin' world with, an he jus' fuckin' looks at it like it's a goddamn bus ticket. I hate this golden guy. I hate them all.* "You owe me wan hunred feefty more. For the fas' servees." *Worth a try,* Armando thought. *Christo, the rich fuck ain't even battin' a goddamn eye, whippin' out the extra bread like I ain't even worth arguing with. Jesus, I hate this golden fucka. An' I hate fuckin' Fidel for gettin' me stuck here.*

The golden one was turning, leaving, no look back, no good-bye. *I don' even exist for this guy. I'm like the goddamn wallpaper, chairs ... toilet. Yea, tha's it: toilet.*

Armando came just that close to not telling Rosen. Just *that* close. But Marquant—or whatever his name was—was a decent guy. He sent Armando business sometimes and, more important, was always polite and gave Armando a little respect. And he'd sounded kind of nervous when he called around an hour ago, like it was important.

"Hey, yore buddee call." That stopped Meesta golden guy. Hey, Meesta Golden was actually lookin' at Armando for the first time. How you like that? "He say meet heem at thee res'rant. Don' go home firs', cause eet take too long an' 'e runnin' late. He jus' meet you there. He say be shore I tell ya. I tol' ya."

Armando definitely had Meesta fuckin' Golden's attention now. The guy looked real surprised, even thanked Armando as he turned in those fancy-sheet stupid-looking 'spensive sandals. How you like that? Meesta Golden thanked him.

*　　*　　*

While the Crab Shack's interior was much larger than one would have guessed from its weathered exterior, its condition was to be expected. The place had definitely been around. All manner of oddities hung precariously from its sagging rafters: a torn fishnet; an old-time diver's outfit, like Rosen remembered John Wayne wearing when he fought the giant octopus, or was it a squid?—no, that was Kirk Douglas in *Twenty Thousand Leagues Under the Sea*. There was also a strange machine with a circular wheel on the side, like the one that pumped air to John Wayne before his line got ripped and the movie ended; a couple of leather dinosaurs—how the heck did they fit in with the ocean motif?—an old-fashioned *Butch Cassidy and the Sundance Kid* bicycle, like Butch rode around in Etta's yard. No one could tell Rosen that *that* tied in with the ocean. *All they have to do is hang Kareem's jockstrap up there and the whole place'll come down*, Rosen thought, swirling his vodka tonic.

Warm bay air flowed through rows of old-style multi-framed windows, sweeping in with it with it fish odors and muffled shouts from the dock outside.

His watch said 6:35. Funny for Papa to change plans because he didn't like surprises, either getting them or giving them. Fred Marquand had made that a cardinal rule for his people at the agency. He was also late, another non-Marquand trait. Maybe it was because Papa was coming through with some heavy information.

Rosen sipped. It was a good drink. The tonic's sweetness balanced the vodka's bitterness. Over his glass, Rosen watched a Key West yuppie in a Hawaiian shirt, white knee-length shorts, Revo sunglasses, and a key ring with a Corvette insignia dangling from his hand doing his shtick for two meticulously tanned women. Both were at least ten years older than the yuppie, but wealth had preserved them well.

It was now 6:48. One of the tanned women opened a purse, giving Rosen a speculative look over her compact as she applied lipstick. When he failed to respond, she snapped the compact shut, rose, and swiveled toward the door.

"Another one of those?" The bartender, a middle-aged guy, nondescript except for a strikingly white complexion, blocked Rosen's view of the departing woman.

Rosen stared at the man, confused for a moment, his thoughts on Marquand. "Uh … sure. Why not?" He tried a smile, but the bartender was already gone.

A three-quarter full glass slapped down in front of Rosen, frosty drops trickling along its exterior. He rolled its coolness between his palms before sipping.

"Hey, you Papa's friend?" The white face loomed close.

"Uh … yes." The bartender had caught him by surprise for a second time. Rosen was sure that he must sound retarded.

The bartender flashed a big white-faced smile. Four gold teeth reflected setting sunlight. "He described ya. Been kinda busy. Glad I remembered—"

"*What?*"

This time it was the bartender's turn to stammer. "Oh y-yeah. Just a sec." He walked across to the register, yanking the top piece off a white notepad.

There was a raucous yell from a skinny brunette waitress whose hair was matted to the perspiration on her pimpled forehead. "Hey, Julie, how about that White Russian and Gimlet?"

"Hold your water, Ellie. I'll be right with ya," Julie waved her off with a flick of his pale wrist and then frowned at the paper before handing it to Rosen. "Here. I didn't get what he meant, but this is just about what he said. Gotta go." The bartender inclined his head in Ellie's direction, rolled his eyes toward the ceiling, and spun away.

Ellie was draped over the service counter, glaring.

Julie shambled toward her. "Yeah, yeah, so what was that order now?" he grumbled, already grabbing for the proper bottles.

Rosen fingered the smudged page. There was a Berlin hotel, a date, and Kharkov's "Koolstrassa" address. Rosen looked at Julie's back with admiration. Not bad phonetics for the Berlin street's name. "How long ago did he call?"

Julie turned. Ellie's glare shifted to Rosen.

"'Bout a hour."

Julie's head snapped back to the drinks. Ellie flashed Rosen a victorious smirk.

"Thanks." He pocketed the note. *And thank you, Papa. Goddammit, you did it! With all your doubts, you went ahead and did it! I love you, old man. Can't wait to hug you. Where are you?* Rosen checked his watch. He decided to relax, think of the positives: he had time, he knew where to look for the bastard, and he had a passport. And he was ready.

Rosen took another cool sip, letting the tangy liquid slosh around his tongue. He grabbed a handful of beer nuts and spun around on his old-time bar stool, popping in a couple of sweet walnuts and even sweeter almonds. After surveying the room, Rosen focused his attention on the large family surrounding Hemingway's keg. The father, a thin, animated man, valiantly endeavored to interest his kids—four of them, none over twelve, Rosen bet—and wife—heavyset and obviously uncomfortable in the non-air-conditioned room—in the story of the author's prowess. Halfway through, the demoralized man threw up his hands and dejectedly followed his kids and lumbering wife toward a Ms. Packman machine next to the restrooms.

It was 7:13. This was no good. He should have realized it when Amando spit out Marquand's clumsy sounding message. It had been a warning: *stay away*. Shit!

Rosen smacked a ten on the counter and darted for the door, brushing by the yuppie, whose relationship with the well-preserved woman had progressed to a point where he might as well be humping her.

*   *   *

Rosen knew from a block away that it was bad: lights revolving and people scurrying. All of the frantic activity was centered around the middle of the next block. Marquand's part of the block. Rosen stopped at the corner, tempted to turn right or left, any way but straight, but he went straight nevertheless. He drove very slowly, a rubbernecker at an accident who didn't want to gawk but couldn't stop himself.

A cumbersome body bag swayed along the very path that Rosen had taken this morning. The path from which he had refused to look back to acknowledge his feelings for the bag's occupant earlier today. Rosen's eyes teared as Marquand's swarming petunias were ground into the slate walkway by the heavy soles of the fire department rescue crew.

Curious neighbors pressed in for a closer look. Three khaki-uniformed men forced them back. Two other officers lounged against their patrol car. A beefy guy in slacks and a sweat-stained shirt listened intently to Mrs. Kower from next door. He scribbled on a tiny pad as she arched knobby fingers toward Marquand's house.

A sixth officer, next to an angularly parked patrol car with a whirling roof light, impatiently gestured Rosen on. The man bent to peer into Rosen's window when he failed to pick up the pace. "Keep it movin'. Keep it moving, huh, fella?"

On the second request, Rosen managed to locate the accelerator. He "kept it moving" all the way past Marquand's corner, all the way past William Street, and Grinnell Street, and White Street—all they way to North Roosevelt and the beach. Then he couldn't keep it moving anymore. The slowly rolling car hit the curb, bounded up, rolled back, idling patiently as Rosen, drooping like a whipped prizefighter, stared at a vast ocean that his eyes were too blury to see.

CHAPTER 15

Craig was pissed. He hated messy operations, and this one had turned out as messy as it could get. There had been no time to call in the local cleanup crew, get rid of the blood, and make the body disappear, nice and neat.

No way in hell with that old biddy next door screaming her bony head off. He almost wished he'd taken the time to off the old bag. She must have had a damn telescope to see what was going on in the kitchen: Eddie couldn't have left the blinds up more than an inch. Chalk that up to inexperience. But the kid had done very well with helping him handle Marquand. Christ, the old guy was strong! Damn strong. Must have been a holy terror in his younger days.

And they couldn't break Marquand. At least not in the short time they had before that old biddy butted in. Craig knew that he would have had Marquand telling him all about Rosen if he'd had another half hour or so. Damn it! Of course, he and Eddie couldn't really go to town on him. They had to make it look like a druggy robbery: sloppy and unfocused; couldn't use hot cooking oil, or pliers, or the bare wires from a plugged-in electric cord. Instead, he'd had to go with the gun muzzle to the kidneys, some cutting and two or three bullets in Marquand's fleshy parts. Still, if he'd only had a little more time, even twenty minutes.

Craig looked over at Eddie, who hunched on the edge of his motel bed. The younger man was still a little white around the gills.

"Hey, what's the matter, kid? Little blood too much for you?"

"Liddle blood. Keeeriste. Dey cudda filled a friggin' blood bank widda stuff." Eddie looked like a mutant cupid, wearing only a pair of boxers adorned with little hearts in tic-tac-toe boxes.

"Hey, we're in a tough business. You can't take it, you go into social work … bus driving. There's plenty of other nice bloodless fields. Only trouble is, they don't pay real well. What'd you make at Fair Oaks?"

"Five sevinty-five a ouwa."

"See? We can always get that job back for you if you want it, kid. Just give me the word. I know it sounds too good to be true, but I can do it for you. Honest. Or maybe you want to go on for an advanced degree in brain surgery. Uh-oh. That's bloody too, come to think of it." Craig gave Eddie an exaggerated shrug. "I guess all the big money is in blood."

"Yeah, well don' worry yaself. I'll do jus' foine."

"I know you will, kid." Craig puffed his cheeks, blew the air from his lips. "Christ, how long does it take them to check the calls the old guy made. I told them it was a priority one."

Craig rose from his bed, absently straightening wrinkles in the spread. The room was done in coral: coral bedspreads, coral lamps, coral ashtrays, coral everything. He hadn't hated coral before they took the room this afternoon, but he sure did now. He walked into the bath—coral, naturally—splashed water on his face and checked himself in the mirror. Christ, his beard was already growing again. He'd just shaved a few hours ago. Must be the heat.

Craig was out of the little room on the first ring, had the phone in his hand on the second. "Yeah. What the hell took so long? I only asked for a few days … Okay, okay, never mind, just tell me. Yeah. Yeah." He scratched furiously on motel stationary for the next two minutes. "That all? Great. Thanks. Sorry about before; you know how it is. Thanks for getting on it so fast. Bye."

Craig sat on his pillow holding the list under his lamp. Eddie moved next to him, craning to see it.

"Here's a bunch to that asshole Kelsey," muttered Craig. "He won't be taking any more calls." *Not unless Kelsey could talk from an empty sewer pipe in a very popular Arlington dumpsite,* he thought. "Only a few others. Guess the old boy wasn't too popular anymore. Sad thing about retired people … Hey, how 'bout this one?" Craig jabbed an index finger with a halfway chewed nail at the last number. "He must have made it just as we were coming in. And he heard us first. I know because he was trying for that fire poker when we caught up with him. This call must have been damn important for him to take the time to make it instead of getting the hell out of there."

"Yeah." Eddie slid closer for a squint. "Yeah." Eddie nodded, bunching his huge neck.

"So glad you agree." Craig smiled a nasty smile. "The Crab Barn. Hmmm. Could Rosen have been there?" Craig rubbed the paper between his thumbs and index fingers as if trying to feel the answer through its texture. He glanced at the digital clock on the TV, then hissed between clenched teeth: "Sheez, even if it was him, those bastards took so fuckin' long with that phone check he coulda had a full-course dinner and split hours ago. *Goddamn!*"

Craig rubbed his eyes and then his teeth. "What's the last call he made before that one? He might have already been worrying. Kinda seemed like the old dude was expecting us from how fast he got in those last two calls. Armando Gutierrez, eh? Doesn't look like he lives far." Craig hissed out a laugh. "Like anything could be far on this little bump in the ocean."

"Yeah." Eddie's laugh was deep, way down in his barrel chest, as if it came out of a well. He yanked on his pants and a tank top, arms rippling. Craig flashed his nasty smile as he ushered Eddie out the door with a sweeping bow.

*　　*　　*

Who the hell was ringing his fucking bell this time? Armando reached over his coffee table—which was littered with beer cans, cigarette butts, and a Frito bag—to turn down the volume on his brand-new Sony thirty-five-inch monitor. The thing had set him back more than a thousand, but shit, what a picture! Like you were there. In this case, "there" was where the Masked Terror was beating the shit out of Igor, the Mad Russian, which was fine with Armando because they were both assholes, and if Igor was moppin' up the ring with the Terror instead, that would have been okay with Armando too.

What wasn't okay was that fucking bell. And turning the sound down as if he wasn't home didn't do anything because the bell kept ringing anyway and he couldn't hear the fucking match. Popping in a mouthful of Fritos, Armando slouched toward the door. He opened it the length of the security chain. It was two white guys that he didn't know. "Yeah?"

"We're looking for Armando," the smaller one said. Not that he was small. Just compared to the other one. *Sheet, the big guy looks like what's-his-name: the Hulk ... Farigmo ... Ferigno.*

"Why?"

"Marquand said you could help us."

More Marquand business. Not that Armando wasn't grateful, even if Meestah Golden was a stuck-up white asshole, and from the looks of these two, they wouldn't be any better, but this was practically night and not business hours. *All-Star Wrestling* was on, and even Marquand should know that Armando deserved a little more respect. "Can't do nauthin' now. You calm back in'a mornin'."

"We need help in a hurry. We'll pay for your overtime."

A couple of hundreds waved in front of the crack. Normally Armando would have jumped, but this was his fucking pride here. These white assholes just thought he was here for them and their fucking money an hell with his time and the Masked Terror and anything that was important to *him*. Well, fuck that.

"Hey, man, I say tomorra. Eet's the best I con do. You come see me 'bou' ten."

Armando had the door almost closed when the sliding end of the chain snapped into his face, cutting his cheek as metal tore and the door exploded open, smashing him back against the tiny kitchen counter. The big guy pinned him there with a huge forearm across his neck. From the corner of his eye, which was about all that he could move, Armando saw the other guy ducking his head out and checking the hall. Then he closed Armando's door softly, jamming one of Armando's metal folding chairs under the knob. It was all very professional, giving Armando the terrifying feeling that these guys might be worse than the Masked Terror and Ivan put together.

*   *   *

With Armando, Craig had been able to take his time. Only he hadn't needed much. The chickenshit little spic told him everything with the first application of hot Mazola oil.

Of course, he couldn't tell them anything during. During, all he did was scream his head off, so they stuffed a sweat sock down his throat. But when they finally yanked the pukey thing out, boy, did he want to tell them all about the passport, all about the picture, all about Rosen.

And when it was over, the little asshole actually looked surprised when they broke his neck before hurling him down the stairs. Like he had expected Craig to thank him and leave. It never ceased to amaze Craig when some idiot thought "If you tell me what I want to know, this can all stop" meant that he would actually get to live. It didn't. It just meant the pain would stop—along with everything else. Marquand had known that.

There was no surprise in that old man's eyes when he died.

Craig lay back on his bed, contemplating human nature and concluding that hope really did spring eternal. Fifteen minutes later, he struggled up, turned off *Arsenio*, and walked to the bathroom. Eddie was already exhaling slowly and evenly from the other bed.

Not a bad day, thought Craig. He lathered his teeth, making sure to work the gums. Very important: working the gums. Gum disease— peritonitis— was the real killer. Cavities you could deal with, but when your gums went, your teeth were history. Craig even had two toothbrushes, one for morning, the other for evening so that they wouldn't get too worn out to do the job. You had to take care of yourself. Eddie just whipped through his brushing. He was in for trouble. Not now, maybe. He was young. But later …

Anyway, it really hadn't been a bad day. Armando Gutierrez's description of Rosen's new photo and new name, Adam Riesen, were already forwarded in to Van Damme. Still, they could easily miss Rosen at the airports or train stations because the search had to be done with limited need-to-know personnel, who had no real authority in the States. Van Damme had gone crazy at the idea of anyone but agency being in on this. Craig wondered why. It had to be an ego thing. Rosen stole secrets from Van Damme's department, and Van Damme wanted to handle it. Okay. But it sure made things harder. They would be unable to do a computer alert to the airlines, cruise lines, and local law enforcement.

Even with their limitations, they had a chance at catching Rosen if he chose a major Southern airport. The guys were already on their way down to cover those. It would be tougher if Rosen grabbed a cruise because of the large crowds. And their chances would be zilch if Rosen moved fast and split in the next few hours. They just couldn't get it together that soon. But if they missed him here, they'd definitely get Rosen in Europe. It was the company's ball game over there—plenty of manpower and unlimited authority.

And Europe was sure as hell where Rosen was headed. Marquand had been very interested in Van Damn's Europe trip. The tap on Kelsey made that clear. Which meant that *Rosen* was interested. Which meant that the idiot probably thought he had a better chance of getting to Van Damme in Europe. Which was crazy. Van Damme's units were authorized to operate over there, did whatever they wanted—no explanations necessary. That proved how crazy Rosen was.

One more thing he would like to do before leaving was check out that Crab Shack, Oyster Shack … whatever, where Marquand told Gutierrez to tell Rosen to meet him. Funny. The old guy not only figured out that someone was comin' after him, but damned if the son of a bitch hadn't managed to save Rosen's ass as well. Marquand *was* good. A legend, just as Van Damme had said. As good as Marquand was, Craig would bet his left nut that he must have left word, or something, for Rosen at that restaurant … but how the hell to find out? They couldn't go in and start asking. Not now, when word of Marquand's death would be all over town. Be too suspicious. Local cops would be all over him and Eddie like a cheap suit because most fuckin' local cops didn't like the agency very much—a territorial thing. And what would Van Damme do then? He'd either have Craig's balls or cut him loose to take the fall if he and Eddie got nailed. No cover was provided for domestic terminations. All agency records of Craig would disappear—yesterday—and he'd be out in the cold. Besides, he and Eddie couldn't shake the whole restaurant staff down after closing hours, trying to find out what Marquand left for Rosen. That many broken civilian bones would be tough to cover up.

What the hell, Craig thought. It'd been a damn good day. They'd gotten plenty done. Why spoil it by getting caught?

Craig rinsed, checked his mouth, grinning, turning his head to one side and then the other. It looked like a good job, nice and bright. And his gums: nice healthy pink, curving down symmetrically upon his teeth. No sign of receding. Eddie's wouldn't look nearly so good when he hit Craig's age.

*   *   *

How much time did he have … How much time? kept tormenting Rosen's mind as he sped across the Keys. Marquand must have talked. Rosen didn't blame him. Company people were good at getting information. Rosen squeezed his eyes shut, trying to expunge the morbid thought: how long had the old man held out? The scene played itself over in his mind. Blood on Papa's beard; pain in the caring, dark eyes; muffled screams behind a wadded cloth gag—

Rosen wrenched his attention away. Deal with the immediate problem. They knew about the passport, about the picture, about his new looks. No doubt about that. If he was ever going to use those to escape, it had to be now. He'd almost gone directly to Key West airport to catch a charter but changed his mind at the last minute. Too conspicuous. Van Damme's people could have already been there, and he'd stick out like a sore thumb in the tiny terminal. He needed a big crowded place where it was easy to get lost. Rosen checked the dashboard digital. It was 9:48, and he was only to Key Largo! At least another hour and a half to Miami International Airport. He hadn't been able to move very fast on the one-lane causeway; too many wobbly boat trailers and lumbering motor homes. He'd hit the highway soon, but the airport was an hour to an hour and a half away, no matter how you looked at it.

Rosen had already ruled out the airports in Tampa, Fort Myers, and Orlando as too far. It had to be Miami or Fort Lauderdale. Van Damme might not have had time to set up surveillance, although the two closer cities were Rosen's most logical departure points. Despite the enthusiastic rhetoric of agency supporters, operations people were not infallible ... especially when it came domestic matters. Oh yeah, the CIA got involved stateside, despite the multitude of oversight committees and watchdog agencies that deluded themselves into believing that they kept the CIA on a tight leash. But with all the restrictions, extra approvals, and cover-your-ass memos, it took more time to set the wheels in motion than in the old days. At least, Rosen hoped so. Anyway, Miami was it. It was bigger and closer than Lauderdale, with more flights at this time of night. He'd take his chances there ... for better or worse.

*　*　*

It was 11:13 p.m., but Miami International was still moderately busy. Spanish-speaking families seeing off relatives, their ranks swollen by second and maybe even third cousins, filed through the ticket lobby. Reddened New Yorkers, who had squeezed out a last day of sun and Mom's cooking before returning to the Apple's addictive madness, rushed for their gates. Unflappable Europeans, returning to the continent with a new repertoire of American-bashing stories, marched by with upraised noses. There were French Canadians, suitcases loaded with the skimpiest of bathing suits for marathon sunbathing on the Hollywood beaches. There were even a few adventurous Japanese eschewing Hawaii for the lure of somewhere new. *Bring 'em on. Bring 'em on,* thought Rosen. *The more the merrier. That's what I need: crowds.*

His quick change in the bathroom went well. Hair tinting at the sink was surprisingly easy (Barbara always made it sound like a big deal— Barbara ... Barbara ... I want you). Then a quick trip into one of the stalls took care of the glasses, mustache, and cheek pads. A guy shaving at a nearby sink did a double take in his mirror when Rosen came out of the stall. Rosen had hidden behind a flower cart across from the men's room entrance, but the man hadn't followed.

Now Rosen stood facing United. Where to go? Where to go? They'd be expecting Europe. They knew about his new passport, and they knew about his interest in Van Damme's upcoming European trip. They had to. Marquand's calls to whoever had been his contact at CIA were all about Van Damme's plans. Whoever killed Papa knew that, because they had either tapped the poor agency guy's phone, beat the information out of him, or both. The same grisly scene played that had been flashing unremittingly since his last look at that dreadful zippered bag carrying Papa's body. Only in place of Marquand, there was a mutilated body with a blank spot for a face. Papa's contact, whose name Rosen would never know.

Rosen winced, closed his eyes, sighed. Another death on his behalf. He indulged himself for just a moment and then forced his brain to cut off the images and think instead. Van Damme and his people would be expecting him to enter Germany from Western Europe, right? What if he came in from the opposite direction? Van Damme wouldn't be in Berlin for another ten days, which gave Rosen plenty of time to get there by way of the Orient. And Papa had given him more than adequate funds for the trip.

Rosen searched for one of the ubiquitous flight information boards. There, over a group of turbaned heads to his right: San Francisco—departs at 11:43, gate C7. On time.

Rosen usually flew dressed up. He didn't know why. His clothes always got wrinkled for no reason. Why did people get dressed up for flying but not for trains or cars? Rosen scanned himself. His slacks were already wrinkled. His short-sleeved sport shirt stuck to his ocean-salty body, itching and scratching as he moved. It was just a little thing, insignificant in all that had happened, but Van Damme was forcing him to react like a lab rat, opening and closing the gates of Rosen's maze at will. He wasn't even able to dress properly for a flight, for God's sake! It infuriated him.

A Latin man brushed by. Rosen reacted automatically with a hard shot to the shoulder. After a mutually stunned silence, Rosen apologized to the disgruntled gentleman, who scurried off muttering. Rosen watched his recent victim burrow between an approaching group of deeply tanned college kids. State-of-the-art tennis racket cases bobbed at their sides, proclaiming their athleticism to all who passed. Rosen paused to envy them, cloaked as they were in youth's transitory invincibility, then he turned to join the waning line at the ticket counter.

CHAPTER 16

The flight was fantastic. Otto Manfred Gruhaber reclined in his first-class seat. First class—could you believe it? They had gotten him, a person who had never been out of the States before, barely even traveled, for that matter, a *first-class seat*. He got champagne— although he had tried to keep the amounts within reason; after all, he was representing the United States Government—at the slightest tilt of his glass. A real glass, mind you, not plastic. Then hors d'oeuvres, steak, scalloped potatoes, and wine after the champagne. Otto didn't dare. That would be abusing Blue's trust. Suppose, God forbid, he babbled about Indigo to the thick-necked blond man sitting next to him. Then his choice of a demitasse or cappuccino and all the fresh fruit that he could ever want. It was nothing short of heaven. Otto tipped his chair back, licked the cappuccino's cinnamon foam from his top lip, and crossed his hands over his full belly. He said no to the breathtaking cocoa-skinned flight attendant when she tried to entice him into an after-dinner liqueur.

Otto's attention rested for a moment on the man beside him. He was extremely fit, business suit and all, but tan and outdoorsy in spite of it. The man had been engrossed in his Steven King novel since before takeoff, exchanging only a few polite jokes about "not being able to eat for a week" before vigorously fanning the paperback to the page where he'd left off. But then, Otto supposed that CIA agents were good at looking as if they were not looking.

Suddenly, Otto felt panicky. Over his objections, Blue had insisted on his wearing a very uncomfortable disguise. First he was given elevator shoes, which, although providing him the never before experienced perspective of a five-foot-eight-incher, nearly caused a headfirst plunge down the airport escalator when Otto miscalculated his first step by the same four extra inches. Next his hair had been blackened and his thick eyebrows shaved down to skinny quarter moons. Still not satisfied, Blue had jammed bulky pads inside his mouth. These not only made chewing difficult but also gave him the appearance of a chipmunk.

In fact, the only aspect of his unsolicited identity change that Otto *did* like was his new German passport and ID, bearing the name "Clause Wertmueller." Otto thoroughly enjoyed pretending that he was a German national.

But had Blue *also* sent someone to protect him? Blue told him that disguises were standard procedure to prevent the Other Side from retaliating against patriotic civilians such as Otto. But was this true? Or was he actually in grave danger? Surprisingly, the frightening revelation tingled Otto's nerves on a level beneath his surface terror, producing an exhilarating sweet-and-sour sensation along with his champagne buzz.

His seatmate shifted Steven King into the pocket in front and plunged into an airline copy of *Business Week*. He seemed oblivious of Otto.

Otto gave up trying to figure out whether or not the man next to him worked for Blue. With Otto's limited experience, he had no way of proving it even if he spent the duration of the flight in speculation. Better to enjoy himself.

He squinted through his oval window. Sun bounded from a solid cloud layer: the flip side of a gray Earth day. How wonderful if one could always soar up into the sun when things became intolerable down there. Otto cocked his eyes upward at absolutely uninterrupted blue. He was happy. Maybe happier than he had ever been. He had a purpose, a *real* purpose. His eyes closed. He slumped against the laminated bulkhead. The engine's low whine soothed him. He should ask for a pillow, but he was just too comfortable to bother.

Sleep cascaded down Otto's brain, across his eyes, and along his neck, numbing his nerves one by one.

Only one little thought interfered for a brief moment, like a vague itch. The same persistent little thought kept finding its way back, no matter how far Otto banished it into the hinterlands of his formidable brain. What had really happened to Ralph Jackson? One day after his call to Blue, Ralph was dead. Coincidence? Lord knew Otto tried to tell himself so—home accidents did happen. But Otto was a scientist, and scientists did not believe in coincidence, no matter hard they tried.

Once again, the little finger of fear poked at Otto's insides. This time he did not savor the sensation.

*　*　*

Otto was right. And wrong. Someone was watching, but it was certainly not the successful mortgage banker from Chicago seated to his right. Instead, a rather frumpy gentleman in tourist class raised his eyes every so often, trying to peek through the curtains to check the back of Otto's head. Doing this was an impossible on two counts. First, the curtains were never open wide enough since first-class attendants went to great lengths to protect their high-paying charges from tourist class voyeurs. Second, Gruhaber's thinning hair stopped six inches shy of the seat top. And if those weren't reasons enough for the frumpy man to stop wasting his time trying to grab a look, where the hell was Gruhaber going to go at thirty-five thousand feet, anyway?

Still, the man could not refrain from looking up every couple of minutes. Maybe he didn't have the nerves anymore. He was pushing fifty-six. Maybe he should think about packing it in. Maybe he would. No need to worry about it now, though. This assignment was nothing. Piece of cake. Just nursemaid the little squirt, make sure he got to where he had to get when he was supposed to. No need to worry about retirement until after this assignment. Suddenly, the frumpy man had a discomforting thought: maybe he had gotten this nothing assignment because the company was thinking the same thing. He hoped not, because if he had nothing else to show for almost thirty years of service—and he really didn't—at least *he* wanted the option of calling it quits first. Millstein immediately decided to resign as soon as he returned stateside.

*　　*　　*

Charles Van Damme stared down at Heathrow. At this altitude, it was a small black patch among London's twinkling multitude of lights. He pushed back the tray table, returning his seat to its upright position per the universal instructions from the crisp voice of the senior flight attendant. She finished with a trite but impressively sincere, "Have a good stay and fly with us again soon."

He stretched his spare frame and wrapped up the spotty conversation with his seatmate, a caricature of a British banker right down to the "wots" and "rightos," promising to stop by if he were ever near whatever quaint little "shire" the tedious man called home. But his thoughts were on the critical week ahead.

Everything was looking good. Gruhaber was already stashed in Berlin under Millstein's watchful eye. Van Damme couldn't help but reflect upon Millstein for a moment. He wasn't given to sentimentality, but he and Millstein did go back at least twenty years. Millstein was shot—used up—no question about that. The sloppy appearance, which had made Millstein the ideal nondescript operative, was now downright slovenliness. But Millstein was still an excellent "nursemaid," and Van Damme was proud of his generosity in selecting the old operative for the assignment. After all, what else did Millstein have but the company? A wife and daughter he hadn't seen for fifteen years. A tiny two-bedroom house in a second-rate suburb, teeming with children and barbecues and all the other accoutrements of modern life that had passed Millstein by. No, this assignment had been a demonstration of unmitigated compassion on his part. Up went his mustache as Van Damme indulged himself in a smile of satisfaction. He had his moments of kindness ... when he could afford them.

Of course, unless Kharkov got cute or Gruhaber got himself into trouble, the little scientist would never know that he had a protector. *Let him enjoy himself in his wonderful 'Bairleen,'* thought Van Damme. The little bugger was so damn accommodating, so eager. Van Damme would have chuckled, but he feared that it might encourage the British banker to resume their imbecilic conversation. Anyway, let Herr Gruhaber enjoy himself. Life had a way of changing. It certainly would in *his* case.

Van Damme mentally reviewed his itinerary. Two days in London, one in Brussels, two more in Paris—possibly three, if he was unlucky. Then Berlin. Berlin and the exchange, where Kharkov got Indigo and Van Damme got everything.

Van Damme involuntarily glanced toward the overhead compartment, which contained his raincoat and attaché case. Silly reflex. Who was going to take them with everyone strapped in for landing?

Everything was looking good. Except ... Rosen. The damn analyst had gotten away again. An *analyst*, mind you! Special Forces training, though.... An analyst who could act. Prior to the past few weeks, Van Damme would have labeled that an oxymoron. You lived and learned. According to Craig, Rosen was probably on his way to intercept Van Damme in Europe, although how could one rely on the effectiveness of an incompetent like Craig? Still, he certainly wouldn't be surprised at anything Rosen did ...

The 747 finished its taxi. Passengers popped up like jack-in-the-boxes, as if missing a minute in the abysmal Heathrow customs lines would spoil their trips. Van Damme never rushed to stand during landing. All you did was wait. This set him apart from the inexperienced. He loved to sit, smugly watching his co-passengers jostle and crunch, going nowhere until the ramps were in place and the doors opened. Then he would calmly get up, edge into line, and disembark at precisely the same time as if he had stood all the while. What sheep people were.

His thoughts reverted to Craig. Craig was slipping. What to do about him? Even humiliation didn't seem to be working anymore. Craig might be outliving his usefulness. It was certainly something to be considered. Not now, of course. Much more important things to consider now. Rosen was also barely worth thinking about at the moment. A few precautions were necessary. That was all. Had to keep focused on Berlin. *That* was the big issue.

He excused himself, edging in front of a frazzled woman who had endured the crush for nearly three minutes to preserve her precious space. She glared but backed up. Van Damme followed the line, passed the "good-byeing" crew, grinning with satisfaction at his successful debarkation strategy all the while.

*　　*　　*

Van Damme loved London. Mayfair, to be more specific. Many parts of London he wouldn't be caught dead in, but Mayfair—a self-contained paradise with Hyde Park, Grosvenor Square, Old and New Bond Street for shopping, Savile Row for clothes, and the restaurants, of course—was perfect. If condemned to spend eternity in one small area, this would be it for him. And never would he complain.

This morning, Van Damme's second in London, was lovely. It was warm and sunny, with a trace of moisture providing the threat of change.

He crossed Park Row to the Hyde Park side, deftly avoiding the chatty throngs entering the massive Grosvenor House or milling in front of the magically lit trees and fountains fronting the Dorchester.

The place had certainly changed in the past twenty years. Only two small groups of the original nineteenth-century homes still fronted the park, huddling together for safety against the towering glass and concrete newcomers. Van Damme glanced across at Upper Brook Street and felt his stomach grow warm. It led to Grosvenor and La Gavroche. What a meal! Thank goodness that he had arranged for a reservation weeks ago. It would have been a tragedy to miss the mixed seafood stew in vermouth sauce, the tender endives, and the decadent assortment of slivers of every wonder on the dessert trolley. Van Damme literally salivated at the memory.

He scurried past the perpetual traffic snarl at Wellington Arch, a misnomer considering the old boy's statue had long ago been replaced by Peace in Her Chariot. He loved the place so much that he'd made a hobby of knowing all the statues and their histories. He passed under the main gate of Hyde Park, into the morning quiet. Birdcalls became discernible above receding traffic noise. Van Damme was delighted to see the trees, smashed and broken from the dreadful storm of '87, finally staging a serious comeback. Ahead was the Serpentine. Even at this early hour, deck chairs holding all shapes and sizes of Londoners lined its grassy shore and a few bright rowboats already coasted over its calm waters. Van Damme regretted that he hadn't the time walk up the bridge that linked it to the Long Water of Kensington Gardens to the west, because its view of Westminster's pinnacles and domes thrusting at the sky was one of his favorites. Unfortunately, he had to partake in his second day of charades at the embassy.

His mood sobered. What a bore. Jamming his hands into his pockets, Van Damme did an about-face, tracing his path back far more rapidly. What a bore. He wished that he could tell the station chiefs and NATO liaison people to forget these pointless planning sessions. That within a few days they wouldn't mean a damn. Things would change irreversibly after Indigo, but none of them knew it. It was a joke. All of the namby-pamby "don't rock the boat" edicts would be dumped, along with the policy-making incompetents responsible for them. Indigo would bring it *all* down. Van Damme loosed a laugh at the clouds.

His buoyant mood might have lasted much longer if he weren't facing the big modern building on Grosvenor Square with the massive American eagle over its front door. Van Damme was always amused by how resentful his British counterparts were of the bird. They claimed it had been put there to symbolically swoop down on the good-old English pigeons that had populated the square long before the United States was invited. Van Damme's forehead crunched down toward the bridge of his prominent nose. How could the British be threatened by the eagle in this day and age? It had been reduced to a parakeet.

He picked up his pace. There were still appearances to keep up for a few more days.

Damn. Another depressing thought hit him. He might not make the galleries on Bond Street if these ridiculous meetings ran too late. With a resigned sigh, Van Damme turned into the embassy.

*   *   *

As much as Van Damme loved London, that was how much he hated Brussels. Practically no tradition left to the place. It was the unconsecrated capital of Europe: administrative center of the European Economic Community, headquarters for NATO. Big deal. All it meant was a lot of modern buildings and a bunch of nattily dressed administrators— "Eurocrats" was the current lingo—sending prices through the roof with their bottomless expense accounts. In many glass and steel sections of the bustling city, the only reminder of its history was the Palais de Justice's classic cupola, scowling down on this architectural hodgepodge from its centrally located hilltop.

More pointless meetings, similar to the ones in London and Paris, had marked Van Damme's days. He found it difficult to feign interest when everything in his life was about to change. Hard to provide feedback when it was all so irrelevant.

The meetings would have been tedious in any event. His colleagues were all treading water, sitting on their hands, keeping low profiles while waiting for the shakeout, in order to determine which former Soviet republics to recognize. That and speculating about how they could sell their spy memoirs as intelligence operations were aborted in a post–Cold War world.

There was a bright spot. Two, really. The cafes were everywhere. They were bright places, open-aired and stocked with the marvelous beers that Van Damme loved. Definitely one bright spot. The other: La Maison du Cygne, of course. Heaven. It was one of the old houses in the Grand Place, where colored floodlights danced along the gilded scrollwork of superb Renaissance architecture. Its marvelous food and fine wine had helped Van Damme salvage one tedious Brussels evening.

He checked his watch. It was 10:14 a.m. Sabena's flight to Berlin left in forty-five minutes. Time enough to call Millstein and find out if Gruhaber was still behaving himself. The concept of Gruhaber misbehaving amused

Van Damme. Some people, you just knew, never misbehaved. Not when they were kids and not when they grew up. Van Damme was positive that Otto Gruhaber was one of those people. Still, he had to check. There could not be any hitches. The day after tomorrow was *it*. Van Damme pushed through the homogeneous crowd, expensively dressed, meticulously groomed, gripping the finest leather briefcases, walking importantly, muttering to similarly dressed people in French, German, and English. He located a bank of a bank of phones immediately past his gate.

Had Van Damme picked the phones four gates farther down instead, he would been in time to see the passengers exiting the Montreal flight. Had he continued to watch, he might have noticed a six-footer with eyeglasses, light hair, a mustache, and oddly full cheeks for his fit build, carrying a well-dressed little boy of four in one arm and the large carry-on of a grateful young woman with the other. But since the tired child's arms clutched the man's neck in a baby-sized stranglehold and its closely tucked head obscured the man's face, it was unlikely that Charles Van Damme would have recognized Arnie Rosen, the analyst, even without his disguise.

CHAPTER 17

Two days before he and Van Damme passed within a hundred yards of each other in Brussels, Rosen's plans changed between the United and JAL terminals at San Francisco International Airport. His first instinct had been to get as far away as possible—hit Japan and then work his way toward Germany. Van Damme's killers wouldn't figure on Rosen coming in from the East, so they'd be less likely to be waiting for him at airports servicing that side of the world.

A great idea. Only one problem: he'd be coming through the former Soviet Bloc. That wasn't a great idea if Kharkov and Van Damme had something going, because if Van Damme had men and contacts in Western Europe, then Kharkov, with his KGB, military, and secret police good old boy network, could field five times as many players. And if *they* caught him, he would disappear—no questions asked—forever and completely.

By staying in the West, he would have a better chance. There were still rules here. It was a little harder to make people vanish. Not impossible, just harder.

Rosen decided that he was too tired to think about it anymore. Tomorrow would be better. He pressed the Sheraton button on the hotel display board near the baggage claim. A voice making a prodigious effort to sound enthusiastic about his arrival told him that the van would be outside at the center divider within five minutes.

He shuffled through the automatic doors, shivering as the San Francisco "summer" night air cut through his thin clothes. Someone had said, "I spent the coldest winter of my life one summer in San Francisco." Who? Rosen tried to think … It was probably Twain. He had said most of America's clever things … he and Will Rogers.

The van caught Rosen dozing against a concrete pillar and passed him. He scrambled after its taillights, cursing. It slowed before two squat powerful-looking women with identically short-cropped brown hair, surrounded by a sea of mismatched luggage. Both wore aids marathon 1990 sweatshirts. The van driver appeared undecided until they gave him a no-nonsense "get the fuck over here" wave of their thick fingers.

Rosen waited, rocking with fatigue as the woman outside hefted luggage to her partner. As she finished, she gave Rosen a look that told him he could never move suitcases *that* quickly, then rolled her thick shoulders and thumped up the steps. Rosen nodded to the smiling young Chicano driver and navigated carefully around the overflowing luggage bin. The twosome scrutinized his every move until he was clear of their precious belongings.

The van trip and check-in were more or less of a blur. Rosen remembered tipping the gabby bellhop; yanking off what clothes he could; and flopping on the big, firm bed.

*　*　*

Dazzling light hit Rosen's eyes. He blinked them open, realizing that he hadn't even closed the drapes. Now he was paying for it. Actually, not. It was close to noon according to the bedside digital clock.

His mouth was filled with used sweat socks. He shuffled into the bathroom and stared into the mirror. A basset hound stared back at him: red-eyed, clear down into his lower lids.

Marquand was dead.

Rosen lowered his head, scooped cold water onto his face, more into his foul mouth, swished it around, spit.

Marquand was dead.

He didn't look at the mirror again. Instead, he shuffled back to the bed. The sheets were untouched beneath the crumpled spread. Rosen had already flung it away and yanked the top sheet down before dismissing the temptation to burrow back in for another twelve hours. Instead, he wandered to the window. Rivers of freeway ten stories down, roads leading in, roads leading out, people zooming along, everyone with a purpose, everyone with a life …

A life.

What the hell did he have?

Where was his life—his family and friends?

He had nothing that those people down there had. No matter how much they bitched, how much they hated their bosses, how much lip their wives/husbands gave them, how much their kids bugged them, they still *had* those things, perfect or not. He didn't. He didn't have any of those wonderful, simple things that all those people whipping along down there took for granted and had no goddamn right to take for granted.

Arnie Rosen dropped the curtain, turned from the window and slipped off his jockeys, fully intending to let a hot shower pulse over him until it jarred the thoughts out of his head and down into the soapy water at his ankles. He fully intended to. Then he passed the bed, and before he could stop himself, he flopped bare ass down, face in the pillows, crying. Not just crying, but *crying*. Sobbing as he never had in his whole life, much harder than the last time that he could remember, when his collie was split open by the careening pickup of a drunken apprentice carpenter.

*   *   *

The crying stopped as it had started: suddenly. There was nothing left. Rosen suffered no self-recriminations as he had when he was a kid. He was entitled to cry. He needed it. The loneliness was *that* great. Maybe the crying would happen again—maybe for a long time to come. He didn't care. He was entitled; he didn't have to make any excuses.

In the mirror, his eyes were puffy red, like Barbara's on those rare occasions when something Rosen did, or didn't do, caused her to let go. Afterward, she'd come out smiling an embarrassed smile, saying, "My eyes are all puffy, aren't they?" while he would be thinking, *She is the loveliest sight I will ever see.* Rosen dwelt on that one for a few moments. Then the clouds around him cleared and he was ready.

His subconscious must have been working on the problem all along, because his course of action was immediately clear: There would be no eastern route. Forget Japan. Up to Canada and over to Brussels— good air service but not as likely an entry point as London or Paris, so it shouldn't be watched as closely—then by car into Germany. It was easy entry to one EEC country from another, and there was no special driver's license required. Then through the Eastern part of Germany—the most dangerous, but in the confusion of reunification, he might easily slip by. Actually, not much of a trip. The German roads were high-speed raceways, at least in the West. And he had plenty of time to get to Berlin.

Rosen retrieved his crumpled pants, unfurling them upon the bed. A mess! He studied the phone, poking at the button for laundry/dry cleaning.

*　　*　　*

The trip to Vancouver was uneventful, except for his whirling mind. Over to Montreal, it was the same, except for some blessed dozing.

Montreal to Brussels did not look promising. A young woman with a boy, perhaps four, sat in the window and middle seats. There would be no sleep for him when the kid got restless—that you could bet on. Wrong. The kid was an angel. Rosen got a solid three hours without his uttering a peep. So solid that he missed his meal and had to beg the aging flight attendant— they weren't all young and voluptuous anymore, were they?—for a snack.

He gratefully tore open his bag of sweet roasted peanuts and had just inserted his fingers for a large pinch when the shy little blue eyes peeked past the woman's chest and lighted upon it. They rose hopefully to Rosen's face, lingered briefly, and then locked back upon the shiny package with single-minded intensity. Rosen sighed and extended the package. The youngster's mother, a pretty brunette, no taller than five-two, declined in broken English, but Rosen insisted. Reluctantly, she allowed the child to accept, demanding a polite "merci" from the musical little voice in return.

After a silence, Rosen decided to try his French. "Where are you going?"

She looked up, clearly stunned that he could speak her tongue. Fairly well, as a matter of fact, and with a decent accent. Hers was the universal concept of Americans: either you speak English or no communication was possible. "I go to Brussels first. Then Paris for two weeks."

"Vacation?"

"Yes." She paused, smiling ruefully. "If you can call visiting your husband's sick mother 'vacation.'"

Rosen smiled. "Your husband left you to do—he'd meant to say "face" but couldn't find the word—it on your own. Or does he meet you there?"

She switched to English. "No. Ah am stook wiz zee job."

He laughed. "Tres bien."

She went back to French. "And you?"

"I'll be going to Berlin."

"It's an exciting time there now." The discarded silver peanut package hit the floor near her feet. She reached down for it and turned to the child. "John-Claude, you will hold this until the lady comes back." The little angel compressed tiny lips into a pout but wrapped his pudgy fingers around the foil ball. She turned back.

"Very exciting," Rosen agreed, keeping the irony in his voice to a minimum. "What is your name?"

"Angelique Verdane. This is Jean-Claude." She nodded toward the pouting child. Angelique smiled, dainty eyebrows raised, heading off the obvious question. "And yes, his father is a great fan of skiing."

Rosen had to laugh again. "You get that a lot, do you?"

"From everyone. 'Oh, like John-Claude Killy,'" she mimicked.

So it went. Rosen's French was going smoothly except for occasional lapses of vocabulary. She charmingly threw in sporadic English phrases with that scintillating French twist.

The French set off memories of Rosen's past. His knowledge of it came a little from high school but mostly from his tour in Europe. Three years in Germany had allowed for a lot of travel.

He'd been too late for Nam—no real regrets about that—but still thought he might want the Special Forces after high school. A major conflict with Jewish parents who expected the usual: college then a law or business or accounting degree. Harriet and Arthur Rosen's tolerant smiles when Rosen first proposed his plan transformed into ferocious opposition as graduation approached and he still hadn't submitted any applications. Not with Ivy League schools or even—heaven forbid—state universities. Rosen's rebellious whim crystallized as their desperation-driven threats intensified. His grades were always excellent and sadistically remained so, which only fueled their anguish.

It had nothing to do with his loving them. They were actually pretty decent, as far as parents went, providing him with a pleasant middle-class existence. They had a nice home in a nice suburb; a nice bar mitzvah, complete with a silver fountain spewing four differently colored soft drinks and a graceful ice swan; braces when his teeth started heading in different directions; a decent used car when he was old enough to drive (he had to pay the insurance); and carte blanche to any Ivy League school that accepted him. It was just that Rosen could not see the point of further education when there was nothing that he wanted to be.

If Harriet and Arthur hadn't pressed and had just backed off and let him make his own choices, Rosen probably would have concluded that the Special Forces wasn't necessary for someone who already had the discipline to make straight As, place second in the state wrestling tournament at 167, and be an honorable mention all-state wide receiver.

As parents, however, they didn't back off, not even when their son threatened to sign up on an exceptionally ugly Saturday morning three weeks before graduation. Until that very moment, Rosen had privately planned to inform Harriet and Arthur that he would be taking a job while attending the local junior college for a year or two and then transferring to a four-year school. He had only been waiting for a face-saving opportunity to deliver the news. Instead, furious at their renewed threats, Rosen stormed out of the house and an hour later was shocked to find himself at the army recruiting office. He listened to a sergeant with acne, not much older than he was, boast about how few qualified for the Special Forces. Rising to the bait, Rosen's pen was aimed at the signature line. Suddenly, his major role model, a bachelor uncle from Cleveland, blasted through the door, pushed past the gaping sergeant and, gripping the young boy by the wrist, dragged him out into the light of day. A month later, Rosen was accepted to Cornell under their late admissions program.

Rosen never regretted it. He made most of his friends who would last a lifetime during those irresponsible years when his most pressing problems were exams and what girl to invite up for the next big weekend. But Rosen never got over the challenge that the acned sergeant had hurled at him four years before. He enlisted three weeks after graduation and no one—uncle, parents, or astounded grad school–bound friends—could change Rosen's mind.

He never regretted that decision either. Rosen enjoyed the physical challenge. He discovered instincts within himself that had been only partially nurtured by football and wrestling: a true appreciation of skilled violence. And he was excellent at it. He had the physicality and temperament and was controlled by a "non-psychotic mind." At least, that was how Sergeant Bammin—nicknamed "Slammin'" by the hundreds he beat, flipped, and stomped repeatedly on the dreaded mats before they developed sufficient skill to at least, partially, pay Bammin back—analyzed his edge over other trainees with similar degrees of physical skill.

"A Hebe yet!" Slammin' could never get over that one. He used it to introduce Rosen to the other instructors in his unusually hyper Southern drawl. "The toughest Hebe this side a Tel-E-vive." Bammin' never had much luck with "Tel Aviv."

Europe had been sweet pickings for Rosen, the South of France, Rhine country, Madrid. Rosen loved it all. And he got plenty of time to see it, especially after he began winning inter-division tournaments for old

Slammin'. You were scored on how many times you would have killed your opponent if you hadn't pulled the blow, wrench, thrust, or kick at the last hundredth of a second. It wasn't that you didn't get hurt; there were plenty of sprains and major bruises. Rosen cracked a rib more than once during his two and a half years of competition. But the travel benefits were more than worth the pain, and if truth be told, Rosen liked the fame that went along with winning.

It wasn't big fame—just within his base at first. Then, as his wins extended to other bases, the whole Special Forces began to recognize his name. Not bad for a twenty-two-year-old visiting a strange base exchange to hear whispered behind him, "There's Rosen. He's odds-on to whip Ortuna for divisional champ tomorrow." It sure was a damn good couple of years. Then Slammin' wanted him to re-up, but Rosen knew that it was time to head back to reality.

Reality was not as pretty as Germany. Not many employers were in the market for someone who could kill with either hand or live off the world's most inhospitable lands without supplies. And Rosen wouldn't take money from the folks, so a full-time graduate school was out.

Finally, he turned to the agency. They too were looking for advanced degrees, but in Rosen's case, they didn't make an issue of this. One possible reason could have been his rave reviews from Special Forces, with whom the agency did more than a little business. They even sweetened the pot by agreeing to finance an advanced degree at night. *That* was the clincher. By then, Rosen wanted a law degree as much as Harriet and Arthur had wanted it for him three years before. He enrolled at Georgetown that fall.

His days were long but interesting, and the nights were as well. However, they made for quite a grind. Rosen never slept before two in the morning on his four school nights, and he was then up early the next day for work. Rosen later wondered how he had ever pulled it off. The answer was a universal one when we marvel at our prior Herculean capacities: youth. Rosen stuck to his punishing regimen through the four and a half years that it took to get his law degree.

Ironically, his parents died in a car crash during his fifth semester, leaving unfinished business between themselves and their son. Although Harriet and Arthur Rosen were thrilled that he had come around to their way of thinking about his education, they never accepted Rosen's resistance to their frequently offered financial aid. They were also positively mystified by his affinity for the CIA. However, unlike their grievous miscalculation regarding Rosen's resolve during the Special Forces fiasco, Harriet and Arthur—to their credit—suffered in silence through their son's latest peccadillo.

He met Barbara one lucky day at the law library. She was a college senior who preferred its tomb-like atmosphere to the frivolity of the undergraduate facility. They were married a year later. Two more years and Eleanor came. That was when Rosen told the agency that he wanted to stay in analysis.

His superiors had always planned for Rosen to go into operations after school. With his background, he was a natural. They gave up after many fruitless "counseling" sessions. Operations was the glamour, the place you made your mark in the agency. Analysis was backup—necessary, but only to enhance operations. The key promotions came from operations, and Rosen had voluntarily switched to the slow track. A shame, they had thought, but that's what family did to some men. The commitment just wasn't there. Too bad. Rosen had known that was what they'd think and hadn't minded. He wanted to come home every night. He had been no more than a year away from going into his own law practice, until now.

The polite bell tone warned him to fasten his seat belt. They began their descent. Jean-Claude pointed and then flattened his face against the window as the miniature wonders of Brussels spun into view.

The odor of sickeningly heavy perfume pummeled Rosen's senses as the elderly flight attendant leaned across to make sure that Jean-Claude was secured. Angelique rattled through her too-big-to-be-fashionable handbag. Out came a gold compact and the inevitable lipstick. She applied rich red to her full lips with the softest sound of friction. Catching Rosen's eyes in the tiny mirror, she turned and laughed self-consciously. Her warm brown eyes revealed flecks of gold. Her somewhat short hair spun away and exposed a perfect tiny ear fitted with a delicate pearl. Her flashing hair's sweetness lingered in Rosen's nostrils.

He hated himself for what he was about to do, but he needed an edge when the plane landed. "Who did you say were meeting at the airport?" Rosen asked as Angelique's head dipped back toward the tiny mirror.

She pouted her lips as she traced the raised center portion with her lipstick. Once finished, Angelique glimpsed her work from all angles. Satisfied, she returned the lipstick and compact to her bag and turned to Rosen, her glistening lips set in a reproachful smile. "The Gentleman did not even listen to me. He pretended, but he did not. Otherwise, he would have remembered that I am here to visit my ailing Mother-in-Law, Madeline, who is by now incapable of moving around her house, let alone coming to meet me at an airport. How ungallant not to remember such essential information."

Rosen laughed into her twinkling eyes. It was a shallow laugh but the best that he could muster under the circumstances. And she *was* delightful. Of course he remembered the story of her in-laws. He remembered everything, but he needed a lead-in for his next suggestion. Raising the back of a wrist to his forehead in mock anguish, Rosen said, "How could I have committed such a horrible faux pas? I have disgraced not only myself but also all of my countrymen, whom I have so poorly"—he wanted to say "ineptly," but the French for the darn word wouldn't come—"represented. There is only one thing that I can do to redeem myself and my fellow Americans." He paused.

Angelique appeared amused and curious.

"Will you allow me to drive you to your aunt's home? You have your baggage and Jean-Claude, and I have the time, so—"

"I do not wish to inconvenience you," she laughed. "The sincere penitence which you have expressed is enough, and I think that Jean-Claude would enjoy the train. I understand it is only a twenty-minute ride to the center of the city—"

"Better yet. I plan to rent an automobile there. Too much of a crowd at the airport. I could accompany you on the metro and help you with luggage. Then you can decide if you want a ride."

She hesitated a moment as she tried to fathom his persistence.

He sensed it and hurried to press his point. "You must allow me to redeem myself," he said with a smile. "It would be nice to have pleasant company a little longer. I have nothing but dreary business meetings to look forward to for the rest of the week."

Something in Rosen's voice won her over. He was sure that he *did* look lonely. "Of course. We would be delighted to have you accompany us, wouldn't we, Jean-Claude?"

"Yes, Mama," the child responded dutifully, indifferent to anything but the enlarging landscape in his window. His response was muffled by the close proximity of his lips to the Plexiglas.

Angelique ruffled Jean-Claude's fine hair. "It is settled, then. We shall have a gallant American escort." She grinned up at Rosen.

With a thump, the plane contacted ground. There was a jolt and then ferocious reverse thrust from the shrieking engines as they strained to subdue three hundred tons of rushing metal.

Although Van Damme's people would be out in force at Heathrow and Orly, Rosen had no doubt that someone would be posted here at Zaventem too. They were much too thorough not to cover all the airports. But they would be stretched thin here, and that was the first thing that he had going for him. Additionally, they might not yet have received copies of his new passport picture. Still, those two alone weren't enough of an edge for Rosen. Now he had a third one. Regardless of whether they knew about his disguise, Van Damme's people would not be looking for a man with a family, and fate had just dropped one in his lap. Or at least in the two seats next to him. As for the car, Rosen really did prefer the less conspicuous city car rental to an airport location.

Rosen let the plane's reversed momentum melt him into the seatback. He sighed deeply. His relief had nothing to do with the safe landing although the surrounding passengers might have assumed as much.

*   *   *

They disembarked at Central Station and entered the streamlined metro. The place was immaculate. Even piped-in music, if you could believe it. Rosen mentally contrasted it to the litter-strewn, vagrant-filled subways of New York, Boston, and every other US city he could recall. The difference was monumental.

During their ride, Rosen got directions to Avis from a well-dressed executive-type figure.

The ride was over too quickly for John-Claude's liking. The child was enthralled by the shiny car's huge windows and whooshing speed.

They found Avis at 145 Rue Americaine easily enough, but a polite argument ensued over Rosen's refusal to supply a credit card. Eventually, the prim little manager, who had been summoned by Rosen's frustrated rental agent, agreed to a substantial cash deposit and the matter was settled. Rosen opted for a Volkswagen outfitted to US specifications.

"She lives near the Grand Place," Angelique said when they left the yard. "According to this map, it's not far. Turn right at the corner."

Traffic whirled by. As in any strange city, all the other drivers seemed to know exactly where they were going and were hell-bent to make it in record time. Crowds clogged pedestrian crossing lanes. Brussels teemed with activity: a purposeful, industrious, no-nonsense populous on the move, aware of its powerful economic role in the world economy.

They barely had time to gasp at the splendor of the Grand Place. Its buildings contained hundreds of delicate elongated windows framed by intricate gold scrollwork, much like the protruding windows of the captain's quarters on an old Spanish man-of-war. John-Claude's gleeful squeals stopped abruptly as hurtling traffic spirited them past to conventional neighborhoods on the far side.

Rosen felt her eyes. "What, Angelique?"

"Why were you looking around so much on the train and at the metro?"

"Who said I was?" Rosen tried for a reassuring laugh while keeping his eyes glued on the maniacs whose automobiles threatened the Volkswagen from all sides.

"Please, *Adam.*" Angelique pronounced Rosen's alias with disappointed impatience. Adam Riesen was the name on his passport. "It was quite obvious."

Rosen shrugged. She wasn't going to buy the bluff. "I thought some people might be looking for me."

"People that you did not want to find you?"

"Something like that."

"That is a yes?"

"Yes."

"Oh." Angelique clutched Jean-Claude, who wriggled at the increased pressure.

Rosen, although paranoid about his driving, forced himself to turn and smile. He shook his head and wrinkled his nose. "Nothing bad, I promise. Really."

Angelique smiled back, but more timidly than before. She did not release her tense grip on the child as she dropped her face back to the map. She looked up and pointed emphatically. "I think that's it over there." It was more a supplication than an observation. "My Mother-in-Law's street. *Yes!*" Angelique practically shouted. "Rue de la Verge Noir. This is where she lives. *That is the house.*"

Rosen wished that she weren't so relieved, but he couldn't blame her.

She hadn't been counting on anyone else's problems.

The house was plain but neat, whitewashed and cozy in the sun.

Rosen envied Angelique, wishing that he too could visit a cozy little place away from it all. But there was none left for him.

Angelique grabbed her bags from Rosen, clutching Jean-Claude's hand firmly in hers as they got through their good-byes. She checked that Rosen had pulled away before turning toward the house.

Rosen watched the woman and boy dwindle in his rearview. Angelique Verdame raised the metal ring on the front door without a backward glance at the departing Volkswagen.

*　　*　　*

Driving without a destination, Rosen happened upon a large bookstore. He wheeled into the closest parking spot and purchased road maps of the Netherlands and Germany. A block farther, he located a small street café. Not much of a coincidence, he decided. There were hundreds of them.

Rosen studied hurrying pedestrians over the foamy head of his beer before concentrating on his route. Two main roads led east. He chose the southerly road through Liege in case he needed a major city before leaving Belgium.

The early afternoon sun relaxed his face muscles while the ice-cold mug tingled his fingers. He should have felt better. Not *good*, of course, but at least a little better. After all, he was still alive and on his way to Van Damme with enough money to get the job done. Hell, if he really thought about it, who would have given him odds that he would have gotten this far?

A bright set of blue eyes all of three feet above the ground stared widely as his mother pulled the little child along by his outstretched left hand. A sudden center sidewalk kiss between two young people in jeans and sandals evoked annoyed mutters from sidestepping businessmen. The sidewalk teemed. Sweet wafts of baking apple and fresh crust from a nearby bakery permeated the warm breeze.

How could he have done such a thing to Angelique? He had used her, endangered her and Jean-Claude for his own purposes. The neighborhood's pleasant aura diminished as guilt overwhelmed Rosen. What the hell kind of an animal would do that? The answer—ugly and oh so clear—was the kind of an animal *he* was becoming, or had already become.

His brief moment of peace shattered, Rosen scooped up the change, finished his mug with a sloppy gulp, and wiped his lips as he hurried, head down, toward the Volkswagen.

CHAPTER 18

Otto Manfred Gruhaber was in seventh heaven. In fact, if there were one, he would have been in tenth heaven. Berlin. Oh, Berlin. More beautiful, more wonderful, more fantastic than even he had imagined! Certainly, there were blemishes. The Kurfürstendamm, originally the trail from the Electors' palace to his hunting castle in the Grunewald Forrest, was now the main thoroughfare in Berlin. It was more honky-tonk and far less dignified than he'd expected. It had endless neon, glass, and steel; fast-food franchises by the dozen; and—he could hardly believe it—peep shows. Few of the dignified prewar buildings were left to counterbalance its inelegant modern trappings.

As for the original Kaiser-Wilhelm Gedächtniskirche at the end of the boulevard, only its broken stump of a tower remained. A newer church to the east and a modernistic chapel tower on the west flanked it. The graphic contrast epitomized Otto's second concern. He was appalled by the city's over-willingness to mask its great traditions in the frenetic trappings of present-day life.

Yet all things considered, Berlin was the most wonderful place that Otto had ever been.

The Kempinski Hotel Bristol, his hotel, was a wonder of old-world service and lavish elegance. And there were the cafés everywhere. Colorful, delightful, sometimes even friendly.

And Otto adored the breathtaking Siegessäule. It was a towering gilded figure of Victory perched upon her high column of dark red granite and sandstone.

But his favorite was the Brandenburger Tor, Berlin's triumphal arch. Otto could almost see the Prussian army pounding beneath its massive columns on their way to or from conquest. He had nearly lost his balance leaning back to stare up at the Victory Quadriga perched atop. It was a two-wheeled chariot drawn by four surging stallions. It was a symbol of defiance that had raced fearlessly toward the old East Berlin and its terrible wall until communism was finally routed.

The only place that Otto would not go just yet was the East. It still smelled of Russians as far as he was concerned. He could feel them lurking just behind the Gedächtniskirche and hovering on the other side of Brandenburger Tor, waiting to grab him if he wandered too far behind the Reichstag. No, Otto wouldn't set foot there until it was time to deliver the Reds' deathblow. He would push them so far out of his dear Germany that they would never return. Then, and only then, could he enjoy the other half of Berlin.

Otto Manfred Gruhaber removed the Indigo plans from the second bottom of his leather overnight bag for the fourteenth time in four days. Carefully separating the thin sheaf of computer paper, he studied and re-studied, testing himself on the function of every bolt, wire, and screw. Otto had no idea how complete his presentation would have to be before Blue pulled the plug on these KGB schemers, but he was resolved to perform his part flawlessly. No one would accuse Otto Gruhaber of falling down on the job. Whatever was required of him—Blue had been vague, probably for security reasons to which Otto couldn't repress a titillating shiver—Otto was sure that his role would be clarified when Blue arrived tomorrow. And he *would* be prepared.

Otto's light was the last to blink out on the Kempinski's fifth floor. It was after two in the morning.

*   *   *

Two hours before Otto finally turned off his lights, Millstein shook his head at the red-eyed apparition glaring at him from the dresser mirror. The little German bastard was driving him buggy. Five goddamn days of nonstop tourism. Here, there, every-fucking-where. If Millstein hadn't been completely sure about packing the company in before this assignment, he damn well was now.

Damn Gruhaber had to see every goddamn nook and cranny of the lousy city. Millstein hated Berlin and what it stood for. Even after twenty-five years of European duty, he still couldn't help but wonder what every Kraut over sixty-five who crossed his path had been doing, say, about fifty years ago. "Ve vuss only vollowing orders." Right, yeah. Bullshit!

And he hated Berlin's arrogance. As if they would have lasted five minutes stuck out here in the middle of Commie Land without the United

States watching their ungrateful butts. Only to hear them tell it, you'd think the bastards had held off the Reds all by themselves for the last forty-five years. Millstein wouldn't have minded one bit if the good ol' United States had turned its back for a minute during the Cold War and—poof—no more haughty fucking West Berlin.

But this little prick Gruhaber was dragging him past every pompous, overblown statue and monument and into every café, hotel, church, museum, and whatever the fuck else in the whole miserable city!

"How's he doing?" Van Damme would ask during his daily call to Millstein. "Is he all right? Are you keeping a sharp eye out? Nothing must happen to him. I'm counting on you, Herb. That's why I put a man with your experience on this. He's important."

And all that Millstein could answer was, "Yes, Chief. Right, Chief. I got him, Chief. Don't worry, *Chief*," while inside they both knew how badly Van Damme was bullshitting Millstein.

It was all over. Herb Millstein had no doubts anymore. The handwriting on the wall was big enough for Mr. Magoo to read. Herb Millstein was through. Over the hill. Done. Nothing but fucking nursemaid jobs now. No way for a man who had over two thousand maximum risk hours on his sheet to be treated. Better to leave now with what little dignity he had left than to wait until there weren't even "nursemaid" jobs left for him.

What kind of a job was CIA operative for a Jewish boy, anyway? His mother had cried for days. His father just shook his head every time they saw each other for years afterward. "My son, the spy," had been his father's constant opener. A weak attempt to make humor out of the family's shame. Not a lawyer like his brother Edwin. Not even a paralegal like his cousin Barbara. And a doctor like his Dad's partner Abe's son? Millstein's parents didn't even dream about that.

No, he was "Herbert—gasp—The Spy." The freak. The mistake that had been dropped on Morris and Tillie Millstein's doorstep by an anti-Semitic stork under the influence.

And damned if Morris and Tillie weren't right. What the hell *did* he have? A crummy pension, some good memories—and a hell of a lot of bad ones. No condo in Florida. No hefty portfolio of mutual funds. Not even a wife. Wives didn't work out well for long-term field men.

And hadn't *that* set Tillie off: no grandchildren. Thank God for Edwin's fertile wife or Millstein would have had to take full responsibility for Tillie's stroke and eventual passing. Kids or not, Millstein would never have had to take the blame for his father's death. A gaudy little secretary at Morris's coat manufacturing outlet on Thirty-Third Street had that honor.

Anyway, here Millstein was, and that was that. At least he'd be getting even with that pricky little German tourist Gruhaber when Van Damme flew in.

After scratching his large hairy belly, Herb Millstein pulled off his yellowing boxer shorts and shoved his veiny legs beneath the covers.

*   *   *

The traffic was driving him crazy. The Kurfürstendamm was one giant parking lot, and it wasn't even rush hour. Irritable drivers muttered out open windows into the late September heat. Pieces of soot from the unprotected coal-burning furnaces of the East settled onto Rosen's windshield.

He stared helplessly at the Mengenlehreuhr, a space-aged clock sculpture perched on the boulevard's wide center island. He tried to recall which of the five light columns were hours and which were minutes—he knew that the blinking ones were seconds—and what on earth the other two were. Mercifully, the traffic moved ahead before he threw something at the damn thing.

The Ku'damm had acquired some class since Rosen remembered it. The same wonderful old stone buildings sat shoulder-to-shoulder with their glass and steel counterparts, but there were many signs of upgrading and rehabilitation. There were not nearly as many strip joints and dives as in the old days. There were now more upscale shops and chic cafés. The Ku'damm had become respectable. What do ya know?

For Rosen, the old Ku'damm had been synonymous with drinking for days on end, friendly blondes speaking precise, if limited, English; bosom buddies he had never called.

The big Kempinski sign snapped Rosen back to the present. Van Damme would be there in three days if Papa's last message were correct. Rosen's restless glance shifted to the bleak half tower of the Gedächtniskirche. Sharp sunlight accentuated its discolored surface and bomb-broken lines. It matched his mood.

Finally, he was at the wide drive of the Hotel Palace. Rosen abruptly swung the Volkswagen out of traffic. It was glaringly out of place among the many Mercedes, but the tactful door attendant appeared not to notice.

Rosen quickly crossed the elegant plant-and tapestry-decorated lobby. No time to admire the surroundings. He needed something. Something highly frowned upon by the upright German government. Something illegal. And he needed it fast. He didn't think that he'd been away too long to figure out how to get it.

Twenty minutes later, Rosen crossed the Ku'damm, heading south on Uhlandstraße. The chic atmosphere deteriorated, and the streets and their occupants became progressively seedier as he approached Lietzenburger Street, the heart of the red-light district. Touted to gullible tourists as "olde Berlin," few Berliners ever set foot in the neighborhood's sleazy honky-tonks. Frumpy shills beckoned toward smoky doorways, where muffled sounds of discordant jazz filtered between narrow openings in scarred velvet curtains. Small groups of American soldiers and Japanese businessmen emerged blinking into the harsh noon light. Jaded hookers, up too early for enthusiasm, halfheartedly tried to coax Rosen over.

This was definitely the place. It hadn't changed from his old army days. Rosen half expected Monty Starks from Newport, Kentucky, or Bradley Green of Memphis, two major drinking buddies, to stagger out of one of the bars, grab his arms, and yank him back through the dirty curtains.

Rosen chose one with swinging doors and a shade better jazz. He pushed inside and bumped into a large red-faced man who was attempting to negotiate the wide doorway with slight success. The man glared for a moment. Then, forgetting whatever grievance he had conjured up, he laughed and slapped Rosen heartily on the shoulders before bumping his way out. Flashing beer signs and fake Tiffany highlighted curling cigarette smoke. The only well-lit object in the narrow room was a longhaired trio—base, piano, and sax—squashed into a corner at the rear. Beer-soaked sawdust stuck to Rosen's soles. The stale air was foul with perspiration.

Rosen stared through the haze, scanning the patrons with decided interest. He finally strode to a specific point along the scarred bar, settled on his elbows, and perfunctorily ordered a Lowenbrau from the multi-tattooed barman. His attention was riveted on the scene to his left.

*   *   *

"Friggin' Army. Fourteen friggin' years. Fourteen friggin' years. Isn't 'at right, Brownie?" Staff Sergeant Timothy O. McKorkle, a short man with extremely wide shoulders and a salt-and-pepper crew cut, wrapped a powerful arm around the skinny shoulders of Corporal Willie "Brownie" Brown, nearly shaking the beer mug loose from Brown's clenched fingers. "Ain' 'at right, Brownie?" McKorkle gave Brown's shoulders an extra hug, sending most of Brown's remaining beer cascading over the rim.

"Y-yeah, Sarge," Brown agreed, primarily out of self-preservation. "That's exactly right. You been in the Army fourteen years." Brown knew where this was leading— he had heard it twenty or more times in the last few months—but he kept his own counsel. He knew that it was killing McKorkle. It was better to let the Sarge get if off his chest again. Unlike Brown, whose uncanny programming abilities put him in great shape for the civilian job market, the Sarge had nothing going but the Army. He knew it. And Brown knew it, although the corporal would rather die than ever admit that to his sarge.

"Fourteen years, Brownie, and now with 'is friggin' Glassnest"— he never did get the word right—"I'm gonna be out on my ass, ain't I, Brownie?"

Strictly rhetorical. Brown knew the script by heart. He signaled the tattooed bartender, Helmut, for two more.

McKorkle tapped the bottom of a pack of Lucky Strikes, expertly extracting two, and jammed one into his yellow-toothed mouth. He flipped the second to Brown. The sergeant grabbed a book of matches that had recently been sloshed over by his spilled beer and attempted three hard strikes despite their unpromising condition. He cursed and heaved them away, digging deep into his khakis for a Bic lighter, which he held shakily near the Lucky's tip. "All 'this goddamn time I give the friggin' Army. All 'is time. I'm a good Sarge, ain't I, Brownie?"

It broke Brown's heart to hear this rock of a man plead for validation. "Damn right you are, Sarge. The best. The best in the whole damn US Army, I say!"

The beers came. Brown slid one over, forcing a cheery note into his reedy voice. "C'mon, Sarge. Drink up. Lemme get that." Brown reached over and fingered the Bic, jabbing its oversized flame at McKorkle's cigarette.

"Damn right I'm 'a best." McKorkle threw out his barrel chest, spinning around to see if anyone would challenge his assertion. "I am 'a *fuckin'* best!" Brown glanced around the dark room. Sarge was running the gamut from self-pity to mindless aggressiveness quickly. Usually the process took at least half an hour; this time it took less than ten minutes. And when Sarge got aggressive, watch out. Six guys once. With his own eyes, Brown had seen Sarge lay out six German punk rocker types. "Punk" but not weak. Most were over a head taller than Sarge. Faster than you could believe, they were lying there holding their weird-colored haircuts, groaning and bleeding. Brown yanking at Sarge; Sarge still wanting to stomp the biggest one a few more times; finally dragging Sarge away just before the droning police siren bore down on them.

"Yeah, Sarge, you're the best." Brown gently tugged McKorkle's arm, turning him back to the conversation. "You *are* the best."

"An' the friggin' Army an' the friggin' politicians don' care. The fuckin' Russkis say, 'Le's be freind's,' an' the goddamn politicians can't wait to kiss their ass. Gonna cut my army way down. I know it. Gonna get ridda all us guys who been savin' their asses fuh years. Gonna take m'job away. I know it, Brownie."

"Nobody said anything like that, Sarge. No orders been given." Brown knew instinctively that he had said the wrong thing. He tried to backtrack. Too late.

McKorkle's little pig eyes screwed tightly into his flushed face. "You *asshole*! Who' you jiving? You kiddin' this white man? Yuh gonna go out an' get yusself a great job. You ain' got nothin' ta worry 'bout. Bu' don' you bullshit me. Don' you sit back an' bullshit the Sarge. Don' you dare pull that shit on me, Brownie!"

At times like this, Brown was never sure whether McKorkle called him "Brownie" out of affection or because Brown was black. Either way, he genuinely liked the sarge. Although the army's attitude toward blacks was immensely improved, many of the older noncoms were incapable of putting aside their lifelong prejudices. Brown's existence could have been considerably harder if the Sarge hadn't been there for him. He had gotten him into computer training—thank the Lord—where Brown's goalless life suddenly took shape. Sarge did it, despite lots of heat from white guys who wanted in. He owed the Sarge big, and Brown knew it was a debt he'd never repay except by keeping the sarge company during these escalating periods of self-doubt.

"Hell, Sarge, I wouldn't—"

"No more, Brownie! I tol' ya ta cut it." McKorkle loomed dangerously as he blinked into Brown's face, his neck muscles rolling and shoulders hunching. A fleshy fist smacked against Brown's mug, skidding it along the bar. Its foamy contents sloshed out for a second time.

It had never been this bad. Brown had never been afraid of the sarge before. He suddenly felt as if he didn't know this man. But afraid as he was for himself, Brown was twice as scared for McKorkle. What kind of a hell was the man going through? Sarge was changing—and Brown had refused to see it until this very moment—into someone who was losing it. *Really* losing it. No point in letting things get worse. He had to think. See if there was a way he could get Sarge some psychiatric help. But right now, he was only making things worse.

"Hey, Sarge, I think I'll head back, okay? Got a project over at base ops. You know how Captain Clemensky gets when he's wanting one of those spreadsheets." Brown laughed somewhat nervously. How could he be so nervous with his best friend in the Army? Not caring for the phony sound of it, Brown stubbed the Lucky into an ashtray full of his spilled beer. The butt hissed, sending up two erratic tendrils of smoke.

"Yeah, get ya ass outta here, Brownie." Sarge's eyes might have flashed regret. Brown wasn't sure. Then the rage was back. "Get outta here, Brownie. Get *outta here!*"

The threat hung heavy between them. Brown shrugged, sidling away from McKorkle. McKorkle's head was back dangling over his beer before Corporal Brown had cleared the swinging doors.

*   *   *

"Damn shame after all you guys have done for your country." Startled out of staring at the gossamer head on his beer, McKorkle whipped his bulldog head to the right, fists clenching.

Rosen raised his palms, a half smile on his face. "Hold it. I didn't mean to eavesdrop, but you were talking pretty loud and I just want to tell you I agree with everything you said."

"Yeah?" McKorkle squeezed the word through a clenched jaw. He was beer-blurry, still not sure that he didn't want to take this guy apart.

"Yeah. I don't trust the Russians either, and I sure don't agree with all this base closings the damn congressmen are talking about. It's stupid. Soon as we let our guard down, the bastards'll be all over us."

"Fuckin' righ'." McKorkle sidled closer. This guy wasn't half bad. "Fuckin' righ'." He lifted his mug, pursing his thick lips as he nodded agreement.

"Hey, you look just about out. How 'bout two more?" The stranger waved his mug and pointed toward McKorkle's. Helmut gave a curt nod from down the bar.

McKorkle chugged the rest, an indistinct "thanks" escaping the corner of his lips.

"What are you going to do?"

"Who the hell knows?" McKorkle grabbed for the fresh mug. The guy was starting to annoy him. Getting too fuckin' personal.

The guy read his mind. "Look, I'm not trying to be nosy, but I need something, and you might be able to help me. Maybe there's a way the army could pay you back a little for all the time you've given it. Interested?"

"Hey, I don' do nothin' ta screw the Army. Got it?" McKorkle swung angrily back toward the bar, cupping his fresh mug in both hands and hunching his shoulders around it.

"It's not the Army. It's the *politicians*. They're screwing you *and* the army. Royally. How many years of service have you given them? And now you don't even know if they're going to dump you or not. By treating you that way, aren't the politicians really shitting all over the army too? I mean, you guys *are* the army. What kind of people would treat you and the Army like that? You and the army don't owe them anything, believe me."

The guy stayed back, not physically pushing, but his low, compelling voice required McKorkle's concentration.

"And," even quieter now, "if things get bad, you're going to need a stake. The Army doesn't have to eat, but *you* do."

McKorkle squared his broad shoulders and pivoted toward the guy. He rubbed two fingers across his right eye and then cupped his palm over his early afternoon stubble, taking a good long time before answering as he fought through his alcoholic haze. Years of experience had taught McKorkle how to overcome a minor buzz like this one. Soon his mind was working. He'd done plenty of deals at the expense of old Uncle Sam even when he wasn't pissed off as he was now. No big thing. But McKorkle had street smarts—always had—and anyone with street smarts knew you never let a sucker know you were anxious. So all he did was shrug and say, good and bored-like, "Mebbe," not giving anything away. Cool like old John Wayne, making the guy do the squirming.

"Look, are you or aren't you interested?"

This guy wasn't squirming. Not at all. More like he was looking ready to go, starting to put his mug down. Street-smart guys also knew when not to push.

"Yeah, I am. What's the deal?"

The guy looked him square in the eye. No little civilian pansy, this one. McKorkle could tell. He knew people. This guy had steel down there where his balls were. You could see it in the eyes. Cold blue all the way down.

"I need a gun."

Blue Eyes said it so quietly that McKorkle wasn't sure whether he had actually heard it or just knew what the request was likely to be. In any event, he wasn't surprised. "Tha's not easy, you know that? Not easy." This time it was McKorkle's turn to stare through squinted eyes, compressing his lips while he perched his chin on his hand, right in front of the stranger's face.

"I know." Blue eyes didn't budge an inch. "How *hard* would you say it is?"

"'Bout a thou' hard."

"How soon?"

The guy hadn't blinked. Maybe the price should be higher. "We keep the deal or we don't have one."

It was eerie, as if the bastard had read McKorkle's mind again. McKorkle tried to lighten things with a yellow-toothed smile. "Sure. A deal's a deal. I need about three days. Military .45 okay?" He frowned. "You ain't lookin' for no weird automatic shit?"

".45's fine. And ammo. But I need it tomorrow night at the latest. No longer."

"Sheet, that's rough—"

"I need time to find someone else if you don't come through. Can you do it?"

"Can I *do* it? Goddamn right I can do it." McKorkle's pride was hurt. When it came to the Army, he could do anything. Anything except save his job. Could he do it? Of course he could goddamn do it! "*Yeah*, I can do it. Where do I call ya?"

"No calls."

McKorkle should have known that. He felt embarrassed in front of those unblinking blue eyes, so he got gruff to cover it. "Yeah, yeah, I know. We'll meet back here, okay? Six tomorrow."

"Six is fine. But we'll meet at Loretta im Garten, near the amusement stalls."

McKorkle blinked. This guy knew his shit. The beer garden was the only respectable spot on the Leitze—plenty of families, well lit, no place to make trouble—in case McKorkle decided to screw him and grab the cash. For a moment, McKorkle's temper flared. The guy didn't trust him. Then McKorkle laughed to himself. Blue Eyes was a sharp operator. "You got it. Six near the kids' games."

The guy turned.

"Uh."

The guy turned back, screwing down near-white eyebrows in a frown.

"How 'bout a deposit?" McKorkle asked, trying to keep a straight face. "I got some heavy expenses."

Blue Eye's eyebrows arched high in an "Are you shitting me?" stare before he turned away again.

McKorkle watched him shoulder his way through the boozy crowd, out the creaky doors. Well, it never hurt to try. McKorkle snickered as he slurped the rest of the head off his beer.

*   *   *

Blue Eyes really had class. No doubt about it. McKorkle sat in a pavilion at the Loretta im Garten, watching manic youngsters bounding across the game areas. Their strident laughter clashed with the soothing rustle of light-festooned trees overhanging the dining tables. The air, warm enough to taste on the trip over, was somehow less oppressive in the festive environment. Loretta im Garten was an oasis in merciless acres of urban humidity.

McKorkle, for all his years on the Lietze, barely remembered the restaurant. He had been here once, he now recalled, trying to impress a fat fräulein named ... Greta. Yeah, Greta: hips that swamped you; boobs like duffel bags; and a box that had seen more traffic than the Lincoln Tunnel. McKorkle hadn't been aware of Greta's promiscuity, her first two attributes being more immediately apparent, so he had tried to snow her by going to a nice place. He should have saved his money. The chunky fräulein would have trotted under the covers if he'd taken her to a McDonald's and limited her to fries and a Coke. What McKorkle's unsentimental reminiscence did prove, besides the fact that you couldn't trust a broad, was that Blue Eyes had class. He knew the only nice place on the whole fuckin' Lietzenburger Street.

McKorkle checked his watch: 5:58. The guy'd better show. Not that it was such a big deal getting the friggin' .45. Hell, on base, guns were as easy to come by as the clap. Showed that Blue Eyes wasn't as smart as he thought. The whole deal took McKorkle less than a half hour. All he had to do was go to Master Sergeant Kirby at motor pool, who owed him one, who went to Mess Sarge Rodriquez, who had a cousin in quartermasters, who had a choice of three no-serial-number beauties just ready to go.

The .45 cost McKorkle—let's see: nothing for Kirby, $250 to Rodriguez, and nothing to the cousin, who Rodriguez must have taken care of. His fee of $1000 less $250 was 300 percent. Not a bad profit. Christ, if he could only come up with that kind of money regularly, he wouldn't need to worry about what the friggin' army was going to do to him. He'd be out before Captain Clemensky's signature dried on his discharge. *Better start thinking like that from now on, Timothy my boy. Better start thinkin' that way starting now. Time to start thinkin' like that all the friggin' time, Tim.*

There was Blue Eyes right on the nose, just as the big hand hit the twelve. *Class act,* McKorkle told himself for the third time in the last ten minutes. McKorkle signaled.

Blue Eyes, looking side to side, finally caught his hand movement. He strode toward McKorkle, passing a table of business-suited locals clinking their steins together to beat the band.

*   *   *

A half hour later, Rosen walked back to the Palace. An army-issue .45 automatic was shoved into the waistband of his pants, its chilly barrel pressing into his right side.

Rosen was as close to elation as his tortured emotions would allow. He had a weapon. He had almost two days before Van Damme was scheduled to arrive at the Kempinski if, pray God, Marquand's message was right. And he had time to rest, which he'd better do now because later on there wouldn't be any.

The air was still stuffy, and legions of spewing autos compounded the problem. The fragile breeze playing across Lorreta im Garten had died as soon as Rosen entered the street. Gray soot, disbursed during business hours, dusted the windows of closed shops.

The Kurfürstendamm was even more crowded now than in the daytime. Restaurant patrons and theatergoers jostled Rosen as they aimed unswervingly toward their destinations. Rosen didn't mind. Soon he would be near Van Damme. Nearer than the bastard ever imagined. Near enough to kill.

*   *   *

Charles Van Damme strolled through terminal at Tegel Airport. From long experience, he opted for the efficient express bus service rather than the queues of growling taxis that flanked the entrances. No matter what city, Van Damme never allowed his agents to meet him. He preferred a settle-in period to gather his thoughts before dealing with the eager-to-please ambitious young ones. And this was even truer in the case of the cynical veterans.

He disembarked at Zoo Station in record time. The trumpeting blare of an elephant caught his attention as Van Damme paused to examine the Pagoda-like splendor of Elefantentor gate. Excited children yanked impatiently at their parents' outstretched arms as they journeyed toward the world's greatest array of mammals. For one reckless moment, Van Damme himself was tempted to ride the energy of the children's enthusiasm under the Elefantentor. How pleasant it would be to be buoyed on the dreams of zoo-bound eight-year-olds. He stood undecided. Then he shrugged and, jamming his free hand into a pocket, turned toward the Ku'damm. As he walked, Van Damme thought he detected a faint pungency competing with the acrid traffic odor. He fancied that he was smelling one of the great gray monsters behind the wall but knew that it could have just as easily been his imagination.

Soon Van Damme was engulfed in the crowded confusion of the Kurfürstendamm's wide sidewalks. September sunlight glinted at him from the windshields of slow-moving traffic. Conversely, brisk-pacing pedestrians brushed rudely by, inconvenienced by his tourist-like pace. Café crowds, more in sync with his leisurely mode, sunned and sipped dewy mugs of white-frothed beer amidst explosions of harsh laughter. In spite of the apparent cleanup and beautification of the boulevard, one or two shabby shills noisily enticed Van Damme into curtained strip show entries with outrageous promises of gratification. An organ grinder's scrunch-faced monkey tugged at Van Damme's pants, tipping its tiny red hat as his coin disappeared into its delicate pink palm. Sweet pastry smells mingled with exhaust fumes in the lifeless air.

The uninterrupted barrage of street noise terminated abruptly. The minute that Van Damme passed into the cool splendor of the Kempenski's lobby, it was as if every person and auto on the great boulevard behind him had been scooped up and carried off by a giant hand. Destroyed in the war and rebuilt in 1952—renovated sometime in the 1980s— the Kempinski retained its original atmosphere of ageless hospitality as if the spirits of past generations of staff still hurried through its corridors, serving joyfully.

A slight bald man with wire-rimmed glasses and a perfectly symmetrical goatee hurried over as Van Damme approached the reservation desk. "Mr. Von Damme. Vot a pleasure to zee you again. Rupert!" His neatly manicure fingers crackled in the direction of a young bellman. "Mr. Von Damme's bag."

The blond youth approached, tugging down on the ends of his gold-trimmed green uniform, gripping the leather suit bag before Van Damme was quite ready to let go.

The manager's eyes narrowed behind his glasses. "Vait over zere!" Ruppert strode leisurely toward the bank of elevators, indifferent to his manager's displeasure.

"Za youth uff today. They haf not za desire, za vill toward perfection." The small man shook his head at Ruppert's retreating figure, speaking as much to himself as to his guest.

"Don't worry, Herr Neimier. The Kempi is as grand as ever. And I'm sure that with you in charge, the service will be impeccable as always." The little man's eyes darted in all directions at once, ever watchful for mistreated guests. Van Damme's compliment failed to register for a moment. Suddenly, Neimier's pinched face brightened as it sank in. "Zank you, Mr. Von Damme. Zank you. Ve zertainly dry."

A raised voice across the lobby jolted Neimier's gaze up over Van Damme's right shoulder. Only a mother retrieving an elegant ashtray from her three-year-old's clutches. Neimier's worried eyes settled back on Van Damme. "Come. I get you checked-in, Zir." He scurried toward the desk. "Martin!" Again Neimier snapped his puny fingers with remarkable force. "Room four seventy-two for Mr. Von Domme."

Another noise. An errant chambermaid tiptoed down the center of the lobby like a deer that had wandered into a camp full of sleeping hunters. Van Damme held back his laughter with immense difficulty as Neimeir sucked in his breath.

"You vill *eggscuze* me, Mr. Von Domme." With an apologetic wave, Nemier rushed at the poor woman, who froze before a semicircle of fully occupied couches.

Van Damme grinned at the hotel manager's rapidly retreating back. "Of course, Herr Neimier."

The dark-haired young man at the desk slid Van Damme's credit card back across the marble counter. "Have a fine stay at the Kempi, Sir," he said in unaccented English.

Van Damme thanked him, signaling Ruppert over. "Take the bag to my room and leave my key at the desk." He handed Rupert some Deutch Marks and walked toward the house phones. "Mr. Millstein's room, please." The white receiver was still warm from previous use. Van Damme wrinkled his nose and moved it away from his face.

After six rings, the operator returned. "I am afraid that he is not in, Sir. Will there be a message?"

"Have him call Charles Van Damme, room four seventy-two, when he gets in."

"Very well, Sir." The unaccented but overly precise female voice clicked off.

Van Damme walked to the public phones. It was safe enough—a thousand calls a day going out of here—little chance of a trace. He took the one on the end, hunching his shoulders away from his neighbors. The call was to a cellular phone. The greeting on the second ring was in Russian. "This is Benheim. My collection is complete."

"The other preenceepal weel be een as arranged." The connection went dead, leaving only an angry buzz in Van Damme's receiver.

Van Damme stared at it a moment before replacing it. Three and a half days until Kharkov arrived. Plenty to do until then, but first a nap. Van Damme believed in naps, especially short ones. Nothing like a nap to get your energy level back up. Five minutes with your head down on your desk was worth two hours at night. Funny that so few people realized how beneficial naps were. That was good actually. It was one of the things that gave him such an edge.

Picking up his key, Van Damme walked toward the elevators. While he waited, he tapped his foot against the marble floor, idly enjoying its rhythmic thuds until the hydraulic doors drowned them out.

CHAPTER 19

Rosen pressed his hands hard against the Volkswagen's steering wheel, stretching his arms and shoulders. Three and a half hours and no sign of Van Damme. Guest after guest went through the Kempinski's shiny brass doors, each saluted royally by the green-clad doormen, but there was no Van Damme in their midst.

Curious police kept eyeing Rosen's parked vehicle there by the side of Berlin's busiest road. But so far, they had not acted.

Where was he? Was he coming? Was this the right day? The right hotel? The right city? Had Papa's contact at CIA been a setup, deliberately giving Papa false information about Van Damme? Instead of being dead, was Papa's supposed friend off on a nice vacation as his reward? Or had the man himself been fed bad information before he and Papa were slaughtered? Or had Van Damme's plans simply changed?

Rosen slapped the wheel, causing it to vibrate with a low-pitched hum. *Shut up. Shut up or you'll drive yourself crazy! Only eleven-forty. Plenty of time for Van Damme to show. Got to believe. Got to believe. Got to believe!*

And what's the worst, huh? What's the worst that could happen if he doesn't show? That's always a good one. Ask yourself what the worst thing that can happen is and you'll realize things aren't as bad as you think. Okay, so what's the worst? I'll find him. I'll find him again, right? That's not so bad. It's not such a big deal. I'll find him again if I have to, and I'll still get him, right? Right. So calm down. Relax. No big deal. No big downside, right? Right.

Wrong. Wrong. Really wrong.

The downside is they get me before I get him. And if he isn't here, I gotta start from scratch, and while I'm starting from scratch, they could be this close to getting me. And if they're this close, then they're damn well going to get me first.

And that's why it is such a big deal and why he—please, God—better be here and better be here soon or, even better, now!

Rosen's hands knotted. His pulse beat hard and fast. His breath rasped through the car, loud enough to obliterate the steady drone of Kurfürstendamm traffic. A tall, emaciated frame separated from an oncoming cluster of pedestrians. It paused as the twin doormen leaped to their doors and entered so quickly that Rosen wondered if it had only been an apparition fashioned from his aggravated craving to see the man. *No. No. Don't go crazy on yourself, Arnie! Of course it's Van Damme. But no limousine? No agency escort?* That was odd. Still, he recognized that arrogantly arched back, the upraised nose, as if the world emitted an odor that Van Damme wished to avoid. It was the Fucker himself. The King of Fuckers.

Before Rosen realized it, he was pushing open the passenger door, sticking out a foot, and reaching back to make sure that the .45 was snug under his belt. All of Rosen's senses focused past the Kempinski's brass-framed doors. He visualized Van Damme swaggering through the lobby and barging up to the front desk past a long line of patiently waiting guests as an obsequious manager kowtowed. Then Rosen saw himself blasting through the front doors, sending green-uniformed doormen flying, tearing down the thick carpet of the deathly quiet lobby. Gasps from seated guests as they realized what was about to happen. The manager's face frozen into a fear-whitened grimace. Van Damme, his back to Rosen, was the only person in the giant room who did not know that he was about to die. Until Rosen's ice-sharp voice cracked out his name. Charles Van Damme, the King of Fuckers, turned as the haughty smile drooped like melting wax as he watched his death approaching in Peckenpaugh-like slow motion.

Rosen's second foot had already made contact with the pavement when he yanked it back in, along with the first one. He slammed his door shut. After slapping his lowered forehead with an open palm, Rosen dug his fingertips into his temples until they ached.

Not like this, Arnie. Not like this. If Van Damme has people in there, you'll never get to kill him. Only you'd be dead. Hell, if that's what you wanted, why didn't you save yourself all this effort and let them kill you before? Think. Why did you come all the way over here? That's right. To catch Van Damme in his dirty little traitor's game so that he doesn't just die—he dies ruined. That's the ultimate revenge, isn't it? Isn't that how you saw it from that first day with Barbara and the kids upstairs? Wasn't that the way you wanted him to die, knowing that his name would be cursed? Wasn't that going to be your revenge? Then don't blow it now. You're too close. A few more days and you've got him. He's meeting Kharkov. Hang on, Arnie. Do this thing right. For Barb and for all of them…

Rosen slouched back behind the wheel. To his left, another sleek black patrol car passed, slowing perceptibly as it drew alongside. Soon he would have to change parking places.

*   *   *

Rosen was sleepy. Very sleepy and getting more so. It couldn't go on like this. Van Damme had done nothing so far. Nothing. Two days and all the bastard had done was stuff himself at fancy restaurants after routine meetings with mid-level intelligence people. Or at least that was who Rosen assumed they were.

One thing that he did know: Van Damme had not met with Kharkov or any of Kharkov's people. And he damn well knew everywhere that the man had been because he stayed up late—no, that wasn't right—stayed up almost continually until three in the morning. After three, he felt safe in assuming that Van Damme would stay put so that he could drive back to the Palace for a few hours of desperate sleep. By six in the morning, Rosen resumed his vigil either hunched in the Volkswagen, hidden behind a newspaper in the sidewalk café in front of the Kempinski, or playing with a pay phone in the hotel lobby. Anywhere that he could groggily commence his surveillance of the *well-rested* Van Damme robustly striding forth to attack another day.

By Tuesday, Rosen made a vow. As he sat in the VW sipping his fourth cup of bitter coffee from his cheap but indispensable thermos, Rosen decided to kill Van Damme no later than five on Wednesday afternoon, whether or not Kharkov appeared. Otherwise, he just might sleep through the bastard's departure on Thursday. Yes, it had to be Wednesday, one way or the other. He was getting too tired to care whether he caught Van Damme passing secrets or not. Too tired.

Rosen's left eye began closing. He didn't want it to. It did anyway. He shook his head and rolled the window down a little more, inviting in the growl of late night traffic. He sucked sharp, moist night air into his lungs. He sipped more coffee, wincing at the aftertaste from his plastic cup.

But it did matter, Goddammit. He *did* want to catch Van Damme turning over documents to the enemy and receiving dirty money. It should be that way. He *wanted* it that way. If he could just hang on and avoid falling asleep and missing the whole thing, it *would* be that way. Only he couldn't risk letting Van Damme escape while he waited for just the right time. If he blew it, he might not be able to catch up with the bastard again, at least not before Van Damme's people caught up with him. And let's face it: killing the prick was the point. Taking him out. Avenging his family. And if it didn't come out just the way he wanted it, well, too bad. You didn't always get everything just the way you wanted it in this world. Rosen almost laughed. Recent events certainly made that painfully clear. He started feeling giddy. Grogginess certainly did wonders for your sense of humor. Van Damme had better do something soon, or else.

Or else. Or else he didn't have to worry about it anymore!

At precisely 11:37, the doors of the Kempi opened, and silhouetted by the lobby's thousand perfectly operating, perfectly maintained lightbulbs was Charles Van Damme. He was dressed not for one of his lavish nights on the town but in working clothes: slacks, windbreaker, and an interesting briefcase under his arm. Rather late for a business meeting. Or maybe just the right time.

Suddenly, Rosen wasn't sleepy. His lips pulled back, radiating waves of energy into his cheeks, eyes, brain. This was it. He *knew* it. Knew it all the way down to his clenched right fist. Okay, Charlie, do your thing. Do it, you bastard. I'll be there. The .45 nudged Rosen reassuringly as he settled back in the seat, hand on the key.

A blue Audi squealed up, rocking to a jerky stop. A door attendant popped out from the driver's side, holding the idling car's door open, bowing in appreciation of whatever Van Damme handed him as he slid in. Van Damme barely waited for his door to be shut before accelerating into traffic.

You haven't used a car before. Got somewhere important to go, Charlie? Rosen threw the Volkswagen into gear, splashing coffee onto the passenger seat as the car lurched away from the curb.

Traffic was still heavy along Strasse de 17 Juni. It lessened considerably as they continued west on Heerstrasse, dropping off to nothing as the Audi turned north on Schonwalder Allee.

Rosen drifted farther back, keeping only Van Damme's taillights in view. As they swung right on the Am Juliusturm, the slender spire of St Nikolai jutted into the moonlight. Seventeenth and eighteenth-century houses presented ornate facades as the Volkswagen clattered along the cobblestones of Old Spandau.

Now Rosen knew where the meeting would be. The Spandau Citadel. How poetic. Bouncing toward a high curb, he cut the lights and turned off the engine. As if on cue, the Audi parked a block ahead.

Shifting the .45 toward his right side, Rosen slipped into a dark windbreaker and zipped it so that the elastic collar covered his face below his nose. From out of the glove compartment, he yanked a matching black ski hat and set it tightly upon his head, rolling the itchy material as far down his forehead as it would go. Farther inside the glove compartment were lightweight dark gloves.

Stepping out of the car Rosen locked his door and began walking in the direction of the Audi. As he slid the gloves over his hands, Rosen was little more than a dark specter in the three-quarter moon's light.

Ahead, Van Damme glided in and out of the shadows of a small forest of chestnut trees. He was almost as invisible as Rosen. As he mounted the narrow bridge connecting the fortress to the mainland, powerful moonbeams transformed his long, slender figure into a grotesque characature. Above him, the mighty citadel obliterated the lower sky, dwarfing Van Damme in its immensity.

Rosen stopped, awed as always by the massive structure that had guarded the river entry to Berlin since 1594. Brick walls strong enough to withstand modern artillery, solidified by tidy rows of moonlight-glinting mortar, towered upward from the waterline. Its angled bastions carved into the night. And there atop the King Bastion rose the Juliusturm, an ancient keep that had protected its early constructors long before the timeless citadel was erected around it.

The magical place had fascinated Rosen during his tour of duty. He spent hours upon hours walking the battlements, memorizing the dimensions, visualizing the dead generations of artillery divisions that defended it. He saw them huddling in their drafty billets and rushing over the bridge for a drunken night in Old Town's sweaty taverns. The citadel had been a good place for Rosen to think, to be alone. *His* choice then. Not now. Now the silhouette up ahead had foisted this aloneness upon him. The silhouette just stepping through the Kommandantenhaus door. The door to the Commander's House that led into the citadel. The door that should, at this time of the night, be securely locked!

A slight breeze flicked ripples on the moat's surface, moonlight flashing from their tiny crests. Night insects buzzed and rattled in the surrounding undergrowth, but Rosen could still hear the silky song of leaves. It was that quiet. His footsteps were next to silent upon the sturdy drawbridge. Soon now. Soon. He tried to hurry. The citadel was a monster maze. It was easy to lose someone in its low-slung buildings and courtyards within courtyards.

Don't I need help? The question dogged each footstep. How many in there already? Waiting? Another question he couldn't answer. Van Damme came alone, but that didn't mean that the Russians had. Didn't even mean that Van Damme's people weren't already in place. What could he do? No way— there was *no way* he was backing off now. *None. Don't even think about it. You're playing this out no matter what. You wanted to do it in spades: catch him in the act; get the goods. Now do it and shut up.*

Very close now. There's the Commander's House. I can see the carvings along its pediment. Hard to make out in the half light, but I know they are the emblems of ancient Prussian provinces. Quit stalling; forget the fifty-cent tour.

He peered in. The opposite door, leading into the largest courtyard, stood ajar. Rosen stepped toward it just as a huge shadow darkened the moonlit drawbridge behind him.

Rosen edged along the far wall until he was able to peek through the open door. Chestnut trees rustled in the courtyard, casting shifting shadows over the hazy buildings that bordered it. Was it his imagination or had the wind picked up a notch? Was this really the way to take Van Damme? Here? Isolated? Get it done right. That's what Marquand would have said. Getting the job done was what counted. Marquand's look when Rosen told him his plan said it all. Marquand would never criticize, but that look …

Rosen's neck ached with tension. He massaged it with his left hand. His right hovered, claw-like, never more than a few inches from the .45 Like what—an old-time marshal facing down the bad guys in the middle of a mud-caked main street? Only trouble was, with the exception of Van Damme and Kharkov, everyone in there would be thinking *he* was the bad guy and they were the marshals.

That was it. *That* was the problem. Why was he here doing it the hard way? It hadn't come fully together in his mind until now. The thing was, if he didn't prove that Van Damme was selling secrets, then Van Damme would die a martyr killed by a crazy. He'd give Van Damme what he wanted most: immortality. For months, table talk across heirloom silverware and long-stemmed cut glass at fashionable Washington dinner parties would be as follows: "Poor Charles, killed by some analyst who cracked up and killed his own family, you know. And just when Charles was about to do great things in Intelligence. Such a shame." Before long, the legend of Van Damme would grow until he became known as the greatest intelligence operative since Bill Stevenson, legendary founder of the OSS and savior of the free world during Hitler's time. Old MI5 pensioners as far away as London would hoist ruby sherries to Van Damme's memory. "Oh, Charles Van Damme. Why, there's no telling how far he would have gone if that madman Rosen hadn't killed him."

That's how legends were born. Rosen couldn't let that happen. A killer and a traitor should not be rewarded. That was why he *had* to do it this way. The end. No more questions. Suddenly he had a revelation. Why should the place be crawling with opposition? This whole affair had to be a secret ploy by Kharkov, as well, because Yeltsin would never condone a KGB recruitment of a top US intelligence operative at a time when his government was desperately courting Western aid. Kharkov, like Van Damme, would minimize the risk of exposure by involving as few of his people as possible. Rosen closed his eyes, praying that he was right. He moved forward purposefully and sucked in a deep breath. No more questions and no more theories. Get on with it. Rosen slipped through the doorway.

Just in front to his left was the Pallas, or Knight's Hall. A low-slung affair, rebuilt in the sixteenth-century from the tombstones of a desecrated Jewish cemetery, it stood submissively in the Juliusturm's massive shadow.

Rosen's eyes swept upward to the Juliusturm. It was a hundred feet of ageless defiance whose eight-foot walls had protected noblemen and their treasures since the twelfth century. A light flashed within. Its door must be open. Van Damme was there. *And* the Russians. Naturally the rendezvous would be at the Juliusturm. Over the centuries, it had always been the center of activity at Spandau Citadel. Why shouldn't modern men also be drawn to its timeless stolidity for their intrigues?

Rosen sprinted into the Pallas's shadow, following its rough, cold wall to the base of the tower. Light from the Juliusturm illuminated a rutted square of uneven courtyard. Rosen edged closer.

The gouged Pallas wall was like fine glaze compared to the ragged outcroppings of the Juliusturm. Rosen held his breath and peered into the incredibly thick archway. A winding wooden stairway filled the tower's narrow confines. He could see nothing but the ancient steps spiraling up and out of sight into deep, dark shadows. Nothing else. Not a sound. Rosen raised the muzzle of his .45 to eye level and tiptoed inside …

A silent shadow glided along the rounded wall across from Rosen. Soft footsteps scuffed against the ancient wood as the shadow made its way down. It was a long, thin shadow.

Rosen's face contorted. Almost of its own volition, his gun rose toward the shadow's left. He widened his stance and locked his elbows. One more turn and a pair of expensive loafers materialized, followed by the stick-like legs, narrow chest, and elongated head of Charles Van Damme.

There was a crushing impact against the back of Rosen's neck that sent the .45 spinning toward the rough stone floor, clattering, bouncing, and clattering again as Rosen's numb body toppled after it. The uninviting stones enlarged seconds before a tooth-rattling concussion.

Cold gray eyes stared down at Rosen from a massive square-jawed face. The face was fairly symmetrical except for its battered nose, which angled pronouncedly left. Rosen shook his head to clear his vision. The nose remained askew. The man who owned the nose looked to be at least six-five, but Rosen's perspective, flat on his back staring up, may have added a few inches. The man with the angled nose's very large shoe—no mistaking that, even from Rosen's position—sat squarely and heavily on the center of Rosen's chest. He tried to rise. The shoe pressed into his chest with crushing force, squeezing out his breath as ridges and points of the rock floor gouged his spine.

"I wouldn't move. Werner is quite powerful enough to grind you into the ground with his foot."

That deep, soft voice. Rosen curved his head backward as far as possible, then arched his back to gain a few more inches of vision. He gasped, catching a brief glimpse of Van Damme emerging into the light before the shoe drove him back down. Then the voice and face were squarely above him.

Van Damme looked down. He was rounder, less angular in the dim light. There was both sympathy and rebuke in his soft voice. "You know, Werner has been following me since I arrived in Berlin. Spelled, of course, by others." Van Damme's head shook slowly side to side, in and out of the shadows. "But the operable point is that you had no chance of getting to me. Didn't that occur to you?" Van Damme paused, then shrugged off the rhetorical question.

He moved slightly back and lowered his head, allowing Rosen to see him more easily from the floor. "You know that you are sick? We should probably provide you with some sort of treatment that would permanently exorcise your devils. Perhaps a lobotomy?" Charles Van Damme's lips rose over teeth that appeared unnaturally white in the subdued light. "Unfortunately, I cannot risk losing you again. You are a very dangerous man."

"I'm not the fucking killer. *You are!*" Propelled by ferocious emotion, Rosen was able to arch upward at Van Damme.

Werner's immense shoe increased its pressure, slamming Rosen back.

Werner ground his heel into Rosen's solar plexus.

Rosen groaned, grabbing at Werner's ankle. He might as well be twisting at a Redwood. "I left … a … letter in th' … hotel safe." Words weren't easy with the staggering pressure on his chest. "If I … don' come back, they … will op'n it an' know … why."

"You may pull your foot up a little, Werner. I can barely hear what Mr. Rosen is saying." Van Damme's mock concern echoed at Rosen from the cold walls. "You've already proven yourself to be suicidal, Rosen. *And* paranoid. Who would believe anything from you? Especially with your well-documented vendetta against me.?" Van Damme bent at the waist, leaning closer, the gaunt lines of his face clarifying even in the murky light. "However, in this case, your mental condition will be entirely moot. You are going to be robbed and killed by two Turkish gentlemen who have been waiting most of the day for the opportunity. They have been promised your car and valuables. I don't know if you're aware of it, but the Turks are considered criminally inclined by most Berliners, so your death won't be very surprising."

"Robbed and killed here? In the early morning. That's kind of suspicious, you asshole."

Van Damme rose and walked away, his narrow back toward Rosen. He wore cuffless tan slacks and a blue blazer. Flickers of light glanced off a row of four silver buttons near the edge of his sleeve as he waved his right arm. "Not here!" There was stridency in Van Damme's voice. Then its register lowered as it smoothed and softened again. "You are going to be stupid enough to be caught in the Kreuzberg late at night. Kreuzberg, I don't know if you're aware, is a *very* bad neighborhood. Lots of dirty little one-room apartments. Crowded. Sometimes only one bath to a whole floor. Terrible conditions. That's where the Turks live. Is it any wonder that they are so dangerous? Poverty and frustration make for violence. I wouldn't be surprised." Van Damme turned, strode back, and kneeled, his voice soft and conspiratorial. "I wouldn't be surprised if you were found floating in the Landwehrkanal. It runs right by that bad, bad area."

Rosen arched his neck, thrusting his face at Van Damme's. "My car? They could get caught with my car. And talk."

"Nobody believes Turks in this city. And you can't seriously think that these illiterate scum know who we are. So there is nothing for them to tell. *Is there*?" Van Damme looked at Werner, nodding in Rosen's direction. "These analysts," he grinned, shaking his head and rolling his eyes. "Let him up. He's too stupid to be dangerous."

The huge man raised his foot after a last vengeful grind of Rosen's ribs.

Rosen sucked in the pain, never taking his eyes off Van Damme.

Backing off five feet, Werner removed a large bore revolver from a black shoulder holster that barely looked adequate to accommodate the heavy weapon. Light glinted off the long barrel. Werner crossed his thick arms, dangling the weapon loosely in Rosen's direction.

Rosen propped up to an elbow, rubbing his chest as his glare shifted to Werner. The big man stared back impassively.

Rosen arched into a sitting position, continuing to knead the injured area with his thumb and splayed fingers. "Why didn't you tell the police about my escape from that front of yours?" He frowned at Van Damme's frown. "You know. Fair Oaks. Don't you think someone will get suspicious at my turning up halfway across the world when everyone thinks I'm still there? Bad planning, Van Damme."

Van Damme barely covered his mouth before yawning.

Rosen wasn't sure whether it was real or just an affectation, but he would have bet on the latter.

The thin man's eyelids lowered as his voice took on the tone of a teacher explaining a concept to a not overly bright child. "In the first place, Mr. Analyst, I wouldn't describe Fair Oaks as a front. Granted, we do have some influence there. Dr. Gorgone, for example, has given us immeasurably valuable information concerning our people's ability to withstand interrogation after extensive sleep deprivation and/or the introduction of certain drugs. For this, the institute has received some very generous grants. But these have been funneled through entirely independent sources. There is no demonstrable relationship between our organization and theirs, I assure you."

Van Damme studied the tips of his long fingers, pursing his lips in displeasure as his thumb caught a rough spot on one of the crescent shaped nails. "Pardon me. Second, you represent a crucial security breach, so it is natural for us to want to handle you ourselves. We obviously can't have outsiders involved because you possess information that would compromise national security. Everyone understands that. The Fair Oaks personnel cannot be faulted for cooperating with us in such a sensitive matter. And even if there is a little jurisdictional squabble in the aftermath—with FBI, for example—so what? Our failure to include them will be attributed to inter-agency paranoia. We've been accused of that before and no doubt will be again." Van Damme stared at Rosen as if he planned to continue but thought better of it and walked toward the tower's entry with a quick nod to Werner.

"Now you can go on with your dirty spying for the KGB. No problems anymore, huh, Van Damme?" Rosen called as the tall man hunched to exit.

The thin shoulders stiffened. Van Damme hovered, half in and half out for a long moment, before backing in. His soft eyes shown moistly as he approached. "It doesn't matter what you think. Do you understand that? What I'm doing is necessary—" He stopped, obviously struck by the intensity of his emotions. Dismissing his own unexpected reaction with an impatient shrug, Van Damme turned and began to leave a second time.

"And killing women and children—a five-year-old little boy and an eight-year-old girl—that was also 'necessary,' you self-righteous bastard? Who the hell do you think you're kidding?" Rosen was up to his knees. A kick from Werner sprawled him back to the hard floor, his ear slapping into a furrowed rock before he defiantly thrust himself back into sitting position. Rosen gulped deep emotion-driven breaths, his injured earlobe dripping red onto the shoulder of his windbreaker as his hate-slit eyes bored into Van Damme's back.

Surprisingly, the gaunt man turned a second time, his face noticeably whiter even in the dim light. A haunting apparition in the castle tower. "Werner, I must have a private word with this deluded man. I'll be fine," Van Damme said as the giant's face contracted. The division chief flicked his right wrist. With the metallic *click* of a spring, a small-bore over-and-under pistol filled his right palm.

The hulking Werner backed into the shadows. Only his eyes reflected occasional rays of light. They were still intent upon Rosen.

Van Damme stepped toward his kneeling adversary, settling on his haunches three feet away. The delicate pistol moved level with Rosen's eyes. "I know that you won't let yourself believe me, but I deeply regret that *that* had to happen." His voice was soft, eerie in the harsh stone surroundings. "I could not have any witnesses. It was *your* fault for interfering."

"'Interfering?'" Rosen's tone lashed Van Damme.

Werner shuffled in the shadows.

Van Damme lowered his voice further.

Rosen was forced to twist his ear toward Van Damme's taught lips, but the words themselves hissed out in an angry torrent from beneath Van Damme's writhing mustache. "You know *nothing*—you're *nobody*—and you haven't the slightest idea what I am or what I do or *why*. How dare you intrude into my world and not expect to pay for it? How dare you judge me or what—"

"You killed my family—*and that gives me the right, Van Damme!*"

Van Damme blinked, long black lashes flicking the tops of his sharp cheeks. He drew in a deep breath. Using his free hand to stabilize his awkward position, he exhaled air slowly through semi-closed pale lips. Breath sweetener assailed Rosen. Van Damme rose partially, knees creaking. "Rosen, this has never been personal with me. Never." He shrugged narrow shoulders. "Well, that's not true. Maybe now it has become that way. But not when all of this started. God, man. I didn't even know you existed during all of those years that we were under the same roof! You just can't …" Van Damme stared upward, tracing the circular flow of the rough-hewn steps before gazing back at the floor somewhere to Rosen's left. "You just can't go jumping into someone else's life like that." His lips tightened. Something went dead deep in the soft eyes. Van Damme rose, turned, and said, "Take care of things." Without a backward glance, he ducked into the night.

CHAPTER 20

"**G**et up!" Werner Kohauer motioned with the gun. Not that he needed the gun. Not at all. Not even with big men. Definitely not with this little toad. How big? Maybe six feet at most. Maybe. What was it in American? Ah, yes: "pounds"—170 pounds or so. It insulted Werner even to have his weapon out for such a puny man. What could this baby do against Werner's might? Still, if anything went wrong, Werner definitely did not want to lose another job.

"You are too brutal for police business!" That was what Herr Captain Dietrich, with his potbelly and big political connections, had told him. There in Dietrich's big office with fancy views of almost the entire city. Too brutal. "A laugh," as the Americans said.

Too brutal. Because he detested criminals, especially the filthy immigrant kind that corrupted German society. The Yugoslavs and Poles and Greeks were bad enough, but at least they were Christians. But the Muslims were dirty little dark people who couldn't speak except for incomprehensible pigeon German; who brought their inscrutable religion with all of its fanaticism; who created tenements out of apartment houses and gutters of their streets; and who were not more than one step removed from criminality at any hour of the day. Too brutal?—because he dealt with them the way they deserved, with strength and finality. It was the only way they understood, and if arms, noses, or jaws got broken, well, that was the consequence of *their* atrocious behavior, not his.

Fortunately, the fat captain in the fancy office had not recorded the details of Werner's recent arrests on his official records. Werner believed that the omission was out of guilt because Dietrich knew that Werner was right. (Dietrich's actual motivation had been the desire to bury as many scandals as possible until his next promotion to an even fancier office.) So the CIA grabbed Werner when he offered his services. And he liked the job:

good pay and benefits. Werner did feel that his opportunities were more limited than those of the Americans, but that was to be expected—it was their agency. Overall, Werner couldn't complain.

And he thrived on the "wet" assignments. Werner was aware that that was the Soviets' euphemism for "terminations," but it had such a pleasant ring to it. Like this one. Too bad that Werner couldn't beat this little man before turning him over to the filthy Turks, but still, it would be amusing to watch them carve him up. For once, these garlic eaters would be doing something useful.

"Up." Werner jabbed a thumb in the air. "Rozan … Rozan … Zat iss Jewish?" The smaller man just glared as Werner's cold eyes ignited. All this fuss about the Jews. They deserved what they got, his father had told young Werner that after he came back from school one afternoon with many questions about mass killings under the Nazis. His father told him that the Jews strangled Germany and deserved to die. All the false tears and bleeding hearts—"bleeding hearts": Werner liked that American expression too. Guilt, which so many of his countrymen professed, made Werner sick. How many really believed it? Anyway, soon, one Jew less.

He marched little Rozan toward the archway, bending briefly to pick up the .45 before pushing him out into the three-cornered courtyard. As they neared the wall, two shadows separated from a group of chestnut trees. "Here he is!" Werner shouted in German. He sprawled Rosen along the rough stones toward two dark men in stained short-sleeved shirts.

From either side, they approached the dazed man cautiously. Moonlight brightened the stubby blades protruding upward from their clenched fists.

I will have to use that plastic bag for his body, thought Werner. The filthy Turks would drive Rozan's body back to Kruezberg in Rozan's car. But *he* would have to drive the whole lot of them to Rozan's car, and no one was going to bleed in Werner's brand new BMW. Not "new" new but secondhand low-mileage "new." It would have been so much more convenient to set the murder up here, but "wet" business had to be credible. And everyone knew the Turks of Kruezberg wandered their district all night looking for trouble. Werner crossed his massive arms, positioning himself for a better view as the Turks moved in.

*   *   *

Rosen shook his head. The powerful push into the rough stones had left him woozy. His nose trickled hot blood over the puffy contours of his lips, his tongue automatically tracing the outlines of his teeth for breakage. His mind fought to clear itself. *You've got more to worry about than broken teeth, Arnie. That monster Werner obviously doesn't plan to kill you himself or you'd already be dead, so it looks as if these little guys with the knives are supposed to do it. Okay, if you don't have to worry about Werner's gun right now, just the knives, it helps to know that, except that the knives are getting awfully close. Actually, one is closer than the other. The one on my right. That's also important to know.*

The nearer man, still shadowy, short with a very round head and a long mustache, held his knife low—not clutched high above his head like the amateurs in a movie stabbing scene—and moved in with sliding side-to-side steps. He knew what he was doing. *Very important information,* thought Rosen. *The other one probably does too—also important to know. Okay, now I have tons of valuable information. Great! How about my using it? Now, before the first guy gets close enough to kiss me?*

Rosen pushed up to his hands and knees. Aiming at the closer man's right knee, his best target below knife level, Rosen tucked his left shoulder and launched a kick, snapping his leg out and up on a forty-five-degree angle, tilting his toes inward and following through with full heel extension, catching the knee just as the man's weight shifted a step forward. The crisp snap at the apex of Rosen's kick echoed lightly in the enclosed courtyard. The ensuing crack of bone and cartilage reverberated resoundingly, but even this was dwarfed by the victim's ringing shriek. The Turk dropped as if a trap door had opened in the courtyard floor. He rolled from side to side on his back, hunching around the useless knee as if by squeezing it tightly enough, he could stop the unbearable pain. He couldn't.

As the first Turk's howls ricocheted from stone to stone across the ancient courtyard, three things happened simultaneously: the second Turk stopped dead in his tracks; Werner commenced screaming at both Turks—no mean feat in light of the downed one's ruckus; and Werner got shot …

*   *   *

Werner didn't know that he'd been shot, at least not right away. He did know several things: one, he was pissed as hell at the stupid Turkish bastards who couldn't even kill an unarmed man with two knives; two, he would end up having to do the job himself, which he really didn't mind; three, he would probably have to finish the Turks too, which, by this time, sounded even better than killing Rozan; four, something big was stinging him beneath his right shoulder, and it was numbing his back. Werner couldn't decide whether to kill the big insect that was stinging him or the three men, first. Having always prided himself on his efficiency, Werner decided to slap the insect while he stalked the miserable Turks. "You imbecilic, worthless garlic eat— Aaaagh!"

The bug, the miserable big bug, must have been a monster, Werner thought. His whole back was on fire. Swatting it had practically paralyzed him with pain ... and blood? *Blood* all over his hand! No bug. No God-awful bug. A bullet. My God, someone had shot him!

Werner turned. His right arm was getting heavy, but not heavy enough so that he couldn't raise his gun. He squinted into the citadel's shadows, seeking out the madman who had tried to hurt him, Werner the invincible. Time enough for the Turks and the Jew when he finished with this fool. Where was he? There must have been a silencer, because Werner had heard no shot. That meant that the fool only had a handgun. A mere handgun, with its little bullets, against him! He would win. Werner stumbled on the rough surface as fire burned along his back toward his lungs. No matter. He was up against a mere handgun. What a laugh—another American expression that he liked.

Werner squinted, pausing to listen. Many trees. Many buildings. Many places to hide. Where? It had to be close, for a handgun's range was not great. His right arm, his powerful right arm, was tingling now, the gun a little heavier than usual. No matter. He would win. There. A movement. A figure separating from a tree not twenty yards away. The fool. Werner moved forward. He had too much to do to get fancy. He would just kill the fool and get back to his real business before Rozan killed the Turks and escaped. That would not look good on his record—the nice record that fat Captain Freidrich had kept so clean for him. Werner had never failed an assignment ... and he wouldn't now. Just get the fool ...

Werner staggered. Where had that one miserable little bullet hit him that he was even effected this much? Fifty feet to his target. Werner raised the gun. It wavered. His gun never wavered. He steadied it with his other hand, something he *never* had to do ...

This time Werner heard the *hiss.* The fool had fired again! It took him in the stomach, grinding through the heavy muscles, the soft tissue, and a good piece of his intestine. Oh, that hurt, but nothing stopped Werner the Invincible.

He lurched badly as he fired, his thunderous shot screeching off the courtyard floor, whining into the nearby trees. He raised his gun again. *Much* heavier this time. Now he was fighting to steady the barrel, resigned to using both hands, firing as his muzzle swung past the dark figure (was its hair white or was that just the moon playing tricks?), knowing he had missed, jerking—although he didn't want to show the other that he, Werner the Invincible, was hurt, as the next hissing bullet, louder now that the other man was boldly walking toward him, bit into him a critical six inches higher than the last one.

Things were starting to pour out inside him now. He'd better finish this fool fast or he'd fail his assignment. Gott, his knees were wobbling. They *never* wobbled. His gun was dropping. He *never* dropped his gun. His eyes hazing, his feet shuffling. None of *these* things ever happened either.

The white-haired fool was very close now. Very brave now. Just where Werner wanted him, where he could get his huge hands on this little, old fool, where ... Gott, Werner the Invincible was falling. That never ...

*　*　*

"You imbecilic—you worthless garlic eat ..." As Werner's voice boomed against the ancient stones two minutes before he died, Rosen's attention snapped from the second Turk toward the enraged juggernaut. Why had Werner's bellow stopped mid-word? Rosen was already to his knees, preferring to meet Werner's charge standing up. He frowned, waiting for the giant's next move. Inexplicably, Werner turned and reached a huge arm overhead, groping for something on his back as he strode off in the completely opposite direction. Then the giant jerked upright as he touched whatever was on his back. A jerk of pain! Definitely. Then he was moving a little slower. Then Rosen thought he saw Werner jerk a second time, although at this distance, it wasn't clear. Then the giant was sort of staggering rather than walking. Then his gun flashed down at the courtyard stones followed by what was possibly a third jerk—it was really hard to see. Then he was out and out tottering. Tottering. Rosen was pretty sure, even in the darkness. Then—son of a bitch—the big bastard fell. No doubt of that from the thud.

Rosen whirled back toward the second Turk. Perhaps he had let the man get too close when he became mesmerized by Werner's behavior? No danger. The man's face was turned in Werner's direction. His jaw extended toward his chest, eyes dull, stubby blade pointed at his own feet.

Rosen backed farther away, positioning himself behind the man's fallen companion before searching the darkness where Werner had sprawled.

A figure separated itself from the shadows near where Werner must have lain. It stopped, apparently to study the giant for a moment, before moving toward them.

It was clearly too much for the second Turk. With a shriek, he bolted for the trees.

Rosen tensed, unsure. Beneath his closely cropped hair, the shadow person's skull looked white in the moonlight. Right height, right build, right hair. Rosen knew. "Whatever you're doing here, Sergeant, I'm glad to see you."

Seconds later, McKorkle's craggy features were bathed in moonlight. "No sweat. Who are these guys?"

"An answer for an answer." Rosen sidestepped the groaning Turk and walked toward McKorkle, but not too close. "What *are* you doing here?"

"I figured you were in on some sort of a scam. Thought maybe I could cut myself in, yuh know, with m' future looking so unpredictable an' all. Been following you, since I seem to have plenty a' free time nowadays. Didn't figure on anything like this." McKorkle frowned down at the Turk. "Hard to talk with all that groaning going on." He squinted toward the Juliusturm, the trees, the distant shadows of the citadel's wall. "Anyone else to be worried about?"

"Just the fellow who ran off. And he only had a knife ... if he hasn't dropped it, along with his dinner."

McKorkle unscrewed his silencer and slipped a long-barreled revolver back into the holster that rode his thick hip. "This isn't going to make me any money, is it?" he asked gruffly. His sour look already anticipated Rosen's answer.

"No."

"Since I already wasted this much time, might as well hear what it was about."

"Saving my life's not enough for you, huh?"

"Not by a long shot."

"Some guys and I had a little disagreement about money. What else?" Rosen checked his knees with lightly probing fingers. Scraped, raw, not much blood. His jaw, pretty much the same.

"Yeah, that's usually the big one. Broads come in second."

Rosen "yeahed" McKorkle back with a smiling headshake.

"That big guy the muscle for some local loan shark?" McKorkle evidently wasn't ready to let it go yet.

"You got it. You must've dealt with some of these solid citizens yourself from time to time, Sergeant."

"You are certainly right." Now that the conversation had shifted to him, McKorkle clearly lost interest. His business was *his* business. He walked back toward the large pile that had been Werner. "We better get ridda this," he called back. "I don't like leaving a mess. The police around here are real persistent. They ain't used to bodies lying around like in Detroit. How 'bout the river? He's a ton, but we oughta be able ta get 'im over the wall."

Rosen walked up thinking, weighing. Getting rid of the body. Was that the right thing to do? If Werner failed to show up or contact him, Van Damme would want to know why. Other company people would be crawling over the citadel. Werner would be found. So would the injured Turk, and a "cleanup" would take place. The police would never see a thing, but the sergeant didn't know that; he thought this was about gambling or loan-sharking. That was the way Rosen wanted it. No telling what the sergeant would do if he knew that the Government was involved. Might even get patriotic and turn Rosen in—or try to anyway. Who could tell? Better to follow McKorkle's suggestion.

Besides, if Werner was found, Van Damme would rightfully assume that Rosen had escaped and was after him again. That put the advantage back with Van Damme. If the division chief didn't know exactly what had happened here, Rosen's chances were better. At least with no bodies, Van Damme wouldn't know who was dead and who wasn't. Maybe he'd think the Turks had killed both Werner and himself. That would be of some help. "Sure. Let's do it." He reached down, gripping Werner's ankles.

*　*　*

McKorkle went for the armpits. Blue Eyes was smart, McKorkle thought. (What the hell was Blue Eyes's name?) He had taken the monster's lighter end. McKorkle "oofed" as he tugged at Werner's shoulders. The massive man was even heavier in death. "Let's mostly drag him, huh?" McKorkle wriggled his arms farther under the body for a better grip, clamping his hands over Werner's incredibly broad chest. "This fucker ... weighs ..." *Screw it,* he thought. *Too hard to talk and carry at the same time.*

Finally, Werner was propped atop the low wall. Far below, the Havel swooshed along, its moonlit eddies swirling around the same walls that had stood up to it for over five hundred years.

"Let's ... do it." McKorkle's breath was sporadic from his efforts. Rosen hesitated; McKorkle didn't. Werner's bulk arched outward in a sprawl of arms and legs. It smacked the wall a third of the way down with a mushy *thump,* causing Rosen's stomach to contract, then splayed outward in slow motion, finally slapping mightily into the rushing water.

"I only give that dive a three point one."

Rosen gaped at the grinning sergeant, who shrugged and then chuckled again at his own joke. "What about the gimp?"

Rosen's face hardened.

"Okay. Okay." McKorkle pushed out his thick palms toward Rosen. "It was just a thought. I'll take him back and dump him somewhere. He'll be all right." He quickly scanned the area, scratching his brush cut. "His other little buddy is long gone; you can bet on that."

"I'm going to lay off betting for a while," Rosen replied straight-faced.

McKorkle stared at Rosen, confused. Then the sergeant grinned. "Very good. Say, what's your name, anyway?"

"Riesen. Adam Riesen."

McKorkle squinted, weighing the name. "Yeah, well, whatever. I'm Tim McKorkle." He offered a stubby hand and gripped Rosen's hard. It was a habitual test of strength that McKorkle employed unconsciously.

Rosen extricated his hand. "Pleased to meet you, Tim. You don't know how pleased. If I can do anything—"

"Nah, that's okay. Say, there *is* something." Rosen waited.

"The gorilla had a real pretty little Beamer. Since he won't be needing it anymore ..."

"Fine with me." Rosen shrugged.

"I yanked these outta his pocket ... before." McKorkle dangled a key ring by its BMW emblem. They tinkled in the citadel's silence. The Sergeant's hardened face beamed with boyish excitement. "I got these friends. By the time they're done with it, it can't be recognized." He shot Rosen an extended wink.

"Good. I'm glad it worked out for you."

* * *

They walked back to the wounded man. His loud moans were now only sobs and what sounded like praying. The words were like no language that Rosen had ever heard.

"I'll help you get him to your new car," Rosen said. Together they lifted the Turk, slipping his arms around their shoulders. There was no change in his soft sobs until his injured leg banged against something in the dark. The shriek left their ears ringing. They switched to a fireman's carry, their hands locked under the man as his leg dangled safely above further obstacles. His moaning receded to its originally tolerable volume.

The BMW was parked just over the bridge, under a group of shadowy chestnut trees. *Werner must have passed me or followed me,* Rosen thought. *But I really don't remember seeing another car except Van Damme's and I hope I would have noticed a car following me when I was on foot. I'd sure better be able to if I'm going to survive. No, Werner must have seen me take off after Van Damme and then gotten here first. He probably brought the Turks with him and sent them on ahead.*

"Hold him a second." McKorkle let the man's good leg down, leaving Rosen to balance him. He tried two keys before the door opened. McKorkle stuck his head inside for a long moment, finally pulling back out, a look of rapture on his normally sullen face. "Smells like sixteen-year-old pussy. Do I have ta put him in there? Okay. A deal's a deal."

They got the Turk in with only one prolonged shriek.

Standing in front of the driver's window, Rosen extended a hand. "Don't squeeze it off this time, huh?"

McKorkle laughed, seeming embarrassed. "The Army." He shrugged. "Hey, what would you have done if I was pulling a—what was it—scam? Shot me, robbed me? What?"

McKorkle grinned his rare little boy grin. "Who knows? Guess I would have played it by ear, but I probably would'a left ya sump'un." He punched Rosen's shoulder and slid into the BMW. "See ya."

The door closed with a sturdy thud. McKorkle's face was a picture of anticipation. Rosen was already forgotten.

"See ya," Rosen said, mostly to himself. He started back toward Old Town.

*   *   *

What a dream. McKorkle laid his hands over the BMW's soft leather, spreading his stubby fingers to maximize the sensation as he moved them in sensual circles. Better than sex? Well, just as good anyway.

And speaking of sex, a car like this sure wasn't gonna hurt. Wait'll that stuck-up Franzie at the Yankee Bar got a look at it. Franzie, that sexy little divorcée, holding out for an officer because "a voman haas to look out for her future," she told McKorkle when he proposed an after-hours get-together. Maybe now she'd see that McKorkle was going places, faster than a lot of those dumb-ass wet-behind-the-ears ROTC kids she put so much stock in. And if not her, so what? There were plenty of others who'd damn well appreciate him. His luck was changing. He could feel it. This four-wheeled beauty was just the start. "The Sarge" was going places.

McKorkle straightened up, breathed in a deep gust of BMW A-number-1 cowhide, and checked his eyes in the rearview. They stared back, glowing, alive, confident. No more uncertainty. Whatever the army did was okay with Timothy O. McKorkle. He'd make out just fine. Best thing that could've happened, this thing with the army. He'd been too comfortable, too secure. A man needed to be shaken up occasionally. Find out what he really had in him, what he could really do when the chips were down.

McKorkle glanced over at the man next to him. The Turk slumped forward, clutching the knee, perspiration running from his face and arms like a river, dripping down toward McKorkle's beautiful leather seat. Normally, McKorkle would have been totally pissed, thrown the fucking little guy out. But not tonight. Tonight he, Timothy O. McKorkle, had had a revelation, seen what he could really be. Tonight he just felt sorry for the little brown man next to him. Someone who could never feel what he felt now. Who never would have one-hundredth of the opportunities that Timothy O. McKorkle had before him.

He practically patted the man's shoulder but stopped short of that. What the hell? He'd even drop the poor bastard off in Kruezberg. The trip would give him a chance to run the Beamer before dropping it off for a face-lift tomorrow.

McKorkle watched Riesen, or whatever his name really was, walking toward town. He passed his own junker. McKorkle decided he would sell it to that corporal … Williams, the one who was always after him about it. He'd have Williams pick it up early tomorrow. McKorkle thought about offering Blue Eyes a ride the few blocks. Nah, it was better to let it end right here.

"Thanks, man," he said to the departing figure. With an Ed Norton–like flourish from Gleason's *The Honeymooners,* McKorkle rotated the key in gradually diminishing spirals until it mated with the ignition.

*　*　*

The wind from the bang slammed Rosen's back like an ocean wave. His body jolted forward, his legs doing a crazy dance to prevent him from toppling face-first onto the rocky road. His ears rang as reverberations of the explosion rattled inside his head. Rosen looked around, dazed and not comprehending the cause until his eyes lighted on the flames shooting upward from the BMW's windows, hood, and even the undercarriage. They engulfed the car, mocking the peaceful night.

He stood frozen. Nothing. Nothing he could do. He couldn't even get closer. The heat was too intense. Crackling started, like a night full of firecrackers, as the car's multiple layers of fine paint blistered and exploded. Rosen couldn't tear his eyes away—it was all so final. The end of McKorkle, without even a chance to save him as *he* had saved Rosen less than an hour before. No mouth-to-mouth; no Heimlich; no rush to the hospital; no anything. Gone. Done. One bright flash. One bang.

Rosen turned and ran. Still shaky, his feet did not always aim straight ahead, but for the most part, he managed to keep them moving in the right direction. His hearing was shot from the blast. He hoped it would recover later. Figured it would. Right now, all that he had to concentrate on was getting to the car and driving away before the crowd arrived. All the residents of Old Town must have heard the explosion regardless of how soundly they slept. Soon the chestnut forest might even catch fire. That would certainly draw some attention. Did the Germans have volunteer fire departments? Rosen couldn't remember. In his days the army had taken care of its own fires, like that inferno at the infirmary when some nicotine addict snuck a smoke just before his sleeping pill kicked in.

Here it was, the VW. There was movement farther down the street: people standing on the sidewalks in front of old narrow houses, straining to catch a glimpse of whatever had awakened them; flashlight beams darting between the pitch-black tree trunks; a robed man jabbing his finger toward the conflagration as another, also robed, cupped his hands above his eyes to peer where his neighbor indicated. To Rosen, the escalating activity was a frantic pantomime choreographed to the violent ringing in his ears.

He turned on the ignition. Unable to hear if it caught, Rosen threw the VW into first and jammed the gas. The car jolted forward. He threw it into a tight U, bouncing haphazardly over the cobblestones and away from the milling crowds. Soon he had cleared the narrow streets and was accelerating across the smoothness of less ancient roads.

Van Damme didn't leave any loose ends. And here Rosen had been worried that Werner's disappearance would alert Van Damme. No problem. Van Damme had taken care of that with his neat little car bomb.

Van Damme's own men apparently weren't having any more luck than those close to Rosen. Hadn't the company always taught you to take care of your own, or was that just more pap for the flunkies, while the big boys played by their own rules?

It was strange, but for just a second, Van Damme, the monster, had almost seemed human back in the tower. Rosen thought he'd detected regret, or something close to it, flickering in those changeable eyes. Rosen screwed a mental lid on his sentimental reflections. He must have been wrong, or even if he had witnessed some vestige of remorse from Van Damme, it would be no more than a jungle cat might experience before ripping apart its overmatched prey. Maybe the lion felt something for the doomed gazelle. Who knew? It certainly didn't stop the lion from killing. At best, Van Damme was the same: a carnivore with a carnivore's conscience.

Rosen accelerated, racing the VW along deserted streets toward the center of Berlin. The echoing of his ears was the only sound in the late night city.

*   *   *

Charles Van Damme arrived at the Kempi by one fifteen. Waving a return greeting to the late-night desk crew, he considered hunkering down onto one of the deep, soft couches and sniffing the strong bouquet of a fine old brandy while watching tipsy revelers straggle in. He decided on bed instead. *Very* important day tomorrow—probably the most in his entire life. Better be rested.

He stepped into the elevator, backing toward his own corner, away from the perfume and cologne of a sleek tuxedo-and evening gown-clad group. They were a tanned, perfectly groomed, young-skinned lot, giggling at in-jokes and comparing notes on the in-seasons at world-class resorts while exchanging unselfconscious fanny pats. Van Damme left them at the fourth floor. He wondered what they would be doing now that there were no witnesses.

He inserted the key, stepped in. God, he was suddenly tired. He sat heavily upon the queen-size bed, avoiding crushing the turned-down spread, and allowed his shoulders to slump forward, rolling his head down, stretching his long white neck. All of these idiotic meetings. They never stopped. Especially here in Berlin, the former undeclared capital of espionage and intrigue. Everyone, positively everyone, in this whole damn city fancied himself a master strategist, from the lowest embassy gofer on up. And now, with the Wall down, there were more experts than ever. And he had had to sit politely and listen, suffering an endless stream of fools. Not for long. Not after tomorrow.

Van Damme wondered if poor Werner had gone fast. Hoped so. A good man for a foreign national. Normally Van Damme didn't like working with them, preferred Americans, but Werner, although an accomplished sadist, had been extremely reliable. Nevertheless, the German represented a loose end. Not so much because of Werner's assignment tonight but because no one must know about tomorrow. And Werner had become much too proficient at keeping track of him. Still, it was a shame. The man had been a wonderful weapon—damn near indestructible.

With a sigh, he forced himself up, walked to the bath. Removing his shirt, Van Damme dug through the contents of his Dunhill toilet kit. He laid a half-used tube of Crest and red toothbrush along the side of the sink.

"How is Gruhaber?" he had asked Millstein just before his trip to Spandau.

"The little asshole stayed in today for a change." Gruhaber had been leading the operative on a merry chase over the last week. Millstein made no bones about that. Millstein was getting old. Too bad. He'd been a good man in his day, one of the best. Not anymore. Old and cranky—and slow.

Not a formula for continued success in the agency. Well, tomorrow was his last assignment.

Van Damme studied his perfect teeth. White as ever—no cigarettes or excessive drinking to spoil them. He wasn't really sure that drinking had anything to do with tooth whiteness, but it certainly sounded plausible. His emaciated chest reflected back at him, white and puny. He had always hated that! He tried weight lifting when he was a youngster. Tried to beef up with milkshakes and protein powder too. Nothing worked.

"It's your thin bone structure," said his mother, his doctor, everyone. "Don't worry about it." But he still did, even to this day. He was strong enough, but he had never been able to make himself *look* strong. He could wear the best clothes, get the best haircuts, and Lord knew he was handsome enough. *Very* handsome. And, of course, he was brilliant. But he would never *look* powerful enough to make himself a perfect package. Even his skin betrayed him. It burned. Then, after the humiliating period of peeling, it reverted to pure white again, enhancing his unhealthy appearance.

Still, he was rich, successful, powerful, envied—a man among men— about to go to the very top. What was being a little skinny compared to all that? Silly. Ridiculous. Van Damme humphed into the mirror, laughing at his childishness. His false good mood lasted for about ten seconds. Then his smile soured and he grabbed a thick bath towel, draping it over his shoulders so that he wouldn't have to look at his chest.

Van Damme's mind changed direction frequently, but always with total focus on the instant subject. His emaciated chest was entirely forgotten. Now Gruhaber was the topic. Millstein said that the little man had been working all day. That was good. For the past two days, they had spent many hours together while Gruhaber talked about angles, formulas, and specifications. Van Damme had listened, but most of it sailed over his head. You could not become a rocket scientist overnight.

And Gruhaber's damned accent drove him crazy. How could anyone have lived in the States since he was three and still speak that way? Gruhaber must have never had a single friend, spending all his time with Mommy and Daddy and the aunties and uncles.

One thing Van Damme knew: He couldn't have explained those plans if his life depended on it. That was why Gruhaber was so important. Lord, how Van Damme had humored the little man over the past two days, acting excited when Gruhaber did, looking impressed when Gruhaber's voice demanded it, nodding sagely when Gruhaber expected it. All difficult enough for Van Damme under ordinary circumstances but infinitely harder in this case because when Otto Gruhaber became absorbed in his work, he neglected to brush his teeth … and Otto Gruhaber was one man who owed it to the world to always brush! In spite of it all, Van Damme had seen to it that Otto was happy and enthusiastic so that Otto would be convincing tomorrow. That was critical. Van Damme was more than willing to tolerate scientific babbling and atrocious breath if Otto was at his best.

He finished with his teeth; splashed his face; applied moisturizing cream to the skin under his eyes and massaged it in with his fingertips, stimulating the weak muscles there. It was a nightly procedure that he hoped would prevent the loose skin from ever sagging.

Rosen's face flashed before Van Damme's eyes just as his head hit the sweet-smelling pillow. Van Damme hadn't conjured it up. He had actually striven to bury the entire incident in the farthest recesses of his ample mind, but here it was. The analyst had been a nuisance, a needless complication. Christ, he hadn't even been aware that an Arnold Rosen existed a month ago. Who had invited this analyst to play God and butt into his life? What happened to Rosen and his family was Rosen's fault, not his. Rosen. Van Damme humphed into his pillow, tossing to get more comfortably situated. Rosen, playing like some kind of amateur detective, nothing better to do with his time than spy on *him,* chief of European operations. Rosen had been out of his mind. How dare he? Yes, he deserved *exactly* what he got. Bigger things were at stake here than some busybody and his ridiculous need to interfere. Thinking he was some kind of a hero. Foolish. *Trying to match me. Laughable. Also a little pitiful.*

Charles Van Damme burrowed deeper into his pillow. He was sorry for Rosen. Sorry that Rosen's family had to die. He hugged the pillow around his ears and willed his mind to shut off. He summoned his powerful calmness, his edge over the rest of humanity: his proven method for dealing with issues more rationally and less emotionally than anyone else. Whatever had happened to those unfortunate people couldn't be helped. The end. He had world-changing matters to attend to. But first for some sleep …

CHAPTER 21

Blue appeared at his door promptly at ten thirty, fresh and impeccable. If there was one word to describe Blue, then Otto Manfred Gruhaber believed the word was "impeccable."

"Morning, Gray." The words flowed out from between the impeccably white teeth.

"Goot morning, Blue."

It was still as exciting as the day when Otto was first contacted. Blue, a very tall, gaunt man had caught up to Otto as Otto walked to his car. Otto's space was always as close as you could get to the bigwig reserved spaces surrounding Sklar's rear entrance because Otto was always the first one at work. In his deep, soft voice, Blue asked if they could talk somewhere in private. The parking lot was filled with black shadows and little else at that time of night, and Otto was terrified. Once Blue had jammed an identification card close enough to Otto's face for him to make out "Central Intelligence Agency," Otto's heart stopped palpitating. Otto drove, with Blue following, to a little English pub on the El Camino.

They both had soft drinks while Blue explained how badly the Central Intelligence Agency needed someone just like Otto, with access to Indigo II. The secret new satellite was "the perfect cheese to bait our trap," according to Blue. Blue had not been happy with Otto's choice of location because he had to constantly raise his voice above the whooping at a nearby dartboard, but he finally said, "Would you help?" Of course, Otto said yes. Otto would have agreed ten minutes earlier, as soon as Blue told him that they were going to catch the Russians doing something underhanded, but Blue never gave him the chance.

Then Blue had leaned close and said, "Do you understand that this must be completely—I mean *completely*—confidential?" Of course, Otto said yes, and they shook hands. Blue paid for the drinks, although Otto offered, and before Blue drove off he said, "You must figure out how to get

the complete plans to Indigo II, not just the part that you are working on."
Otto said, "I already know how." Blue said, "Good. If there is any trouble,
we'll cover you, but don't forget that this is *completely* confidential." Then
Blue slid his long legs into his car and said, "You will know me as 'Blue.'
You will be 'Gray.'" That had really thrilled Otto. Then Blue drove off in
his white rental car, leaving Otto staring after his taillights and wondering
whether the last forty-five minutes had really happened.

"You have *all* the plans?"

"Right here, Blue." Otto patted his leather case. It had two brass snaps
and was made of soft calf hide stained from years of use. It was a gift from
his mother just before she got sick. It was still hard for Otto to think of
her and the D-word in the same sentence.

"You're *positive?*"

Blue had a way of emphasizing certain words when talking to him that
made Otto feel like a child, but Otto had never reacted. The mission was
far more important than engaging in minor personality clashes. Today
was the decisive moment, however, and Otto's nerves were already raw.
"Absoloootley."

Blue's quick frown gave Otto a guilty twinge of satisfaction. Otto was
proud of himself. He had made his point in the least confrontational of
ways, the way a good team member should.

Blue's perfect smile returned. He had understood; nothing more had
to be said. Otto's admiration for Blue soared to new heights. What a good
team they were!

"Better be off," said Blue.

They walked the two blocks to the S-Bahn at a brisk pace. The
morning air was unseasonably cool, hinting at autumn not far off.

A modern graffiti-less bus appeared almost immediately. There were
few passengers because commute hours were over and because the majority
of workers commuted west rather than vice versa.

The Tiegarten's splashes of green swept by to their right, first
consistently and then intermittently as outposts of the city began to
encroach. By the time they crossed the snaking River Spree, the mighty
park was no more than a distant bluish haze.

The bus driver whined up and down through his gears as they recrossed
the Spree twice more. Moments later, they disembarked at Friedrichstraße.

Otto darted his head right and left, but everything that he had heard
was true. No frowning guards in depressing brown uniforms tramped over

to study their passports. No guards anywhere. Until now, Otto hadn't really believed it possible that Berlin was no longer divided, at least not at his gut-level emotions. The Russians giving something up that they had owned lock, stock, and barrel for over forty years—how could it be? Bad economy or not, it was inconceivable to Otto that they would really do this without NATO pushing them out block by bloody block. Otto's mind was spinning as he trotted after Blue.

There had to be a devious reason that the bloodthirsty Russians would do such an uncharacteristic thing, and Blue must know what it was. Otto's eyes darted nervously. That's what this was all about: a trap, which the CIA had set to prove that the Russians were still the Russians, regardless of their crocodile tears of repentance. The horrible realization hit Otto that the vicious brown-uniformed guardians of the detested Wall had not gone home after all. They were actually hiding behind every fluttering curtain and partially opened door, poking each other's ribs, drooling and laughing as he and Blue wandered into their midst.

Otto pounded forward to catch up with Blue. The thin man walked tall and sure. He knew better. The set of his shoulders buoyed Otto. They *would* get the goods on the Russians, foil them regardless of the odds. Otto's shallow chest swelled. He tugged his narrow shoulders back, glaring at the fearsome buildings ahead with new resolve. Sniffing back a drop of mucous that was about to roll from his nostril, Otto hugged his mama's precious leather case and hurried onward toward his heroic destiny.

*　*　*

Otto loved the Unter den Linden on sight. Not that he hadn't read about it in a hundred books and viewed it through a thousand pictures, but here before him was the very avenue that the royal electors used as they rode to the hunt from the royal palace. Otto also knew that long ago, rows of nut and lime trees were planted along its entire length, ergo its name: "Under the Lime Trees."

Otto gaped at the great buildings that lined the broad boulevard. Once or twice, he actually had to remember to open his eyes and look. *You idiot,* he laughed to himself, *forget your old habit of visualizing these marvels. Here they are before your eyes!* The little man spun around, trying to capture the entire panorama, but he failed. It was just too much for his eyes to take in, but he kept trying. He looked guiltily back at Blue, but Blue didn't seem to mind. He just stood there watching Otto, slightly amused, maybe, but certainly not angry or impatient.

They stood on the center island with six lanes of traffic scooting by. Otto raised his hand to shield his eyes. Directly west was the Brandenburger Tor, where the GDR flag had flown until recently. Through the trees, Otto discerned the sun-hazy shapes of former communist ministries and embassies. They were too modern to be interesting, even if he hadn't hated what they represented. But to the east, above the huge bronze rump of Frederick the Great's horse, past the broad shoulders and flowing cape of the great king's statue, that was where he wanted to be. Among the classic buildings of the great German empire.

"Haff ve time?" Otto asked, not daring to hope. To his delight, Blue shrugged, waving "go ahead" with long, delicate fingers.

Unsure how much time they had before Blue would pull him away, Otto hurried past the statue and across three lanes of traffic. There, to his right, was the opera house. Its stone was a startling white, and sunlight exploded off its gilt trim. Behind it, he caught a glimpse of the tan columns and bluish-gray dome of St. Hedwig's Cathedral. Across the street was Wilhelm von Humboldt University, with the likeness of its founder seated proudly in front, the thin shadow cast by a street lamp rippling along its white pedestal. It was all so wonderful that he had to glance around faster and faster to get it all in.

How much time left? Faster. The Arsenal. Oh, the Arsenal, the oldest of all. Just look at that luminous brick, dozens of detailed statues of warriors and maidens protruding like the quills of a huge red porcupine. The history … think! Yes, 1695. It had been the storage house for the arms captured by victorious Prussian armies. It was a museum now.

There was only one flaw, one problem. Otto had done his best to try to forget, but the fact kept pushing back at him. Intruding. Dampening his enthusiasm. Not totally. Certainly not totally, but somewhat. Otto had to admit it. That fact. The fact that he could not force back for the life of him was that the whole place, almost every last building, had been rebuilt by *them*, by the Russians and the GDR. They had reconstructed these divine relics with their filthy bloodstained hands. These marvels, gone forever, piles of meaningless brick and rock, except for their tainted hands. The hands of butchers! Otto wrestled with his insoluble dilemma. In order to appreciate all this, he had to acknowledge that the Russians were capable of doing something worthwhile. His euphoria deflated like a punctured balloon.

"Time to go, Gray." Blue's smooth voice was a lifeline, dragging Otto up from his dark depression.

Otto checked his watch. Eleven-fifty. Forty-five minutes had flown by. He looked up at Blue. The thin man waited, a tolerant smile on his fine lips. It was the same tolerant smile that had punctuated all their interaction lately, as if Blue were a father humoring his little boy. Otto experienced a moment's irritation, fought it back, curiosity getting the better of him. "Vy haf ve valked around here for zis long?"

"I thought you'd appreciate the opportunity. I'm sorry that you didn't."

Was that more mockery in the unfathomable hazel eyes? Otto couldn't be sure. "I ahm very appreziative, but I do not zink it vass only done for me."

"You are right, Gray." Blue's delicate hands went up, palms outward in a gesture of surrender. His thin body bent closer, conspiratorially, as if a great secret were about to be revealed. "'Just be a tourist.' That's an important rule when you are out of your own neighborhood. It is never wise to rush to an important destination when you don't know who may be rushing after you. Get the idea?"

"Uff course." Otto's depression and his irritation with Blue's patronizing attitude disappeared in the excitement of their shared intrigue. "Ve vant to zee if ve ahr being followed before ve continue."

"Exactly right." Blue's smile broadened. He patted Otto's narrow shoulders.

"Vell, ahr ve okay to go get zem now? I ahm prepared." Blue was really proud of him. Otto could tell. Blue was wonderful. Otto would show Blue. He would carry out his side of the meeting flawlessly. Not that there was much to do, not much at all. Describe Indigo to the Russians; elaborate on the plans if they had any questions. No subterfuge, no deviousness, no acting. Frankly, he had been quite disappointed yesterday when Blue described his role. Otto was not to engage in a brilliant gambit against the Russians, as he had fantasized. No subtle half-truths, quarter-truths, or even outright lies. "Nothing," as the old bromide went, "but the truth." It had been a colossal disappointment. Still, he would do his job and do it well, unchallenging though it was. After all, this wasn't a matter of ego. National security was at stake!

"Good. I think we're all clear. No one's followed, so let's get it done." Blue's long arm was back around his shoulders. Two companions, off to do their duty. Otto beamed up at Blue, his little legs spinning as Blue's comradely pressure propelled him toward a row of high-rises to the south.

Otto's stomach remained remarkably calm—until the shadow of the first faceless concrete-and-glass tower crossed his shoes.

Blue must have felt Otto's shoulders curl inward toward his neck. "You're doing fine." The calm face beamed down at Otto even as Blue's grip on his shoulders tightened. "We're almost there … and you know your part perfectly. So don't worry about it. I'll take care of everything else. Once we get what we need"—Blue's left hand waved up and off toward unseen possibilities— "others will take over. There will never be a moment's danger. I guarantee it." Another powerful hug.

Otto pulled away, back arching. "I ahm not affraid." His shrill voice hardly supported the assertion. "I just vant to be zure of my responzibilities. Zat iss all."

"Of course, Gray. I know that. Of course I know that." Blue's fine eyebrow's contracted over the long straight nose. "Do you think that I would take anyone with me who was afraid? Of course not." Blue's delicate right hand waved off the absurdity of the idea.

Mollified, Otto attempted to mirror Blue's smile. But he did not reply. His voice would have betrayed the terror clogging his insides.

*　*　*

They stepped into a high-rise. Otto couldn't have picked it out from any of the others if his life depended on it. They were all gray concrete and glass. The stairs to the far left of a drab little area, which Otto supposed was the building's excuse for a lobby, were also concrete. They were flanked by a flimsy, metal railing whose spokes alternately bent in and bowed out in a pattern of deliberate destruction.

Otto had no idea whether the building had an elevator, but in light of its overall dilapidated condition, he was happy that Blue elected to walk. They opened the fire door off the third-floor landing. Cooking smells, mostly unpleasant, oozed out from under drab green doors along the one-tone gray corridor. The cheap industrial-quality carpet, meant to match the walls, failed by at least three shades.

Despite the building's mammoth proportions, not a single inhabitant was visible. No sounds either. Aside from the odors, it could have been deserted and condemned to be brought down by a wrecking ball within the next five minutes.

Otto's thumping heart echoed down the drab corridor. He could not believe that Blue didn't hear it; he expected the thin man to turn any second, place an elongated finger to his lips, and give him a monstrous "shush." But Blue continued walking, each long stride gobbling up twice the carpet that Otto could manage, head erect atop his swan's neck.

Suddenly, Otto hated Blue. So confident, sure, in control, while Otto could barely keep from wetting himself. Who had given Blue the right to rope him into this insanity? He was no spy, no hero, just someone who minded his own business and was good with a computer—that was all! How dare Blue trap him this way? Why, Otto had never even planned to stay in the United States. He never really felt at home, if the truth be known. It was only circumstances that had kept him there. His sick mother. A decent job. That sort of thing. Not love or desire. Nothing like that, so why should he be here risking his life for a country he didn't even care about? It was crazy.

Otto's palms were hot and cold at the same time. The nerves in his forehead were twisting, tightening, squeezing his temples. Clumps of his hair clotted to the perspiration on his forehead. He must run. Get out of here now, before it was too late.

Otto glanced this way and that, gently and carefully so that his tall captor wouldn't notice. Nothing. No exits except at each end of the interminable corridor. Too far. Too far. He'd never make it. Blue would have him in his sights. Blue had a gun. All these crazies did. And Blue would use it, without a second thought, before he'd gotten ten feet! Otto was shaking now. He was trapped. He was dead—

Rap ... Blue's knuckles against a sick-green door. A creak as it swung slightly open, another as it opened halfway. My dear God. My dear, dear God! It was too late! Otto's foot crossed over the jamb. He hadn't wanted it to; it just happened. Or maybe the light but purposeful shove from Blue had helped.

The apartment—for although tiny by Otto's standards, that is what it was—was furnished like the office of a starving accountant. Its living room was dominated by a massive oak table, scarred and gouged from age and misuse, set near a narrow window laced with dried trails of dirty rain. Three equally mistreated chairs, of what once might have been a larger set, sat at careless angles. Dividing the room approximately in half, and facing the table, was a shiny brown vinyl couch of newer vintage. Angling across its back like a jagged bolt of lightning was a large tear through which white stuffing escaped. A brass coat tree stood to the right of the door. Its arms were the trunks of intricately detailed elephant heads: a valuable antique, completely out of its element. No doubt an item confiscated by the KGB, speculated Otto.

A small man, smoking a long, thin cigarette of the type enjoyed by American women, stood near the window. Although his face was pinched into what Otto supposed was a welcoming smile, it looked more as if the man had just tasted spoiled milk.

A second man sat on the couch. A tiny halo of white scalp glowed from the center of his short brown hair as he propelled himself upward. His immensely broad shoulders were too large for his outdated black jacket. They tugged the material across his chest so taught that Otto was sure that one deep breath would rip the seams in two.

"Welcome, Charles."

So that's Blue's first name, thought Otto. *Very fitting. Yes, definitely a Charles, now that he thought of it. Forget that, Otto. Who cares?*

The small man's face pinched together even further. He gestured with the long cigarette toward two of the chairs, reaching for the third, himself. It scraped across the threadbare area rug as he spun it toward the table. "Please sit, gentlemen."

"Thank you, Nikolai." Blue—now Charles—walked toward the table, stopped, turned. "Come *on*, Clause," he said with a tight-lipped smile, "I want to introduce you." The soft eyes did not smile.

Otto edged forward.

"This is Clause, *my* expert. Clause Wertmueller … Colonel Nikolai Kharkov."

The little man drew in his face again, this time in a frown. His skin was extremely white. There were pink blotches under his eyes and near his chin. He was not at all Otto's idea of a Russian military man, who were all supposed to be hulking and robust. "You are German?" His voice was annoyingly high, like those of the stereotyped Natzi interrogators in grade B war movies.

"Only by birth. He's an American citizen working at one of our top research centers," Van Damme replied before Otto could respond.

"Ah." The Russian colonel's pinched frown transformed into his pinched smile. "And this is Sergei, *my* expert." He inclined his head toward the large man standing to his left.

Sergei's broad Slavic face betrayed nothing. Dead eyes staring, unblinking. He gave a curt nod.

That would by my idea of a Russian colonel, thought Otto.

"Charles"— Otto suddenly preferred that to their code names, because this wasn't a glorious game any longer and hadn't been since they left the Unter den Linden—motioned to Otto, saying, "Take the chair near the colonel. I'll sit back here since I'm not contributing anything." He walked to the couch, sat with a crunch of vinyl, sprawling long legs toward the others.

"You are too modest, Charles. You are a major contributor." Kharkov's laugh was positively shrill.

Charles (*What on earth is his last name?* Otto wondered in spite of himself) joined in. Inside jokes? Otto didn't like that. And the horrid Russian spoke better English than *he* did. Suddenly, Otto felt the outsider. The two men before him had much more in common with each other than with him. Otto wondered how the impassive Slav felt about it, if he was capable of feeling anything about anything, which Otto doubted. He looked at him standing there by his boss like a robot.

"Sit down, please, Clause." Charles's voice was pleasant enough, but Otto did not turn, did not want to see what Charles's eyes were saying. He sat. His wrist itched. He scratched. Now the other wrist. He scratched that one. Now the arms. He looked down. Red bumps were popping up, three on one arm, four, no five, on the other. Little things were moving on him. He pushed at one. It hopped high and away. Fleas. Oh my God, *the place was full of fleas*! Lord, what next? Otto sighed, scratched again, and gave up, his little shoulders sagging even farther than usual.

Kharkov stubbed out his cigarette on the table's edge and had another in his mouth simultaneously. He pulled out a pair of thick gold-rimmed reading glasses, arranged them over his hawkish nose, and stared at Otto.

And Otto stared right back at the Colonel—well, not exactly "back." Lower, actually, toward Kharkov's highly buffed designer shoes. Otto took the opportunity to study Kharkov's apparel, which fit much better than Sergei's and was infinitely more stylish: blue blazer, pale blue shirt, gray slacks, and expensive-looking black loafers. That was a surprise. Kharkov looked much more like the lace-up type.

"*Clause!*" Charles's voice broke in, a trifle less patient this time. "I think that Colonel Kharkov would like to see Indigo now."

Otto sighed, laying his precious leather case on the worn table. He fumbled with the snap, which he could normally disengage in his sleep, finally clicking it open, practically ripping Indigo's first page in his attempt to make up for the time lost. The sheets rattled noisily in Otto's shaking hands before he finally managed to flatten the first three in front of him.

The big man, Sergei, came up behind Otto, peering down, imprisoning Otto between his bulk and the massive table.

"Th-this is … the …" Otto could not recall how he got through the first page of preliminary specifications and materials, but somehow, he did. The giant grunted deeply and frequently, disconcerting Otto so that he had to retrace his thoughts constantly. Things got even worse when the giant needed a clarification. He would lean, crushing Otto against the table. But that wasn't the worst of it. Sergei had horrendous body odor. Still, Otto was surprised to find that Sergei asked very insightful questions, probing questions. Positively *interesting* questions.

Amazingly, by page four, Otto was actually enjoying himself, relishing Sergei's reactions to the laser applications; to Indigo's ability to pinpoint the most insignificant land target; to the speed with which it could hone in and lock on, despite the most adverse atmospheric conditions. By sharing his knowledge with Sergei, Otto found that he had fallen in love with the ingeniousness of Indigo II all over again. It was truly a scientific breakthrough.

Otto almost wished that he could pull the last two pages out and really dazzle Sergei, but that would never happen. It was not the plan, and as Otto's adrenaline pumped, he knew—absolutely knew—that everything was going along 100 percent according to plan, Charles's plan. (Otto would find out his last name when this was over. Certainly they had been through enough to trust each other that much.) Charles had been right. Charles knew his business so well. How could he have doubted a professional like Charles? How could he have been frightened like a little baby? No wonder Charles was treating Otto the way he was: hard and cold. It was the only way that Charles could get him through this. Charles knew that. Charles was going to bring him through this easily! It was all Otto could do to keep from turning back toward Charles and giving him a big wink.

Ten more minutes and Otto looked up, settling his chubby arms over his little chest. He arched his back against the firm chair, looking first at Kharkov, then back toward Charles, searching for a sign, a hint of admiration from the tall man. Charles's delicate face was blank, impassive. He scrutinized his fingernails, giving no indication that he was aware that Otto had finished.

That's why Charles was so good. Otto had to hand it to him. No nerves. Still, when would Charles ask? It was time for him to ask so that shortly thereafter, the door would fly open and Charles's men would charge through, capturing the Russians and the plans for their missile and, most important, ending this nightmare so Otto could go home.

"Isn't there something more?"

It took a moment to register. The Russian Colonel asked for "something more." Otto pretended not to hear.

"I beg your pardon, uh … Clause … but wasn't there another facet to Indigo II? For instance, doesn't it have a new type of interlocking optic system that allows closer viewing than current systems?"

"N-no. That's it." Otto tried a smile, but his lips twitched instead.

"A missile targeting capacity?" Kharkov's smile compacted his features until they were mostly indistinguishable. His screechy voice remained scrupulously polite.

"Uh …" How could Otto keep ignoring the Colonel? Why was Charles just sitting there? Why didn't he ask for their plans for the Amphora missile? That's what he should be asking for. Otto's job was done. He had given the Russians a rudimentary briefing on Indigo to wet their appetites. They were now supposed to reciprocate with a similar synopsis of Amphora so the CIA people could rush in and steal their plans and Otto could leave this wretched place and go home to wonderful California so that maybe, if he ever felt safe again—six months, or a year, or ten years from now—he could stop torturing himself about what *really* happened to Ralph Jackson and, even worse, *why*? So for God's sake, why didn't Charles whatever-his-last-name-was say, "Okay, Russians. Now it's your turn? What have you got?"

Silence. All eyes on him.

Otto looked from Kharkov to Charles. Charles to Kharkov. Finally, just Charles. Otto's sweating hands were sticky. He barely breathed …

"Show them the rest."

What? Otto screamed inside himself. *What are you saying?* Was this a trick? Had Charles really said that? His stomach clenched like a fist. His right fingers tore anxiously at his left fingers. He felt as if he hadn't breathed in minutes.

"*Show* them the rest, Clause."

No question: Charles *had* said it. The thin lips had moved, and the deep voice had spoken calmly, quietly, assuredly.

"But …"

"Our friends are entitled to *all* of our information." So maddeningly calm, so reasonable …

"We can't expect theirs without giving them *all* of ours," Charles continued in the same placid tone.

My God! My God! What was he fighting for? The Russians wanted the plans; Charles wanted Otto to give them the plans. At least, it looked as if he wanted Otto to give them the plans. Otto didn't know anymore; he didn't have any idea what was going on. God, it just wasn't fair. He didn't know *what* to do. Look at Charles, sitting there like a Buddha, staring back at him. Otto fumbled with the clasp, dragged out the final two sheets, and dropped them upon the others.

Sergei tugged off his jacket, threw it toward the end of the table, and leaned over Otto again. The odor was too much for Otto. He pushed his chair back and managed to rise before Sergei engulfed him. With a weak smile, he stretched, walking to the far side of the table. His knees wobbled. He rested a shaking hand on the solid wood to hold himself upright.

"This is the Caretaker System," Otto began. "It picks up the frequencies of pre-launched missiles and guides them to laser-identified targets." To him, his voice sounded as if it were pouring through wadded cotton.

Twenty minutes later, Sergei grunted and walked toward where Kharkov sat smoking. Both spoke in Russian, nodding, shrugging, and frequently gesturing toward either Otto or the section of table where the Indigo plans sprawled.

Otto snuck occasional looks at Charles. The gaunt man stared straight ahead, acknowledging neither him nor the Russians.

The Russians' guttural conversation halted abruptly. Kharkov's chair tore at the disintegrating rug as he shoved it back. Otto could actually hear its frayed fibers snapping in the deathly quiet room. The colonel rose, removing his thick-lensed glasses with effeminate delicacy. Otto couldn't help wondering why Kharkov had bothered to wear them. Sergei had done all the reading. All Kharkov had done was blow globs of smoke in their direction as they tried to concentrate.

Kharkov stared at Otto. His watery gray eyes blinked back the smoke from a fresh cigarette. Otto's breath, already short, stuck somewhere between his lungs and the lower part of his neck. His eyes dropped, and he began studying his hands as if he had never seen them before. Finally, he swallowed and looked up, but now Kharkov's eyes were on Charles.

Charles returned Kharkov's gaze, unblinking, hands loose in his lap, as relaxed as if he had just slipped off a massage table.

Silence.

Suddenly, Kharkov smiled, forcing the cigarette in his teeth toward the ceiling. "Sergei says that everything is completely in order. Sorry for the extensive review, Charles. I hope that it did not inconvenience you." His apology in no way extended to Otto. That was quite clear.

"Not at all, Nikolai. You have to be sure we aren't putting one over on you, we sneaky Americans."

Kharkov tensed, searching the aesthetic face of Van Damme. Suddenly, he convulsed with laughter, his peculiar screech bounding across the sparse room. "Oh, Charles, you Americans with your sarcasm. They never could teach us that in our courses at the institute." He shook his head, still snickering. "We would all have been discovered within our first week of deep cover, if they had ever actually sent us over to America, all because we didn't laugh when we should and did laugh when we shouldn't."

Charles smiled back. "It wouldn't have even taken that long, Nikolai. We knew about your deep cover training, and the names of all its participants, two weeks after it started. You wouldn't have even gotten out of Canada."

Kharkov's laughter sputtered and died. His face reverse pinched into a frown. "Yes. Well, on to business." He walked toward a corner of the rug and tugged upward, revealing a dusty section of floor. The KGB colonel squatted and, forming a diminutive fist, pounded its edge against the wood. *Thwack.* A one-foot square section of floor popped up. Kharkov shoved his jacket sleeve up, reached into the hole, and removed a plain red office folder. As Kharkov rose, his knees gave a loud creak. Crimson-faced, he stalked to the table and threw the folder down. Sometime during his journey, his cramped smile had resurfaced.

"Our side of the agreement, Charles. The plans for Amphora. Your man may verify them now." He looked at Otto. "Ask whatever questions you have. Sergei's English is not as good as mine is, so if you don't understand something, I will translate Sergei's answers. Take all the time that you need."

Kharkov jammed out his latest cigarette on the table's surface, leaving a circle of smoking ashes. He whisked them to the floor with a flick of his hand and crushed out their glowing residue with his heel. "We used to be able to get all the army tanks that we wanted, but never ashtrays." Kharkov waved Otto back to his chair. "A little background, in case Charles hasn't filled you in." He waited for neither conformation nor denial. "Amphora is a cluster missile, which means that it has the capability of splintering into upward of forty minor—no, mini-missiles—if it senses the heat or motion of an alien object before it reaches its target. In other words, anything sent to neutralize it will cause it to multiply. Its sensory range is approximately three hundred yards, as I understand. You will no doubt find the exact distance somewhere in this file."

Kharkov dug into his jacket and produced another cigarette. He looked surprised that Otto had not yet opened the red folder by the time that he had lighted up. "You may begin *anytime* that you wish." Kharkov's face squeezed into his odd smile as he turned toward the CIA man. "Now *that* was good sarcasm. I think so, don't you, Charles?"

Five minutes into it and Otto was totally enthralled. The propulsion system was at least the equal of American technology, although the heat-triggering device was definitely cruder. Sergei, with Kharkov's aid, gave meticulous descriptions of the operational factors. In less than a half hour, Otto felt sufficiently confident of his working knowledge to assure Charles that the plans were not only authentic but complete.

"You're sure?" Charles's voice was coarse from his long silence. "You are *absolutely* sure?" *You'd better be,* was the clear implication.

Otto followed his index finger slowly, carefully, across all four pages of circles, lines, and numbers, top to bottom. "Yess."

"Thank you, Nikolai." Charles yanked his long legs in so that he sat upright on the couch. "And thank *you*, Sergei." He saluted the big man who stood next to Kharkov's chair.

Kharkov muttered in Russian. Sergei stepped forward and half-bowed toward Charles, which was precisely when Kharkov shot him. The previously impassive face contorted, the large hands groped for the heavy table, slid off its edge, the heavy head smacking its wooden surface with a hollow crack. A second *pfft* from Kharkov's silenced gun slapped Sergei sidewise onto the floor. A whistling came from either the large hole in Sergei's chest or his nose. Otto was too terrified to analyze where. It stopped abruptly as blood bubbled from Sergei's mouth.

Otto gaped, then gaped wider, shaking his head back, forth, back, forth. "No. No. No," flooded from his mouth in a monotonous stream. At least he supposed that it was coming from him, because neither Kharkov nor Charles was saying anything.

They stared at him.

Otto would have likened the two men to scientists contemplating a rat that had been hopelessly stymied by its maze—if his mind had been clear enough to draw such analogies—however, at this instant, Otto's mind was a bowl of oatmeal.

He could not tell how long he had remained in this comatose state, but it could not have been too long because when he revived, the others were in their same positions: Charles leaning forward on the couch and the colonel sitting stiffly in his straight-backed chair, with his gun loosely cradled in his right palm.

Ralph Jackson's image slapped into Otto's brain. Unfortunately, Otto now knew *exactly* what had happened to Ralph. And he fervently wished that he hadn't acquired this knowledge so suddenly or with such certainty. Otto's lip vibrated as a major tremor passed through it. Then again. Then a spot on Otto's temple joined in. He blinked at Charles through watering eyes.

The gaunt man sat bolt upright on the couch, searching out Otto's befogged stare. He slicked back his perfectly arranged hair with his right hand and then drew his fingers along his mustache, downward, until they cradled his chin. "There have been a few changes. The cavalry won't be charging in." Charles's eyebrows arched high as he flashed a remorseful smile.

Otto found his voice. "Vot ahr you doing? Vot in Gott's name are you doing?"

"Let *me* explain, Charles." Kharkov sounded more like an overeager student than a KGB colonel.

"Be my guest." The CIA man reclined with a wave of his palm.

The Colonel carefully folded his unused glasses, slipped them into his jacket, simultaneously removing his tenth cigarette of the session. He frowned at it, lighted it anyway, gazing at its upward spiraling smoke as he spoke. "Both Charles and I believe that our nations must maintain strong intelligence." Kharkov used his cigarette to gesture toward the documents in front of him, dissipating the lazy spiral of smoke into erratic fragments. "Take these weapons, for instance: Amphora and Indigo. Both of our countries are obviously still producing devastating weapons of war. With all the changes, *nothing* has changed." Kharkov puffed, looking toward Van Damme for agreement.

The thin man nodded on cue.

"Those currently in charge don't agree. They play at politics, endangering our security while they indulge their sentimental fantasies. Charles and I will use these"—Kharkov again jabbed his cigarette toward the plans—"to prove to our countrymen that preparedness is the only security ... and that neither of our present leaders are inclined to provide it." Kharkov rose. He circled the table from the opposite direction from Sergei's pooling blood, hopping up to sit on it directly in front of Otto so that his heavy breath tickled the sparse hair of Otto's scalp. Kharkov tugged his sharply creased trousers up at the knees, inadvertently drawing his gun level with Otto's eyes.

Otto froze. The gun was short and compact. Although Otto understood its technical operation, he still found it amazing that one discharge from the meager instrument could fell a monster like Sergei.

"Pragmatists such as Charles and I know that lasting peace between our nations is impossible. Someone will gain the advantage and use it against the other. It is the world's history." Kharkov's gun rose and fell as he emphasized each point.

Otto's eyes became transfixed by the dark hole in its weaving barrel. It was like staring into a cobra's mouth.

. "Only strong intelligence can prevent one side from being taken by surprise, and strong intelligence requires strong leaders. Men like Charles … and our General Yermakov."

Kharkov stared at Otto, trying to determine what? Otto wrenched his own eyes from the cobra's mouth/gun, hoping to take his cue from the man. Did Kharkov expect understanding? Admiration? Whatever those chilling gray eyes wanted, Otto would give. Whether or not it would do him any good … Well, better not to think that far ahead.

"Yes. The Colonel's eyes blazed down at him. "*Strong* people!"

Otto finally worked up the nerve to break eye contact and turn toward Charles. Charles's patrician face was clear and untroubled.

Kharkov dashed Otto's waning hopes. "Charles agrees. Totally. In fact, *he* contacted me. I was suspicious, I will admit, but after a series of tests— he gave me the first page of the Indigo plans months ago—I realized that he was a …" Kharkov's flexible countenance screwed together as he fought to recall the word. "Yes, a *kindred* spirit." Kharkov bestowed his prune-like smile upon Charles while enthusiastically wielding his gun before Otto's nose. "After that, there was … uhh … no stopping us."

Kharkov took a long, deep puff. The smoke from his nostrils and mouth poured down upon Otto's upturned face. Otto stabbed at his eyes with a shaking hand, but the KGB man did not notice. His eyes were locked above Otto's head as he recalled machinations that the lowly scientist could not possibly fathom.

"We devised a plan with two 'spies.' You and …" Kharkov flicked his cigarette hand over the table's edge. Otto had no doubt that he was referring to the two large soles protruding from beneath. "Charles will make Amphora public knowledge in your country, proving that, despite my nation's hardships, we are still your enemy. America's propensity toward paranoia will force its leaders to appropriate massive funds for intelligence—"

"Who zays zat vill be enough to change everyzing?" The interruption shocked Otto as much as Kharkov. How had he had the nerve? Otto gaped up at the Russian, wringing his perspiring hands as he awaited the consequences of his impetuousness.

The gray eyes crackled fire down upon him. Then, unbelievably, the Russian smiled. "A very good point. We anticipated that this still might not be sufficient provocation, so we have arranged for your defection as an additional incentive."

Otto's hands stopped twisting. "I didn't def—"

"Oh, but you did. You did. Two days ago. That's right, isn't it, Charles? Certain items were placed in your apartment. Notations on airline flights to Berlin on a writing pad from your company. Also, a business card from an insurance agent who is suspected of being one of our people by both the CIA and FBI. The man actually is KGB and has just been recalled. Since no one must ever challenge the credibility of your defection"— Kharkov shrugged indifferently—"he is about to have a fatal accident on his new assignment." With each point, Kharkov leaned closer, pinning Otto back against his chair. "Lastly, a page of the Indigo II plans will be found under your mattress. Not very bright of you, I must say." Kharkov tsk-tsked not eight inches from Otto's face. His tobacco breath made Otto wince. Kharkov reacted, pulling back and glaring. His voice was sharper now, strident even by comparison to its normally abrasive pitch. Kharkov obviously wanted this over.

Otto cursed himself for antagonizing the man. In the next instant, he realized how little that mattered.

"You are well-known for your anti-Russian sentiment, I understand. Some people may wonder why you would defect to us, but not many. You have no friends. Most of your family is dead or too old to be credible. When the evidence is found—ah, yes, I forgot to tell you: there will also be a sizable amount of unexplained money passing in and out of your bank account—the consensus of opinion will be that you were cleverer than anyone could have guessed at concealing your true motives."

Inadvertently, Kharkov pulled closer again, then, appearing to remember Otto's reaction to his breath, he jerked stiffly back. "How do you think the American public will react when only three weeks after they learn that we are developing the Amphora missile, Russia steals—right there from the heart of their beloved California—the most spectacular innovation in military satellite technology since its invention? "You will actually be seen in Russia very shortly. Ah, wrong word … *Briefly*, I mean, as my leader, Alexi Yermakov, breaks the news about US production of Indigo. The Russian people will become as outraged as the Americans were about our Amphora missile. They will get even angrier when American agents kill you in transit to Moscow. That, and the CIA's theft of Amphora." Kharkov frowned at Otto.

Otto hunched his shoulders as Kharkov's gun rose toward his face.

"You stupid man, why do you look so confused? How do you think that I shall report this incident? Think!" Kharkov peered down into Otto's face and then shook his head as he went *phuuuh* with his taught lips. "I will say that I arrived slightly too late to prevent Sergei from selling state secrets to the CIA. Had my reform-minded superiors provided me with sufficient support, I would have been able to save Amphora as well as killing"—he pointed the muzzle of his gun toward the corpse beneath the table—"this traitor. Believe me, anti-American sentiment will hit new heights in the next few months, and General Yermakov will sweep these wretched reformers from power. Then, if all goes well, I could become head of my organization or even minister of the interior."

Kharkov settled back, arms crossed, momentarily engrossed in the contemplation of his bright future. His forgotten gun drifted toward the ceiling. The Russian regained his concentration, fixing his gaze and weapon back upon Otto. "Of course, Charles too will benefit from the laxity of his superiors, who allowed Indigo to be compromised. In fact, I should think that there will be a new CIA leader before too long." Kharkov looked up over Otto toward the couch and asked with his prune-like smile, "Have I got it right, Charles?"

"Almost, but not quite." A difference in Charles's tone. Lower. The voice very, very quiet.

Otto was about to turn when he was riveted by the dramatic change in Kharkov's expression. The creeping smile melted; every facet of the cramped little face drooped. In opposition to the sagging of his body, Kharkov's gun hand jerked frantically upward.

The *pfft* came from Otto's left. This time he understood what the sound portended. He was not in the least surprised when the right side of the Russian's blazer erupted in red, nor when Kharkov's ascending gun spilt from his rigid fingers and flopped on the carpet.

"You think I don't have … security … people here? You … think I am … that … stupid?" Kharkov's voice came out in hoarse spurts between his rasping breaths. His left arm hugged his oozing right side, his entire body slumping in that same direction.

"Not stupid, but certainly a trifle naive." The CIA man was rising now, his silenced weapon, far longer than Kharkov's, pointed directly at the wounded man's middle.

Two shots rang out from beyond the closed front door. Two seconds later … another shot.

Silence.

"I suspect that you don't have security men anymore, Nikolai." Charles shook his head as a mocking smile engulfed his chiseled features. He approached the table, brushing by Otto without acknowledgment.

The Russian listed severely toward his right, propped on a spasmodic elbow.

"Didn't it occur to you that I could get what I wanted without giving up Indigo? Why would I give your miserable government such an edge?"

The Russian's elbow gave out. He flopped over on his side so that the thin man had to bend over him, his voice rising, competing with the Russian's jagged breathing. "I'll have it all. That's the best way, isn't it?" Van Damme skidded Kharkov along the table, out of the way, and scooped up the papers. They crackled crisply as he crushed them together. "Capturing Amphora plus thwarting the theft of Indigo. Not a bad day's work, is it, Nikolai? Of course, I'll have to space them out and pretend that they were separate operations. Even I would be suspect if two such intelligence coups happened simultaneously … don't you agree?"

Charles had dropped his voice, but Otto heard him just as clearly. He realized why: Charles no longer had to compete with the KGB Colonel's breathing.

Charles lifted Kharkov's wrist, concentrated a moment, shrugged as he dropped it. Kharkov's limp hand hit the table with a thump. "Not much of an audience," Charles reflected. He frowned down at Otto, as if noticing him for the first time, and walked past Otto's chair and toward the front door without a word.

"So z-zat … vas how ve do it?" Suddenly, Otto was alive again, his breath, ignored during the drama, coming in gasps. "I vish you voot haf told me vat to expect. This vas really qvite frightening. But very eggzciting. Yess. Uff courze, zeeing men kilt—zat iss not zomething I vant to zee again."

Otto couldn't stop talking. Bolts of electricity were rolling up and down his nerves. Relief. Yes. Relief after such fear. It was all going to turn out right. After all. Charles planned it. Should have told him, though—not fair to put him through all this—but so what. So what! Everything would be all right now, except … what was that the KGB murderer had said? Russian "security people." *Oh my God! Right outside the door. Oh my God! And Charles was going to the door; not just going toward it but stalking toward it. Don't!* God, he was *opening* the door—*wait!*—Otto threw up his hands, mouthing the word that he was too paralyzed to voice. Then he shut his mouth, watching, hugging his shaking hands. Charles knew. Charles knew everything. He planned for everything. When would Otto learn? The man walking into the room with the gun in his hand was American. Charles had his *own* security! Charles knew everything. *Just relax, Otto, you idiot, and leave it all up to Charles.*

"Mightn't a silencer have been more appropriate, Millstein?" Charles said softly to an older man, who looked more to Otto like a shoe salesman than someone who might have just killed a host of Russian agents. Charles turned his back on the man before he could reply.

"I didn't have time to find it." The gravelly voice was defensive. "You left for here earlier than you said you would."

"I paid for that mistake, Millstein. I had to sit through that KGB egomaniac's life story until it was time for you and Dahlvans to move in. Has Dahlvans secured the lobby?"

"No, Mr. Van Damme. One of the Russians got in a lucky shot—"

"Dead?"

The older man nodded.

So *that* was Charles's name: Van Damme. Otto was too overwhelmed by his discovery to dwell on poor Dahlvans. Yes. That fit perfectly. "Charles Van Damme." So very right. A name, a man that Otto wouldn't ever forget. No, Otto chuckled to himself, he certainly wouldn't. *Shush now. Listen. Memorize everything that happens here so you can remember during those boring, boring years ahead—thank God for them. I couldn't take this every day, but shush now, so you can remember—*

"Suppose there were others?" Charles Van Damme shot back over his shoulder. "That gun of yours would have brought them running from blocks away, Millstein."

"Nah. They're more short-staffed than we are." The older man's voice was stronger now, more confident. "Anyway, the opposition didn't exactly authorize Kharkov to have this meet, so he wasn't exactly in the position to requisition an army—"

"All right, all right." Charles Van Damme waved off the other's comments before turning back to face him. He shot a thumb in Otto's direction. "He goes to the safe house." Van Damme quickly reviewed the sets of plans, rolling each page as he spoke. "Things will settle down in a couple of weeks. Take the car I left here yesterday. Leave right away. Talk to you soon."

Otto stopped Charles Van Damme midway through the door. "Vait, I vant to come—"

"You can't." Charles Van Damme's thin lips curved painfully upward in a transparently false smile.

"Vy not? I vant to be done viz zis." Otto waved stubby fingers at the room, tears in his eyes. The stench of death—there really was such a thing, not just an author's fancy—was creeping into his pores like noxious gas.

"Too dangerous. KGB will be all over—"

"Vant to go home ..."

"Trust me." Van Damme's smile was a plaster mask, cracking instantly as he turned and rushed out the door.

"Let's go, Otto." Millstein barked in a gravelly voice that sounded as if he wasn't well and wanted to be done with this and everyone involved. That frightened Otto. Maybe that was why his puffy face was so sour. And maybe that was why he wore that filthy, heavy raincoat in this summer heat. The man's red-veined eyes shot through Otto as if he weren't even here. That also frightened Otto.

Suddenly, Otto thought back to the evidence in his apartment. And the manipulation of his bank account. And Charles Van Damme's bragging to the dying Kharkov of how neatly Otto's upcoming defection was going to fit into his plans. Fear, much worse than any he had experienced in the last horrible hour, tugged at Otto's organs. He wasn't ever going back home! Moisture seeped down his right leg. *Gott, I've wet my pants,* Otto observed dejectedly. Weighed down by this ultimate humiliation, Otto shuffled out as the man in the shabby raincoat motioned toward the door with that enormous gun.

CHAPTER 22

Almost three hours to the minute before Charles Van Damme shot Nicolai Kharkov, Arnie Rosen watched him exit the Kempinski from a strategically located seat at the next-door café. Rosen exhaled from between pursed lips, thankful that he hadn't missed Van Damme in the swell of pedestrians parading past the Kempinski.

Van Damme planted himself squarely on the sidewalk, probably defying the human river pouring by to muss one strand of his hair. Rosen marveled. Not one scurrying passerby even noticed the towering man whom Rosen had vowed to destroy. They had their own concerns: where the best prices were for fall sweaters; what to have for lunch, meat or fish; whether to take that new job in Bonne. Every one of them wrapped up in his own world. A few might be mildly interested had they known they trod the stage of this deadly drama. Might even be sufficiently intrigued to mention it during cocktails. But even they would push it aside as newer tragedies lit their TV screens. *How alone we all are,* thought Rosen. *How many people would care about what happened to me as much as if their home teams lost the play-offs?*

A chubby figure clutching a blond leather briefcase hurried from the hotel and burrowed through the crowd until he was abreast of Van Damme. Together they melted into the pedestrian flow.

This must be it, thought Rosen. The shorter man wore baggy pants with one pocket hanging out and had hair that looked as if he'd just stuck his finger in an electric socket. Not to mention a thick plaid shirt that was much too hot for a day like this. He had to be a researcher or scientist, the sort of person that Van Damme would need if he were authenticating something complex and detailed to the KGB. Like plans.

Rosen laid his *European Herald Tribune* on the table and overtipped the waiter, who had never become too discouraged to stop in front of

Rosen's three-hour-old bottle of mineral water every fifteen minutes and ask, "Would Mein Herr like anyzing else?"

Rosen's initial instinct was to stay close behind so that he wouldn't lose them. Still … following Van Damme too closely had its drawbacks. Last night at the citadel, for example. "Fool me once, shame on you. Fool me twice, shame on me" … and all that.

Sure enough, a frumpy-looking guy shouldered his way into a group of well-dressed women as he hurried after the pair. The women—middle aged but well-preserved, with nice calves and strong behinds—stopped to glare at the stubble-bearded man who had brushed their high-styled suits with his stained raincoat. He ran their gauntlet, unfazed, concentrating only upon the tall and rather short man up ahead.

Rosen frowned. Certainly not the quality of a Werner. Was Van Damme running out of good help? Still, Papa had always told him that some of the best operatives were the old warhorses. It was a tough life, and it took a lot out of the field men, Marquand said. Only the best ones managed to reach old age. If that were so, this guy had to be good—better remember that!

Rosen rose hesitantly, still unsure what to do. What if Van Damme had put a tail on the tail, ahead of him? Yet he couldn't afford to find out without losing them in the crowds. He was up and moving. Pungent people odors mingled with stale auto fumes. He brushed the back of his hand over the .45. He had become so used to it by now that he was immune to its pressure and had to check regularly.

The shabby man shuffled his way north toward the S-Bahn. Wonderful. Beautiful. Less crowded now and easier to follow the wrinkled raincoat, even catch glimpses of Van Damme's lofty head thirty yards past the tail's slouching shoulders. Bus coming. Had to speed it up a little. The two in the lead were already in position to climb in, but the frumpy man was still sixty feet from the short queue. Suddenly, Van Damme's tail stopped. Just stopped.

Fuck, no! He's not getting on. "Another trap" flashed in pink neon letters across Rosen's mind. Had he been following too closely? *Idiot. Dumbbell! They saw you. Anyone would have.*

Rosen spun, half expecting a team of goons to be converging on him; grabbing him; hustling him off, feet dragging, to the Landwehrkanal; laughing at how old Werner must have really slipped to let an idiot like this get the best of him at the citadel; still chuckling as they launched Rosen headfirst at piles of rough debris bobbing upon the canal's scummy surface.

Nothing.

No one threatening behind him. Unless you wanted to count a spindly old woman walking a short-legged dog with fading fur. Or two early teens, blond as the sun, accelerating hand in hand toward Van Damme's bus.

Rosen turned forward. *What do I do? Go around him and get caught between him and Van Damme like I did last night? Or wait and lose them? Suppose the guy in the raincoat isn't following them any farther? Suppose someone else picks them up when they leave the bus?*

Rosen swiveled right, left. Just a broad stretch, flooded in midmorning sunlight that highlighted sprinklings of ash soot filtering down out of the high wind currents from the unscreened factory chimneys to the east. There was no way around without revealing himself to the man in the raincoat.

Rosen dug his nails into his moist palms. They were stepping into the bus. Only a few more people and then it would roar off into traffic. One or two more stops and it would pass the former site of the Wall …

One or two more stops! Could he get on ahead? Crazy. No way. Unless he could outrun a bus. Forget it. Take out the man ahead … How 'bout that? Without a scene? Without Van Damme seeing? No way. Great. Van Damme had just sat down near the window, within easy view of his man. Was that a look Van Damme gave the tail? Had the sloppy guy nodded back? Was he turning toward Rosen? Rosen looked away, studying the mutually tottering progress of the old woman and her old dog. He couldn't help thinking that whichever one died first, the survivor would soon follow.

He turned halfway back, shielding his face with his hand. Van Damme was facing away, undoubtedly talking to the little man, and the one in the raincoat apparently didn't know Rosen existed. He had to make his move now. Rosen started toward the tail. The man was about five-eleven, slightly shorter than Rosen but considerably wider. Rosen's right hand snaked toward his back and into the windbreaker. His fingertips brushed the .45. Thirty feet left. Twenty. No! The shiny door slapped shut. With a monster cough, the bus rocked away from the curb.

Shit! Shit! Rosen sped toward the crumpled raincoat, wanting to smear it red, stomp it into the sidewalk, hear its wearer groan and grunt. He was being stupid, knew it, but didn't care. This guy had ruined it for him, after all this. Goddammit, he didn't care! Ten feet away …

The raincoat began moving. Away from him—won't do you any good, buddy—and toward another bus! Right behind the first one. It reminded Rosen of New York, where you waited and waited on Fifth Avenue, then five busses would pop up all in a row. *So the efficient Germans aren't any more efficient than the inefficient New Yorkers, when it comes to busses, huh?* thought Rosen. *Bad for Berliners; good for me.*

The raincoat scrambled up. A few stragglers followed. *Hurry, the doors are already closing! The driver's probably pissed off that he had to pick up anyone at all. I guess the second bus is supposed to have the easy trip.*

Sure enough, the driver shot Rosen a resentful look as he forced himself through the half-closed doors. Rosen smiled in return. The bus lurched forward, Rosen lunging for a pole to keep from hurtling down the aisle. *Bus drivers always win,* he thought.

Raincoat had a little better luck. He staggered against a bulky man in smeared work jeans before toppling into an empty seat. Averting his head, Rosen hurried past, finding a seat on the same side, three rows behind. Raincoat slouched down so far that his thinning salt-and-pepper hair disappeared beneath the seatback.

Rosen was positive that the tail had not made him. Through the broad front window, Rosen watched Van Damme's bus shimmy around a curve toward the Bahnhof Zoo stop. Ten minutes later, Van Damme and the short man disembarked at Friedrickstrasse.

Despite knowing, rationally, that East Berlin had ceased to exist, it was emotionally incomprehensible to Rosen that Van Damme and his companion could just get off the bus and go about their business. No armed guards pored over their travel documents; no dogs yanked at their chains, trying to tear into them; no jeeps blocked their way. And most amazing of all, no Wall.

The man in the raincoat took his time, letting the other passengers disembark first. He allowed four men in overalls; two executive types; one knockout blonde; and two elderly women in shawls, which had seen better days, line up to leave before wearily rising.

Rosen let two more passengers slip in between Raincoat and himself. Where the hell would Van Damme be by the time this lumbering clod got moving? Rosen gnawed his lip, forgetting about the false mustache. He tested it with his finger. It hadn't slipped.

Raincoat lolled his way forward, maddeningly slow. He appeared to have no interest whatsoever in keeping track of the pair ahead.

Rosen ducked to peek out the window. Van Damme and the short one were disappearing behind the buildings of Friedrickstrasse. He slammed his right fist against the seat back. What the hell was this guy waiting for? Raincoat finally clambered down, reached into his pocket, and pulled out a chocolate bar. Its foil glinted harsh sunlight as he ceremoniously peeled the wrapper.

The bastard had all the time in the world. What the hell was going on? Suppose this was the end of Raincoat's tail? Suppose another tail was picking them up on the Friedrickstrasse? Rosen's forehead was sticky. He swiped at it. Couldn't wait any longer. Rosen veered right to distance himself from Raincoat, darted past, shooting a quick look back at the man. Raincoat was engrossed in the remains of his chocolate bar, chewing slowly and deliberately, oblivious to Rosen, Van Damme, and the world. Was it possible that Raincoat's shift was over? Or was he just good—waiting for Rosen to move ahead so that he would be trapped between Raincoat and Van Damme?

Rosen forced himself to walk, not turning until he was around the corner, peering back from behind a stark concrete building. Now Raincoat was feeding the scrubby gray pigeons that waddled and pecked their way across the plaza. Soon word had gone out, and every pigeon in the area was bouncing and bobbing toward Raincoat. They circled and clucked for his largess while he stood in their midst, arms extended, like a messiah bestowing a silent benediction upon his followers. Whatever was happening, Raincoat was out of the play.

Rosen shoved himself from the cool concrete, squinting into the bright sunlight flashing off of the building's plain white surface. There, crossing the street, a block, maybe more, Van Damme's tall figure followed by the bouncy round one whose little legs pumped to keep up. Rosen gained on them, no more than 120 feet away by the time they hit the green expanse of Unter den Linden.

Twice Rosen darted into doorways, peering back, scanning the street for the man in the raincoat. He zipped around a corner for a third look. Nothing. The man was not following. He'd bet his life on it. Frowning at his unintended irony, Rosen resumed his pursuit.

*　*　*

An hour later. A whole goddamn hour later and what? A walking tour. A walking tour with the little guy jumping around like a kid at an amusement park and Van Damme acting like his daddy. The only difference was that the little guy hadn't dragged the chief of the European Division off to buy him an ice cream—yet.

Rosen sat on a bench under the lime or chestnut trees, whatever they were, glaring at the ridiculous-looking pair. After cracking every knuckle for at least the third time, he was seriously considering sneaking up as they approached that Soviet War Memorial and shooting Van Damme—on the hour—in honor of the historical now-defunct "changing of the guard," performed by the East Germans religiously during the occupation.

Still, what was in that case the little guy was squeezing for all he was worth? It couldn't just be a picnic lunch. Rosen had to be right. This was what he'd been waiting for, and he *knew* it. That case contained the plans that the traitor was going to sell to the KGB for money—or narcotics or whatever his payoff was. Maybe a commission in the KGB. Who knew? *Just wait a little longer,* he told himself. *You're right on the verge of bringing that stiff-necked bastard down.*

Rosen stared at nothing in particular for a long moment before pulling a crumpled pack of Juicy Fruit from the windbreaker. He fiddled with the foil wrapper, extracted one slightly stale piece, and chewed it slowly, letting the sudden sweetness seep over his tongue to the farthest corners of his mouth. Nope. Van Damme would still die as planned. This had to come out right. He would wait....

And wait …

And wait …

His watch. Van Damme was looking at his watch and talking seriously to the little guy. Rosen leaned against Friedrich's statue with its stone cool against his warm cheek. They were coming straight across. No more aimless meandering now. They cut in front of the westbound traffic under the center island's first row of trees, then the next, then across the eastbound lanes toward a cluster of faceless concrete high-rises.

Rosen crossed, spitting out the gum as he hit the south side of Friedrichstraße. The two were really moving. Had the infallible Van Damme killed too much time? Was his planning off? Was he running late? Good. Rosen prayed that Van Damme's stomach was knotting up right this minute. Let the stomach acid pour, God. Make it burn.

They hustled past the twin cathedrals. The little guy slowed down as if he wanted to look, but Van Damme bent down and said something.

They kept moving. Rosen detected a change in the little guy; his enthusiasm was gone. Something was happening, as he wasn't bouncing anymore. "Dragging" was more like it. His shoulders, although nothing much to start with, were scrunched in more now, making him look like a walking pear. What was happening? Was the little scientist getting wind of things? Had Van Damme given him another story and only now confessed the truth? Or was he getting cold feet? God, Rosen would have loved to be up there listening.

They took a quick right at the next corner. Rosen speeded up now that they were out of sight, cutting across the street so that he could backtrack to the corner and peek around before committing himself.

There they were, staring up at a tall building close to his corner. He pulled back then and inched forward so that he could see with his left eye. The little guy was really not into this. His back was stiff, and his shoulders pointed away from the building toward the street. His round face was frozen with fear. Van Damme pressed an arm around him, half coaxing and half forcing the little man inside.

Rosen edged closer, ready to bolt after them when Van Damme cleared the doorway. As Van Damme and his reluctant companion disappeared, Rosen started but stopped dead, clutching the building's rough corner.

Farther down, hidden by Van Damme and the little man until they entered the doorway, was Raincoat and a second man. Raincoat chewed on something—maybe a toothpick; it was hard to tell at this distance— as he and the other stared up. *They must be looking at the same building,* thought Rosen. *It's big. I'll bet it runs a third of the block, and they're at the far entrance.*

I can't move until Raincoat does. Rosen's breath leaked out fast, and his nails scraped the wall's rough edge. *Move, damn it! Go on in so I can.*

Raincoat wasn't cooperating at all. He slouched against the big building near the center of the block while he picked his teeth, or sucked a piece of candy or whatever, but he was not moving. His partner, younger and far more CIA looking, stood nearby with his hands in his pockets. Were they down here to keep watch for the whole time Van Damme had his meeting somewhere in that vast building?

I can't wait for them, Rosen thought. *Can I get into this closer entrance without them spotting me? Pretend I'm a tenant? It's definitely an apartment building. Nah, don't be ridiculous. How can I take that kind of chance? Okay…find another way in. That's it. Run around the block and see if there's an alley. How long'll that take? What difference? I'm not doing any good here.*

He turned and started in the opposite direction.

And stopped. How are you going to find them by now, huh, genius? That building is un-fucking-believably huge! You think Kharkov has his name on the tenant directory? Rosen rubbed his palm hard over his left eye and worked it down across his nose, mouth, and finally his chin. He slid back toward his original spot near the building's edge. Time passed ...

More time passed, and Rosen still had no solution.

Two young boys approached, dressed in faded but neat shorts. They stared up at Rosen, mouths agape, and then giggled as they crossed the street on which Raincoat and his partner stood, turning back midway to stare at him a second time before scampering off in a trail of tittering laughter.

Rosen froze. Had Raincoat seen? Were he and the other man walking up the block to check out what the kids were laughing at? Should he chance a look or cut across the street into a doorway? Damn, this was going all wrong! He should have shot Van Damme and forgotten the rest. Just *killed* him. He wasn't a spy, and he wasn't trained for it. He was a hand-to-hand killer and an excellent tracker: good for the jungle but not here. Why was he doing this to himself? Seeing Van Damme dead should be enough. If it wasn't, it was too bad because that was *all* he was going to be able to accomplish. That is, if Raincoat wasn't after him by now. He dug back for the .45, yanked it out, and let it lead his head around the corner.

Raincoat wasn't coming; Raincoat wasn't even looking. Raincoat was checking his wrist with his baggy sleeve pulled back for a better view of his watch. Raincoat squinted up toward one of the higher floors, down at his wrist again, then dug his right hand deep into a baggy pocket and entered the building. His partner reached into his well-tailored jacket and followed.

Timing. Raincoat was *timing* his entry! He wasn't a lookout. He was part of it. Rosen leaped around the corner and ran past the first entrance and toward the second, where Raincoat and his partner had disappeared. He hugged the .45 under his left arm. He had to catch up because Raincoat knew where Van Damme was!

Rosen stopped at the entry, propped a hand against the glass door, and pushed. Two yellowing shrubs in fungus-overgrown wood planters bracketed him. Rosen could almost hear them pleading for water ... or death.

What if he waited down here and caught Van Damme coming out with the money? That would do the trick. It'd be a lot safer for him than charging into some room upstairs. But number one: He wouldn't know the odds. Van Damme could come down flanked by half the KGB and the bastard would get away while Rosen was being mowed down on this miserable side street. Number two: If Van Damme was defecting, then same deal. At least if he followed Raincoat up, he could get an idea of the odds first and then decide how to handle it.

No time to think anymore. Raincoat wasn't waiting for him to decide. *Pretty soon, I'll lose him, too. Put up or shut up, Arnie.* He pushed the door the rest of the way.

Plain metal stairs were straight ahead. No frills for these folks. The lobby, if you could call the ten-by-ten area a lobby, was covered in the lowest-grade carpet Rosen had ever seen. It was like what movers put down to protect elevator floors. Black cigarette burns dotted its surface, with three recently discarded butts forming a triangle near its center. A third shrub, the terminal triplet of the two outside the door, suffered beside a yellowing floor length mirror to his right.

A heavy step rang along the metal stairway and then another step perhaps a landing and a half up. Raincoat and his partner weren't exactly light on their feet. Rosen grabbed the railing, testing the first stair. It would be quiet enough, especially with the racket from the two above. Rosen took the stairs two at a time until he was almost to the second floor.

Their footsteps above became quieter and slower. *Getting close, huh?* Rosen thought. He heard the sound of a softly opened door. *Click.*

Moments later, there was a second click.

Rosen moved quickly to the next level, pried open the red fire door ever so slowly, and turned the knob first to avoid his own click as it released from the jamb. He pressed his right eye into the opening. Raincoat moved carefully down the corridor. There was an exceptionally large stain dead center between his shoulders. It looked like coffee. How do you get coffee between your shoulders? The raincoat reflected light from the long rows of naked fluorescents, giving it an eerie translucence. The man crouched closer to the wall.

Rosen could see his partner hugging the same wall, twenty feet farther down. Raincoat must be the senior of the team, for the younger one had gotten stuck as the point man. The younger man moved forward in a half crouch with his gun angled upward at forty-five degrees, the muzzle at eye level, and his left hand down and back for balance. He stopped at each set of doors, listening, gently trying the knobs, first the left one and then the right, before creeping ahead to repeat the process. Three or four before the end, he stopped for an extra long time. Thinking or listening? Listening.

His gun angled higher as his left hand pushed the door.

Raincoat closed the gap quickly and surprisingly silently. The young one slipped carefully in. Raincoat was crouched in the hallway, sighting his weapon through the open door. What the hell was going on? Wasn't Raincoat Van Damme's boy or was he here to break things up rather than help Van Damme? It had never occurred to Rosen that Raincoat might be a good guy tailing Van Damme.

Rosen had the fire door almost open when the gunshots echoed back at him. He blinked. He didn't know why they'd surprised him, but they had. Was Van Damme dead? Was this the end of it? No. He *had* to be in on it! He raised his gun and pushed through, lunging back almost in the same motion.

Raincoat was backing out of the apartment. He turned and flattened against the corridor, eyes and gun sweeping the area. After a long moment, he seemed satisfied. Raincoat proceeded toward the opposite door. He had just about reached it when he suddenly jerked his head up, wheeled, and pointed his gun back toward the apartment he had exited.

A hand grabbed the jamb high up. Then a body lurched out. The new man was big, wearing coveralls and a shockingly white polo, and was in terrible shape even from where Rosen was standing. His legs were stiffening, causing him to totter as if he were leaning into a stiff wind. He struggled to keep his balance as he fought to control his violently shaking gun. He rocked back against the doorjamb, using the last of whatever was keeping him up to raise his weapon. Raincoat watched as if fascinated by the dying man's heroic efforts. Then, like a child bored with the antics of a mortally wounded insect, Raincoat walked forward and punched his gun into the other's face. This time the *crack* was quite loud. The dead man flew back through the doorway, arms and legs windmilling.

Raincoat turned and peered down the corridor toward Rosen's fire door and then retraced his steps to the apartment diagonally across. The door must have been opened for him because natural light settled over his face and chest. He stepped in.

Rosen tiptoed through the fire door. Slowly down the hall now … slowly. *Real slowly, Arnie.* Who had Raincoat shot? KGB? What did that mean? If Van Damme had a deal with Moscow, then Raincoat was anti–Van Damme if he'd just killed one of Moscow's people. Very good. But suppose he just shot a person, or persons, who were after Van Damme? Then he would be pro–Van Damme. *How can I know until I see what Raincoat's doing in that apartment? And that may be a little late if Raincoat is Van Damme's boy.*

Rosen took a second step, and the carpet made a sucking sound. He crouched, ready for doors to swing open. *How do I know all these apartments aren't filled with players watching me through the peepholes?* Rosen wondered. *Probably saying to themselves, "Who the hell is that guy? He's not one of ours. Must be one of theirs." Any second, one of these doors could pop open and … My lungs hurt. Gotta remember to breath, Arnie. Passing out won't help.* He sucked in two long draughts, whiffing someone's not-too-promising dinner. *Whew, whatever happens, at least I won't have to eat that.* He compressed his lips and wrinkled his forehead. Rosen thought, *Where did I learn to make jokes during times like this? Must have been to loosen up before those combat tournaments. I'm certifiable.* He shook his head, moving forward.

He was halfway there. It was a long corridor with lots of ugly green doors. *When you get to that first open one, you've gotta look. Suppose whoever's in there isn't finished? Not the guy who got it in the face—he's finished—but suppose there are others. Can't afford to have them at my back.* Rosen was to think about the next minute long and hard in the following weeks. It was the moment when he was *that* close to taking a shot at Van Damme. Of course, there were no guaranties that he would have hit him at that distance, especially with Van Damme moving as fast as he was, but at least Rosen could have given it a try. Maybe if he hadn't been gaping at the first apartment's grisly occupant, or if his reflexes had been army sharp, or …

But none of that changed what happened next. The door past the one where Rosen stood crashed open, and a tall, gaunt body hurtled out toward the far exit with rolls of white paper coiled under its arm. Rosen froze as he fought to shift his attention from the corpse in the apartment to the fleeing figure.

Perhaps he had been shocked into inaction by the discrepancy between the scenario in his mind and what actually transpired in that instant. Maybe it was because he had already relived the scene so many times— walking into the room as money and documents changed hands; grabbing the money and documents; shooting Van Damme repeatedly—that his mind could not adapt to reality.

Regardless of what might have happened, what *did* happen was that while Charles Van Damme escaped—easy as you please—Raincoat stepped out of the same apartment with the little guy in tow. Rosen, knowing damn well whose side Raincoat was on now, thumped down the hallway in the opposite direction as he tried to find a place to make a stand against Raincoat. Then Raincoat's gun was kicking up carpet chunks at Rosen's calves; Rosen was turning, dodging, and sprawling just as Raincoat's next shot caught the wall where his head would have been. Then his own gun was bucking and splattering the ceiling over Raincoat, showering plaster on the agent's scanty hair, while the little guy sprawled his hands and arms, trying to cover all of himself at once. Rosen finally remembered to prop his hands against the floor so that his next shot was accurate.

The bloodstain on Raincoat's chest rapidly grew as large as the coffee stain on his back. Raincoat staggered, looking confused as if trying to remember something extremely important. He then turned toward the exit but spun too far, pitching headfirst toward the opposite wall, his hands rigid at his sides. The *crack* of his skull reverberated back down the corridor.

Silence then except for the little guy's sobs. Rosen could have sworn he heard the sound of a quietly opened and closed door somewhere behind him. He wheeled, but the corridor was vacant. Rosen rested his head in his arms for a moment, too spent to worry about what came next.

Then he began worrying despite the frazzled impulses roving his spine. What about the open apartment with the corpse? He rose, spinning toward the wall and hugging it as he worked his way along. When he was within twenty feet, Rosen leveled his gun muzzle at the backlit doorway. He inched forward to the eerie rhythm of the little man's staccato sobs.

There *was* a second man—not much better off than the one with no face and little brain left—lying inside the door. This one was sprawled half off a gaudy flowered couch next to the wall with his stiff fingers hopelessly reaching for a holstered gun slung over a nearby chair. Rosen tried to avoid the faceless one, but like a rubbernecker, he gawked at the bleeding mess of a head in spite of himself. As he backed out, he saw the sole of a shoe off to his left. The young CIA-type sat in a corner. There was a conclusive hole beneath his neat blond hairline.

Rosen withdrew with a sigh and trudged toward the open door across the hall with his gun loose at his side. He doubted that there would be anyone left alive in the apartment where the Kharkov meeting had taken place. Rosen took little satisfaction in finding that he was right. There was a body on the table with another under it.

Out in the hall, Raincoat also didn't move. His head was jammed against the wall, facedown, in the kind of impossible position that only one past caring can maintain. Rosen contemplated the corpse. *Whoever you were, pal, you weren't on my side.* Suppose he was? Suppose Raincoat was after Van Damme and Van Damme was escaping, which could explain why he had been running his ass off for the exit? Suppose Raincoat was bringing that little whining wreck over there on the floor in for interrogation? *Shit. Did I just kill a good guy?* Rosen wondered. *Great. More proof that I'm an out-of-control psychopath. That'll help the cause.*

Rosen shook his head, puffed out his cheeks, and exploded the trapped air through puckered lips like a trumpet player without his mouthpiece. It was all so damn hard. His shoulders drooped. The .45 was a hundred-pound anvil at the end of his arm. It was just so damn hard to do it all on your own.

You wanna quit? Go ahead! It was that damn voice—the one inside— that knew just what to say. *You want to quit on them?* Rosen's mind visited the bedroom of his house. Barbara and the kids were in the same positions in which he'd placed them, only their eyes moved, following him as he plodded from the chair to the dresser to the window. *You want to quit? Quit—*

"*No!*" Rosen roared toward the little man, who had finally begun to totter to his knees. The sight of Rosen bearing down on him sent him back to the floor, feet and arms drawn together, a chubby whimpering fetus.

"Get up," Rosen snarled.

The fetus didn't move.

"Up!" He yanked the fetus by one of its fleshy arms.

The twisting of its flesh in his grip motivated it to yelp and rise.

Rosen stared down at the top of the cringing head. Light from the open doorway reflected off a circle of flesh surrounded by clumps of dark hair that protruded in multiple directions. "Look at me, you bastard!"

Slowly, the pudgy face turned up. The eyes were red from crying. Viscous fluid trickled from the pig-snout nose.

"You better stop crying and start talking," Rosen said with his face an inch from the other's. *My God, we really do talk in clichés,* he thought as the words left his lips. Rosen jerked at a *squeak* over his shoulder. Another door, or maybe the same one as before, opened slightly and closed fast. Not a good place for interrogations, he decided. "Come on." He yanked the quaking man toward the exit and onto the metal landing. He should get out of the building right now. He knew it. But the little snot nose— "Will you wipe your nose?" Rosen barked as the other dragged a white hankie from the pocket of his slacks—was so frightened that Rosen wanted to question him immediately. Answers might be tougher to get later, when the man got his confidence back. "Where did Van Damme go?"

"Ch-Ch-Chahrlz?"

"Van Damme … Charles … I don't give a shit!" Rosen accompanied this with a vicious shake.

"I … don't know." The red eyes implored Rosen.

Damn, the guy was good. "You were with him all morning. You're not going to insult me by telling me you just met him?"

"No, I vouldn't." The little guy tossed his head mightily back and forth, fending off confrontation.

"You're a local, aren't you? You were Van Damme's contact for the sale of the plans … You set things up with Kharkov?" Rosen yanked again, shaking the little body until its teeth clicked sharply together. "I'm not gonna drag this out of you one word at a time. Start goddamn talking until I stop you. Where did Van Damme go? What was he doing here? Why all the bodies?"

"I do not know vere he vent … but ve vere here to zhow za Roossians … zees Kharkov, Indigo II." He shook his head while dabbing at his nose, but quickly pulled his handkerchief away when he saw the storm in Rosen's eyes worsen. "He told me it vas a trap, a ZIA trap to catch za Roossian KGB bigzhot. I vass to help, get za plans from my company. I vork on zattelites." He shot the hankie back up to amplify his explanation. "I ahm from za United Shtates. I ahm a zitizen." He waved the hankie hand, and the other one, to counteract Rosen's skeptical frown. "I ahm, a *U-ESSS zitizen*," he said indignantly.

"Keep your voice down." Rosen's glare, and the .45, squelched the little man's rebelliousness.

"I ahm sorry. I vill." His voice dropped to a whisper. "Zen … I don't know. Evreyzing vas different in zere. Ve got plans"—he shook his head, squeezing his light eyebrows down to his nose, forming a lopsided circle with his lips—"then zey got plans. Mr. Kharkov shot this man who was helping him read our plans; Mr. Van Damme shot Mr. Kharkov …" The man's voice trailed off as the tension shifted into his frenzied little hands. They darted up and then flopped to his lap like wounded birds.

Rosen stared down at the little bald spot again, waiting.

"I don't know zat man who zhot at you. He vas taking me to a ... a save houze. At home, zey made my apartment look like I vuss a defector. Ze faked my bahnk account to look like a vuss a shpy. I think zey vould haf killed me zoon." The moist eyes rose timidly, probing Rosen's face.

Hell, Rosen didn't know what to believe. He needed time, and this definitely wasn't the place. Had to get this little sack of tears somewhere where he could really get into it with him. Sure, the little guy was scared, but that didn't make him Mr. Straight. Operations people were good under pressure, trained to think on their feet. *Don't be a sucker for red eyes and a running nose, Arnie.* "Turn toward the wall, hands against it."

"Vot?"

The man sounded terrified. Still, how could you really tell? "Against the wall—and keep your fucking voice down!" Rosen spun him, shoving hard between his shoulder blades. The little man's hands pawed the wall, barely preventing his face from hitting it. "Hands higher. Hurry!"

The little hands swam upward.

"Spread your legs."

"Vot? Vy? Vy—"

"Do it now."

The little man lurched as he worked his unsteady legs farther apart. His ankles folded inward like a bad ice-skater's.

He's wearing elevators, thought Rosen. *Wonder how much else is a disguise—and why?* Rosen patted all the way from armpits to ankles. The little body tightened as Rosen passed his hand along its crotch. Unarmed. *Strange,* thought Rosen. "Let's go." He spun the guy back in a clumsy pirouette. "Walk downstairs. Stay very close and a little in front. I'll tell you where to go."

The red eyes stared up at him. Nothing but despair showing. The nose still trickled.

"Nowww!"

They moved clumsily downstairs, the little guy stopping almost every step in case Rosen's orders had changed, Rosen prodding with the .45 to get him moving again. By the bottom, they had achieved a sort of workable coordination. They stepped into the bleak lobby. It duplicated the one that Rosen had entered on the opposite end, except that the cigarette butts on the floor no longer smoldered and the wretched plants were already out of their misery. Rosen pushed through the glass door, blinking his way into the early afternoon sunlight.

Rushing footsteps came from the left. Now the right. Hands forced his arms to his sides. He was pinned between husky bodies as his short companion whimpered like a wounded puppy. Faces, more distinct as the sunlight's effects lessened, thrust into Rosen's. He did his best to screen his fear as he glared back.

"You two check upstairs," was commanded in guttural German. Two of the eight surrounding them separated and shouldered their way into the lobby.

Rosen hoped that they would keep talking. His German was good. Maybe he could find out more since they probably assumed that he did not speak their language.

There was no more conversation. One command from a beefy blond man in an alligator shirt and pre-1960 chino slacks and they practically flew back to the corner and up Friedricstrasse. His four captors were very good. To nearby pedestrians, they appeared to be a group of friends hurrying to Wiener schnitzel and beer. No casual passerby would notice that although the outer two laughed heartily, the inner four, hidden by the others' broad backs and shoulders, were having none of it. Adding insult to injury, the man in the rear occasionally jabbed Rosen in the kidneys with Rosen's own .45.

A quick right at Unter den Linden and they practically sailed toward a monstrous white concrete building, split by towering rows of narrow dark-tinted windows. It loomed harsh and frightening in contrast to the delicate mother and child marble statue in front.

Rosen marveled at how efficiently they were hustled through the crowded lobby and down a side staircase. Three levels beneath, they shoved him down a narrow corridor where he had to duck his head. His captors flanked him front and back. Solid metal doors set into the corridor's rough brick lined their way. Alligator Shirt, in the lead, stopped before one. A humorously large antique padlock hung through two shiny metal loops, one attached to the tarnished metal door, the other to the metal jamb.

Alligator Shirt removed a narrow key from a crack in the mortar to the door's left and inserted it. The ancient lock snapped open with a crisp *click*. The door was not nearly as efficient. He elbowed it, then shouldered it, before it began to budge. The excruciating screech of metal against stone chilled Rosen's spine. Forcing it three-quarters of the way open was enough work for Alligator Shirt. He turned back, scowling as he wiped his forehead with the back of a hand, rife with curling blond hair. Alligator Shirt signaled toward the black interior.

Rosen was hurled forward, tripping over the jamb, plunging toward the dust of the concrete floor. He was able to break his fall with open palms. They smarted from the impact. Rosen whirled as he heard an "Ohhhhh," throwing up a reflexive forearm as his diminutive companion catapulted toward him, arms whirling. He caught the little man squarely across the thighs, deflecting him sidewise.

The man who'd pushed Rosen laughed, slapping the back of his companion, who had flung the little man. The proud winner of the impromptu shoving contest grinned and joked with those in the corridor behind. After a last peek by Alligator Shirt, they worked the heavy door closed, inch by screeching inch.

Rosen stared helplessly as the corridor light narrowed to a sliver, then disappeared as the door thumped shut. The unrelenting blackness was underscored by the finality of the snapping lock.

CHAPTER 23

osen struggled to his knees, rising quickly to relieve their stinging. Both must have been badly scraped by the fall. Well, what was the old joke: At least they'd keep his mind off his hands, which weren't in such great shape either.

He edged slowly forward, palms outward to ward off obstacles. It was so dark. No crack of light from under the door. No reflections. Nothing but unending blackness. The floor felt smooth. Probably cement. A few cautious steps more and Rosen sensed something large and close. Amazing how you could see without seeing, like those defensive backs who used to want to separate him from his head after a catch. But he could always anticipate their angle of attack and spin away, minimizing the impact.

Don't go nutty on me here, Arnie, let's stick to business. Just touch whatever it is in front of you—carefully.

The metal door's rough surface crumbled as his fingertips dislodged flaking paint, but otherwise, it was solid. He worked his way to the right. No sound except his cautious shuffling and the ragged breathing of his fellow prisoner. The wall was brick, similar to the corridor. Occasionally, Rosen would involuntarily yank his hands back as they encountered the sticky softness of a spider web. After eight paces, he came to a corner and plunged into a forest of gooey fibers that seized his eyebrows, nostrils, and lips. His face contorted as, spitting and cursing, he clawed them away. There was a gasp from the man on the floor …

Thunk. His shin cracked into a box. Wood, he guessed.

"Shit!"

"Vot?"

"Shut up!" The last thing he needed was that little bastard getting conversational right now. Damn. Rosen reached down, rubbing the sore shin. Where the hell was that sixth sense he'd been so damn proud of a few minutes ago?

The little guy was back to his gasping breathing. Good. Rosen felt around. Yep, wood box, just about mid-calf high, perfect for creaming a leg. He continued, working around the box and back toward the wall. There was another box within a step. It was bigger than that first little sucker, with wire bands going around it. Rough surfaced. "Shit."

"Vot?"

"*Shut up.*" Wood splinters—the thing was full of them. More boxes … Careful. Six more paces, around a whole stack of boxes this time, and he came to the back corner. A huge pile of boxes, all shapes and sizes, were stacked floor to ceiling so that he had to detour from his path along the back wall.

The little guy's breathing followed him as if he were watching Rosen's progress in the pitch-blackness.

The wall on the far side was relatively empty except for a desk with office chairs stacked atop. Rosen felt cold concrete, just like the other side. Probably the back wall would have been the same, if he could have gotten close enough to touch it. Soon he felt the rougher, warmer brick again, telling him that he had made the full circle to the front wall.

Rosen took three gliding steps until his fingers hit a metal conduit. He traced it downward.

Snap …

The little guy did an exaggerated pantomime of an owl blinded by a flashlight. Once he had recovered, he stared wide-eyed at Rosen.

Wouldn't you know it? Rosen thought. *A damn light switch at precisely the end of my walk. Aren't those things supposed to be on the right side of the door?*

It was definitely a storage room, dusty and unused. Several crates lay around randomly, coupled with the haphazard stacks of those against the walls. Rosen surmised that little of any importance was kept here. The crates were mostly lettered in German, one or two in Russian. The lighting was ample: three large fluorescents in metal brackets, chicken-wired for protection, mounted on the front and two side walls close to the low wood ceiling. There were vent grates in the sidewalls near the lights, but these were too small to be entered by anything larger than a squirrel. No windows. The rear crates reached nearly to the ceiling. Nothing but solid wall showed in the occasional gaps between the stacked rows. No other openings, so far as he could tell. Hell, they were below ground down here. What'd he expect, a nice picture window?

Rosen made one more halfhearted attempt at the door and then returned to the room's center. He chose a crate, sat, and studied his injured hands. They were red and scraped, some thin lines of blood across the lower palms. He yanked up his pant legs. His knees were raw but not bloody. He let the pant legs slide back down, then rubbed his nose. His mustache was slightly askew. Rosen laughed to himself and yanked it off, enjoying the little man's expression. How much good would it do him with his new hosts? He fingered its gummy surface doubtfully but slapped it back into place more to rid himself of it than for any expected benefit.

His attention shifted to the little man on the floor: arms locked tightly around his knees and forehead dug in atop in an attempt to shield himself from events gone hopelessly out of his control.

"How'd he get you to sell out? What'd he promise you?" Rosen said. "Money? Was it blackmail? What the fuck would make someone like you do that?"

The disheveled head shot up. He squinted hard at Rosen, as if he hadn't really seen him until this moment. "Zell out? Vat are you talking about?" His head drooped, the flurry of anger subsiding into lethargy. "Zell out," he mumbled into his knees.

Rosen studied the round head. Light reflected from the nearly perfect circle at the scalp's center so that although the unruly hair was definitely brown, it seemed to radiate a lighter aura. The little ears were red along their upper edges and protruded quite far.

Rosen's lips pulled taught. "Yeah. That's what giving state secrets to the enemy is *usually* called. You got another name for it?"

"I vouldn't do zuch a thing."

The voice was so low and muffled that Rosen only grasped its meaning as it echoed back through his brain. He leaned closer, pushing back on the little man's forehead, forcing the red-rimmed eyes up to his. "What did you think you were doing? *What the hell did you think you were doing?* What are you? One of those nuts who—"

"I vas helping us against the Russians, dahm you." The little man wrenched his head away, shaking Rosen's hand off by leaning his torso as far back as possible. Pushing up to his feet with a sedentary person's awkwardness, he stalked toward the door.

"Yeah, right. You steal plans and try to tell me you're 'helping.' Who's gonna believe that shit—"

"I vas helping za *Z-I-A!*" Rosen's cell mate spun back on the final word, nodding emphatically with each letter.

Rosen's entire forehead drew down over his eyes. He cocked his head. "How?"

"Ve zet a trap vith the Indigo II specifications. This Roossian vas nefa zupposed to keep them." The perfectly round face jutted forward, eyes clashing with Rosen's, lips tight as he crossed his putty-like arms firmly over his protruding belly.

"Why the disguise if you're such an innocent bystander?" Rosen stared pointedly at the other's shoes.

"He told me it vould protect me from reprizals later on. Changed my hair, my vace ..." The little man dug violently into the side of his mouth with pincher-like thumb and forefinger, extracting a flesh-colored substance similar to what Rosen had used to distort his own cheeks. He stared at the glob, then squeezed it in his pudgy grip and hurled it at the wall. "Yah, my proteczion. Very, very vunny."

Rosen moved closer gently, slowly, halting several feet from the man.

"What was the plan?" he asked softly.

The little man's face clouded over. Internal resolve that had bolstered the weak chin dribbled away like so much water. He resembled a gasping fish. The chubby red hands fluttered away from his chest and dropped like stones. "I ... don't know. It all got changed around."

"How? Tell me." Rosen's voice remained soft. His eyes were no longer hostile, only intensely curious.

His cell mate's rounded back straightened. His reddened eyes narrowed. "Who are you?"

Barely a pause: "CIA."

"Then vy vould you shoot Mr. Van Damme's man?"

"It was a rogue operation. Unauthorized. I'd show you my ID"—Rosen hunched his shoulders as he rotated his palms upward—"but it got grabbed with the rest of our papers."

The little man's thin shoulders rolled forward, drooping as his spine returned to its normal slouch. "Yess." He smiled sadly, like someone who has just been informed that he doesn't really own the Brooklyn Bridge. "I zuppose zat iss vy everyzing vent wrong."

Rosen stared at the floor, allowing his cell mate to acclimate to this outrageously altered vision of reality. "He vuss going to haf me killed." The little face flushed as shock turned to anger.

"It won't happen. Not now." Rosen ventured even closer. The little man did not back away. "We'll work this out."

The red-rimmed eyes looked up, needy, like a hungry puppy's.

Rosen walked to a crate, scraped it along the floor toward the one that he had been using, sat on the new one, and patted the original. "Tell me what happened."

The little man hesitated, deciding. He fluttered a futile hand and shuffled toward the empty crate, dropping heavily upon its edge. The crate tottered. He seated himself more securely and trapped his restless hands between his knees. Rosen noticed that the man's arms were devoid of muscle, like twin tubes of white dough.

The little fellow started in a trembling voice, gaining anger as he continued. With the anger came confidence, until his voice rang across their cell.

Rosen stopped him only to clarify who Ralph Jackson was—or, more properly, had been—and to give him an occasional soft "Go on" when the little man's emotions threatened to swamp him.

"Und zey are going to make *me* look like a devector. Me! And all I vanted to do vuss help." The rage was strong now, the little hands winding and twisting with a palpable rasping. Suddenly, they shot up toward his face. His doughboy body crumbled forward at the waist, sobs working their way around his rigid fingers.

Rosen sat still.

Soon the little man's heaving shoulders quieted. Shortly after, his hands dropped, moisture reflecting from the spread palms. More glistened on his cheeks. He tried for a grin, but his lips froze in a straight line. "Zorry—"

"Don't worry about it. You had a right. You've been through a lot." Rosen watched the hankie pop out, waited for the long nose blow to finish. He asked, "Is there any more?" as the hankie was stuffed back into the other's pocket.

Rosen's cell mate shook his head, sagging at the shoulders again.

"What's your name?"

"Otto." Muffled.

"Hey, Otto …"

Otto kept his head down.

"Hey, *Otto*, what's your last name?"

"Gru … ha … ber." Low. Muffled.

"What's that? Growhuber?"

"Gru … haber."

"Groohaver?"

Otto's head snapped up. "Gruhaber. *Gruhaber*—"

"That's better." Rosen smiled. "I'm Adam Reisen."

An indifferent nod.

Rosen reached over, rested a hand on Otto's tiny slouched shoulder. "Once we're out of here, you … you and I have got to get that story out." Otto looked around slowly at the walls, the ceiling, finally at Rosen.

"Yess. Out auf here." "We will. No problem." Rosen shrugged off the possibility of any other outcome, hoping that he sounded convincing. "Then they have to know about Van Damme."

"Don't they *already* know?" Otto gaped. "You zaid you ver ZIA. Zis vas a … vat … 'rogue operazion'? Now you zay they don't even know about him." Otto shook Rosen's hand off his shoulder and gazed around. "Oud of here." He shook his head slightly, snorted, shook it harder, hunching his shoulders. "An den vat?" he said, as if he really didn't care if there was an answer.

"Don't worry. I promise we'll get out of this and get Van Damme. I'm CIA too, remember?" Enthusiasm had not been Rosen's strong suit lately. He hoped that he was succeeding in dredging some up for Otto's sake.

Otto turned toward Rosen. "He iss a very powervul mahn, yess? More powervul zan you?"

"Not once we tell the right people about Indigo—"

"Powervul men do vat zey vant, yess?"

"Not this time."

"Vy? Zis is zo different zan all uf history."

"Look at me. *Look* at me, Otto."

The round head turned. Tears hung along Otto's pudgy cheeks. It was hard for him to keep his eyes on Rosen because they kept clouding over.

Rosen leaned close, attempting to fix the man's gaze. "Do you think you can be safe ever again until we stop him? Think about his plans. Is he going to let you live away your life in front of your computer? You think you can just say you don't know him anymore and that he doesn't know you … and that will make it true?"

"I leaf zings alone. I lif …" At least Otto's eyes were connecting with Rosen's now.

"Sure. He'll just sit in that big office, waiting to take over the whole CIA, and think, 'Otto knows enough to keep quiet. He won't say anything. Not even when he has a drink. Oh, oh, how do I explain how the Russians will almost steal Indigo in a few weeks if Otto isn't a defector? Oh well, I'll just have to think of something else. Can't have anything happening to good ol' Otto.' That's the way it'll be, right, Otto?"

"You ahr right. Okay. You ahr very persvuasive. You should be proud. Goot. Now I ahm totally terrified."

Rosen searched the other's face. No laugh? No smile? He had no clue as to whether the other knew that what he had said was very funny.

"We'll make it. Don't worry—"

"I just vant to go bahck to my computer."

"You will. You will," Rosen grinned at the top of Otto's bobbing head as it retracted back into his shoulders. He had his proof. Finally. Right here, slumped in front of him, his un-fucking-believable proof! *Van Damme, Van Damme. I'm comin' for ya,* sang inside Rosen's head. *I don't give a fuck what—I'm comin' for ya!* "Don't worry, Otto buddy. You *will*!"

*   *   *

Arnie Rosen's euphoria lasted only until the ferocious scraping of the metal door scoured the optimism from his mind. How long had it been? He wasn't sure. Certainly more than an hour. Three or four? He looked at his watch. Less than two. Funny, it seemed longer, but then, there wasn't much to occupy you in here.

The big door opened quickly, despite its protests, faster than Rosen would have expected it could with the obvious bad fit. *That* was the first thing that worried him. Soon Rosen understood why the door was giving in so easily. A very square man, not so much tall as immensely wide, propelled it the final distance as if its lack of alignment were nonexistent. *That* was the second thing that worried him.

The huge face, broad-cheeked, with a nose that had been broken so many times that it could no longer be properly reset, was blank and impassive as it grunted at the man in the alligator shirt and his companion. They both carried uncomfortable-looking straight-backed chairs, which the square man directed them to position between Rosen and Otto. His tiny green eyes reflected the overhead lights as he monitored his men's progress. They glowed with sullen malevolence. *That* was the third thing that worried Rosen.

*   *   *

Captain Dieter Moder, formerly of the GDR, now of the Unified German Republic, was unaffectionately called "Hitler Moder" by his men, usually when they were either very drunk or very confident in whom they were confiding. And Moder was in a far fouler mood than the one that had earned him his nickname. The fact that in *his* district such a thing could take place! Never. Never had there been an "incident"—to hell with that polite word—*six* unexplained murders! He had maintained twelve years of tidy order. Ten with the party and almost two, since. The only exceptions were the antics of those crazy espionage people, and they didn't count. No policeman could be responsible for those psychopaths.

And if that weren't bad enough, Americans were involved. During these times. When he couldn't just bring them to headquarters, like the old days, and beat them until they begged to confess. No. Things were different, thanks to that idiot Yeltsin. Moder had to be handle this quietly until the true facts were ascertained. No improprieties would be tolerated with the American eagle hovering above his land, a large money bag suspended from its ugly beak. The Americans were now his "friends." Unbelievable. So anything involving Americans had to be airtight before charges were leveled. That was the word from above.

But "above" didn't know about this yet. Didn't want to know, more than likely. Lousy bureaucrats, always wanting to keep their asses clean. Well, that was fine with him. No interference, just the way he liked it, here in a nice secret little room in the Ministry of Foreign Affairs. All alone, away from the little toadies at headquarters and their spying reports.

A good thing Fritz—Moder glanced toward the man in the alligator shirt—had realized that the terrified caller from the murder scene apartment house mentioned "American English." A good man, Fritz. Moder studied the younger man, wondering how soon he would have to arrange things so that Fritz faltered. One couldn't have Fritz's reputation becoming too widespread. However, that was for another time. Right now, Moder was going to get to the bottom of this. Oh, yes. Then the pains in the ass "above" could spend from now until hell figuring out how to handle the politics. Once his job was done, he didn't give a shit.

Moder glared at the two who had dared to commit murder in *his* district.

*   *   *

The next few days had not really been so bad, as Rosen contemplated them in retrospect. Sure, some sleep deprivation: the door screeching open; lights jamming on; their senses numb as men with rough hands roused them from their mildewed mattresses, hoisted them into those unyielding chairs, and screamed accusations in their ears. By now, Rosen had become so familiar with the repetitive sequence of questions that he didn't have to fully wake to answer. He had also learned to contend with a rigid bathroom schedule—eighty feet down the hall and to the right— which had demanded painful abstinence before his body acclimated to the routine. Rosen's only remaining complaint regarding the bathroom routine was that he and Otto had to leave their stall doors open to their captors' views, regardless of the nature of their needs. Still, everything considered, things had not gone too badly—until today.

Today, Moder, "Captain Moder," as he insisted on being called, who had previously been satisfied to glare balefully from under his thick, low forehead at both the questioners and questionees, pushed his bulk off his chair and got more involved.

Moder's first slap, ringing through the room like the crack of a bullwhip, nearly took Rosen's head off. Immediately after, Rosen's cheek caught fire. It was the first significant use of force applied to them. "There will be no more lies," Moder said, as unemotionally as if he were ordering a sandwich. For all his brutish looks, Moder spoke limited but flawless English. "You see these papers?"

Rosen couldn't. All that he could see was an overstuffed manila envelope swinging toward his face. He barely blinked in time to prevent one of its corners from piercing his eye. Moder followed through, sending the envelope spiraling toward the crates at the rear. It bounded off one, hitting the concrete with a *splat*.

"They are as fake as this." Moder's thumb and forefinger darted for Rosen, pincher fashion. Soon his false mustache followed the discarded envelope's trajectory. "No more stupid stories about Russian KGB agents, you understand?"

Rosen winced as Moder poised his huge palm, but he tried to explain that it really was the truth, taking another poleax blow for his trouble. After twenty or so more questions, each followed by a similar token of Moder's dissatisfaction, the left side of Rosen's head lolled at an oblique angle to his right shoulder. It felt as if cotton wads had been surgically implanted beneath the skin in his face. Nothing was the same shape as before: his ear; his jaw; the edge of his cheek, which protruded so far that it engulfed the corner of his left eye. One of Moder's men still pinioned his arms behind his chair, but there was little point.

All that Rosen could do was dangle helplessly as questions, thuds, and screams now emanated in rhythmic succession from Otto. Otto blubbered, "Roossian agents" during pauses in the sequence. "Roossian agents, I svear!"

Smack.

"Aiiih!"

The process repeated itself.

"Two were Americans. They had drivers' licenses from Pennsylvania and Ohio, USA. The others, ordinary citizens of the Soviet … a Russian republic. We have their identifications. I want no more lies. Are you CIA? Why did you kill them?" Moder repeated in his impassive monotone.

"Check, Goddammit." It had escaped Rosen's swollen lips before he knew it. A response to Otto's useless agony. It must have been an instinct to protect one who was less able to cope than he. Whatever his stupid reason, it had come out. Not once but twice. "Check their goddamn identifications. How can you not check their identifications?"

Rosen paid. He knew he would when he heard Moder's chair scrape the concrete. Rosen couldn't see the granite-block face—didn't want to lift his head to try—but he couldn't prevent himself from visualizing Moder's green pig's eyes glowering with rage. Compared to the anticipation, Rosen welcomed the numbing crunch. He didn't remember much after that. Maybe he had gotten hit again, maybe not. There was only a simple buzzing, a monster fly let loose in the room—or in his head.

* * *

It was quiet again. Dark.

I ought to talk to Otto, give him some encouragement, thought Rosen. *Give him some good words about the future and keep the poor little guy's spirits up. After all, I need Otto when we get after Van Damme again. But I just don't feel like it, not right now. Later, when I feel a little better. Right now, I just want to sleep …*

* * *

Captain Dieter Moder sat back of the standard issue desk in his small office. His sheer denseness dwarfed both so that he resembled a large mammal penned up in an undersized cage. The Americans, CIA or not, stuck to their story. Even the little one, who didn't seem a very likely agent and had no pain tolerance whatsoever. Moder smiled. He enjoyed the man's yelps. Would such a person be able to hold to such a tale: KGB colonels trading in secrets with American heads of intelligence, unknown to either of their governments, if there weren't an element of truth in it? *Paahh,* thought Moder, *I must be getting soft. I'll work harder tomorrow and get at the truth, even if I have to break every one of their bones.*

It couldn't hurt to verify the identifications of the other four. Two Siberians, an Uzbek, and a Georgian had been found in addition to the two CIA corpses. It would take a couple of days. Any nonmilitary, non-intelligence inquiries were low priority, and communication with the arrogant KGB stank even during high priority investigations. But still …

Moder grabbed an old computer printout of detainees from the preunification period. Economic crimes, mostly, trading in D-Marks, selling Western blue jeans and decorated T-shirts near the edges of the Alexanderplatz. The usual silly little things that took up most of his time. He frowned at the barely legible columns on his screen. Miserable Russian computers. They couldn't do anything right. Still …

Moder put the sheets down and reached for his dial phone. It couldn't hurt to check.

*   *   *

Moder got smarter after that first day—he worked their bodies instead of their faces. Less evidence with the bodies. Knotted towels could be used, terribly painful but few marks, except for a bruise or two.

The sessions actually became a perversely welcome interlude for Rosen between coal-black periods of inactivity. They were tied to their chairs all the time now. The only distractions, aside from Moder's sessions, were his own ragged breathing and Otto's sobbing.

Deep in their subbasement, the night cold inhibited their sleep. It penetrated their thin clothing and invaded their bodies. Their poor circulation, induced by long periods of immobility, no longer provided a defense against it. By now, their skin had become their enemy: a clammy wrapping which caused constant discomfort regardless of their level of exhaustion.

The cold was even worse during what Rosen supposed was daytime. The mighty door, for all of its creaky fit, allowed a constant stream of air-conditioning from whatever machinery serviced the outside corridor. It raked their bodies continually on its path toward the rear wall. Rosen's sinuses were soon so swollen from the cold that needles shot down his forehead and into his eyes each time that he moved his head.

Otto developed a perpetual cough, deepening and hollowing as their captivity lengthened.

Moder's questions never varied significantly: "Are you CIA?" Then, "Who killed whom?" When this second question was repeated daily, Rosen determined that advanced West German ballistics testing had not yet been embraced by the former GDR. Then, "Who took these so-called plans?" Then, after his daily tirade regarding the preposterousness of their stories, coupled with a few gratuitous punches, "What were you selling or buying, and where did you hide it?" Rosen had thought this a curious way for Moder to finish up, but by the third day, he understood. Moder had been so preoccupied with apprehending black marketers under communism that he was unable to conceive of any crime not having its roots in economics.

And all that Rosen could do was to yell at the beginning of every session and gasp out by the end, "Have you *checked* yet?" For which he invariably paid …

*   *   *

The results came in shortly after Moder's sixth interrogation session. He hunched in his tiny office, frowning at his big hands. Two knuckles on the right one were red and swollen. He reread his notes for the third time. His handwriting was surprisingly delicate, *y*'s and *j*'s finishing in grand loops. Of the two Siberians who had presumably been killed seven days ago, one had actually died in the Great War, the other during the Stalinist purges. The Armenian was, according to Moder's information, thought to be a victim of the recent earthquake, although verification was impossible at this time. And the real Georgian had died of injuries incurred during KGB interrogation over the distribution of antigovernment literature six years earlier. There was no additional information on the two dead Americans, but that wasn't surprising. Moder's low-level inquiry would not warrant research about Western nationals. Anyway, he would bet a week's pay that they were probably nothing more than slimy American drug dealers, most likely with false credentials.

Damn! He didn't need these problems. A pencil cracked. Pieces jutted out at skewed angles from between his fingers. Moder stared at his hand, confused, until it dawned on him that he had destroyed it. So they weren't two Siberians, an Armenian, and a Georgian, at least not the ones whose identification papers he had in his middle drawer. False identifications were not easily obtained, unless the dead men had needed them for official purposes or could afford their heavy prices in the criminal marketplace. Men who might traffic in American cocaine, for instance.

Moder stuck a fingertip into his ear, working it deeper. He removed it and surveyed the results before flicking off the red-brown particle with his thumb. If they were Russian government people, even KGB, they had to be minor players. Certainly not high-ranking colonels. Moder came as close to laughing as he was capable. Imagine *him* inquiring whether Nikolai Kharkov was missing! He could just hear himself now: "Oh, he is? Well, I know just where you can find his body. By the way, comrade—am I still allowed to call you that?—Kharkov turned over the plans to a major Russian weapon to the Americans. It was supposed to be an exchange, but the American who is the director of the European Division for the CIA— yes, that is right—seems to have outsmarted your colonel because he got to keep *all* the plans."

That was all Moder needed, to become the laughingstock of these arrogant Russian security people who looked down their vodka-reddened noses at anyone who tried to do his job, who had not been born Russian. Not born a *big city* Russian, actually. Oh, yes. Quite a laugh on Dieter Moder. All the way back to *his* superiors, many of whom were still quite cozy with their old KGB bosses. And then on to the men under his command. No, thank you. Still …

It wouldn't hurt to put out feelers, find out if anything was going on. These dead had to belong to someone. Maybe some KGB games that had blown up in their own faces? Actually, embarrassing the KGB was a rather pleasing prospect. This time, Moder did smile: a kind of lopsided leer, the right side of his lips turning up, the left remaining stationary. How funny. Mopping up for the KGB. Oh, yes, police on Moder's side of the former Wall still worked with the KGB. Hell, the party was down now, but no telling when it would come back. You didn't burn your bridges in his business. He found himself excited by the prospect of a resurgent communist sphere of influence. Things had been so damn boring since Berlin's Communists had discovered their democratic roots. Moder reached for the phone.

*   *   *

Captain Uri Grigov worried as he traversed Drezhinski Square toward KGB headquarters. Old Lubyinka Prison was as dismal as ever in the waning summer. No hope for its exterior. Ages of unsavory machinations within had indelibly suffused it with an aura of doom.

Not so with the gaudily remodeled interior, commemorating the KGB's ostensible change of image. As usual, Grigov stifled the desire to throw up as he entered what could have been the lobby of a concert hall or opera house. Its exaggerated opulence was calculated to prime the hoards of tourists flooding daily into Moscow's number one attraction for his agency's public relations pitch.

He could almost catch the lilting tones of one of the handpicked guides, any one of whom could have walked straight out of a movie screen, as she gave the canned presentation to her doting group. Grigov had heard it so often, he could repeat its major points by heart: This former nerve center of Soviet security is just another government agency subject to the prevailing political philosophy. Now that the state is committed to democracy, our administrators are delighted to forsake their distasteful security functions for much more constructive programs. We are primarily a department of the Ministry of the Interior, helping to implement the difficult transition that our nation is undergoing. Some of us have been assigned to army units whose responsibility is to guard our internal borders during these difficult times. And so on.

For the hundredth time, Grigov repressed an insane notion to crash the captivated group and sell someone a Moscow bridge. Instead, he limped across parquet floors and oriental rugs toward the stately marble staircase.

Nothing else today would be funny. He had lost Kharkov.

Grigov's boots tattooed the slick marble corridor in their customarily ragged cadence. Since the accident, he had almost become used to the delay as his dragging right foot caught up with his healthy left. A little souvenir of Afghanistan. A hidden "Butterfly", the toy that his people dropped from helicopters for tantalized Mujahideen babies to retrieve and blow off their extremities, had caught up with one of its creators. Ironic. More so, because Grigov had been there only briefly to establish his cover as a liaison between the army's intelligence wing, the GRU and the KGB. He had been scheduled for one lousy week; however, his stay was extended by three months in a miserable undermanned field hospital. Yet even in his worst moments, when the wound reeked from puss and perspiration and the pain was a sharpened bamboo shaft poking through his spine at his brain, the KGB man had been surprised to find that he still preferred his torment to an armless child's lifelong nightmare.

Grigov yanked open one of a hundred similar doors and entered a tiny windowless office. He had to squeeze between the old wooden desk and the wall to reach his seat.

His office at GRU headquarters was larger, but his dual assignment required a KGB base of operations as well. Five months earlier, Grigov had been ordered to ascertain the degree of hardline sentiment within the Red Army, consequently his posting to the GRU. What none of his superiors knew was that he was also performing this function within the parent agency, the KGB. A big job, but he had plenty of time now. Katlana had left shortly after her first glimpse of his mangled foot. It wasn't the foot, per se. That had just been the straw that broke the back of their failing marriage. Summer/winter romances didn't always work, despite the songs. She was twenty-four to his fifty. Grigov had long suspected that the turning point in the relationship had come four years earlier, when his blonde ballerina stopped complaining about his outrageously long working hours. Grigov never blamed her for wanting more out of life than an old workaholic cripple; could have made things difficult, especially when his sources revealed a daytime love nest with a promising young Ukranian transfer to the Moscow Ballet. He never gave revenge serious consideration after his initial vodka-fueled rage had dissipated.

Grigov had recently targeted Kharkov as the main offender. The Colonel was using his dual status to act as a go-between for hard-liners in the army, the GRU, and the KGB. Now Kharkov was gone. Who knew what trouble the man was up to at this very moment? Grigov was supposed to know, but he didn't. Not a good situation for the man to whom he reported, a few short metro stops from the Kremlin—or for Grigov's career.

CHAPTER 24

Savin puffed repeatedly, the meerschaum bowl growing hot in his palm. He smoked frenetically like this only when he was angry. As the overworked tobacco grew bitter to his tongue, he made an exaggerated effort to gently lay the pipe on the wide press table. His real inclination was to smash it down, sending pipe shards and resin spewing out over the smug faces lining the briefing room.

It was too early to talk about Amphora and what it meant to East-West relations, but damn Culcane, sitting like a smirking Buddha to his left, had leaked it. After that, the reluctant president had no choice but to authorize Savin's press conference. On Capitol Hill yet, with Culcane, the soon-to-be head of foreign relations, in attendance. And if all this weren't humiliating enough, Charles Van Damme was there to answer questions on the operation itself. How had Culcane known?

Savin glanced past Culcane to Van Damme. The man had modestly downplayed his role in the daring theft of Amphora, attributing its success instead to the courage of Agent Millstein, who had neutralized the opposition and unfortunately was missing in the line of duty. Pencils flew at Van Damme's every resonant word: a new press darling in the making. Had *he* been the source? Savin found it hard to believe that a man like Van Damme, who lived for the agency, would violate its code of privacy.

There could have been plenty of other causes, thought Savin. *Hell, nothing was sacred anymore. Leaks everywhere. My God, private corporations would never tolerate the appalling lack of confidentiality rampant in the government.* Whatever the cause, Savin was stuck feeding these jackals information that should have been analyzed and sanitized for months before it broke. The poor President had barely been given time to confer with his Russian counterpart, who was understandably outraged at having such a bombshell dropped into his lap with no time to verify its bona fides.

"Does this mean that Russia could be working on a host of other weapons like Amphora?" The question came from a large woman in an obsolete pageboy, whose imitation tortoiseshell glasses were equally out-of-date.

"We presently have no knowledge of any other major weapons research taking place," Savin replied.

"But you didn't know about Amphora until a few days ago."

Oh boy. He'd let himself in for that one. Savin toyed with the idea of refilling his pipe.

"Do we currently even *have* the intelligence capability to determine what Russia might or might not be working on at the moment? Or any of the other Commonwealth republics either?"

Savin's new tormenter was Arlen Franco of the *Post*. How could you win with this guy? If you adequately funded intelligence, he'd cry paranoia. If you didn't, then it was lack of preparedness. Savin detested the glint in Franco's beady little bird's eyes. The stained seersucker jacket, part of Franco's phony I'm-too-damn-dedicated-to-care-about-my-appearance image, didn't help either.

"Our intelligence capabilities are perfectly adequate, in light of present funding levels. We interdicted Amphora, didn't we?"

"Due lahgly to Mr. Van Damme," interjected Culcane.

Savin had left himself open for that one too. Maybe it was time for horse breeding instead of public service. "We all work on the same team. Charles Van Damme's success, as I'm sure that he would be the first to admit, comes from the effort of many people behind the scenes."

Savin nodded toward Van Damme, who smiled agreeably. *If the Chief of the European Division was conning him, he was doing a superb job*, thought Savin. There had even been the right degree of embarrassment in Van Damme's normally controlled face as he bustled into Savin's office to warn him, just before the rumors of the surprise press conference erupted across Langley.

"How will this affect relations between our two countries? Will aid be withdrawn?"

Stupid question. You always got them as time ran out and the desperate second-raters tried to make points with their editors.

"That is a matter for the president and his advisors. I am certainly not qualified to speculate on such matters."

"Senator Culcane, how do you think we will respond?" This bush-league reporter was not going to let up.

"I agree that the Pres'dent aynd Congress must decide such mattuhs, howevah."

Yes, Culcane, thought Savin. *You aren't about to miss the chance for a juicy "howevah," are you?*

"We at Foreign Re-lations …"

Already sounding like old Senator Chase has retired and you're running the show, aren't you, Culcane?

"We will considah this matter *vera* ca'fully in ouah consultations with the pres'dent."

"And now, ladies and gentlemen, I thank you for a very stimulating session." Savin relished Culcane's scowl. The Southern blob had been working up a head of steam for a second Gettysburg Address. "I am afraid both Mr. Van Damme and myself have scheduled other appointments." Savin never had a problem breaking up corporate meetings. In fact, these press people were pussycats compared to a cantankerous group of shareholders. He rushed out with Van Damme in tow. The chorus of whines from those he'd failed to call brightened his mood immeasurably.

*   *   *

Van Damme reclined into the moderately comfortable seat of Savin's company car. The glass shield between themselves and the extremely lethal driver was reminiscent of a limousine, but that was as far as it went. Savin, in keeping with his reputation for frugality, had scrapped a long tradition of sleek black limos for a Ford Taurus. The sides were armored, of course, and the glass could stop automatic weapon fire without shattering, but essentially it was still a Taurus. Good Lord, the man had no class.

Conversation had been polite but strained on the drive back to Langley. Savin obviously had questions about Van Damme's role in the Amphora leak, but he was too much of a gentleman to question a high-ranking subordinate without proof of misconduct. Fine with Van Damme. He could do without Savin's small talk. There was a lot to think about.

The driver kept to a smooth fifty even though everyone else was passing. Another of Savin's rules for maintaining low visibility.

Fine again. Van Damme didn't care if they did twenty. What he *did* care about: Millstein and Gruhaber were missing. No doubt about it now. Even over-the-hill Millstein should have been at the safe house hours ago.

Van Damme had stewed all morning. Even his meditation hadn't helped. He should have already picked up on this problem, would have, except for all his recent heady success—his ducks lining up so fast that even he had been dazzled. Stupid. Losing control meant losing the game. How could he forget one of his cardinal rules?

What on earth went wrong? How many times had Van Damme wondered as he tried to keep up appearances with Culcane and Savin, and now those ridiculous reporters, while his insides echoed with maddening questions? Had the Russians picked them up? Or the Germans? Was Millstein breaking under torture at this very minute? Revealing what? Van Damme's relationship with Otto? That was all Millstein knew ... and Van Damme could handle that. He'd gone over his options enough times to feel confident ... if he only knew where Millstein was, and if he was still alive.

Van Damme caught a quick movement out of the corner of his eye as the gate guard waved them in. Was it his imagination or had the man's perpetual slouch vanished as he recognized the Director's car?

If Gruhaber was in the hands of the former GDR police, then he might as well be in the KGB's hands, because the ex–East Germans still played on both sides of the fence. And the little man would certainly tell them about meeting with Kharkov and Van Damme's fatal alteration of their agreement, the minute they said "boo" to him. No problem there. All that would prove was that Van Damme had created a brilliant scheme to steal Amphora, during which some enemy agents died and our agents died. No problem, again. Agents died every day, for far less reason than something of the magnitude of an Amphora.

Gruhaber would also tell them that Van Damme planned to stage his defection. How could the Russian government use that? If they publicized it at home, it was bound to intensify anti–US sentiment. They wouldn't want to do that. More likely, the pro-glasnost forces would leak the story to the US State Department. Less messy if Van Damme could be dealt with internally. But why should that work? Who would believe the word of a terrified civilian like Gruhaber, in Russian custody, against Van Damme's own? No, no threat there.

At worst, Van Damme would have to scrap his follow-up plan to frame Gruhaber for defecting with Indigo. A shame since a second anti-Russian revelation within the next few weeks would sound the death knell for Russian-U.S. relations. Fortunately, the Amphora phase had gone well enough to assure him a promotion to deputy director and enrage the Russian hard-liners. Still, the Indigo scandal, right on its heels, would really put major funding back into the intelligence program, not to mention driving Yermakov over the edge into a Russian civil war.

If Millstein wasn't captured, where the hell *was* he? And *where* was Gruhaber? Had Millstein killed him? Were they both dead? Van Damme's long nails gouged the seat's cheap fabric. He turned to see if Savin noticed, but the older man merely stared out of his heavily tinted window.

Van Damme had already put the word out scrapping Gruhaber's defection scenario. Even while those press jackals back on Capitol Hill tore at Van Damme's scraps of information, the little programmer's bank accounts were being reversed and the evidence in his apartment eliminated. Indigo would have to remain a dead issue until Millstein and Gruhaber were located.

The car was stopped. Savin was already half out, frowning at Van Damme's trancelike concentration. With an apologetic shrug, Van Damme skidded his long legs through the open door.

Ragged sunlight ricocheted into his eyes from the main building's windows. Heavy heat clamped down upon his scalp. Even the birds were too drained to sing.

Van Damme hurried along, careful not to pass up the slower-moving Savin in his desperation for the building's dark coolness. All he had to do was find out what happened to Millstein and the Gruhaber and everything was under control. Van Damme made a conscious effort to smile at Savin's bobbing back. Next he forced himself to suck in a deep drought of hot, moist air. He began to relax. Yes, he *would* find Millstein and Gruhaber, if they were to be found. Even for an "unofficial" operation like this, he had plenty of surveillance men and informants inside Germany and Russia. He'd know whatever had happened to the two within a week.

*　　*　　*

Had Captain Uri Grigov waited another eight hours, he could have read about Amphora and Kharkov in the wire services. Not knowing this, he plumbed the depths of Lubyanka, arriving at a level that never had and never would be seen by thrill-seeking tourists.

The KGB's central communications center remained perfectly intact. In the pre-reform days, orders that were too sensitive for conventional diplomatic channels were beamed to operatives in embassies spanning the globe from inside its subterranean walls. Some would have sworn that similar messages still emanated from streamlined satellite dishes. They would not necessarily have been wrong.

Grigov was reasonably sure that Kharkov was in or near Berlin. The extremely important man, to whom Grigov had appealed for help, had been able to ascertain this by making three quick phone calls. He had shared his information with Grigov, but his thick eyebrows had squatted above the bridge of his nose for their entire interview. Nothing was said, but the Captain knew that he did not want to be the object of such a frown ever again.

Grigov marveled at the labyrinthine complex's relative silence. Banks of computers replaced rattling, buzzing transmitters that had previously transformed the center into a B movie director's version of Frankenstein's laboratory. He worked his way through the technological maze until he stood behind a straight-backed young man with a rigid, blond brush cut. "Sneaking in Pacman again, Roshenko?"

The young blue-eyed face swiveled quickly, literally lighting up as its owner recognized Grigov. "Captain, a long time. Are you back with us?"

"No such luck. Still wiping the noses of GRU toy soldiers. But I wonder if I have enough credits left over for a favor?"

"For the best operations officer I ever trained under? Always." Roshenko's eyes darkened in concentration. Playtime was over.

"Sit, Roshenko. *Sit*. I'm not grading your exams anymore." Grigov pushed a clutter of papers from the edge of the next desk, straddling its corner. "I have to locate Colonel Kharkov. Some sort of silly interdepartmental nonsense not worth discussing." Grigov flung out an open palm in dismissal. "He was supposed to be in Berlin."

Without response, Regoff swiveled toward his screen and commenced a steady clacking on the loose keys.

Grigov watched over the man's broad back, marveling at the speed of screen changes as incalculable possibilities flashed by.

Finally, Roshenko spun around, shoulders slumped forward, lips pursed. "Nothing, Sir. I checked the embassies in all the surrounding countries as well. Are you sure he is in Eastern Europe?" Roshenko hunched his shoulders and winced before Grigov could reply. "Of course you are, Captain. Forgive my thoughtless question."

Grigov shook off the apology. "Try accidents, deaths … any incidents involving Russian citizens … or even Warsaw Bloc nationals." His bad foot began to throb. Too much standing in one place made it throb, but then, so did hanging it from a desk like this. The nerves were gone, except for the ones that transmitted the interminable buzzing like a bashed funny bone. "Call me at this extension. I will be there until I hear from you."

Roshenko absorbed the request-turned-demand without comment, flinging himself at his computer like a demented pianist.

*   *   *

An hour later, the shrill ring of Grigov's phone vibrated the walls of his tiny office.

"Captain?"

"Yes, Roshenko."

"Only one thing so far. An inquiry by Berlin police about four nationals with false IDs, killed in an apartment house in Berlin over a week ago. Also two Americans … We don't know about their IDs. It was buried in Karinski's low-priority stack. Everyone figured it was just another drug deal gone sour."

"What was the address of the apartment house?"

"Let me see. Kuhlstrasse, number 44, Sir."

"Kuhlstrasse? Kuhl … yes! I'll bet a month's pay that's one of the apartments that we kept in East Berlin for meetings between control agents and their foreign national recruits. We used to have dozens of such locations. "Roshenko, you are a star in our black hole of inefficiency. I owe you a swim in vodka." Grigov slammed the instrument. His bad leg knocked the side of his desk, but the captain barely noticed the pain in his haste to leave.

*   *   *

He was in East Berlin by three fifteen, thanks to a speedily arranged military flight into nearby Schönefeld Airport. Grigov sympathized with civilians. The same trip by Aeroflot into Tegel, Berlin's main airport, could have taken up to two weeks to arrange, *if* there were no complications— which there always were.

Moder was clearly surprised by the status of his visitor, his granite-block face drooping before he recovered. The dimensions of Moder's office reminded Grigov of his own, but he sensed that had Moder known, the captain's grudging respect would have been instantly withdrawn. Grigov kept the office analogy to himself.

They hurried down to view the bodies. Definitely Kharkov. Try as he might, Grigov could not resist an uncharitable thought. He had never seen Kharkov looking better. He had no idea who the others were. Descriptions were coded back to Roshenko. It was 4:12.

News of Savin's press conference broke at 4:43.

Grigov crucified Moder on the spot. Not that he had any authority to do so, but he did it anyway. Moder, forgetting that world events had made them equals, reacted with the instinctive subservience that Grigov had counted upon. The policeman kept muttering something about "I did not want to embarrass myself." Something else about *"My* district." The Russian captain literally slapped him to get him moving away from his desk and out of his perspiration-fouled little room.

Together they crossed the Unter den Linden toward the Ministry of Foreign Affairs. Bright lances of afternoon sunlight rebounded directly into their eyes from the building's narrow windows. Summer birds, invisible in the thick leaves overhead, trilled and warbled. Early patrons milled under a café's yellow-and-gray awnings, their laughter harmonizing with its splashing fountain.

It was probably all very charming. Grigov didn't care.

They confronted the two battered men at 5:13. One had a nasty cough.

Grigov asked for their documents. Moder lumbered toward the rear of the room, foraged behind a wall of boxes, and returned with a large envelope with two mashed-in corners. The KGB man rifled through the contents, noting that both wallets were devoid of currency—an inexplicable phenomenon for international travelers. As he laid the envelope with its contents on a nearby crate, the Russian captain determined that he would educate Moder on the virtues of honest law enforcement when he finished interrogating the prisoners.

By 7:20, Grigov was jetting home. He slid his fourth antacid tablet onto his tongue, tried to suck it, but ended up chewing it instead. His lips puckered at its chalklike taste. Grigov's chronically painful foot was suddenly the least of his worries. The acid washing up out of his undulating stomach was far more uncomfortable. Yet the KGB man would have gladly embraced his pain for eternity to avoid facing the extremely important man's awful frown for the second time in less than twenty-four hours.

Chapter 25

After the visit from the Russian Captain—at least Rosen thought the man was dressed in a captain's uniform—things got slightly better.

The constant drafts stopped, and Rosen was encouraged. It meant that their captors were taking precautions to prevent Otto's hacking cough from worsening. The implication was that they did not wish to kill Otto and Rosen—at least not at the moment.

The beatings continued, but the Neanderthal with the huge fists didn't seem to have his heart in it. *Either someone was taking his and Otto's story more seriously*, thought Rosen, *or Captain Moder wasn't getting enough sleep.*

"Cough seems better." Rosen smiled weakly. His right eye was so blurry from swelling that Otto appeared to have two left ears.

"Yes." Otto's desire to communicate had all but disappeared over the course of their ordeal.

"Zhut up!" Karl, their guard at the moment, apparently knew only one English expression, delivered with blaring intonation. He never hit, but he snarled a lot. One muscular arm bore the name "Ula" inside a three-masted schooner. Karl always brought their evening food, usually late and always cold. Rosen was not sure if those were Karl's orders or if he was simply indifferent to the condition of their cuisine. Tonight the fare was spicy sausage, boiled potato, and a little warm beer served on the customary school cafeteria–type tray. Karl bent near Rosen's feet to set the tray down so that he could untie their hands. It was a ritual that he followed every night, with the tray never being less than a foot or more than two feet from Rosen's right shoe. Karl never seemed to have a gun; he just had a long police nightstick. With their legs tied, he really didn't need one, except tonight.

The edge of Rosen's stiffened right hand slashed into the back of Karl's thick neck, dropping him face-first onto the sausages. Their soft brown insides oozed out from beneath his cheek and nose.

Otto gawked as if trying to reconstruct the events that had reduced Karl to such a state.

Rosen worked his other hand loose. "Someone didn't do a good job on these knots this morning. I was hoping that Karl would stick to his routine with the tray … He seemed kind of compulsive."

By then, Rosen had unraveled the cords around his ankles. Next he checked Karl. If he didn't suffocate in the sausage, he'd be fine in an hour or two. Rosen went to work on Otto's wrists. The little man creaked up from his chair, nearly tripping as he forgot that his feet were still bound. Rosen sat him back down and began digging into the thick knots that hugged Otto's ankles.

Otto was up again, staring at Rosen like a lost child looking at a police officer. He hacked repeatedly, bending at the waist as if Moder's huge fists were still pummeling his gut. He finally straightened, heaving and teary-eyed.

"Can you make it, Otto? We have to get out of here."

"Zertainly." Otto thrust his tiny shoulders back, eyes slit in determination.

"Then stay close to me." Rosen was positive that Karl hadn't locked the door; he was too confident to bother. Sure enough, it grudgingly creaked open. Although he was reasonably sure that their guards worked individually, Rosen prayed that no one else happened to be in the corridor. The opening door was a fanfare announcing their exit.

The corridor was empty. Elongated shadows cloaked rough wooden doors whose padlocks glowed eerily in the dusky light.

Rosen quickly ducked back in, almost knocking Otto down. "That's following me a little *too* closely, Otto. I've got to get back over to Karl for a second." Rosen reached down for the man, hoisted his dead weight up into the chair that Rosen had recently occupied, curled the rope around the upper part of Karl's arms—which dangled along his sides—yanked tight, looped it around Karl's chest, and yanked a second time. Once Karl's feet were done, Rosen tugged, checking to make sure that the bonds would hold. He then removed Karl's right shoe, yanked off his grimy sock, and wedged it into Karl's slack jaw.

Rosen squinted toward the back corner and then dashed into the shadows, returning with the battered manila envelope that the Russian captain had recently placed upon a crate. Rosen inserted his fingers into its mushy mouth. "Here." He handed Otto his passport and wallet. Rosen reached in a second time and removed his own wallet. He then balled the ruined envelope and pitched it back into the shadows. He dug hesitantly into the interior compartment of the wallet. "Hey, Otto, what do you know? The Germans only ripped me off for about half. How 'bout you?" Rosen waited for a response, but Otto merely gaped at the objects in his palm without recognition.

Rosen reached for Otto's wallet. "Here, let's see … You've got some money left too. Well, all right!" Rosen slid the wallet into Otto's front pant pocket. "Better let me have that too." He plucked the passport from the little man's feeble grasp and jammed it into Otto's other pocket. "Now we're set, Otto old buddy. Oh yeah, one more thing." Rosen dangled the false mustache that had been stuck to the envelope between his thumb and forefinger. "Has *this* seen better days?" He picked at its surface and then held it to the light. "Hopeless." With a flick of his wrist, he banished it to the same shadowy oblivion as the manila envelope.

Back at the door, Rosen craned his head out once more and then motioned for Otto to follow.

Their progress was slow: Rosen moving ahead along the wall, peering as best he could down the hazy corridor and then signaling for Otto to catch up. Twice they had to stop for Otto's coughing jags to subside, with Rosen hugging Otto's feverish face to his own chest to muffle the furious hacking.

The hall widened as they reached the stairs. Lighting from above looked far more reliable. *Probably fluorescents*, thought Rosen. He parked Otto out of the light and crept up. The next level looked like more storage, although the ceiling was higher and the corridors wider. Above that, there was a garage level. Good enough. Garages had exits. Anything higher and they would run into the main entry area and possibly night attendants.

A quick peek into the massive garage confirmed that very few government employees burned the midnight oil. One or two solitary vehicles stood among acres of white-lined stalls like metallic cows in a vast concrete pasture. The odor of gasoline from inefficient engines persisted like an invisible cloud layer. Rosen's cheek brushed the door's cold metal as he withdrew his head.

Moments later, Rosen had Otto by the arm. By the third level, he had Otto's arm over his shoulder so that he lifted him in unison with his dragging rear foot. With each faltering step, Rosen worried more and more about the little man's ability to continue. "Can you make it okay?"

"Yah." Otto flapped an impatient left hand.

They entered the parking garage. Although he made a valiant effort not to, Otto shuffled every fourth or fifth step. The sound of his scraping foot bounded hollowly across the limitless concrete. As they approached a small door next to the closest huge roll-up door, a sequence of loud *clicks* escaped a green metal housing mounted shoulder high against the wall. Both men started but then sighed as only air-conditioning commenced *whirring*.

There was no alarm on the small door. Rosen had feared that it might be an emergency exit. If it was, they hadn't outfitted it with an alarm. Rosen tugged it open. A wave of humid air poured in.

They stepped out onto a wide driveway. To his left, superimposed over moonlit clouds, Rosen recognized the dome of Saint Hedwig's Cathedral. The Unter den Linden would be to their right. Their shoes flicked pebbles across the asphalt as Rosen and Otto advanced toward the sporadic drone of cars passing along the nearby avenue.

*　*　*

"Hitler" Moder snapped three more pencils in succession. His tiny office seemed even smaller after his humiliating confrontations with the recently departed Russian Captain. Imagine being forced to bungle an interrogation *in his very own district*. His meaty fists flung files and papers across the three feet from his desk to the wall. They cascaded to the floor in tangled confusion. Then his giant chest expanded and he let out a huge sigh. One good thing came of this mess. Fritz, who was responcible for the prisnors, will be held accountable for the sloppy ropes around Rozen's hands and Rozen's escape, even though they were actually quite tight until *my* final inspection. He cocked his square face toward the room next door that housed his staff. *Sorry, Fritz*, he smirked, *you won't be taking over my position until you are an ancient, and probably not even then. Too bad, you ambitious little bastard.*

*　*　*

Mercer and Hobbs picked them up right away. Mercer did anyway. He was much smarter than Hobbs, who sat behind the wheel stuffing his face with a smelly cheese sandwich loaded with mayonnaise, most of which was oozing out along his lips like toothpaste.

Who the hell else would be shuffling down Unter den Linden at this time of night except them? The only other people around were Berliners from the west closing down the Operncafe after a night of slumming in the eastern part of the city. And *they* sure as hell weren't walking like these two. Not with that caravan of Mercedes straddling the curb.

How the hell did that little Gruhaber get out? That's what Mercer wanted to know. Nobody just walked out of those storage rooms in that Foreign Ministry monstrosity. The basement storage rooms were a little secret that former East German Keystone Cops hid from Bonne: a nostalgic carryover of the good-old days of political assassination and unrestricted torture. What a laugh. Every rookie from every intelligence service—even the Italians—knew they were still used for *special* interrogations. And who the fuck was this guy with Gruhaber?

Something was *definitely* wrong. No Millstein, a clean escape that couldn't happen in a million years, and some guy who wasn't supposed to be there helping little Gruhaber stumble down the street.

He and Hobbs were supposed to be routine surveillance in case Millstein and Gruhaber showed. Carter at Berlin Station had figured the two would turn up at either the ministry or the morgue if they were still in the eastern part of the city, so he gave Mercer and Hobbs the ministry and two other guys the morgue.

They hadn't been told why they were looking for the pair. Probably not a kosher operation, but Mercer didn't care. Half of them weren't, and he'd lost his virginity too long ago to worry about it. And Hobbs. Forget Hobbs—that prick was so twisted that his hard-on looked like a corkscrew. The point was that nobody had really expected to see Millstein and Gruhaber again—at least not on their feet—after all this time. This surveillance circus was just for show, Mercer had figured. Probably to keep some big shot up the line happy.

Now this. *Just my luck*, thought Mercer. *Stuck with a loser like Hobbs and this turns out to be the first surveillance in the last two friggin' years that I actually see somebody I'm supposed to be looking for. Great. Just great! At midnight, yet.* "Hey, Hobbs, our guys are walking."

"Uhmff … huh?"

"Get that shit out of your mouth. Most of it's on your shirt anyway. I *said* that our guy is walking."

"Yeah. Where?" Hobbs stuffed the sandwich back into its greasy paper sack. He dabbed mayonnaise from his lips with the back of his wrist and wiped it on the seat.

"*There!*" Mercer pointed, jamming his finger repeatedly against the windshield as Hobbs gaped like a fish staring out of its glass bowl.

"Holy shit. How'd they get out? An' who's the other guy? That ain't that old fart Millstein."

"Who knows? All I know is what we gotta do."

"Yeah. What?"

"Wait until they get past the café; there are too many people there. Maybe on a side street or when they get to the trees near the statue. Then we grab the little guy and take out the other—nobody said nothin' about keeping anyone else except Millstein."

"Okay." Hobbs turned the key. The lights snapped on.

"*Get those fucking lights off! We're sitting here parked at the curb and you flash the fucking lights. Why don't we just yell, 'Hey, we're coming to get you! Don't you know anything, Hobbs?*"

"Keep your pants on; they went on automatically. We drive so many cars that you never know what they're gonna do so fuck off! Those turkeys ain't thinking 'bout anything now 'cept getting their asses the hell outta here." Hobbs twisted the end of the turn signal. The lights popped back into the hood.

"How the fuck do you know, huh? You think it takes a genius to wonder why a damn parked car has people in it this time of night? It doesn't. It just takes someone a little smarter'n you … which is just about anybody."

"Ah, fuck off, Mercer. You worry too much. That's why you got no hair."

Mercer hated that. No matter how badly he screwed up, Hobbs always had that comeback. It shut Mercer up every time. He hated losing his hair, and he hated any reference to it. Fucking Hobbs with his gut and body odor—and just about every other loathsome characteristic known to man—had *hair*, which always put him one up on Mercer. It wasn't fair. "Okay. *Okay.* Let's keep it on business." Mercer felt Hobbs's smirk burning the side of his face, but he refused to turn toward his partner. He wouldn't give Hobbs the satisfaction. "Wait until they pass, then ease out and swing a U. No one'll give a shit this time of night. No traffic. We go down a ways and then come back toward 'em—"

"What the fuck?" Hobbs did a classic double take, his fish eyes gaping.

"Step on it. *Step on it, you asshole*! The bastard's grabbing that guy's Mercedes, yanking him right out, fer Christ's sake! See, Hobbs. *See, you shmuck*! He must have seen the lights."

"Shut up, Mercer. I don't need to hear a lot of crying. You know that's what they call you? '*Crybaby* Mercer.'"

"Fuck you, Hobbs. I just take my job seriously. Not like a fuck-off like you. *Will you get going*? They're already turning. *Move*!"

The big Mercedes squealed from the curb, cutting straight out and then screeching left toward the tree-lined islands. Its sprawled owner rose shakily, too stunned to react for a moment. Suddenly, he erupted into manic hand waving and shouting. A berserk penguin in his disheveled tuxedo.

Hobbs tried a U, nearly buying it from a passing van.

"Will you watch out!" Mercer swung his arms around as if he were warding off killer bees. "How are we supposed to catch 'em if you get us killed, you moron?"

"Shut up, Mercer. Just *shut up*!" Hobbs skidded the Toyota around, jammed into third. The Mercedes was already turning on Friedrichstraße.

"Better keep it respectable until we get a little farther out. Don't want the police in on this." No more bullshitting now. Mercer was calm and Hobbs was too. With all their hassling, they were actually a pretty good team.

Mercer reached under the dash and pulled out his Colt Maxi-Comp. Strands of silver electrical tape, which had held it in place, clung to its nickel exterior. Mercer stripped them off with a series of sharp crackles. He rested the weapon on the back of his forearm and sighted the Mercedes through its special scope. "The other guy's driving. I can either get him or a tire. I'd rather get him, but the little guy has a better chance if I go for the tire." Mercer shrugged over at Hobbs. "I don't know. They said keep him alive … if we can. Hell. Get me close and I'll see what I can do."

* * *

"Son of a bitch is trying to get to the airport," noted Mercer. They had chased the Mercedes in silence with Hobbs intent behind the wheel and Mercer fine-tuning his scope.

The Mercedes was moving fast along Straße des 17. Juni. Sure enough, it swung right across Charlottenburg, heading for the Wedding district.

"He'll be on the Avus extension soon. If we can pull up, I could get a good shot there. The blown tire would take care of both of them. Carter said we only had to *try* to get the little guy back alive. No point in jumping through hoops ta do it, right?"

"If we can keep up with him in this piece of shit," snarled Hobbs.

"You can do it, Hobbsey." Mercer grinned at his partner. When it came to the actual action, *he* was the cooler one. It was only the little bullshit details that drove him crazy. The big stuff he could always handle.

As soon as they hit the high-speed road, the Mercedes accelerated away as if Mercer and Hobbs were standing still. Those clowns in the Mercedes might think they had gotten lucky and hit an autobahn, but Mercer knew it was just a short extension road and not one of the streamlined monsters that laced West Germany.

Hobbs gamely put the Toyota through its paces. In addition to being out-horsepowered, the embassy mechanics had done a lousy job of tuning the car. As Hobbs accelerated past seventy-five kilometers, it began bucking. "Just great! Why the hell don't they just give us skateboards?" Hobbs pounded meaty palms against the steering wheel. It vibrated with a monotonous hum.

"Hey, Hobbs. We didn't think we'd be chasing these yahoos, did we? Just keep 'em in sight … We got plenty a chance at the airport. There ain't even gonna be any crowds this late."

No sooner had Mercer spoken than the control tower of Tegel Airport materialized out of the darkness. Three-quarters of the way up its nearly invisible base sat two stories of bright rounded windows, capped by what looked like a lantern top. It could have been a flying saucer whirling in for a landing. Below, night mist diffused window light from the massive terminal building.

"What's that asshole doing now?" Hobbs squinted, bobbing his head up and sidewise to keep the Mercedes in view as it weaved between extended rows of parked vehicles.

"Look." Mercer's stubby finger jabbed at the windshield. "The bastard's running for the restricted area. Son of a bitch knows we're here an' he can't get by us to the terminal. Thinks he can lose us out on the runways in the dark. Let him try. Easier for us. Nice and isolated. I *love* it." Mercer jiggled the Colt in front of Hobbs's nose. "I've got an infrared scope for this baby. That asshole's in a world of trouble now, an' he don't even know it."

"Shit!" Hobbs smacked Mercer's gun away with the edge of his hand.

The Toyota squealed off to the right before he could get it under control. "You are one crazy bastard, Mercer," he said, without looking at his grinning passenger.

Mercer reached for the cellular and dialed. "Carter, that you? Believe it or not, the pigeon is actually flying. Yeah, the little guy with the weird name. He showed about forty minutes ago. I'm *not* shittin' ya. Him and some guy I don't know … not Millstein. I told ya, dummy—some guy I don't know! I *know* Millstein … Okay, forget it." Mercer put his hand over the mouthpiece and looked at Hobbs. "What a numbnuts," he whispered before putting the phone back against his ear. "We're at Tegel, following 'em toward the runways. Have the others back us up at the terminal … Yeah. Catch ya later." He clicked the receiver back into place. "Numbnuts," he muttered to himself.

The Mercedes jumped off the apron, bouncing along the rough grass and weeds that bordered the runway. From off to his left, Mercer caught the wheezing roar of a firing jet engine. Flames danced from its maw, projecting shadows of parked aircraft across their Toyota. "Okay, Hobbsey. His ass is ours now. We can move as fast as he can through those ruts and shit, so let's do it!"

The Toyota lurched as it lost traction, then dug in, kicking out a spray of grass and weeds as it bounded after the Mercedes.

*　*　*

Rosen fought the wheel as the heavy car bounced and banged over uneven soil, rocks, and small bushes. Otto gripped the dash, his wide eyes riveted upon surrealistic splashes of terrain flashing chaotically in their lurching headlight beams.

Rosen had spotted them as soon as he and Otto had cleared the ministry. Pretty amateurish flicking on their lights like that, but he had to admit that since that initial mistake, they'd done pretty well. Although he'd been able to stay ahead, he couldn't shake them. Couldn't have made it into the terminal with Otto limping before they caught up, either.

Rosen had no doubt that whoever they were, they were armed, so his only chance was out here, car against car. His was bigger and heavier. If he could outmaneuver them, he ought to be able to put the light Toyota out of commission. He glanced at the rearview mirror. The Toyota's lights were bouncing as if they were on springs. *Good, you bastards*, Rosen thought with grim satisfaction. *I hope your teeth shake out.*

Rosen saw what he was looking for: an auxiliary taxi strip with vacant planes lined for morning flights. Lots of room for hide-and-seek among those huge wheels and broad wings. There was a big United 727 along with three Lufthansa monsters, plus some others too dark to identify. He cut the wheel sharply. The heavy vehicle lurched, its rear swerving as if it were spinning into a 180. Rosen hunched up his shoulders to his ears. Had he expected too much from even a Mercedes?

Otto yelped, "Gott in Himmel!"

The rear wheels bit, and the Mercedes righted itself. It shot off the dirt and bounced up the tarmac apron, squealing toward the shadows of the towering, silent aircraft.

*   *   *

"What the fuck? Now he's going for that plane parking lot over there. This guy must be panicked out of his mind, hey, Hobbsey?"

"I guess." Hobbs was too busy wrenching the bucking wheel to analyze the mental state of their quarry.

"When we get them backed up on the other side of those planes, we leave the car. You take 'em left; I'll go right. We'll use the semiautomatic stuff in the trunk. Either of us can stop 'em if they try to go around … an' we catch 'em in the crossfire if they try up the middle. We're so damn far away from that terminal that we could fire mortars and no one would notice."

"Yeah. *Yeah!*" The Toyota flew off a high patch of rugged grass, hitting the tarmac on two wheels. Hobbs down-geared, grunting as the steering wheel vibrated clear through his locked elbows, his shoulders, and into his lower jaw.

"So let's herd them down toward the middle," Mercer said.

Hobbs, perspiration trickling everywhere—even into his ears—gaped at his partner as Mercer casually lowered his window like a commuter approaching a tollbooth. Mercer rested his left forearm along the window's edge; he laid the Colt gently upon it, bent to line up his eye with the scope, and slowly squeezed the trigger three times. One shot ricocheted behind the Mercedes, kicking up a minute shower of sparks. The next two ignited the tarmac near its right front wheel. "That should do it." Mercer grinned, blowing imaginary smoke from the Colt's muzzle in a clichéd imitation of a victorious gunslinger.

"Yeah, you're the greatest shot west of the Pecos, Wild Bill." Hobbs dug into his nostril with a knuckle. "Let's wrap this up, huh? Before they get back in them fuckin' weeds again. My nuts are aching enough already."

"We'll take care of your valuable balls, Hobbsey. Just a little farther." Mercer began to snicker but stopped as he squinted through the windshield. Suddenly, he pulled back, eyes widening until he thought that his lids would tear.

"*Haaaaaabsssss!*" Mercer pointed with the Colt, frantically spiraling its barrel in an erratic circle.

"What the fuck—" Hobbs's face mirrored Mercer's. Twenty feet ahead, an aircraft fuel truck rolled slowly from behind a Lufthansa jet's huge wheel. It moved toward them, dark and silent, like a miniature offspring of the great plane.

Mercer's hands shot up to protect his face, but the ripping yellow flame tore through his fingers, frying his eyes as he catapulted through the windshield and into the inferno beyond.

*　*　*

He smoothed back his fine blond hair that he wore, against all regulations, in a short ponytail. Ignoring the heat, he strode from his protected spot behind the Lufthansa jet's enormous tire toward a shadow-draped Porsche. Outracing the Mercedes and the now molten Toyota had been easy once he was sure of the Mercedes's destination.

He settled his average-sized frame into the low bucket seat and waited. The sweetness of rich leather was tantalizing. This was not the kind of vehicle that he could ever dream of driving back home. He worked the shift lovingly, savoring its precision even in the stationary vehicle.

The Mercedes idled a safe distance from the raging flames. *Its occupants must be too stunned by their good fortune to move,* he thought.

Good fortune. No such thing. Loosening the little truck's fuel valve, removing its wheel blocks, releasing the emergency brake: *that* was their good fortune. That and the slight downslope on which the truck was parked. And of course, excellent timing on his part.

The Mercedes backed up hesitantly and then made a wide arc back toward the terminal. He followed without lights, keeping far enough behind so that the synchronized whine of his engine remained out of hearing range.

Parking was easy this time of night, and he had no trouble keeping them in view all the way to the United counter.

Off to his right, he spotted two others with an undue interest in his quarry: definite problem.

He scanned a nearby departure board. They must be taking the 1:15 flight to New York. It was the only one leaving before dawn. Departure wasn't for another thirty-five minutes—plenty of time.

The ticket vendor pointed across the counter, and the taller man's head revolved in the direction of her finger. He turned to thank her and then walked directly toward a blue-doored men's room. The smaller man stumbled along at his side.

The two who had been watching followed. They both carried long raincoats folded neatly over their arms. It was humorous. They looked like nonidentical twins trying to dress alike. The blond man knew that what was beneath the raincoats was anything but humorous. He arched his neck, flexing his meticulously developed shoulder muscles. The ponytail swung and then settled back as his right hand flicked forward, sending a long, thin blade sliding down into his palm. His fingers shielded its glint from those hurrying by.

Twenty minutes later, the blond man followed the two Americans through security. The long blade had been safely shoved deep down into an overstuffed trash receptacle in the men's room. He wondered how long it would be before the blood from the two adjoining johns pooled out onto the tile floor despite the paper towels that he wadded around the dead men's wounds. It was not that he was worried. He never worried—was only curious. No matter how stopgap his methods, he would be at least thirty-six thousand feet in the air before the first scream rocked the terminal.

CHAPTER 26

Billows of cigar smoke spiraled up from Culcane's desk, engulfing dust particles that bobbed in the window light. The offices of less secure senators had understated white walls and sparse decorations. With public outrage billowing over fiscal abuses, their occupants preferred to have visitors relay tales of austerity to their constituents. Such was not the case with Culcane's prestigious front-row office in the Richard Russell Building. Abundant vases, oils, and antebellum furniture—including a massive gun case with eight gleaming shotguns suspended at precise intervals—crowded its ample dimensions.

Van Damme stared across Delaware Avenue, where Capitol Hill office workers hunched over brown-bag lunches on the low stone wall surrounding a large fountain.

"We got the Pres'dent ahn the run, son." Culcane's voice had a harsh quality, despite his Carolina drawl. "You gonna be the next depity directah a op'rations within a week aw so. Pres'dent's 'bout redda to lean all ovah Savin raht nah. Polls ah showin' people want a strong man in intell'gence—this Amphora scared the shit outta them—an' you that man."

Culcane's soles pivoted in rhythm with his speech. With his feet atop the huge desk, the rest of him was below eye level so that Van Damme could only respond in the direction of the most recent smoke columns. "Well, I am certainly looking forward to serving in that capacity, Senator. And I appreciate all of the help that you and your friends have given me. Without you, the President wouldn't know I exist."

"Nah, don' be so modest, son. You the one thet showed us what the Russkies ah up ta."

"Yes, but without your help, no one would have ever known I had anything to do with it, Senator. You know, as well as I do, that the credit always goes to the top."

"Mebbe you ah raht." Culcane's feet skidded off the desk. Sheets of white paper followed, gliding through the rays from the window on their descent toward the maroon carpet. Culcane's head popped up, pig eyes glowing through the halo of smoke. "In thayt case, theh is a little favah you could do fo' us … if you wuh so inclahned."

Van Damme was not so surprised that a "favor" was forthcoming as by the early nature of its timing. "Yes, Senator?" He hoped that sounded sufficiently noncommittal.

"Well, Chahlie"—Culcane was oblivious to the involuntary tug of Van Damme's shoulders at this aberration of his name—"ah don't know what the Russkies have got in mind or evun if they got the stomach fuh any more fightin'. But ah do know that a lotta my frens—an' therefow *yaw* frens"—he jabbed the glowing cigar toward Van Damme—"could get a big edge if they was ta know what was going on in Eastun Europe. Yuh know, lotta people heah an' in Europe gonna be spendin' a lotta money ovuh theh. He'ps ta know whethuh it's gonna be a good inves'ment oh not." Culcane pursed his thick lips, studying the glowing cylinder of ash before looking back up at Van Damme.

Van Damme sucked in a deep breath and immediately regretted it. Tendrils of pungent smoke assailed his nostrils, even at this distance. He had known that this was coming. Better to set the ground rules right now. He hadn't gone through all this just to become someone's boy; had never become Jefferson Pelt IV's boy; would not be Culcane's either. Van Damme's spine stiffened as he let the breath escape slowly through his lips. "If I can do that without compromising national security or my agency, Senator."

Had Culcane's eyes flashed? Did the square head jerk back slightly? Van Damme could not be sure. Culcane's responses were minute, if they happened at all. Before Van Damme could read the man further, Culcane's flesh oozed back into a smile, obliterating any vestiges of his real feelings.

"A co'se, son. We admahr your integ'ity. Tha's why we behin' yuh. Ah onluh meyant if—"

"If I can, of course I will. Anything to help the people who are helping me serve my country."

"Apraypos a that, Chahlie. Some people think you could go higher in se'ving ya countrah."

Van Damme's pulse throbbed despite his attempt to relax. "Such as what, Sir?" He forced his fingers to loosen around the slim wooden arms of his chair. His shiny wing tips looked very distant.

"'Lected office, a co'se. Why, ya got almos' as much reco'nition as ol' Ollie Nawth … an' without one-hun'eth the press an' TV exposhuh."

Van Damme almost spoke, checked himself, remembering the golden rule: Never interrupt when things are already going great.

"Yep, ah sure do see yuh in thet roll. Lawd knows the pahty needs some new blood." Culcane crushed his butt into a green glass ashtray bearing the party emblem. "But fust things fust. Le's get you effec'ively runnin' the CIA opahrations. Savin'll fuss, but with us ta back yuh, the Pres'dent'll sit him down an' have a haht ta haht. Lotsa good exposhuh fo' ya. Aftuh thayt, be plennya time fuh ya ta move ahn up."

Van Damme stifled a wild impulse to lean back, slip his hands behind his head, and kick his feet up on Culcane's desk. This got better and better. "I'll leave myself in your good hands, Senator." He rose, extending his right hand.

Culcane leaned forward as far as his stomach would allow, managing to give Van Damme a three-quarter grip. The senator's palm was like moist dough. "Tha's raht, son. Yuh leave it ta me. You an' the pahty gonna do jus' fahn tagethah." The flesh around Culcane's right eye swelled shut in what Van Damme supposed was a wink. Then Culcane's dark eyes glazed over. Their meeting had ended.

*　　*　　*

Light diffused through myriad crystals into a swelling rainbow. The chandelier was immense by normal standards, merely appropriate to the dimensions of the Pell dining room. Van Damme wished that he had the courage to inform the table that he intended to spend the remainder of the evening cataloging every one of its twinkling teardrops, diamonds, and spheres. That way, dinner would be over without his ever having to set eyes on Richardson Pell. But then, Felicia wouldn't sleep with him for at least a week. Besides, was it his imagination or had the old curmudgeon been unusually civil? Van Damme wrenched his gaze from the pleasing glass fragments and contemplated the figure far down at the head of the table.

A vulture—that was Richardson Pell IV. All the way from the heavy head hanging far forward over the narrow, pointy shoulders to the arthritic clawlike hands with their curving yellow nails. They reminded Van Damme of talons, the way that they snagged dazzling silver chafing dishes laden with bright steamed vegetables and mounds of parsley-dotted potatoes.

Even Pell's rheumy blue eyes had a dead quality, as if very little that they saw was processed by the brain. Not true. Everything was processed and *reprocessed* by that hyper-powered computer mind of Pell's. Nothing escaped its analysis—not in business and not in private life.

To Pell's right, his wife, Fiona, a sparrow to his vulture, small, pale, jittery, forever warding off both real and imagined affronts with a staccato "Oh, that's all right, dear. That's all right." Had Fiona ever been the woman in the old man's life? Van Damme wondered. Certainly not after Felicia.

His gaze swept quickly by the three brothers: middle-aged squash players, past their starting-to-lose-it wives, to Felicia, who, according to Pell's decree, always sat on his left. Coincidentally, this was usually as far away from Van Damme as the extended table allowed.

"Felicia tells me that you may have a try at politics, Cha'lls." Van Damme detested Pell's blue-blooded rendition of his name worse than all of the other hateful variations put together. Pell's voice crackled like a sawed limb about to give way, proof that even vast wealth could not adequately insulate one against cancer of the larynx. The operation had succeeded in removing the bubbling mass, but portions of Pell's throat had come with it.

"Very premature, Sir." Van Damme twiddled the end of his mustache. He dropped the offending hand into his lap as soon as he realized. He could change world events without blinking an eye, yet he was self-conscious about his every move in front of this old bastard. "'Deputy Director is my immediate goal. If that goes well, then—"

"We need a *politician* in the family. Haven't had one since my grandfather was lieutenant governor. Everyone is too busy making money. We're good at that." The vulture eyes rested on Van Damme's far longer than usual. "You could bring credit to the family—*as* a politician."

Van Damme inventoried the extraordinary number of insults with which old Pell had just zapped him. Cutting him off midsentence. *That* was commonplace—the old boy didn't get many points for that one. How about belittling his anticipated appointment as DDI? That had been good! Give Pell a rating of six. And implying that Van Damme was no good at making money, that was worth at least a seven." Telling Van Damme that he might *finally* bring credit to the family—give the old boy a nine on that one. Total: 22. *Not bad for four and a half sentences, you old bastard.*

"Well, we'll have to see—"

"We could bankroll your campaign royally. Contributions from the companies. Political action committees. Of course, others too will also be overjoyed to help get a right-thinking man into public office." The talons flexed.

Van Damme mentally paraphrased Pell's last statement: 'Others' had damn well *better contribute plenty* if they knew what was good for them.

"And the …" Pell's voice just stopped. It did that often now. His bony cheeks reddened in frustration. The talons worked furiously. The rest of the table hurriedly found coffee to stir, salads to finish, lips that needed wiping. It was unforgivable to acknowledge Pell's residual throat problems.

"The family," Pell continued matter-of-factly, "will provide all other funds necessary." He scanned the table, daring opposition. Only nods of agreement. "The family *needs* a politician of stature, Cha'lls. We have been too long without a presence in that arena."

*　　*　　*

"Daddy is awfully proud of you. I've never seen him so enthusiastic." Felicia's hand rested on Van Damme's accelerator leg. The Lincoln's dash glowed warm green; the road was soft and yielding; Pell's J&B twenty-year-old scotch radiated messages of well-being to his brain.

"Sure. Now that I might do something useful for the Pells with my wasted life, like become a politician." He couldn't bring himself to sound angry about it. Everything was going too well. Why not the politics? He could keep the Russians in their place forever once he took high enough office. He would prevent them from ever jeopardizing the United States again. With Pell money, he was a shoo-in. Why not? It all fit.

Van Damme slid Felicia's fingers toward his crotch. She left them there, rubbing small circles over his organ. He smiled, accelerating toward home. Everything was going just right!

CHAPTER 27

Van Damme thought that the meeting with the president had gone unimaginably well, considering that Culcane had practically blackmailed the chief executive into having Savin replace his current Deputy Director of Intelligence, Martin Alstead, with Charles Van Damme. But President Clendon was a great politician. His cordial smile never wavered during their brief session in the Oval Office. Possibly Clendon was secretly relieved. Elections were less than a year away, and the President needed a popularity boost.

Culcane had argued that Van Damme's appointment would provide that. And to boot, the President would not be blamed by insiders for disloyalty to his man, Savin, because everyone knew that Van Damme's mushrooming visibility was a plus for the party. Culcane had poked a stubby finger in Clendon's direction. "A absolute win-win fuh ya, Mistuh Pres'dent."

By the time that they had finished shaking hands, Van Damme would have sworn that he could see Clenden's wheels turning over the new possibilities. After all, he *was* a politician. All that was left now was next week's announcement by Savin and he, Charles Van Damme, would be the new deputy director.

*   *   *

Van Damme strode through his outer office, catching a surprise glimpse of his delectable intern Shelley's creamy thigh as she bent over a low green file cabinet. Despite his preoccupation, tingly warmth emanated from Van Damme's groin.

"Mr. Craig is waiting, Sir," came from her wind chime voice.

Van Damme tried to take his cue from Craig's sitting posture—a sure indicator of his subordinate's success or failure—but found himself too elated by the results of his meeting with the president to pursue this advantage.

"Did you find them?" Was there a smug cast to Craig's mouth? If so, Van Damme would make him pay dearly, but not now.

"Millstein's dead. One of our nationals in German intelligence says he was carried out of the apartment along with the other stiffs, but some dumb-ass local cop—yuh know, one of those old liners who's waiting for the second coming of Stalin—was sitting on the information for a goddamn week. Our man couldn't make a positive ID 'til last night."

"What about Gruhaber?"

"He escaped from this same dumb cop last night."

Van Damme breathed a long, relaxing sigh. He strode slowly around the massive desk, delicately lifting his pants at the knees before settling into his soft swivel chair. So Gruhaber was all alone. No Millstein to back up his story. Just Van Damme's own word versus the little German's. And once Van Damme resurrected his account of thwarting Gruhaber's sale of Indigo to the Russians, it would be his word against that of an obvious traitor … and since traitors were fair game, he had the firepower to make sure that Gruhaber didn't live long enough to get into a pissing contest with him.

The gaunt Chief of European Division clicked open his Fabergé egg. Light bounded off the tiny roofs. Should he implicate the Russians in espionage to steal Indigo again? Did he really need it? Or was he far enough ahead of the game already? Overdoing was always a risk. Van Damme had been in the business long enough to recognize that right this moment, he was making a career decision. Was there more to this than Craig had told him? "Strange. I'm surprised that a little hothouse flower like Gruhaber could even buckle up his booties by himself, let alone escape from a bunch of former GDR security pros." Van Damme casually clicked the egg open and shut.

"He had help."

Van Damme reset the egg into its lacquered wooden base. "Who?"

"We think it was Rosen." Secret glee livened Craig's dead gray eyes.

"*What!*" escaped Van Damme before he could clamp his gaping mouth shut. Control. *Control.*

"Mercer and Hobbs called in from Tegel, just before they slammed into an oil truck—"

"What did you—"

"That's what I said, Mr. Van Damme. They drove into a damn fuel truck. I don't know any more than that. But Mercer called it all in—said they were chasing two men who'd come out of the Foreign Ministry

Building and stolen a car. One of the descriptions was definitely your little Otto, and the other one sounded a whole lot like Rosen."

Control. Van Damme's hands clenched spasmodically. Thank God he had replaced the Fabergé. If he'd had it in his hands just now … "How could Werner fail?" he queried, his knuckles white. "Why does this Rosen keep coming back?"

Craig surreptitiously observed Van Damme's every movement, like a grade-schooler peeking up his teacher's dress.

"Didn't they ask for backup?" An insipid question, but Van Damme needed time to get his thoughts in order.

"Of course. Those two were found dead in the airport men's room. Stabbed. Never even got their weapons out."

Van Damme began to pivot toward his big tinted window, stopping midway. Craig would be able to see his expression reflected in the glass, and he definitely did not want that. Instead, Van Damme rose, looping around the far end of his desk, away from Craig's line of vision, and walked to his prized Seraut painting. He took a long while studying it; at least he hoped that was what it looked like to Craig. In reality, he couldn't have pointed out the strollers from the trees. There was a crinkling of leather behind Van Damme, and he knew that Craig must have turned to watch him. *Steady, Charles. Don't let him see. Keep it in … Keep it all in.* The figures in the painting began to distinguish themselves from their grassy background. A moment later, his carotid artery stopped twitching. Good. He turned and walked back to his desk, smiling pleasantly at Craig.

"This Rosen. Much more to the man than meets the eye," Van Damme said matter-of-factly after he reseated himself. He laced his fingers behind his head and reclined the chair as far as it would go. His control was back. *Rosen has turned into a worthy opponent,* he rationalized. *Why make the situation so negative? Look at the positive side. The analyst is making your life more interesting.*

Was that disappointment in Craig's face? Van Damme was amazed to discover that he really didn't care. He spun away, licking his upper lip as he studied the triple arches of the headquarters auditorium. Their gleaming whiteness was apparent, even through the heavily tinted window. His pursed his lips, raising his gaze to a field of fragmenting clouds. "I have good reason to believe that Otto Gruhaber is in possession of a set of the plans of the Indigo II spy satellite, which he recently stole from his employer, Sklar Industries. I believe that he intends to turn them over to interests who are unfriendly to our nation. In short, he is a traitor who is planning to defect. *That* makes him fair game. And Rosen too since he is helping him." Van Damme pivoted rapidly back to face Craig. "Reinstate the evidence against Gruhaber. You follow, of course?"

Craig leaned forward, lips pinched, nodding. "Yeah, I get it. Except these two aren't in Europe anymore. They're on their way to Kennedy."

"How do you know?"

"Only flight to the states, then."

Van Damme's upper lip tightened. "Maybe you expect me to call in the Federal Bureau of Inves—"

"Yeah. I know." Craig put up a hand before Van Damme could continue. "We've already taken out—what is it … six people? Here. Stateside. Where we're not supposed to be playing. That's not counting the eleven or so civilians on the interstate. So what's a few more, right?"

Van Damme cupped his fingers and clapped. It was a hollow popping. "Very good, Craig. When you resolve this situation, I will arrange to fly their bodies back to Europe on one of our cargo flights. We need to do everything by the book for this to work."

"Great. We use one of our Bahama charter outfits and everyone thinks that we killed Rosen and the German over there on our turf." Craig reached for a jade paperweight, turning it to catch the window's light. "Nice move."

"Put that *down* and get some men up to Kennedy. *Now!*"

Craig lowered the jade, but very slowly. "I already have. Not to worry." He pushed up, arching his back in an elaborate stretch. "Four contract guys. Eddie's one. He's the guy I used when we interrogated those guys down in Key West—"

"The man's name was Marquand. Mr. *Fred Marquand*. Don't forget it again. He was a better man than you could ever hope to be—one of the best the agency ever had! He wasn't just some 'guy.'"

Craig's eyebrows screwed down in confusion. After a moment, he shrugged and his horse face slipped back into its usual noncommittal stare. "Okay … sorry. Anyway, this Eddie is good. Takes the initiative—"

"He'd better be. I do not want to hear Rosen's name again until he makes the news … as a dead spy. Do you get my drift?"

"I'll take care of things. Not like your boy in Europe—"

"You've had two chances at Rosen already: on the interstate and in that sanatorium. Don't forget *that*, Craig!"

Craig clearly fought not to respond as he reached for the door, but a tremor in his shoulders gave him away. He left without a word.

Van Damme settled back, smiling at the closing door. His resurrection of the plan to implicate Gruhaber in a bogus theft of Indigo had been forced upon him quickly. Now that he could reflect upon it calmly, he was glad of his decision. When he thwarted the Russians this second time, by preventing them from stealing Indigo in concert with Gruhaber, many things would happen, all good. First, what little American sympathy for Russia remained after the Amphora incident would evaporate like water on a hot griddle. Second, the snowballing Van Damme mystique would gather momentum for his ultimate venture into politics. Third— Van Damme had waved the corresponding finger as he formulated each point—Gruhaber would officially become a Russian spy, with Rosen as his accomplice. Then he could devote as many people as he needed to catch and kill them, with little risk to himself, provided that their bodies could be secretly transported back to Europe. And he had certainly arranged *that* on more than one occasion.

Van Damme smoothed the edges of his mustache with the tips of his middle fingers. Here was the best part, he was thinking with a satisfied grin: the KGB and the Red Army would know that Gruhaber's defection was a fraud, because neither of them had anything to do with it. Yermakov, the Soyuz Party freaks, the other hard-liners, and the xenophobic nationalist groups would go absolutely crazy. Why would the CIA set them up after the Amphora rhubarb unless the United States was looking for excuses to intervene militarily? The root of all Russian paranoia was a fear of being attacked. Their history was replete with invasions. With NATO the only viable power in Europe, the Russian siege mentality was rampant. Yermakov would perceive it as a now-or-never opportunity for seizing power and reuniting Russia—and maybe the other republics as well—against the West. It was a natural. And once a died-in-the-wool Communist like Yermakov, or even some equally crazed fascist type, took over, bye-bye Western economic help. And, most of all, bye-bye Glasnost Conspiracy.

The thin man tipped his chair forward. There was a mild *twang* as the springs contracted. He rose and walked to the Seraut. It was truly surprising how much a mind under pressure could affect reality. When he had feigned interest in the painting to hide his emotions from Craig, it appeared as a hodgepodge of hellish dots. Now it was a window to his future: a nice Parisian vacation, just he and his wife, to celebrate his appointment as DDI. Charles Van Damme tipped his lanky torso closer to the canvas, mentally substituting himself and Felicia for the merry strollers in the dappled park.

Chapter 28

Customs was torture for Rosen. As the line inched along, he became more and more convinced that a cadre of company contract killers, armed with everything from lethal hypodermics to garrotes, was massing in the passageway immediately past the inspection area. If he concentrated hard enough, he could hear their collective breathing whistling from its dark mouth, like air from a severed windpipe. The well-tailored man in line behind him—had he been there the whole time, or had he just positioned himself to prevent Rosen from escaping once they entered the tunnel? How about that sleek woman eyeing him from two rows over? Was there a semiautomatic weapon in that oversized leather handbag of hers?

No nerves for Gruhaber. He moved zombie-like each time a suitcase clicked closed and their line trudged forward. The whole flight had been like that. "Otto would you like coffee?" No answer. "Otto, how about some lunch?" Silence. Eventually, Rosen would have to snap the little man back into a functional mode, but right now, maybe this was better. At least Rosen could make decisions for both of them without any arguments.

The air-conditioning was overworked in the crowded terminal. The pungent body odors of his fellow passengers were increasingly noticeable. Rosen was convinced that he was no better after long hours in the cramped flight. Shrill complaints from the head of the line crackled backward. They were contagious. Soon passengers behind and to his sides took up the call. A deeply tanned man in an outrageous Hawaii shirt groused to his blonde companion with the spectacular cleavage about "hitting the goddamn rush hour traffic into the city." *Yeah, I should have your problems, buddy,* thought Rosen as his eyes gravitated toward the black passageway for perhaps the thirtieth time.

Finally, they were there.

"Nothing to declare" brought a bored look from the gaunt inspector. "No luggage" got his attention. The man gestured Rosen through with a jerk of his stick-like arm and an I'll-be-watching-you look.

Rosen corralled Otto, and together they melted into the 150 others shuffling toward the tunnel.

*   *   *

Forchetti and Mosk picked them out as soon as they cleared customs, sliding in behind Rosen and Gruhaber—neat as you please—before they had even reached the tunnel. Bam. Forchetti's gun jabbed into Rosen's back; Mosk's, the same with Gruhaber's. Rosen instinctively slowed down until Forchetti whispered what he'd do if Rosen didn't keep moving. The little guy just coughed. It sounded bad. Forchetti hoped he wasn't contagious or anything.

They marched along through the crowds. *Funny how you could do practically anything you wanted in a crowd,* Forchetti thought. Hell, he and Mosk could use fast-acting nerve relaxants that snuffed the heart in fifteen seconds flat and practically be in their car before any of these stupid griping passengers realized that Rosen and the other guy had just become meat. That was how *he* would have done it. But Eddie said they needed the bodies, and lugging stiffening corpses through a crowded airport was another story.

Gru ... whatever his name was, was out of it. Bumping along like a little robot. Forchetti could probably tell him to walk in front of a car and he would. The other one was a different story. Could be trouble. Forchetti kept alert, never letting his Taurus .38 Special vary more than an inch or two from the center of Rosen's spine.

Before long, the main terminal mushroomed over them. Where the hell was Rodriguez? Forchetti scanned the bank of glass exit doors, halting Rosen with a hissed "stop" and a jab of his weapon. Bright hunlight haloed each entering figure. How the hell was he supposed to pick out Rodriguez in all that glare?

Far to his left, Forchetti caught a windmill movement. Yeah, there he was. Eddie and the car would be parked in front of that door. "There he is," Forchetti called to Mosk. They nudged Rosen and Gruhaber toward Rodriguez.

Rodriguez, a big olive-skinned man with a missing eyebrow, should have known better and let the others pass him first. Instead, he fell in on Rosen's left. Forchetti, distracted by Rodriguez, let the Taurus waver slightly. Another mistake. Rosen's left elbow caught Forchetti's gun hand, jamming the .38 off at a harmless angle as he pivoted toward Rodriguez. He came up into the big man's testicles with the top edge of his flattened right hand, following with his right knee, finishing his pivot with a vicious forearm to Forchetti's nose as he shoved the convulsing Rodriguez between Otto and Mosk. Grabbing the little scientist's arm, Rosen dove toward the exit door.

He broke my fucking nose, Forchetti thought in disbelief. Salty-tasting blood cascaded down his lips. He swung the .38 toward Rosen's back. Fuck Eddie; I'm killing the bastard! The gun's sight was dead center. Forschetti couldn't miss … but his finger wouldn't work. He could not get it … too close … on that fucking trigger. It must have something to do with … that … pressure on his back, numbing him all the way up. God. Old Mosk was already down on his knees. If he didn't know better, Forchetti'd think someone used … one … of … those killer relaxants … on …

*   *   *

Holy shit! Eddie couldn't believe it. *Here comes that asshole Rosen barreling through the terminal door, taking out a group of nuns—scattering 'em like fuckin' bowling pins and lugging this little runt by the arm right between two seventy-year-olds with those Hawaiian flowers around their scrawny necks, who're about to lift their bony legs into the back seat of a Checker Cab.*

Eddie's head pivoted back toward the terminal. No Rodriguez. No Mosk. No Forchetti. Jesus H. Christ! Just great! Three real pros. They were all ready for Rosen; knew just where the bastard was gonna be. What the fuck could go wrong?

"Git after da son of a bitch!" he barked at Davilla. The Nova shot away, screeching around a braking Hertz van; chasing two suitcase-laden pedestrians, eyes white with fright, back to the curb. The Nova crunched over their hastily discarded blue Samsonites as it rammed its way into traffic behind the Checker.

Eddie glanced toward Davilla. The pale little man's hands were relaxed on the wheel. His index finger tapped in time with some tune in his head.

"Nice goin'. Why don'cha attrack some attenchun aw sompun'?"

Davilla just smiled. One white-capped tooth glistened among its tobacco-yellowed neighbors. His finger continued tapping without missing a beat.

Eddie turned toward the back seat. Formaker sat unperturbed, slicking his salt-and-pepper hair back with perfectly manicured fingers. The handle of Formaker's Smith & Wesson Combat Magnum peeked out from under his expensive suit jacket.

Off to the right and seven cars back, an airline catering truck scooted out of Kennedy onto the Van Wyck Expressway. It had been much farther behind a few moments before, but despite the congestion, the man with the blond ponytail had no trouble gaining on the Nova. In the rear of the van, trays of chicken parmesan and beef stroganoff, supposedly destined for hungry passengers en route to London, clattered in their metal racks.

Leo Rostow, the employee who normally made Speedway Food Service's deliveries to British Airways, lay stuffed between a vacant skycap desk and the glass windows of the terminal. Unlike Forchetti and Mosk, Leo would revive within a few hours. He would be unable to give the police any information of consequence when interviewed at his Flushing apartment because he did not have the slightest idea what had happened. But by the time he got together with Max, Oscar, and Sy for an evening of gin rummy, Leo would have concocted such an elaborate tale of daring and courage from strands of information volunteered by his police visitors that by the seventh telling, his friends would say, "Enough already!"

*   *   *

The cab's clattering progress over the miles of metal rods that comprised the surface of the Queensboro Bridge vibrated Otto's brain awake. He was amazed to discover that for the life of him, he could not explain how he had gotten from Berlin to this flimsy metal funnel into Manhattan. Had this particular bridge not opened every episode of his favorite TV rerun— *Taxi*—Otto still wouldn't have had a clue as to where he was.

There was Rosen, tense-faced, squinting back through the cab's rear window, turning and muttering to the driver, peering back through the window again. During Rosen's final conference with the large-knuckled cabby, Otto was sure that a fifty had passed over the seat. The vehicle accelerated, causing it to skitter even more treacherously over the bridge's slick grating.

They burrowed through eastside traffic. Otto barely had a chance to relax after the bridge ordeal before his heart was palpitating again. New York pedestrians seemed to enjoy baiting the cab, like arrogant matadors tantalizing a charging yellow bull. Otto's horrified attention was occasionally interrupted by the awful cough that lanced deep into his chest. Each incident left an ache that never completely subsided before another attack re-aggravated it. Was he going to die? Did he even care?

As they progressed across town, smartly dressed women with pastel shopping bags gave way to scurrying men with hot-looking three-piece suits and briefcases who, in turn, relinquished the sidewalks to hustling hoards in leather, with earphones and boom boxes. Otto looked up to see the frenetically flashing billboards of Times Square.

Rosen reached across to open Otto's door. After waiting in vain for Otto to respond, Rosen shoved him out. Otto sucked in thick heat saturated with exhaust fumes, cigarette smoke, and the aroma of baking pizza. He began coughing. Rosen grabbed his wrist, even as he hunched over from his most recent spasm, tugging him along the teeming sidewalk toward olive-colored railings that led down paper-cluttered stairs into the urine fumes of the New York subway system.

*　　*　　*

"Let's giddafuck outta heah!" Eddie yelled at Formaker. Eddie elbowed the door open. "Ya coicle roun' heah 'till we tell ya wheah de're goin'!" he yelled back at Davilla as he barreled toward the subway entrance.

Eddie took the stairs two at a time, at the bottom scattering three leather boys, with flowing blond hair and too much mascara, at the bottom. He squinted hard, acclimating his eyes to the sudden gloom. The station teemed with as many people as the crowded streets above. Eddie's eyes darted everywhere at once, absorbing smoky images and then rejecting them. Wait. Yeah. Over there, hurrying toward the shuttle. "C'mawn." Formaker followed, unruffled as if he were heading for a shooting session at *GQ*.

The Shuttle. Good idea, Rosen, thought Eddie. *Takes maw people aroun' than any subway in the world. Easy to get lost on da shuttle.*

The platform was filling up fast. Heads craned to watch the little train, whose only job it was to take passengers between Times Square and Grand Central Station--four long blocks east—rattle into its berth.

Eddie spotted Rosen farther down the platform. Then the doors hissed open and a flood of disembarking passengers plunged through the waiting crowd. Eddie and Formaker fought through the mob, shouldering their way into the car before all of its occupants could leave, confounding disembarking stragglers as they stormed toward the next car.

Yeah, there was Rosen. The little creep must be there with him, but how could you see a midget who hardly broke five feet in this crowd? Shit. Rosen must have seen them. He was dragging the squirt—there was Gruhaber for just a second—toward the next car down. Eddie caught an old guy hogging the doorway with a good shot in the ribs as he blasted through. He crunched shoppers and three-piece-suits as if they were so many mannequins. Fuck 'em if they were gonna stop him from getting at Rosen. He looked over his shoulder. There was Formaker, right behind him, gliding through the crowd without a collision. The bastard even had kind of a smile on his face. How the fuck did he do it? *This guy Formaker was really smooth,* Eddie thought, half in admiration, half in jealousy, as he bowled over the last couple of riders in front of where Rosen ought to be.

Damn. Rosen had made the next car. Fucker was flying! Eddie smacked a blond eight-year-old out of his mother's grasp and plunged on.

The shuttle's doors were struggling to close. Too many shoulders and butts jammed against them. Good. Now they had them. No more cars after the next one. Oh, fuck! The bastard was trying to squeeze out of the doors! There he went. Sheet! Eddie pushed frantically toward the door nearest him, but it was too late—too many frigging bodies. He couldn't make it in time.

Eddie looked around. Formaker was knifing toward the next door down, like a shark through a school of mackerel. Foremaker was gonna make it! Five more feet. Shit! Two three-piece-suits with bleary eyes from a four-martini lunch were hassling Formaker. Bastards wouldn't get out of the way. Eddie rushed to help, but gave up in time to spare a large woman with rhinestone sunglasses who blocked his path. It was just too late … The doors had finally bumped close. The train immediately squealed away.

*   *   *

"Folla 'em if dey come up da friggin' steerway," Eddie's voice screeched through Davilla's walkie-talkie. "Folla dat basta'd 'til we cin git back from acrawss town. Ya heah? If dat fucka takes anudda subway insteada' comin' up dem steers, we're shit outta luck!"

Davilla swung the Nova back along Forty-Second and angled toward the curb in front of Grand Central. He had no problem parking since there were No Parking signs everywhere. A lot of exits, but he had to choose, so he stayed where he was tapping all ten fingers in time to the song playing in his head.

*   *   *

"Is everything all right, Craig?"

Van Damme's voice was hushed, hard to hear over the line. *He must be calling from Culcane's office,* thought Craig. They had some kind of a meeting set up for today. "Sure. Everything is okay."

"I take it that that means *both* packages have been picked up at the airport."

"That's right."

"Let me hear you *say* it, Craig. The press conference is on in fifteen minutes. I have to know that there won't be any problems when I break the news of Gruhaber's defection."

"The packages have been picked up."

"And are they *secured*, Craig?"

"Yes."

"Fine." Craig could imagine Van Damme's glorious teeth lighting up Culcane's office. "Have to get off now." Van Damme's voice dropped even lower. Someone must be near. "The Indigo show"—Van Damme's excitement surged through the line despite his hushed tones—"is about to begin."

Craig stared at the silent receiver. Should he have told Van Damme that he hadn't heard from Eddie yet, more than an hour after Rosen's plane had landed? It had arrived on time. The airline confirmed that. Craig laid the receiver down into its cradle and stuck the tip of his left index finger into his mouth. He delicately nibbled the edge of his nail and then withdrew the finger, checking for other rough spots with the underside of his thumb. It was nice and smooth.

What the hell had happened? Six guys to pick up Rosen and the geek. There couldn't be any problem. Damn Eddie was just stringing it out, having a little victory celebration before he called. Hey, it was the kid's first solo. He'd chew Eddie's ass out when he called. Nothing could have gone wrong.

Craig knew he couldn't have told Van Damme anyway; he could not have stood to hear that arrogant voice implying that he had fucked up again. That's all you got from the guy. Not "thank you" or "nice work." No way. Only when something got screwed up. Then you heard plenty: all those nasty little digs. But when Van Damme fucked up, like not taking care of Rosen and Gruhaber in Europe, then old Van Damme just brushed it off like nothing. Craig hated that about Van Damme: he treated you like the goat at the drop of a hat, but *he* never made mistakes.

Craig's fingers encircled the receiver. Years of training told him that Van Damme had a need to know, but then he would have to listen to the man's shit, when ninety-nine times out of a hundred, *nothing* was wrong. What hell there'd be to pay if Van Damme had to scrap his press conference when nothing was wrong. And nothing *was* wrong. Even if there were, Craig would get it taken care of before Van Damme knew. Craig pulled his hand from the receiver. He just couldn't stand to listen to any more of Van Damme's shit.

*　*　*

Davilla's fingers stopped drumming halfway through his silent rendition of "La Bamba." There were old Rosen and Bruhabber—or whatever the little guy's name was—popping out of the old IRT. On the far side, across Forty-Second, going west.

Davilla eased the Nova away from the curb. Blaring yellow cabs dominated the heavy traffic. He did his best to keep an eye on the two as they bobbed out from under triple-feature theater marquees, past shuffling street people in drooping raincoats, punk rockers with orange-and-purple Mohawks, flashy pimps, and low-level drug dealers trafficking with their spacey clientele.

He ran the light to keep pace as Rosen and the other guy dodged Seventh Avenue traffic. Davilla began to feel uneasy. Traffic thinned out halfway toward Eighth Avenue, but that didn't help Davilla's mood. Now he was sure. Rosen was headed for that goddamn zoo of a Port Authority Bus Terminal. Davilla reached for his gun. He could swerve over and maybe get them before they crossed Eighth. It was a tough shot with the Beretta, considering the distance, not to mention oncoming traffic and the other pedestrians he might have to whack to get them, but it was doable. Davilla's biggest problem was the crowds he'd attract. He'd have to leave Rosen and Bru—*whatever*—where they lay, and Eddie's orders were to take possession of the bodies.

Davilla puffed out a gust of air from under his pencil mustache, slamming the wheel with an open palm. Jamming the Beretta back into its underarm holster, he yanked the wheel right, skidding the Nova onto Eighth. The right front wheel groaned as it pressed against a bright red curb. An equally bright yellow hydrant sat within a handshake of the passenger door. *Screw it,* Davilla thought. Let them tow the damn car; it was untraceable. Anyway, he had bigger problems. He slid from the Nova, not bothering to lock his door. Davilla hunched his shoulders and went diagonally west across Eighth, toward the soot-smudged monster that housed the commuter busses servicing the counties of Southern New York and North Jersey.

*   *   *

The press conference was going smooth as silk. Savin had begged off, claiming a touch of flu, but it was common knowledge that the director of central intelligence and the President were in violent disagreement over Van Damme's attendance.

Not that President Clendon himself had been thrilled at authorizing Van Damme to be the one to announce that the Central Intelligence Agency had evidence that the Russians had subverted a member of Sklar Industries' Indigo research team. His initial reaction had been to keep the incident quiet for the time being, fearing a further escalation of anti-Russian sentiment. But Culcane would not hear of it. "The American people must know of this great dangah, suh," was how he told Van Damme he had put it. Culcane's threat was clear to the President: either you jump on the bandwagon with me or I'll leak it and you'll be left looking like you're covering up for the Russians. Clendon knew when he was licked. And since Van Damme was the CIA to the man on the street by now, Clendon barely flinched at Culcane's suggestion that the division chief be there to break the news.

In fact, by agreeing with Culcane's "suggestion" and aligning himself on the popular side of the Russian issue, Clendon, the eternal politician, had placed his friend Savin in an untenable position. Protocol would have the DI revealing the Indigo theft, not Van Damme. Richard Savin would never sit still for this insult, ergo his failure to attend the press conference. Van Damme was willing to bet, just as Culcane had jovially speculated when he called Van Damme's home last night, that the director of intelligence's resignation would be on the President's desk by noon tomorrow. "Fo'git 'bout thet Dep'ity Di-rectah position, son. You gonna be th' new Di-rectah at Intell'gence, less'n ah miss mah guess."

Culcane's prediction bubbled through Van Damme's dreams—in exact dialect—the entire night. Not that Van Damme couldn't have run the show effectively as DDI, but *Director*? It just proved what you could do when you set your goals high and had a superior mind to see them through.

The only annoying part of this ideal situation, thought Van Damme, *was that Culcane insisted on holding the press conference here in his office so that there would be no mistaking the fact that he, Senator Jim Culcane, was very close to rapidly developing events.* A more spacious conference room at the Capitol would have been far preferable. Many of the press were relegated to the tiny anteroom where they could barely hear, much less participate. Even within Culcane's office itself, the acrid odor of wall-to-wall bodies was becoming noticeable.

"How did the CIA come to suspect Mr. Gruhaber, Mr. Van Damme?" This from the leggy blonde elbowing her way to the front of the jostling crowd. Van Damme hadn't a clue whether she worked for the *New York Times* or some two-page sheet in the Midwest.

"Mr. Gruhaber had been absent from work for over a week without any communication with his employer. This was highly unusual because his attendance record had been exemplary over the previous eleven years. Based upon the extreme sensitivity of Sklar's projects, we and the Federal Bureau of Investigation attach great importance to even the slightest behavioral irregularities involving the employees in that company. Together—although I should point out that the Federal Bureau of Investigation has primary jurisdiction in domestic matters—Van Damme acknowledged Horace Krause, a broad man dressed in standard FBI gray, and we concluded that Mr. Gruhaber has left the country."

Van Damme smiled somewhat sheepishly. "Sorry. That was a bit long-winded, but I'm rather new at this. To be brief, a search of Mr. Gruhaber's apartment revealed that he had been contacted by a known Russian agent. We next discovered that Mr. Gruhaber had made a number of unusually large deposits over the past three months and that just before he disappeared, he cleared out his bank accounts. I am not authorized to go into complete detail, but I can assure you that there is sufficient evidence for both ourselves and the Bureau to believe that Otto Gruhaber has defected."

"Where can he defect?" A skeptical tone from a *Village Voice* type farther back.

"Try Cuba, for one. Or Red China. Or how about the same groups in the Republic of Russia who developed the Amphora missile? The one that is capable of raining down sixty to one hundred smaller missiles, even if it takes a direct hit. Or friends of the leaders of the unsuccessful coup that took place in Russian Georgia not long ago. Or General Alexi Yermakov and his extremist followers in the Red Army. Or any number of fascist types who are gaining a following among disgruntled Russian voters. Or the members of the Communist Party, who still hold most of the key positions in government and industry. But my guess—and this is unofficial—is that Gruhaber is working with radicals in the KGB, possibly in conjunction with the right wing of the army."

Van Damme paused. He was exceeding the bounds of his authorization, and he knew it. Culcane was seated to his left, at the center of his huge desk. It was clear that the senator immediately understood Van Damme's concern, and he gave him a reassuring thumbs-up, well below the crowd's eye level.

"Remember, no matter what we would like to think, there are very powerful forces within Russia who have the arms and training to turn glasnost around. The current Russian President's popularity is eroding. If these other groups can win over a few of those who are undecided—and there are plenty of those—then we could be facing a very hostile Russian nation before long. There are also the KGB and the military, who fear that there will be no work if they are disbanded—a most valid fear in light of the present economic disaster. There are others who view the present leadership's course of action as relegating Russia to the status of a third-rate power—a development that many in this country would never stand for if the situation were reversed. There are also plenty of those who don't trust us. Surely you don't think that all of those years of anti-US propaganda weren't believed by many Russians. And if the plans to one of our new weapons becomes public over there, how will that make them feel about the United States? How did we feel about Amphora over here?"

Van Damme turned back toward the leggy reporter. Her lower jaw hung, revealing wrinkles, which she was too absorbed to hide. He lowered his head, pretending to need water. Actually, he was listening. The room was so silent that it seemed no one was even drawing a breath. Van Damme sipped slowly, tantalizing his audience by carefully replacing his glass on its small coaster. When he looked up, the leggy blond had vanished back into the subdued crowd.

A lanky man with the pallor of an undertaker broke the group's collective trance with his high twangy voice. "Mr. Van Damme, we in the state of Kansas labor under the impression that our tribulations with Russian Communism have satisfactorily concluded. Is it your premise that this has not transpired?"

Pitifully pedantic, thought Van Damme. *Self-conscious about your little hick town background, so you're going to dazzle us big city folks?* Van Damme crunched his eyebrows down over his nose. "Is the gentleman asking if the Communists could return to power?"

Spotty laughter from the audience.

The questioner's complexion became almost normal, which Van Damme assumed represented a blush in one so pale. "We have heard a lot of speculation about how the *people* over there won't allow a return to totalitarianism. Remember the *history* of the Russian people and those in the other republics. For the past seventy years, they have accepted their lot. They would fall back into line without a peep if the tanks start rolling and we, and the rest of the world, won't do a thing about it. Not any more than we did in Czechoslovakia, or Hungary, or even if we thought that a coup had deposed Gorbachev. We will sit here ringing our hands. Then, after a suitable period of mourning, we will blithely enter relations with their new government. Oh, there may be a few human rights protests, maybe some threats of economic retaliation, but soon it will be business as usual. Think about it. Isn't that exactly how things would happen?"

Van Damme stared hard at the group for a full minute. Then he reached up, rubbing his lips, a tolerant smile on his face as his long hand slipped down to cup his side. This questioner, too, had slumped back into the crowd.

"Was Mr. Gruhaber a member of the 'Indigo team?' What is that?"

Van Damme searched the room but was unable to locate the question's author. He addressed the group near the gun case since the voice had come from that general direction.

"I'm already in enough trouble for venturing so many of my opinions." He mugged at Culcane, who made a gun of his thumb and forefinger and aimed at Van Damme, wringing tense giggles from a few members of the audience. As Culcane's hammer-thumb descended, more of the crowd broke into relieved laughter.

Van Damme clamped his hands over his heart, evoking yet another round of guffaws. He waved them off, serious-faced again. "I don't think that I had better compound my offenses by commenting upon classified material."

"Such as?" The reporter near the gun case turned out to be a thin man in an uncomfortably hot-looking Harris tweed.

Van Damme laughed with the others. "Sorry." He raised his graceful fingers to ward the man off. "I *will* say that it is not the kind of information that we want out of our safekeeping—"

"Does that mean that we are *still* working on new weapons systems?"

Van Damme gave the thin reporter an exaggerated squint and waved him away. Uproarious laughter this time. *This is easy,* thought Van Damme. *Actually sort of fun. I thought it would be a lot harder.*

"Did Gruhaber have any accomplices?" a deep voice boomed out from somewhere toward the back.

A tricky one. At first, Van Damme had toyed with the idea of bringing Rosen into the equation. Gorgone, over at Fair Oaks, had been showing signs of cracking, complaining about nonstop pressure from a local cop who wanted to talk to Rosen. The little administrator couldn't pretend that Rosen was under treatment for much longer. Fortunately, he wouldn't have to. Soon Rosen would be caught and killed while helping Gruhaber try to deliver Indigo to the KGB. A paper trail of links between the two men was already being arranged. Officially, the agency would postulate that Rosen's agitated mental state had been due to his guilt over the Indigo plot, causing him to kill his wife because she confronted him. Van Damme might have to take a little heat for not bringing in local law enforcement and the FBI after Rosen's "escape" from Fair Oaks, but not much. Van Damme would explain that Rosen had posed a threat to national security and that the fugitive's immediate departure from the country made him the agency's responsibility. As for Gorgone, Van Damme would laud him for his patriotic cooperation. End of story. Except, of course, that Gorgone represented a loose end ... for now. "That is a matter which I am not at liberty to discuss at this point," Van Damme replied straight-faced.

"Does that mean that there might be others implicated at a later date?"

"Come awn, gen'lemen ... an' laidahs." Culcane brandished a pudgy palm at the reporters. "Ah thaink you got e-nough fa now. Mr. Vayn Damme's got a lotta wook ta do. Le's give him a chaince." Culcane nodded to three sparkly-eyed all-American aides, who gently but firmly shooed the group out of his office.

CHAPTER 29

Davilla elbowed through a collection of bald teenagers cloaked in white robes, chanting up a storm in front of the Port Authority's entrance. No sooner had he cleared this obstacle than a foul old crone in disintegrating clothes clutched at him with a scaly claw of a hand. Her mouth widened, revealing toothless brown gums. A gust of vile breath blew up his nostrils. "Ga a qua'ter?"

Davilla shook her off, gagging as he sprinted forward. The good old Port Authority Terminal was in full bloom.

They were up ahead, passing the row of dingy ticket windows, not stopping to buy. That was good news for Davilla. If there was anything he didn't need right now, it was a one-hour bus ride to Hackensack, New Jersey!

Rosen and … "Gru"—that was easier than trying to remember his weird name—weren't exactly sauntering, but they didn't seem to realize that he was behind them. Occasionally Gru would stop and gape at the many outlandish denizens of the terminal, who neither knew nor cared that they were being stared at, while Rosen waited patiently for a moment or two before tugging him onward.

Davilla kept thinking how easy it would be to sidle up close behind, drop them, and disappear into the crowd before anyone realized. But that would mean that their bodies would get picked up by the local cops, and *that* was not the plan. Davilla would have to wait for Eddie and Formaker to get back. There was no way he could carry off two corpses by himself.

The scurrying footsteps of a thousand commuters echoed back from the vaulted ceiling. Rosen and Gru were going straight through to Ninth Avenue. Dingy sunlight framed them as they approached the doors. Great. Maybe he could hit them out on the street, if old Eddie would get back. His foot stuck to the floor. Davilla lifted his shoe. A glob of gum crisscrossed his sole like a pink spiderweb. Geez! They were already out the door. Davilla tried to ignore his sticking right foot as he hurried after them.

There was a squawk from his pocket. Outside the entrance, he whipped out the walkie-talkie, jamming down the send button as he brought it to his lips. "Eddie, where are you?"

"We jus' gawt back." Eddie's difficult accent was worsened by static. "You gawt 'em?"

"Yeah. We're leaving the Port Authority, crossing Ninth on Forty-Third. The car's on the northeast corner of Eighth and Forty-Second, in front of a hydrant. Key's where I usually leave it."

"Awright. We'll pick it up if it ain't been towed. Check ya inna coupl'a minutes."

Davilla was about to shove the instrument into his pocket when a large splotchy hand settled over its top.

"What a hell iss 'at thing?"

The man was at least a head taller than Davilla, but he wobbled side to side, then front to back as he spoke. Davilla easily yanked the walkie-talkie out of the wino's grip, simultaneously shoving him back with his left hand.

"Heeeeey." Foam bubbled from between the man's lips as he staggered forward, arms groping for Davilla.

Davilla stepped back three feet and whipped his right toe directly into the wino's testicles, the wino sinking to the stained sidewalk in slow motion as Davilla spun away, zigzagging across Ninth Avenue between furiously honking automobiles.

Rosen and Gru had put a lot of distance between themselves and him during his tussle with the wino. In fact, they were almost to the next corner. From Gru's slightly out-of-control forward lean, Davilla was sure that he was being yanked along by his companion, which meant that Rosen had spotted him ... which also meant that Davilla had better figure out a way to slow them down until Eddie caught up. He checked the street in both directions. Traffic and pedestrians were barely apparent in this depressed area, where grimy brown tenements had deteriorated into hollow storefronts and shells of living quarters. Ahead, the elevated West Side Highway hummed above the docks of the Hudson River.

Davilla slid the walkie-talkie under his jacket. The Beretta emerged in its place.

* * *

"Son, you shaw you gonna find this Gruhabah an' them Indagah plans befaw the Russkis do?" Culcane rolled back in his swivel chair, kicking his surprisingly small feet up on top of his huge desk. Clouds of gray smoke billowed from his freshly lit cigar. "'Cause if yah don't, we ah gonna lose all the groun' we gained ovah this Amphora thaing."

"Don't worry, Sen—"

"Ah mean, raht now, you ah a shoo-in fuh Di-rectah 'cause eva'one thinks yaw Supahman. But folks is funnah. You don' caitch this Gruhabah an' you ain't anabuddy's hero anymaw."

Van Damme waited for two massive puffs on the cigar to make sure that the senator was finished.

"I understand that, Sir. I can assure you that he will be caught and that Indigo will be returned. Believe me. I even suspect that my operation is going to catch a dangerous escaped criminal along with him—"

"No details, Son." Cigar smoke waggled side to side as Culcane waved his chubby palms. "Until you have *results*, ah don' wantah know. Tha's how we sen'tuhs keep outta trouble." Culcane's grin compressed his fleshy face but did nothing to warm his cold little eyes. "Nah go ahn an' git about yuh business. Ah got wook ta do."

A blast of cigar smoke streaked toward Van Damme, dissipating inches from his face. He rose and left. Neither man attempted a good-bye.

*　*　*

Davilla sprinted now, making good progress. He didn't think that he could have caught Rosen alone; the guy moved pretty well. But having to drag Gru along was really slowing him down. They were no more than half a block ahead now. He considered taking a shot, maybe catch one of them in the leg, just to slow them down some more, but there was too much traffic rattling along under the elevated highway. Didn't matter. As long as he kept them going toward the docks, he'd get them, because after the docks, there was nothing but the big dirty river.

Rosen slowed down and waved an arm at oncoming traffic. Davilla gave it all he had. If Rosen got a cab, it was all over. He slowed, smiling, as Rosen looked back and then lugged the little man through a gap in the traffic. *Just try to get a cab in New York when you need one, huh, Rosen?* Davilla laughed to himself.

Little Gru was really dragging. Rosen looked like he was holding him up as they bobbed between a brown UPS van and a silver-sided bus.

There was a loud honk to Davilla's left. The Nova. "Whea's the fucka?" Eddie's foghorn voice drowned out the highway traffic as he arched his bull neck through the open window.

Davilla gestured toward the docks with his Beretta.

"Git in." The Nova skidded toward the curb as Eddie flung open the back door, Davilla clutching for a handle and swinging himself in as the car accelerated.

"Over there." Davilla pointed toward a concrete dock with tidy rows of parked cars stretching far into the Hudson. Formaker screeched on the brakes to avoid a graffiti-encrusted bus.

"Take 'er easy, Fawmaka. Did the guy make any cawls?" Eddie turned toward Davilla.

"No. He didn't have a chance to."

"See, Fawmaka. We don' needa have a accident.… Da guy's just runnin'. He don' know where he's goin'. Le's jus' not have a accident. He'll be dere atta end a dat nice lonely dock. Poifect faw us. Jus' take ya' time."

As the light changed, the Nova crossed beneath the highway's whoosh and rumbled up the pier's concrete ramp. Not a sole moved over the dazzling white expanse except for two distant figures: a tall and a short one, stumbling past thousands of cars in the direction of the hazy New Jersey shoreline.

The Nova skirted vehicles of every description as it rolled along the massive pier … including a silver airline catering van whose engine was running.

Two-thirds of the way down, the parking area gave way to a series of windowless maintenance sheds. A row of concrete posts, connected by no-nonsense metal chains, blocked vehicular access.

"Sheet. Leave th' fuckin' caw heah an' we'll gedd 'em an' drag 'em back." Eddie already had the door open. "Davilla, stay widda caw in case dey come aroun'." He and Formaker disappeared behind the first row of buildings.

*　*　*

Back in the bus terminal, Rosen had spotted the man following them. Despite that, he had let Otto stop from time to time, understanding that the terrified little man was on the verge of collapse. Although Rosen had succeeded in creating the illusion that they were safe, for Otto's benefit, stopping long enough to call Mark Hickey had been out of the question. The man with the thin mustache would have been on them before he could dial. If Rosen had had any remaining doubts about whether they were being followed, the fight in front of the terminal doors eliminated them. Soon after, the man with the mustache had gotten bold enough, or desperate enough, to pursue them with a gun. There had been no place to hide during the chase to the river. All he passed were boarded brownstones, barren storefronts, and gutted ruins. He tried for a cab, but that had proven hopeless.

A minute ago, others had joined his pursuer, in a car. Now trying to run down the avenue beneath the West Side Highway was out of the question. No. It was either the dock or getting shot down from a speeding Chevy. A black-and-white episode of *The Untouchables* careening 1930s Fords, with machine gun tracers sparkling from their open windows, played jerkily across Rosen's mind.

They wove in and out of cars, vans, and cycles, Otto stumbling along beside Rosen like a collapsing marathoner. Waves slapped against the piers beneath the dock, softly sucking at the wooden pilings before slipping back into the river. Above, ragged seabirds floated on puffs of polluted air.

They stumbled past the parking area. Only windowless sheds now, recently painted, clean, and white, even in the smog-filtered sunlight. They stopped short. It was the pier's end. A two-story concrete building, solid on the bottom, with opaque windows lining its upper floor, barred their way. On either side of the structure, three sagging metal chains stretched from large rings set into the building to stout posts at the pier's outer perimeter. No Trespassing signs dangled from the imposing metal links at five-foot intervals.

Rosen slid between the middle and upper chain. He coaxed Otto to do the same. Otto stared at him, uncomprehending. Finally, Rosen tugged at the little man. Chains clanked and rattled as Otto's neck, stomach, and knees smacked them during his uncoordinated journey through.

Rosen peered up at the building's windows. No angry face appeared to chase them away. CITY OF NEW YOUR PORT AUTHORITY is in special type gleamed from large brass letters on the building's side. Whether the building was fully automated or just not in use at the moment, Rosen intuitively knew that there were no spectators behind those one-way windows to witness, or thwart, the deadly scenario that might transpire momentarily. They were all alone. Rosen glanced toward the river. Clouds of brackish smoke from Jersey industries wafted across the Hudson toward Manhattan. Their ethereal contours ebbed and flowed, buffeted by gusts of cold air from the river's murky surface. He knelt, tipping his torso over the pier's edge. All he saw was a row of barnacle-crusted pilings. Rainbow-colored oil slicks clung tenaciously to their rough surfaces, shimmering out of the clutches of receding swells.

Rosen darted toward the building's edge and peeked around the corner. Two men snaked toward him. One was hulkingly powerful. Rosen recognized him instantly. Eddie, from the sanatorium. The race through the subway enabled him to snatch only quick glimpses of his pursuers, so he hadn't realized until this moment. Great. How was he supposed to fight that monster? And on top of it, both were armed.

* * *

"Dey gotta be aroun' da otha' side a' da' buildin'. Ya go dat way, Fawmaka. I'll take dis side. Fergit da liddle guy. He ain't nuttin'. We both go fer Rosun." Eddie signaled Formaker left as he broke off to the right.

Formaker glided toward the edge of the big building at the end of the pier, soundlessly slipping through the chains. The Magnum rested lightly in the crotch of his hand, as suited to him as one of the fine Cabernets in his highly respectable wine cellar. He would finish this fast and get out of New York by early evening. Formaker couldn't stand New York, and he really couldn't stand Eddie. The man was an absolute clown; he hadn't even suggested that they time their attack to take place simultaneously, which would increase their advantage over a single adversary like Rosen. Was the agency so far down on its luck that they had to resort to people like this? Well, he was tired of freelancing for the agency anyway. The South Americans paid better, the work was steady, and your money went a lot further down there. This was definitely his last job for the CIA.

Formaker reached the side of the building. It looked as if it had just been painted. Carefully, so that he wouldn't rub his suit against the wall, Formaker tiptoed toward the far edge. Once there, he listened. All he heard were the sloshing waves. He was grateful for his Revo sunglasses. Otherwise, the glare from the river would have been blinding. But then, that's why he brought them, wasn't it? He prided himself in always being prepared. Formaker straightened his vest and tipped his Magnum around the corner …

*   *   *

Otto hurled his shoe just as the head with the salt-and-pepper hair appeared above the long gun barrel. The heavy elevator model missed badly, smacking the wall a foot above the well-groomed man's ear, but it caused more than enough noise for the man to react. The man jerked his gun hand up for protection, allowing Rosen to slide beneath the big glinting weapon, clamping it with his left hand as he pounded a bony ridge of knuckles into the man's chest with his right. The man gave ground as they grunted and puffed until they disappeared behind the building's white corner.

Terrified of the huge one, whom Rosen said would be coming from the other end, Otto scurried after the combatants.

The man that Rosen was battling wore a suit! It was inconceivable to Otto that anyone would wear a *suit* to kill people. This suit was becoming very bloody as Rosen pounded the man farther and farther along the chalky wall. His only concern seemed to be trying to tear Rosen's hand from his gun. Each thud of Rosen's knuckles drove the man in the suit closer to the rutted concrete of the dock, yet his free hand kept clawing at Rosen's. Bloody gouges opened where his nails ripped Rosen's flesh.

Otto stared, transfixed. They struggled almost silently, despite the pain being inflicted. Footfalls from the front of the building broke Otto's concentration. They were heavy enough to be heard above the river's noisy sloshing. Otto darted past the combatants, too terrified of the raging monster who would soon appear behind him to worry about the waving Magnum.

Suddenly, the other stood there, huge muscles bunched, and nostrils flaring. The gun in his hand looked ludicrous. Why would such a massive man even need anything but his own strength to rip them into shreds? Otto half expected the monster to bellow out a terrible rumbling laugh, toss his weapon away, and lumber forward, gripping Rosen's head in his bionic hands, tearing it from his living body, leaving only the pulsing stump of his friend's neck. To Otto's surprise, the muscled monster behaved just like anyone else. He lowered his gun, sighting it calmly and deliberately at Rosen. Even more surprisingly, the gun over which Rosen and the other man fought flashed first as Rosen wrenched it free and fired in the same movement. Rosen ducked behind his opponent as the muscled monster's gun spat back.

Stains spread simultaneously across the muscled man's chest and the suited man's shoulder. With a roar louder than the second firing of his gun, the monster staggered backward. This time red spray spewed from Rosen's human shield's head. Otto crouched, warm wetness spreading along his crotch as Rosen sighted his own huge weapon and then let it droop over his human shield without firing again.

The muscled man wobbled back … and back … and back, twisting just before he pirouetted off of the edge of the dock. The quivering handle of an undiscernible object protruded dead center between his shoulder blades. After an inordinately long time, there was a resounding splash.

Rosen pointed the Magnum toward the space where he'd seen Eddie topple into the river's gray waves. Then there was a gasp behind him. Dropping Formaker's seeping body, he spun, bracing against the wall as he pointed the Magnum at Otto—and the blond man who stood behind him. The blond man's left elbow encircled Otto's neck, while his right hand pressed the point of a stubby, black throwing blade against Otto's throat.

Chapter 30

Smoke from Tippy Lawrence's Gitane curled upward toward the redwood beams above Van Damme's library. Tippy only wore European clothes, only used European items, and only drove European cars because, according to Tippy, everything about the United States was "Too, too *de'clase'.*"

Van Damme tuned out Tippy's rantings about her newest literary find. Tippy was always "finding" brilliant, undiscovered poets, painters, or authors who, predictably, lost their talents as they lost their allure in Tippy's bed. Instead, he concentrated on the gap between Tippy's tanned and well-muscled legs.

Tippy's husband, Arthur, food critic for close to a hundred newspapers, described a particularly delicate sauce that he had recently encountered in a small bistro "in Baltimore, of all places."

Felicia managed to look as intrigued, as if sauce were something she actually cared about.

If Tippy just moved slightly forward toward the light, Van Damme would be able to see all the way up to her—

"Sirrr."

Goddamn Hodges. Just as the horrible evening showed its first signs of promise.

"*Yes,* Hodges?"

Arthur didn't miss a beat about his sauce, but Tippy scrunched her knees together as if punishing Van Damme for the interruption.

"Senator Culcane is on the phone. He said to tell you that it was quite important."

At the sound of Culcane's name, even Arthur paused for a moment.

Felicia used her reprieve to flash Van Damme a wink.

Tippy's eyebrows rose appraisingly as he uncoiled from his chair.

Excuse me," Van Damme said, smiling what he hoped was a humble smile. "I'll take it in the den, Hodges." He walked quickly toward the stairs. "Hang up when I get on."

Hodges's annoying "Verrry gooood, Sirrr" bounded up the stairs after him.

"Senator?"

"Hah's it goin', Chahlie? Hope ah'm not distu'bing anathaing special." Culcane sounded as if he couldn't have cared less.

"Not at all. What can I do for you, Sir?"

"Nah tha's not ezac'ly the quession. Its maw what ah can do fuh *you?*"

This game playing was irritating, but Van Damme forced a smile into his voice. "You've already helped so much. What else could you—"

"Make yuh Di-rectuh of th' Cent'al Intell'gence Agency ... startin' tommarah."

Van Damme drew the receiver away from his ear. He turned the earpiece toward his face as if he could glimpse Culcane's face through the perforations.

"Chahlie, you theah?"

Van Damme yanked the receiver back to his mouth. "Yes, Sir. Just a little surprised." Van Damme patted long fingers against his fluttering chest, calming himself. "How, Senator?" was the most eloquence that he could muster.

"It seems that Di-erectuh Savin has resahned, possiblah due to his recent disagreement with the Pres'dent ovah yoah press confe'ence. Although he claims it's fo' reasons of health."

Van Damme let three deep breaths slide in and out before continuing. The nerves on top of his hands throbbed all the way into his fingers. "Do you really think that the President would recommend me? I don't get the feeling that he is exactly in my corner."

"He don' zac'ly have a choice, Son." The Senator's soft accent grew harsh. He did not like having to explain himself to a political neophyte. Culcane resumed at an even slower pace than his normal drawl, like a schoolteacher addressing a particularly ungifted student. "Ouah polls tell us that the nation wonts tighter intell'gence aftuh thet Aimphora thaing. Raht now they don' trus' the Russkis futhuh 'en they can shot put th' Kremlin. An' you ah the man they see as helpin' us stay ahead a 'em. Now ouah Pres'dent's no dummah. If he sees that the wind's a blowin' for a strong intell'gence to countah the Sov'ets, tha's jus' what he'll do regahdless a his pus'nol feelin's. Fac' is, he's playin' fer the gran'stands. Wan's ta git yuh approved yestiday, sayin' we cain't affoed a di-recta 'less CIA du'ing these crucial tahms. Wants ta git ya appointed in two days, startin' day aftuh tomarrah. Ah tol' him you'd be readah."

"God! What do I have to do to help, Senator?"

"Nuthin' raht now, Son. Ah'll do a little lobby'ng with the See-lect Committee on Itell'gence to trah an' get ya a fast approval."

"Will you be able to get the liberal Democrats on the committee to support me?"

"Sho' will. Me an' the boys ahlreadah been twistin' a few ahrms. Liberal Democrats read the papuhs too. Cheeriiist. 'Specially now this Indagah sat'llite thaing has got the rest'a the folks up in ahms thet wasn't befow."

From his position near the desk, Van Damme winked at his image in a gilded mirror set between two crammed bookshelves. *This is going better than even I could have imagined. I'm going to the top on the very first try. 'Do not pass go. Do not collect two hundred dollars. Go directly to the Director's office'.* The wolf smile spread so that his mustache brushed the receiver. Van Damme scrupulously fought down the swell of victory warming his insides before it squirted up into his throat and into his voice. "What will I have to prepare for, Senator?"

"Mainluh watch out fuh those holliuh-than-thou types of the Kenneduh 'an Biden ilk. We'll prep yuh tomarrah."

"I'll be ready, Sen—"

"You got that fellah that stole th' sat'llite caught yet?"

"I have my best men on it. We should have it wrapped up in a day or so."

"Does thet mean you *have* o' *have not* caught 'im?"

Were Gruhaber and Rosen safely back in Europe yet? Van Damme hadn't heard from Craig. Didn't know. Culcane would drop him like a hot potato if the Indigo situation wasn't sanitized before the select committee hearings. He had to give Culcane something to keep the momentum going for his appointment. "We're sure that he had an accomplice." By mentioning Rosen, Van Damme created issues of agency jurisdiction that he hadn't wanted to answer until the matter was closed. Still, it was his best delaying tactic under the circumstances. "A rogue from our agency who recently escaped from a psychiatric institution ... maybe with *outside* help." Van Damme allowed the innuendo to drip along the telephone wire.

"Mah God, those Rooshan bastahds 'ul trah anathin'. What a blockbustah we' gonna deliver when these hens come ta roost."

Van Damme imagined Culcane's tiny pig eyes disappearing in rolls of fat, forced upward by his lascivious grin.

"Jes' be shore yuh don' flub it, Son. We cain't getcha in if ya fuck this thaing up. Wouldn' even want ta."

Now Van Damme visualized the Senator's eyes as wide and beady: a cobra tracking a mouse. "No problem, Senator." Why were his palms wet? "I assure you that we will capture both parties, if this agency man *is* really working with Gruhaber and the Russians, *plus* the Indigo plans intact— *and* in time for my appointment." Van Damme's voice resonated through the receiver. No one could doubt him.

"Awright, Son. Then we ah ready. An' *you* ah the man we want ta keep those sneakin' Russkis in lahn."

"You can count on—"

"Ah know. See ya at the prep'ration meetin'. Roun' 'bout twelve. Hear?" Van Damme stared at the receiver. All that emanated was a low *buzzz*.

Rude bastard! He left the room and walked down the stairs. Was the carpeting even thicker than he remembered—cloudlike, in fact—or was he just high from his amazing success? Even *he* couldn't have predicted that things would go this well. If Craig, with enough contract labor to overthrow a small sheikhdom, had done his job, then Charles Lucien Van Damme was the next Director of Central Intelligence.

Van Damme squared his shoulders as he entered the library, nodding pleasantly to his wife and the Lawrences. "Sorry." He smoothed his mustache, screwing up his forehead as he leaned intently toward the chunky, florid-faced man on the couch. "Tell me about that sauce, Arthur. Where was it, Baltimore, of all places?"

*　　*　　*

A cool gust slid off the river, ruffling the blanket of steamy city heat. It wafted across Rosen's taught fingers, briefly drying his grip on the Magnum. Perspiration flowed back between his fingers immediately, but the Magnum remained steadily pointed toward the precise spot where the blond man's face appeared over Otto's right shoulder.

"Kill him and you're dead."

"I do not want to kill him. I just want you not to shoot me before you listen."

"Listen to what?" Rosen nodded sharply toward the space where Eddie had disappeared. "None of your friends wanted to talk to me." The blond man did not fit with the others. And that knife was a duplicate of the one buried between Eddie's shoulders.

Otto wore the glazed look of someone who just didn't care anymore. He dangled from the blond man's forearm like a dead goose in a butcher's grasp.

"Let go of him. *Then* we'll talk." Rosen shrugged away Formaker's body, which had saved him. Its ruined head thumped against the concrete, leaving a bloody smear on the gray surface. The corpse rolled halfway over, but its sprawled legs prevented it from toppling onto its face.

Rosen rose, extending the Magnum to arm's length.

The knife's tip slithered upward to the corner of Otto's eye.

What the hell am I going to do? Rosen's mind tensed in desperation. Otto is my only proof against Van Damme. If he kills Otto, I don't have a prayer unless I get incredibly lucky and shoot Van Damme before a thousand CIA bloodhounds kill me. If I lower the gun, he whips that knife at me. Rosen stared at the blond man's eyes: pale blue and emotionless. No way to read the truth about his intentions in those babies. *Geez, if I lower the gun and he lowers the knife, as good as he is, he can flip it underhand and nail me without my getting off a shot.* The Magnum was getting heavier by the second, weighting Rosen's right arm downward. Could the blond guy see the tremors shooting along his wrist toward this elbow? If we both drop them, how do I know that he doesn't have a second knife ... or a gun? Rosen's arm was shaking now, aching all the way up his shoulder, but if he propped it with the other hand, that might look as if he was getting set to shoot. The aching ran up into his neck. Christ, the damn man's eyes didn't even blink. Rosen sucked stiflingly humid air in through caked nostrils. "You toss your knife and I'll toss this." Rosen circled the Magnum's muzzle skyward.

The man extended his knife outward, but his left hand remained firmly against the little man's throat. Otto tried to wriggle free but the man's hand contracted. Otto yelped and stopping squirming. The implication was clear: he could kill Otto with or without the knife if Rosen reneged on their agreement.

Rosen's Magnum arched over Formaker's tangled body toward the end of the pier. Its clatter crackled out over the grimy Hudson.

The thin knife sped toward a coil of coarse rope leaning against a small storage shed thirty feet away. In less time than Rosen could blink, it quivered sunlight from the center of the rope's wooden spool.

"Who are you?" Rosen tried to speak slowly and calmly. It was not easy.

The blond man released Otto's neck, gently as a lover breaking a caress. Otto staggered free. The man ignored him. "It does not matter."

"Why are you helping us?"

"People I represent are opposed to your CIA division man's policies."

Rosen rubbed damp fingers against perspiration gathering at the corner of his right eye. He stepped toward the man. His hair, weighted down by perspiration, drooped into his eyes. He felt comical—embarrassed—in front of the imperturbable stranger. "How do your people know about him?" Rosen asked petulantly. His flopping hair was irritating, but for some reason, he refused to give the man the satisfaction of seeing him swipe it away.

"He affects their well-being as well as yours."

The man's accent was so neutral that he had to be a foreigner, well schooled in the language. But no matter how keenly he listened for telltale inflections, Rosen could not pick up a hint as to the man's national origin. Rosen stepped closer, stuffing his hands into his pockets in an attempt to appear casual, while doing his best to blink away his clinging hair. He decided to throw in a half smile for good measure. "How?" This time his voice was sincere, interested.

The blond man was having none of it. "It is irrelevant. We do not have much time." Although the man glanced side to side, nothing in his posture indicated any fear whatsoever. "I have something for you that can help all of us."

Rosen's pulse quickened. Could this be true? Was he finally getting a break? Some chance against Van Damme? "Show me." He was very careful not to lunge toward the man, although every nerve in his body was about to explode. Even Otto's attention had shifted from his sore neck to the blond man.

For the first time, the man moved toward Rosen, stopping three feet away. His expressionless face and ice-blue eyes contrasted sharply with his frivolously bobbing ponytail. He reached inside his loose-fitting shirt. There was brief crackling of tape tearing from skin. Then his hand reappeared.

Otto quavered like a tiny woods animal, fascinated but prepared to bolt.

"Here … Take it! The man jabbed a plastic pouch toward Rosen. Pieces of yellowed tape dangled from one corner. "Here are documents showing that your friend"—the man nodded toward Otto without disengaging Rosen's eyes—"was arrested by German police outside of the apartment house where Colonel Nicolai Kharkov and five others were murdered, at *exactly* the day and time when your Mr. Van Damme was appropriating information about the Amphora missile. Also included are the records of yours and Mr. Gruhaber's subsequent interrogation, including full documentation of times and location. Reunification or not, former East German police are very jealous of their jurisdiction. This particular Captain's notes are quite inclusive." He jiggled the packet again.

Rosen reached for the pouch, dropping it to his side without so much as a glance at the contents. The man's face clouded over for just an instant before he regained his rock-hard impassivity.

Rosen didn't notice. Shoulders slumping, he shuffled away from both men, following his feet toward the water's edge. He stared down at rainbow oil slicks riding the swells near the dock. After a few moments, Rosen began to rub his fingertips slowly across his eyes, desperately trying to conceptualize his next steps after this latest, and worst, disappointment.

"It vil proof I vas vith Vohn Dohm in za Berlin apartment, so people vil know I ahm not a traitor and dot he haas lied about me."

The shock of hearing Otto speak a complete sentence spun Rosen around. Except for monosyllabic grunts, he hadn't heard the little man's voice in days. Rosen approached, shrugging off the hope in Otto's face. "Not necessarily." His tone was harsh with his own disappointment, causing Otto to blink and retreat a few paces. Rosen softened his words, but they still flew out with depressing clarity. "He'd know that you never got to the safe house with that man. Millstein, you said his name was? So he could have scrapped the evidence that you were stealing Indigo; sent the team to sanitize your apartment; changed your bank statements back again; left your reputation as good as it was before.

Rosen snapped his fingers, the scenario proceeding before his eyes as if he were Van Damme himself, working it out in his museum of an office. "Then he tells everyone that you were helping him and that he lost you when the Russian backup teams came in shooting. As far as he's concerned, you're dead. So he gives up the Indigo idea, at least for now, and makes you a hero. The Amphora scheme alone could still be enough to get him what he wants, whatever in hell that is."

"Yesss, but—"

"And if you show up alive"—Rosen wasn't hearing Otto, only his own burgeoning hypothesis—"he leads the parade in your honor: 'Otto Gruhaber, the man who helped me capture Amphora from the Communists, has miraculously returned. Thank God.' Van Damme will be kissing you on your chubby little cheeks before you know it. And if you try to tell your story, he'll say the strain of it all got to you. Face it, Otto, who wouldn't believe that a poor little computer genius—whose life's biggest fear was losing data during a power surge—wouldn't go off the deep end after what you've been through?"

Rosen glanced toward the blond man. He had moved to within earshot but otherwise appeared completely detached from their heated speculation.

"Oh, my Gott!" Otto's head shook side to side.

Rosen's face was back in Otto's.

Droplets of perspiration emerged from the little programmer's thinning hairline, losing themselves in his heavy eyebrows, reappearing to cascade down the crevices of his puffy cheeks.

"Suppose Van Damme says that he went along with you because he already knew that you were a traitor who planned to steal Indigo. So he used you and your plans as bait for Amphora. Once it was over, he was going to bring you in, but he lost you during the fight with Kharkov and his people. *And* he saved the Indigo plans that you were ready to sell to Kharkov! You know what happens then? You show up now and they arrest you before you can open your mouth!"

Rosen towered over Otto like a victorious prosecutor grinding up the defense's star witness. He threw up his hands, glistening palms outward. "Sorry, Otto." Rosen dug stiff fingers through his perspiration-matted hair. "Sorry, Otto. It's just that that son of a bitch has us *again*."

"My Gott." Otto's narrow shoulders retracted into his fleshy red neck. "I could still be called a traitor. Efen after survifing."

Rosen gained strength from the drooping little figure. He had always felt the strongest when others were faltering. Rosen raised the plastic pouch high and nodded to the blond man. His other hand lighted briefly on Otto's shoulder. "I don't know what this can do for us, but whatever it takes—"

"I have done the most that I can. However you use this information, or *if* you do, is up to you. I must leave." The blond man strode toward the coiled rope and yanked the dark blade free. When he turned back toward them, it had disappeared. "Here. You cannot walk the streets covered in blood." The man peeled off his garment and reached it toward Rosen.

"We'll get it done." Rosen strode forward for the raincoat, not sure whether he intended to shake hands with the blond or not. "And thank your ... employers." He couldn't let it go. "Who are they? Are they here in New York?"

"My friend, they are everywhere." The man vanished behind the glaring white wall of a shed.

"Thanks," Rosen mumbled toward the pocket of steaming air where the man had last stood. He walked over to the Magnum, leaned down and grasped its grip, then rose and slid the heavy weapon into his waistband. His skin puckered at the sun-warmed metal's touch. "You ready?" Rosen walked back to the little man, who was toweling off his soaking face with his shirttail.

Otto grimaced during the process, as if his own improvised hygiene disgusted him. "Ya," he said, daintily tucking in the ringing wet portion of his shirt as if he were trying to prevent it from touching his skin. Once finished with his project, Otto sighed and, flattening his back against a nearby shed, allowed himself to sink gradually toward the ground. "Vot cahn ve do? I ahm zo tired uf running. I do not care anymore."

Rosen caught Otto under the arm before he reached the concrete. "Get up ... *now!*" The little man wobbled upward, watery eyes gazing fearfully at Rosen. Rosen felt a savage tremor ripple through Otto's fleshy biceps. "You're not giving up. You understand? No more whining and no more complaining." Otto hacked, his little body bobbing around the fulcrum of Rosen's arm. "And control that damn coughing! You're not going to die, at least not from that." Rosen felt a twinge of guilt at that one, but he needed an asset, and all the little man had been so far was a liability.

"Van Damme has conned you ... framed you ... tried to kill you. Do you *like* this man? Do you want to make his life easier or harder? Do you want him to succeed with his lousy little plan or help stop him?"

Otto's body was jerking, but no longer from his fit of coughing. Shamefaced, Rosen unclasped Otto's arm. How long had he been shaking the little man in tempo with his tirade?

Otto wobbled back a step, massaging the spot where Rosen had gripped him.

"*Don't you care?*" Rosen hollered across the sweltering gap between them. "Don't you want revenge? Aren't you a man?"

Otto's tiny chest heaved as he blinked back through the summer heat. "Yess," he hissed. "Yesss, I ahm a *mahn*!" Inside, the mortar was crumbling—mortar that had bonded his emotions into patterns of conformity so that he would be accepted; mortar that had trapped his outrage so that he would not rail at the injustice of being small, heavy, and different. What difference had his hard-earned restraint made? He was betrayed, hunted. Still not a member of any team, except maybe that of the man who stood before him. Rosen. The man who had carried him this far in spite of his pitiful helplessness.

As a child, his poor Aunt had fought the Russians as they ravaged her repeatedly. Otto was positive of that from every nightmare in which the incident zoomed through his psyche. She, a child, had fought and fought until she had had nothing left to fight with. Her suicide had not been a result of giving up without a fight but of giving everything and still losing. Could Otto say the same? No. His death would be by avoidance— repugnant to his brave child-Aunt in heaven.

"I am a man." Otto raised his chin and strode toward Rosen, mustering all of the dignity that his beaten little body could draw from his newly rejuvenated soul.

They walked side by side. There was the Nova! They ducked behind a shed, Rosen grasping for the Magnum, frowning at the quiet shape behind the wheel, motioning Otto to wait before darting toward another shed that was less than ten feet from the vehicle. Rosen crept around it until he had a perfect bead on Davilla's bent head. He frowned again. Davilla seemed to be leaning to reach for a fallen object between his feet. Rosen knew better. As he approached the partially open driver's window, the stench from the dead man's uncontrolled sphincter drove him back. Once again, Rosen was awed by the blond man's efficiency.

Rosen replaced the Magnum and trotted back to Otto. They gave the Nova a wide berth as they proceeded toward the humming traffic beyond the hazy pier.

Chapter 31

"What the hell are you doing out of Fair Oaks? I've been working with this cop, Amos, on the DC force to get that little weenie of a director Gorgone to make you available. Tomorrow we're filing a habeas corpus through an attorney I know down there."

Mark Hickey's voice rang through the receiver, undiminished even by the roaring background traffic. Rosen smiled back at the instrument, grateful that he had caught the busy trial lawyer in his office.

"Gorgone is the *assistant* director," Rosen corrected inanely.

"Whatever. So where are you and when do I see you?"

"Is the Algonquin still around?" Rosen was referring to a charming drawing room–style lounge where he and Barbara would meet Hickey, and whoever was Hickey's showpiece female of the month, on theater getaways to New York.

"You bet. The city will be a rock garden before that place closes." Mark Hickey's voice dropped. For all his good-natured repartee, he surely knew that whatever was coming was deadly serious. "Half hour, okay?"

"Give me an hour to do a little shopping." The hairs on Rosen's chest adhered to his bloody shirt, pricking him each time he moved. "I'm not exactly dressed for the Algonquin or anywhere civilized right now."

"Are you okay, Arn—"

"Yeah. And thanks for making the time—"

"Cut the crap. All I've got is a pre-trial conference over a fired corporate CEO's golden parachute. Worth about six mil to my client. No biggie. By the way, I can't tell you how sorry—"

"I know, Hicker."

"And I'm not asking, but …?"

"No, Hicker. I didn't go crazy and kill—"

"I know, I know. Sorry. Would you rather come here?"

"Nah. You trying to get out of buying me a drink?"

A gusty laugh exploded out of the earpiece. "See you there, pal."

"And no one else is to know, right?"

"Gimme a little credit, Arn. Of course not. Bye."

*   *   *

The Algonquin Hotel's lobby was a throwback to finer more refined times, when splendid carriages and shiny black Ford motorcars lined its curb. Its lounge still managed to retain that turn-of-the-century elegance. Rich wood paneling highlighted by sparkling crystal light fixtures dispelled the tawdry midtown frenzy, while splendid velvet chairs and settees muffled overexuberant conversations. The place had always been, to Rosen, a sanctuary from New York's manic sadness. Surprisingly, it still had that effect upon him. He could feel the throbbing of his nerve endings slow and then stop, even before a white-gloved waiter clinked a hearty brandy snifter down before him. Rosen swished the amber liquid against the bowed sides, releasing the potent Southern Comfort vapor. As it escaped through the vessel's wide mouth, its pungent power exploded into his nostrils.

Mark Hickey strode into the room. Hickey strode wherever he went. He still had the erect powerful figure of his heavyweight crew days, when his Cornell team swept England's Henley Regatta: the world championship of rowing. Hickey favored double-breasted suits because they accentuated his large shoulders and thin hips. A flag of red hair drooped above one eye. It had been Hickey's trademark since Beth Middleton, Cornell's cutest Delta Gamma and Hickey's second-semester freshman love, implored him to keep it that way after one of his windy practices on Lake Cayuga.

Three smart-looking female matinee-goers traced Hickey's progress to Rosen's table before resuming their self-conscious cocktail poses.

Hickey scanned Rosen with concern. "Hey, you look fine. I was worried after what you said on the phone ... Although, Arn, polyester slacks?" Hickey's nose wrinkled up toward his flawless eyebrows.

"That's all they sell on Forty-Second Street, Hicker." Rosen waved off Hickey's unspoken question. "It's a long story so shut up and listen," Rosen said as Hickey slid his chair up to their tiny marble-topped table. "Mark Hickey ... Otto Gruhaber."

Hickey's large hand shot out, then hesitated. "Gruhaber ... Aren't you the one who's stealing American secrets?" Only a slight wrinkle above his wide-set eyes altered Hickey's expression. He was probably the most imperturbable person that Rosen had ever known. Even during a punch-out with three Ithaca College football players after too many beers and too many insults had made a peaceful disengagement impossible, Hickey had never changed expression as he broke two of their noses and received a fractured jaw in return.

"What are you talking about?" The Southern Comfort sloshed dangerously close to the snifter's mouth as Rosen slapped it down with a sharp *ping*. The liquid slowly retreated down, leaving a rainbow residue along the glass's interior.

"Charles Van Damme held a news conference today. Actually, that over-the-hill redneck Culcane held it at his office, but Van Damme was the news—as usual." Hickey signaled a nearby waiter, silently mouthing, "Dewar's and water." The man nodded and did a 180 toward the bar. "He said that the Russians were after some secret plans. Don't you work for Sklar Industries?" Hickey's intense brown eyes bore into Otto.

"Yess." The little man squirmed, fingers undulating around his glass of mineral water. This lawyer was supposed to be a friend, but he sounded more like that awful police officer who arrested them in Berlin.

"Van Damme said that they had evidence that you were working with Russian spies; that you were missing; and that it looked as if you were headed for Europe to rendezvous with them."

Rosen rocked forward onto his elbows, compressing his lips. He frowned at Otto. "So Van Damme decided to set up the Indigo scam after all."

"How coot he haf the nerve? Ve thought he vould gif it up vonce I escaped." Otto's busy fingers had quieted. They now lay flattened against the tabletop.

Rosen reached for his glass. "He figured with all the contract people he had after us, we'd be caught and killed. Then they'd ship us back to Europe where we would get 'officially' killed trying to pass the plans to the KGB. That way, Charles Van Damme—captor of the Amphora missile— becomes a hero all over again." Rosen leaned back, sucking air across the warm liquid in his mouth before letting it trickle down his throat. "Hicker, you thought I was still in Fair Oaks, so I assume that they didn't tell that cop, Amos, or anyone else, that I escaped three weeks ago."

Hickey jolted forward, engulfing his side of the small table. His expression didn't change, but the emotion in his voice was unmistakable. "*Hell no!* That head honcho—Gorgone?—kept stalling Amos. Told him that you were too disturbed to see anyone. Amos wasn't buying it. He kept after Gorgone. One day Amos's captain calls him in. Tells him to lay off. It seems that Gorgone got all the way up to the commissioner, himself. Convinced him that outside pressures could throw you over the edge. Forever. The captain told Amos that Fair Oaks was strictly out of bounds and if he went back again, they'd bust him." Hickey shrugged. "Everyone's scared of lawsuits nowadays, even the cops."

The white gloves appeared and Hickey grabbed for the drink. When the waiter was out of earshot, Hickey stared intently at Rosen. "What the hell is going on?" Hickey flicked his dangling clump of hair aside with his free hand: a habit when he was preparing to concentrate.

"Hold it a second, Hicker." Rosen tapped Otto's fingers, which drummed on the table sporadically. "Otto, I'll bet Van Damme was going to have his stooge at Fair Oaks claim that I'd only *just* escaped." Rosen's eyes rolled upward as if he were watching the scenario of Gorgone's perfidy playing across the ceiling. "Then Van Damme will make up this story that the reason I went bats at CIA was because I was helping you steal Indigo and the pressure cracked me … or Barbara found out and I couldn't deal with it … Something like that. So now he has the perfect excuse to get me too." *Crack.* Rosen pounded a fist into his palm.

Thinking that he had been summoned, the white-gloved waiter glided toward them.

Rosen smiled apologetically as he waved the man off. "Sure. He'll tell everyone that I escaped to get my share of the payoff when you sell the Indigo plans. Then he'll make it look like his people killed us in Europe to stop us from getting the plans to the Russians. It's perfect." Rosen counted off his remaining points by tapping his three left fingertips in succession with his right index finger: "Van Damme becomes a hero all over again. He gets rid of us. And he gets the United States pissed off at the Russians for something they never did! It's beautiful." Rosen lifted his Southern Comfort in a mock toast. "And Van Damme will say that his people were in hot pursuit of me going to Europe so they didn't have time to notify the local authorities here." Rosen drained his glass.

"A goot plan." Otto's head bobbed vigorously. As a mathematician, he clearly appreciated the precision of Van Damme's logic. Rosen's scowl punctured his enthusiasm as it dawned upon Otto that the more foolproof Van Damme's plan, the surer his own death. He avoided Rosen's eyes by tearing the corners off his cocktail napkin.

"Hold it a second. What the hell is going on here?" Hickey's huge hands joggled the table. Peanuts from the overfilled bowl cascaded across its marble surface. "Charles Van Damme is a national hero. *My God*, his confirmation hearing for CIA Director starts in a day or two!" He glowered, first at Rosen, then at Otto.

"*What*! You're talking about Charles Van Damme, the CIA division chief?" Rosen realized how ludicrous the question sounded even before Hickey's reply.

"Yeah. That one. Where the hell have you been? The guy's been on the news every day for weeks. Christ, he's got higher visibility than Trump and Ivana." Hickey stared into Rosen's eyes as if seeking some glimmer of recognition. After a moment, he shook his head, sighing. "This guy found out that the Russians were still working on some horrific missile that could multiply into hundreds of baby horrific missiles even if it was shot out of the air. So he single-handedly stole the plans—right out of the KGB's hands. That got all our starry-eyed politicians to realize that the Russians aren't sitting around waiting for Democracy with open arms. That's why the old director is out and Van Damme's in."

Suddenly, Hickey sniffed and then wrinkled his nose. He spun, glaring at the tinted hair of a small man at the adjoining table. The man had dipped his cigarette daintily back over his narrow shoulder so that the tendrils of smoke floated everywhere but into his own face. Hickey fanned at the offending white trails with a flat hand. Soon they dissolved into the air.

"Clendon would never appoint Van Damme—"

"I mean, sure," Hickey continued, as if he hadn't noticed the dazed look on Rosen's face or the aimless shaking of Rosen's head. "There's all that stuff about Savin's health and all. But you can bet your ass that Clendon watched Van Damme's popularity skyrocket and decided it was time for a more aggressive guy over at CIA. Clendon's no dummy, and the handwriting's on the wall. This country doesn't trust the Russians." Hickey threw down a quick sip, licking the excess from his lips. He worked the moisture off his glass with the ball of his thumb.

"But ... Director of Central Intelligence?" Rosen accentuated each vowel, as if that might help him comprehend. "No division chief has ever made it to the Director's desk."

"Hey, on top of everything else, Van Damme's got some heavy duty rabbis. Culcane, of foreign relations, for one. Clendon would be a fool not to jump on Van Damme's bandwagon, even if he hates the son of a bitch. And he probably does. No president likes *having* to nominate someone, but Clendon doesn't have a choice. Why, hell, if this Indigo thing comes off, Van Damme could probably take the presidency. Clendon better watch out next term, I'm telling you."

"Vat about *glasnost*?" Otto's mouth hung at an odd angle, as if a powerful tranquilizer had neutralized the muscles.

"Are you kidding? A lot of people here would just as soon bomb the Russians after this Amphora deal. They figure—and I'm not so sure that I don't agree—that Yeltsin can't hold it together and the bad guys in the KGB and the army will take over soon, probably without a fight, if they promise to give the Russian people a little food. Many of those poor suckers probably see 'Democracy' as a fancy term for 'starvation.' And not too many tanks will have to roll before all those independent republics will be playing dead, as they did before Reagan and the Wall. Face it, friends, glasnost will be dead and buried before we've had time to pay our respects." Hickey drained his glass, thudded it down, and flicked a raised index finger toward the waiter in one continuous motion.

"Van Damme set Amphora up, Hicker. Yeltsin probably doesn't even know Russia had the missile. It was just a little game between Van Damme and his paranoid counterparts in the KGB, and Van Damme won it all."

Hickey rocked back, crossing his large arms. He fingered a loose peanut, dropping it back onto the table as he licked his lower lip. "How do you know?" He rocked back toward Rosen. "I never believed those things they said you did, Arnie. Knew the ... 'Brain' was the best person to help you. When Topper died, I started getting involved. I was willing to take whatever time it took to get you out of that sanatorium and cleared." Hickey tentatively fingered another peanut, but it soon dropped, rolling within inches of the first one. "Now I wonder. You're making some outrageous charges." Hickey's deeply tanned face furrowed as he toyed with his large ring. Its star sapphire glowed icily, despite the room's warm tones. "How the hell do you know all this when you've been cooling your heels who knows where?"

The white-gloved waiter laid another Dewar's before Hickey, smoothly sweeping the old one up with only the faintest tinkle of ice against glass. "Gentlemen?" He looked down at Rosen and Otto, who both declined. The waiter vanished with a smile as pleasant as if they had ordered a magnum of champagne.

Hickey leaned close to Rosen. His voice hissed through nearly closed teeth. "Arnie, you better start making sense. And *soon*. Or friend or no friend, I'm outta here!"

Rosen had a horrible sensation of losing it all. Here was a lifelong friend, drinking buddy—Jonathon's godfather, for God's sake—ready to get up and leave. Was he sounding and looking that off the wall? Suddenly, Rosen wanted to rest. Drop his head to the marble table and roll his hot cheeks on its invitingly cool surface. What chance did he and Otto have without Hicker?

A vision flooded into his mind. It was a huge Van Damme, arms and legs spread apart like a mighty colossus, laughing thunderously down upon a mouse-sized Rosen, who quivered beneath each rumbling gust. Would Van Damme always keep getting bigger and bigger, while he shrunk away to nothing? No, Goddammit! *No*! This time Rosen's face loomed large into Hickey's as he glared back. "Now you just listen to me, you hear? Just shut up and *listen*!"

*   *   *

Hickey chewed the ice from his third drink as Rosen finished. "And you were there during all this?" Hickey scrutinized Otto's dumpy figure, as if noticing the little programer for the first time.

"Yess." Otto half rose, chubby red hands webbed out on the table. "I ahm not a traitor." He nodded abruptly toward Rosen. "Zhow him za arrest documents."

Rosen's curled his eyebrows in surprise at Otto's uncharacteristic peremptoriness, but the little man was oblivious to his friend's reaction as he glared straight ahead at Hickey. With a shrug, Rosen dug into his waistband, sliding out the plastic packet. It tugged at his skin as he removed it and passed it to Hickey.

Hickey hesitated, as if it contained something alive. Finally, he curled his sturdy fingers around it.

"Records of Otto's arrest outside the apartment building in East Ber … just Berlin—that's still hard to get used to—where Van Damme killed Kharkov. And my arrest at the same place."

Rosen couldn't avoid a smile as Hickey snapped open a pair of black half-lensed glasses and held one of the long pages up toward a brass light fixture next to their table. He was reminded of the plethora of fraternity tales chronicling Hickey's legendary penuriousness as he watched the ultra-successful attorney squint through the cheap drugstore magnifying lenses. Despite his poor equipment, Hickey finished quickly, fishing into the packet for further material. Next he examined a letter-sized pink paper.

Hickey slid off his glasses, dangling them aimlessly in front of his face as he talked to himself. "Van Damme could push the Russians right back into the Communists' hands—or the Fascists. The Cold War: worrying about missiles dropping one warm summer night, all the shit we thought was over, all over again." He dropped the hand with his glasses into his lap, thrusting the pink paper toward Rosen with the other. "Suppose these were setups to bring Van Damme down? We can verify these, I'm sure—"

"Come on, Hicker. There isn't any *East Germany*, anymore. Why the hell are they going to play ball with the Russians and lie about this?"

Otto rose up all the way. He leaned across the table toward Hickey, like a card-cheated cowboy calling out a tinhorn gambler. "Gehrmans hate Rooshians! Ve alvays half; ve alvays vill. Zer may be a vew communist collaborators, but za Gehrman Government vould never auzenticate zese records for za benefit of za Russians. Not now zat ve are free uf zem forever." Otto sat. He grabbed for a napkin, dabbing at imagined patches of perspiration on his forehead. "Ve zhould be able to easily half zem verified, iff you vish."

Rosen shrugged at Hickey, trying to diffuse the impact of Otto's rancor without undermining the validity of his points. "Not only that, Hicker. Give me the time and I can dig up every bit of proof I had against Van Damme in the first place."

"If he has your files, why couldn't he have destroyed all the records by now?"

Rosen rubbed a hand across his cheek. His fingertips massaged an eyebrow as he thought. "He could have removed some if he had time. He's been very busy the last two weeks. He might not even have bothered. I mean, it's not as if anyone I've told my story to has taken me seriously. But even if Van Damme did cover his trail, he can't wipe out phone company charges or airline reservations. And he can't change his own travel records. They're already logged in too many places. Nah, it may take a little while, but I can get him, *if* I can access the company data banks. Believe me, Hicker, I can."

Hickey scratched under his sleek razor cut, kicking up a few red strands, patting them precisely back into place. "I do. It's just … I kinda wish I didn't. We've got one hell of a job ahead of us."

Rosen leaned back, willing the tension out of his shoulders. He winked at Otto, then turned back toward Hickey. "So what do we do now? Van Damme has a lot of help." Embarrassed by the magnitude of his understatement, Rosen crossed his eyes for his companions' benefit.

Hickey let out a gusty laugh.

Even Otto smirked.

"We get to the right people." Hickey's smile vanished as the tension-breaking interlude passed. "And if these work out"—he tapped the plastic package in front of him—"we've got him." Hickey raised his sleek eyebrows as he looked from Rosen to Otto, back to Rosen. "First I'd better get you somewhere safe while I figure out who we dare contact. This may go deeper than just Mr. Van Damme." Noticing Otto's face clench, Hickey added hurriedly, "Hey, it's probably just *his* fucked-up idea." He waved a large palm in front of the little man's glazed eyes. "I'm a lawyer. Being negative is my business. What can I say?"

"What about you? I don't want you ending up like … Larry." Rosen had dropped his head so that the last few words were almost inaudible, but he knew that Hickey knew.

"Yeah. Poor Brain. Got a case he could finally be proud of." His voice rose. "Those bastards got him 'cause he was going to blow this open!"

Two of the sleek-suited matinee-goers raised their heads, staring.

Hickey shot them a little boy grin as he waved his hands in apology.

They smiled back. The third, and prettiest, joined in dazzlingly as her companions tittered into her lavishly earringed ears.

"That's why we've been so damn helpless." Rosen slapped the side of his fist down. The marble was wet from an overflow of Hickey's scotch. Rosen withdrew his hand, absentmindedly rubbing it along the side of his trousers. "All we've been able to do is run. I'm sick of it!" He looked at Otto. "We *both* are."

Otto nodded his grim face and then ducked it away as he began coughing.

"You should have someone look at you." Hickey reached over to pat Otto's heaving back. "You both should."

Otto rose, swiping at the perspiration on his flushed forehead. "I do zat *after* ve haf exposed zis man. Doesn't do me any goot to haf myzelf cured if I vill be dead vrom a bullet tomorrow."

"Makes sense," Hickey laughed, raising the last of his scotch in a toast to the little man. His face stiffened. "We all better take care." He lowered the glass gently. "I can get a friend's place in Pennsylvania, maybe a hundred miles from here. You'll use one of my firm's cars. I'll be down tomorrow. Make sure you're not followed. I'm sure you know how, Arnie. I'll do the same. We should be okay there for a couple of days, until I can make arrangements.

Hickey's sense of urgency suddenly seemed greater than that of either of the other two. *The fear is only hitting him now,* thought Rosen, *while Otto and I have been living with it every minute of every day.*

"Let's go!" Hickey slapped down too much money, brusquely shaking off the waiter's inquiry as to change. Extremely un-Hickey-like, noted Rosen. Even more un-Hickey-like, the lawyer failed to acknowledge the upturned faces of the three attractive women as he hustled his companions through their perfumed aura. They hurried past subdued conversations and clinking glasses, ignoring the cheerful "Please visit us again" of the eager desk clerk as Hickey shouldered them out of the revolving door.

CHAPTER 32

olling hills lolled beside their windows as their car cleared Philadelphia's congestion and navigated eastern Pennsylvania's grassy oceans. Rosen had never driven a Mercedes before, but that was all that Hickey's firm had available. Rosen didn't mind. It was like steering a cloud.

"Ve zhould be close." Otto squinted at the map Hickey had slapped into their hands as he hurried them out of the immaculate garage fourteen stories below his Park Avenue offices. The whole transfer from Hickey's car to the Mercedes had taken less than five minutes, with Hickey exhorting them to even greater haste as he spewed last-minute instructions while practically pressing on their accelerator to hurry them by the attendant's booth. Rosen had never seen Hickey like this. His friend was literally perspiring as he hustled them off. As he wedged the luxurious car into crosstown traffic, Rosen remembered thinking, *Mark must know that we're in bigger trouble than even I realize.*

"Yess. Vest Chester iss zat vay." Otto jabbed a stubby finger toward a green-and-white route sign. "Only tventy miles."

*   *   *

"Vat a qvaint place." Otto's face spun from side to side as he studied the little brick shops along West Chester's narrow main street. "All of zese buildings must hov been built two hundred yearse ago. Look ot zat gingerbread along za roofs."

"Very nice, Otto. Now where the hell is the turnoff to the college?" Rosen kept both hands clutched to the soft wheel as he narrowly squeezed by parked cars on one side and oncoming traffic on the other.

"Zhould be right ahead a mile or two." Otto's eyes still dwelt on the peaked roofs of the narrow brick buildings. Animated conversation from a jean-clad group perched upon the steps of an Ace hardware store wafted through Otto's window, as did laughter from behind the flamboyant barrier of a brimming flower kiosk.

"Thanks," Rosen shot over toward the engrossed little figure. How the hell had Otto become so damn relaxed? When the little man made up his mind to be cool, he was *cool. You're quite a guy, Otto,* thought Rosen.

"Zere iss za college. Turn right ot za next shtop zign."

Now, the homes were modern and sprawling, approached through wide circular drives; ringed by pristine white fences; covering the gamut from ranch to Cape Cod; sitting comfortably on one to four acres—the ultimate phase in West Chester's evolution from Continental Army outpost to horse country mecca.

The home at the end of the long, rutted drive into which they turned was entirely out of context: a traditional wooden farmhouse with a badly settling veranda, drooping shutters, and yellowing paint. Only its high-tech aluminum screens hinted at the present era. Unsettled dust sprayed from their tires as the Mercedes jolted closer. Rosen stopped before a long shed with three garage-door-sized cutouts. Dim silhouettes of a tractor and pickup were distinguishable within its shadowy interior.

"Just like a visit to Grandma's, huh, Otto?" Rosen slid out, walking to the corner of the shed. "Nothing but fields in the back. Wonder if it all belongs to this." He pivoted, staring past the scraggly grass yard toward the distant road. Pinking sky already blurred the outlines of the gentle hills to the south.

"This friend of Hicker's may have the schlockiest house on the block, but he also has a ton of land." Rosen reached for a glowing daisy, tugged away a few petals, watching them spiral down toward the grass like aircraft-less propellers. He turned toward the wide stairs. "Let's go see what we have to buy before the stores all close."

A wooden plank screeched as Otto stepped onto the veranda, causing him to dance precariously at the top of the stairs.

Rosen had to laugh. "It was a good warning to the farmer. Lot of these old houses had a loose board or two like that. Better than a burglar alarm. Don't fall back on me now. There may be a few more between you and the front door."

"Ya. Ya. Okay." Otto moved forward, toeing each board before setting down his full weight.

Rosen strode past him, reaching for Hickey's key. The large doorknob was heavily oxidized, rough to the touch, but the key slid in smoothly. Someone had recently squirted the lock with graphite. A trace darkened the tips of Rosen's fingers as he withdrew the key.

They weren't prepared for the old farmhouse's interior. It was straight out of *Home and Garden*: gleaming hardwood floors; a glossy white built-in bookcase, desk and entertainment center that spread along one entire wall of the spacious step-down living room; a red-tiled country kitchen with a center island big enough to house a six-burner stove and electric barbecue and still have enough counter space to butcher a small steer; and a master bedroom suite with carpeting so thick you could lose a small dog in it.

"My Gott. Who vould half eggshpected zis from za oudside?" Otto shook his head as he zapped channels on and off with the fifty-inch TV's remote.

"We don't need a thing," Rosen called from in front of the oversized refrigerator. "There's enough here to feed the Philadelphia Eagles for a month. Hickey sure knows the right people." He slid two chicken potpies from the freezer. "Come on in and get something to eat, Otto. They may even have frozen bratwurst in here."

"I hate bratwurst," Otto called back, pausing to admire Raquel Welsh in a stone-age loincloth, fighting off a flying dinosaur. He snapped off the picture as the pterodactyl carried her superimposed likeness toward its ineptly animated brood, wriggling atop a painted-in mountain. "But I vill half a little zomething … and zen I vill sleep very nizely," he assured Rosen as he entered the dazzling kitchen.

*   *   *

Rosen woke as a thin sheet of sunlight inserted itself through the crack between his curtains; traced a path along the fibers of the rich pile carpet; slipped up his sheets; and settled upon his upturned face. The clamor of insects, which had bombarded him through the partially opened window during the night, had yielded to a bird orchestra ranging from the piccolo of sparrows to the bassoon of crows. It was nearly eleven. Rosen rushed to wash, dress, and fly out into his first peaceful morning of recent memory.

The hills glowed with reflected sunlight. Ridges of distant grass undulated in the warm breeze like waves of a tropical ocean. A monarch butterfly flitted past Rosen's nose, pursued by a second, their rust and black wings forming a bobbing bow in midair as they linked briefly before the chase continued and they spiraled up and up into the warm haze. The birds, which had so vigorously serenaded Rosen a short while before, seemed to have lost their enthusiasm in the escalating heat. They drooped on the wires crossing the backyard from a tall wooden pole to a point above the rear door, erupting into animated twittering only if a neighbor encroached.

Rosen trotted slowly toward the distant hill behind the house. He assumed that the property continued that far since he could discern no fence demarcating the glaring fields. Sweet summer air poured into his nostrils: hay and clover.

The complicated-looking Adidas, which Rosen had borrowed from the bedroom closet, were two sizes too large. The poor fit forced him to reduce his strides, but the erratic contour of the fields would have slowed him down regardless. *It doesn't matter,* he thought. *It's just so good to have the sun on my face and to feel my arms pumping.* His right running shoe wedged momentarily in a chuckhole hidden by a floppy overhang of tall blue-green stalks. Rosen staggered, but recovered with only a slight twinge in his ankle. Out of self-preservation, he rotated his face away from the sun and concentrated on the ground.

Despite the near disaster, Rosen's mood remained three stages above buoyant as he thrashed through the crisp, high grass toward the soil-streaked hillside.

*   *   *

A Lincoln Continental jolted along the driveway at dusk. Otto and Rosen were engaged in their third chess battle of the day—if one could call Otto's previous twenty or so move checkmates of Rosen a battle. Rosen leaped from the onyx board, causing his king, queen, and a few of their henchmen to totter, and dashed toward the living room window.

"Its Hickey," Rosen called back to Otto as the little programer steadied the pieces.

Otto replaced them in new game formation. There would be no more chess tonight. He joined Rosen at the curtained window. The Lincoln parked directly behind the Mercedes, its wide chrome grill practically kissing the Lexus's rear bumper. *Why so close,* Otto wondered, *when the area in front of the shed was wide enough to park five cars side by side?*

"Holy crap, he brought that cop!" Rosen's eyes protruded angrily in the sun's flattening rays. "What the hell … *You* answer the door!" Rosen raked his hair with stiff fingers, then shoved Otto forward. "C'mon—c'mon. That's the cop who arrested me. I'll be watching from the back. You don't know where I am, okay?"

Otto nodded, sucking in a deep breath. Would anything ever go right again? Never mind. He trusted Rosen. *They* would get through this. "Ya. Ya. Go." Otto shuffled toward the door as footsteps reverberated along the wooden veranda. He hesitated, his fingers caressing the door handle's smooth circumference.

Hickey's face appeared through the stained glass square. The glass's color and texture, like a poorly lit Picasso, distorted his features. The heavy door grated open.

Behind, and to Hickey's left, was a thin black man with slacks that looked as if they had been creased by a steamroller. His shirt also appeared to have been put on just before he stepped from the car. The tip of his maroon-and-blue striped tie reached exactly to his belt buckle.

Hickey, by contrast, looked frazzled. His shirt bloused at the waist and was laced with creases. Hickey's jacket sprawled across his shoulder from a casual index finger, while the other's rested neatly over his left forearm. A black leather holster snugged inconspicuously between the jacket's glistening lining and his shallow chest.

"Hi, Otto." Hickey's large shoulders grazed the doorway as he barreled through. "This is Detective Amos." Hickey's head pivoted from one side of the living room toward the other. "Where's Arnie?"

Otto smiled weakly at the thin black man. "A pleazure to meet you, zir. I do not know vere he iss right now, Mr. Hickey. He might be oudt running or zomething."

Hickey's eyebrows squirmed down toward the bridge of his nose. "Little dark for that, isn't it, Otto?" Cupping his left hand around the side of his mouth, in an exaggerated imitation of someone shouting across a long distance, Hickey called, "C'mon, Arnie. I know you're heeeeere! The nice lieutenant is here to help us."

Silence.

"Aaarnie." Hickey's voice went falsetto. "I *meeean* it."

Rosen strode out from the hall, face burning. "Okay. *Okay*, jerk! Why the hell did you bring him?" He flicked a rigid thumb in Amos's direction.

"*Because* he can help."

"Yeah. The last time he and that big partner of his tried to help, I almost got killed." Rosen's glare shifted from Hickey to the police officer.

Amos stared back, his dark eyes unblinking. "Detective Francis isn't with me. I'm doing this on my own, and I need to hear Mr. Hickey's story from *you*."

Amos's bass voice resonated in Rosen's head. The man's calm, which was too consistent to be real, antagonized Rosen. Without warning, his mind flashed an image of Amos's concerned eyes during his visit to the hospital, but Rosen angrily repressed it. Rosen's lips curled. "Why would you care now? All *you're* looking for is an arrest."

Amos arranged his coat over the arm of an extended leather recliner sitting beneath a chrome floor lamp that arched as gracefully as a stalking crane. He smoothed the faintly graying hair above his delicate right ear before pursing his thin dark lips. He spoke without resentment. "Because of that whole scam at Fair Oaks. All that secret stuff. Them not letting me see you. It all jibes with what Mr. Hickey told me."

"Well, what do you know?" Rosen drew close to the officer. "Someone *finally* believes that I may not be out of my mind." His voice became a whisper as he stared down at Amos. "It would have been nice if someone would have believed me before—"

"Okay, Arnie." Hickey inserted his broad frame between the two, placing large palms on Rosen's shoulders, gently backing him up. "Let's not take it out on Lieutenant Amos. He *is* trying to help now. And we sure need it." Hickey's boyish smile glistened in Rosen's face.

The pressure of Hickey's heavy hands relaxed Rosen. He let them sit there for a moment, comforted by the contact, before shrugging them off. "Okay, Detective Amos, this is Otto Gruhaber." Rosen flattened an upraised palm in Otto's direction. "The man who is supposed to be selling the Indigo satellite to the KGB at this very moment."

"Pleased to meet you, Mr. Gruhaber." Amos played along with Rosen's irony, half bowing toward Otto. Then his face became serious again. "I'm sure that you have some proof of your identity."

"Uff courze." Otto scurried toward the policeman, fumbling with an ancient wallet. Cards and crumpled papers protruded from every crack and crevice. "Here iss my Viza und a library cahd." His hand shook as he proffered them to Amos. "Here iss alzo an inzurance cahd." In his anxiety, Otto violently plucked the card from its worn pocket. Scraps of paper, dog-eared business cards, and plastic IDs rained upon the carpet as the overburdened wallet gave out. The little programer stared openmouthed for a moment, then hunkered down on his hands and knees, scratching and tugging his lost treasures from the thick pile carpet.

Amos briefly studied the items in his hand before smiling down at Otto's gyrating back. "Thank you, Mr. Gruhaber. *These* will do for now," he said loudly, halting Otto, mid-reach, from handing up yet another ID. Still grinning, Amos turned toward Rosen. "Why don't you catch me up on what happened since we saw each other? Mr. Gruhaber can finish restocking his wallet in the meantime. Then I can go over things with him later."

"Here's a good spot." Hickey patted a sprawling three-piece sectional that surrounded the high stone fireplace at the far end of the room. "Anyone want a drink?" Bottles clinked inside of a chest-high teak liquor cabinet as Hickey poked around for his choice. Both men declined as they made for the mountainous pillows of the sofa.

*   *   *

When Rosen and Otto finished, Amos jiggled his thumb along the side of a Sprite can that glistened with pearls of accumulated moisture, thinking. The piercing *razz* of cicadas penetrated the house as if it had no walls. The dapper police officer finally looked up. "That is unbelievable! Charles Van Damme is only days away from becoming the new head of CIA."

"If you're going to do one of your non-believing bits again, why don't you just leave and let us handle it? This isn't your jurisdiction anyway." Rosen's eyes bored into Amos.

Amos took a long sip. When he lowered the can, he was smiling. "Mr. Rosen, I didn't say I didn't believe you, did I?" He paused, placing his Sprite on a glass end table next to a stack of cork coasters and four neatly fanned *Business Weeks*. "I just might. And *you* are going to need me." Amos jabbed a pink nail at Rosen's face. "You don't know who to trust. *Anyone* could be Van Damme's friend because he's America's number one hero right now. There are thousands of nuts out there who'd blow you away in a second if they thought you wanted to hurt him." Now Amos was up, jabbing his finger at them both. "I'm going out on a goddamn long limb even thinking of helping either of you—and you're right: this isn't my jurisdiction—and you know what else? As far as the world is concerned,

I'm not only consorting with a murderer now, but a *spy* too! Not very good company for a black dude on the fast track to captain."

Rosen blinked. So Amos really could raise his voice like anyone else. All that calm quiet control was just a lot of crap, just as he'd figured. Well, he'd tell Mr. I'm-Doing-You-Such-a-Big-Favor where to get off …

"Arnie!" Hickey's voice was shrill. Rosen turned toward the distant section of couch where Hickey sprawled, both hands circling his third or fourth drink. His friend's broad face approximated the color of the swatch of red hair dominating the center of his forehead. Ice tinkled as Hickey's big hands twitched. He looked flustered. Scared. What the hell was going on? The Hicker never got flustered. And scared? Impossible.

"Arnie." Hickey's voice came out gravelly and slow in what must have been a massive effort at self-control. "Stay calm." The lawyer raised a palm and smiled, acknowledging his own recent transgression. "Lieutenant Amos can help us with protection until I can get to the right people. He's right: we have to be very careful whom we trust. There's no telling how deep Van Damme's power base goes." Hickey's glass was to his lips and back in his lap so quickly that the clinking of his ice was the only evidence that he'd actually taken a sip. "God. If that crazy redneck Culcane is actually in on this, then we've got to watch out for his far right cronies too!" Hickey finished his drink with a quick toss of his head. "We need the detective, so be nice and ask him to stay. Okay?"

Rosen studied his friend. When had he seen Hicker drink like this? Back at the Algonquin and now here. Had Hickey drunk this heavily the day of the Rosen's last barbecue? Rosen fought through the awful memories, trying to recall. He could not remember Hickey having more than a couple of beers. Heck, in the old days, Hickey was always the driver because when everyone else was blotto, Hickey was straight. Part of that clean-cut athlete image his friend was always so proud of. Hmmm. Hickey couldn't keep his eyes off his Rolex either. Another sure sign of nerves. What had happened to Hickey—the rock? Rosen speculated whether his mind subconsciously refused to negatively update images of the people it loved, like the Hicker. *If I acknowledge his deterioration, will I have to face my own?* Rosen tried to separate the mythical "Hicker" from the one who sat before him. Had life inevitably ground Hickey down, or was the present situation just too much for him?

Rosen's analysis was interrupted by a soft sucking sound. From the corner of his Eye he could see Otto clasping and unclasping his sweaty palms. Better make peace with Amos for everyone's sake, he decided.

"Detective Amos"—Rosen tried a smile, although he was sure that it came closer to the hollow grimace of a Halloween pumpkin—"I *do* appreciate the risks you are taking. And I, as well as Otto and Mark, would be grateful if you would help us."

"How can I turn down such a *heartfelt* request?" Amos took a seat, burrowing until the couch's mountainous pillows engulfed his slight body. "How 'bout a drink, now, Mr. Hickey? They must have some port in that monster." Amos stared the liquor cabinet up and down. "It's bigger than some of the Seven-Elevens in my neighborhood."

Hickey rose. His smile was back, but Rosen could see the tension throbbing beneath as clearly as if Hickey's skin had been peeled down to the nerves.

"I'm sure we can accommodate you, Detective. Yes, sir, here's a beauty." Hickey flourished a graceful green bottle. Its gold label flashed light as he lowered it toward the marble countertop.

As he stared into its interior, Rosen decided that calling the massive piece of furniture a "liquor cabinet" was like saying that the *Queen Mary* was a "nice little boat." There were three tiers of bottles, eight abreast, plus a full complement of gold-rimmed glasses of all the popular shapes and sizes, suspended from rows of wooden fittings inside the doors. A chrome sink was set into its broad marble counter. Rosen calculated that the value of the massive antique, plus the cost of adapting it to its present use, would add a family room to the average home.

"And for me, another scotch." Hickey clinked bottles and glasses. After a minute or two, he spun around, hoisting his and Amos's drinks. "Anyone else?"

Otto asked for a mineral water. Rosen declined.

When they had all settled back, Hickey withdrew a long cigar from his jacket. Rosen smiled. Cigars had always been an amusing anomaly to Hickey's spartan existence. Unexpectedly, Rosen visualized Hickey's freshman roommate. The poor kid was an ascetic engineering student from Kansas who preferred bitter winter treks to the distant library to asphyxiation in their smoke-saturated dorm room. Hickey removed a matchbook from his pocket. He bent the match and ignited it one handed: a favorite trick of his. The flame swelled and contracted as Hickey puffed the cigar's dark tip into a vibrant orange. For the first time, Hickey seemed to relax. He blew a gust of white smoke toward the ceiling, following with a slow sip of scotch. "Anyone else care for one of these?" Hickey wiggled the glowing cigar above his face.

"Sure," said Rosen. It was a reflex—an automatic response triggered by memories of secure times, when only good things lay ahead and life was a fearless adventure.

Hickey looked surprised. Something sad flashed behind his eyes. Then he covered it with a smile. "Here, Arn. You always were a mooch." Hickey winked as he reached a second cigar toward Rosen.

Rosen reflected on the sadness in Hickey's eyes as he crinkled off the cellophane. He sniffed the musky leaves before biting a bitter notch into the cigar's tip. Had Mark also been remembering the old days … and had it just hit him too that they couldn't ever go live there again?

"How 'bout a light, Hicker?" It came out phony, Rosen's attempt to sound cool when his insides ached with the ultimate realization that—no matter how he yearned—he could never experience those days or those feelings again, except through eroding memories.

The matchbook sailed in an erratic trajectory, bouncing near his right shoe. As he reached down for it, Rosen realized exactly how far he and Hickey had wandered from the days when anything was possible. He fingered the matchbook, slowly tracing the raised silver image on its cover with the inside of his thumb. A very unusual logo: a wall overlain with three delicate vines that spelled the restaurant's name in flowery script. Rosen stared at Hickey, wondering if the dancing yellow match flame camouflaged the hatred in his eyes.

CHAPTER 33

Craig's hands strangled the wheel as he flew across the Delaware River into New Jersey. They had remained frozen in position—white-knuckled and rigid—since he had requisitioned the vehicle after his heated confrontation with Van Damme this morning.

Never, but *never*, had it been this bad between them before. Van Damme had opened by calling him a liar. Straight out, no ands, ifs, or buts. "I don't tolerate people lying to me, Craig!" It happened the minute he'd walked into Van Damme's office. The bastard had been standing there by this fucking antique globe showing the world back in Alexander the Great's—or some other big deal conqueror's time. Van Damme was big on conquerors, probably thought he was one, and he was spinning the damn thing with a skinny finger as he told Craig in that icy-calm voice what a miserable incompetent Craig was; how Craig had lied to him about Rosen and Gruhaber being taken care of; how he, Charles Van Damme, would be in trouble with his congressional backers if Rosen and Gruhaber popped up here in the States; and how he'd have Craig's balls for lunch if they did; and worst of all, how this amateur, Rosen, had made monkeys of Craig and Craig's people.

Van Damme's contempt had dug into Craig like a burning knife blade, searing every organ in his body as he sat straight faced, having to take it. God, what torture! And Van Damme could do it so well. Like he enjoyed it. Only this morning, Van Damme hadn't seemed to enjoy making Craig squirm. *This morning* he was just icy and angry, and Craig was frightened, because the Van Damme he saw earlier today would snuff him in an instant. No questions. No remorse. This morning Craig had gone from being Charles Van Damme's favorite—Van Damme's boy that he *had* been—to a nonentity whom Van Damme would as easily kill as look at.

All because of Rosen. Craig was losing everything he had worked for because of Rosen. Here was Van Damme on his way to the top. Director of the entire damn CIA, and Craig, who should be climbing right along with him for doing all his dirty work, was about to be shit-canned! All because of goddamn fuckin' … Ooooh, how he was getting to hate the name Rosen.

The worst thing was that Craig had lost Van Damme's respect. Funny … but beneath it all, that was what hurt the most. Sure, Van Damme abused him. Plenty. But Craig knew that Van Damme humiliated him to manipulate him, to get the most out him, because Van Damme had believed in him. This morning Van Damme talked to Craig as if Craig were a low-life contract employee, a nonentity, scum.

Craig's guts clenched tighter than his knotted hands as he contemplated the emptiness not being Van Damme's boy would bring. Like when his father, the celebrated heart surgeon, shut him out because he didn't have what it took to get into medical school. From that day on, Jordy, his little brother—Dean's List at Brown and hell-bent for a top med school—got all Dr. Randolph Craig's attention, while Craig was just another loser as far as his old man was concerned.

How about Coach Crumrine? God, Craig's mind wouldn't stop. He had been Crumrine's "boy" too. He, the all-conference QB on the surprising Shaker Heights rich kids team, which had plowed through all the tough Niggers and Dagos and Polacks of Cleveland to get a crack at the even tougher Nigger, Dago, and Polack steel workers of southern Ohio. A week before the regionals, Craig's knee was kicked out in a freak pileup during practice. After that, Crumrine didn't know his name. Oh sure, Crumrine came to his hospital room for show. Every day for a while. But Craig could tell that his coach was looking right through him; knew that Crumrine was calculating, even as he told Craig how the team wouldn't be the same without him, what new sweeps he could install for the super-fast sophomore who had taken Craig's position.

Well, Craig wouldn't let it happen. Not this time. Van Damme *would* count on him again. No little punk like Rosen was going to keep Craig from moving right along with Van Damme to the top.

Craig's eyes swung to the rearview. Two large unsmiling men sat in the back of the company Regal, cold eyes on the darkening countryside, thin, mean slits of mouths pressed tight. The man to Craig's right was a clone of the others. No more than twenty words had been exchanged since the trip began over two hours earlier. The only sounds were the whisper of passing cars and the raucous throb of fast moving semis. That was fine with Craig. He wanted to concentrate on his hatred.

* * *

Rosen toyed with his steak. The others' knives clicked frantically, separating every last pink-red section from the shiny T-bones.

"You and Otto will come down to DC within the next two days, as soon as I line up a safe house. The narcs owe me for a tip I gave 'em on a coke deal between some Jamaicans and a very unsavory group from Latin America." Amos skewered his last piece of steak, shoving it into his mouth. "And those guys have more witness safe houses than the Feds." Amos poured milk into the French roasted coffee, which Otto had brewed with loving care, until it was level with the top of his hefty mug.

Otto winced.

"I know it isn't the classy way to drink it, but I just *luuuve* milked-down coffee." Amos toasted Otto before taking a long swig.

"Good one," Hickey laughed, a little too loudly. He seemed to notice the others staring. Redness suffused downward from the dollop of red hair on the lawyer's forehead to the flesh surrounding his jaw. "Anyway, I'm going to set up a lunch appointment with two friends at Justice, followed by a meeting with our liberal senator from Manhattan. Hell, I practically ran his campaign." Hickey looked toward the ceiling as if his itinerary were written on the plaster. "Then I'll consult with the attorney who's representing one of my client's sons on cocaine charges … He was with the FBI until last year." Hickey's enthusiasm seemed to heighten with the mention of each new enterprise. "Hell, with all that high-powered advice, we'll know our options. Then we can *move*." Hickey's large fist hovered over the creamed spinach.

Despite his bitterness, Rosen conjured up a ridiculous image of Hickey slamming it down and sending a shower of green goo across the table. Rosen studied Hickey. Had he always sounded so much like a lawyer and had Rosen just never noticed before? Another thing bothered him. Except for this recent burst of animation, Hickey had been nervous and subdued. Not at all in character with someone who sounded as self-assured as Hickey currently did. Rosen knew why. After dinner, he said, "Otto, that was a great meal. Clear out of here and have a drink with the detective. Mark and I will take the kitchen detail."

* * *

"Hey, why'd you stick us with this?" Hickey flicked a fleecy gob of soapsuds from his hand. It missed the chrome sink and floated downward onto his cordovan Bally loafer. "Damn it!" Hickey kicked his foot until the suds fluttered off.

"That matchbook you used. Very interesting design on the cover." Rosen slipped the last mug over two spokes on the top shelf of the dishwasher, thumped the door into place, and cranked the knob to wash. There was a muffled rattle as the first slush of water rocked the looser dishes. Rosen pivoted toward Hickey, dug into his pocket, and brandished the shiny matchbook.

Hickey shrugged and lowered his bare arms back into the soapy water. He pulled out a large pan and attacked it with a Brillo Pad, scraping first lengthwise and then side to side with a rapid motion that made the pan hum. "Yeah, I suppose so." Hickey concentrated on a stubborn spot, rubbing the Brillo into a bright red blur.

"Where did you get it?"

Hickey stopped. The skin beneath his red lock of hair wrinkled as he studied Rosen. "I don't know. Some bar in New York, I guess." He raised the pan, readying himself for another crack at the tenacious speck.

"I don't think so." Rosen's voice softened but his eyes bored into Hickey. "But I *do* know where they come from … Mark."

Hickey's patient smile flattened like a badly leaking tire. Rosen never used his first name unless there was trouble between them. "Okay. Where?"

"A very intimate little restaurant. This unusual design … It's the wall that surrounds the restaurant. A very old *brick* wall …"

Hickey spun back to face Rosen. The pan that he had worked upon so diligently clanked against the side of the sink, then, weighted down by a torrent of soapy water, thudded against the bottom.

"Okay. So what? Shouldn't we be talking about more important things?" Hickey's alcohol breath, short and rasping, buffeted Rosen's face. "Like getting out of this with our heads still in place?"

"But we are, old buddy. You see, these matches have a whole lot to do with our situation." Rosen's shoulders squared as his hands dropped straight and quiet to his sides. His voice was soft, but his words became more precise, clipped. "In fact, they explain everything—"

"Arn, what the hell are you talking about? You're not making sense. What do stupid matches have to do with anything? Christ, you'd think you'd been the one who was drinking instead of—"

"You see, old buddy, *these* matches"—Rosen raised the glossy pack until it reflected shards of light upon the bridge of Hickey's nose—"come from a very secluded little restaurant near Langley … Virginia … the kind that only the locals know about."

"What the—"

"And guess who is one of their best customers," Rosen continued quietly, his eyes blazing above the extended matchbook.

Hickey stood two inches taller than Rosen. For a moment, he pulled himself up to his full height and glared down through vein-lined eyes. Suddenly, he sagged, backing against the kitchen's center island. He placed both palms down on the butcher block and settled his rump between them. Perspiration glistened on the darkening circles beneath his eyes. "I don't know, Arnie. You tell me if you want to keep wasting precious time on this nonsense."

"No, guess. *Guess* you son of a bitch!" Rosen planted an open hand squarely on Hickey's heaving chest and shoved.

Hickey sidled crab-like—hand-rump-hand, hand-rump-hand— toward the far end of the island, past the blackened metal grill where charred steak fragments and browned fat strips still clung. "I don't know. *I don't know*! Hickey's reluctance to let those in the other room hear caused his words to come out in a hissing whisper.

"Van Damme, Hicker. Charles *Lucien Van Damme!*"

"You're crazy! You think *everyone's* working for Van Damme!" Safely around the far side of the island, Hickey tried a tentative smile. He waved an open palm toward Rosen. "Hey, Arn, I think you need to see someone about this. You are totally paranoid." A vein throbbed under Hickey's right eye.

"What'd you do, Hicker? Meet him there before you came to visit me and … my family? Quite a coincidence. Not seeing you for at least a couple of years … then you show up just before I'm ready to blow the whistle on Van Damme." Rosen strode down the island. The veins along his tensed biceps protruded, blue and jagged.

"You're crazy!" Hickey, backing away toward the hall door, pointed a finger directly at Rosen's eyes. "I shouldn't be helping you. You're just as sick as they said you were!"

Rosen kept coming. "Yeah, *you* show up and the next thing you know, Van Damme knows just where to find my file." Rosen moved through the doorway to the hall as Hickey backpedaled into the master bedroom. "What'd I do, Hicker, let the cat out of the bag after a couple of brews? Natural to trust a *friend* and say something I shouldn't have—"

"You're certifiably—"

Rosen lunged past the bedroom door, sailing it shut with his right hand, closing the gap between Hickey and himself as the bigger man backed toward the bed. He grabbed Hickey's tie by its loose knot, hauling the wide-eyed face to within inches of his own. "I'll kill you right here if you don't tell me the truth … for my family. You remember them?"

Spittle flew into Hickey's face, but the big man didn't blink.

"'Pretty people,' you said. Well, believe me: they weren't very pretty when Van Damme's contract killers got through with them—"

"I never … knew what would happen. He told me it was an internal security issue." The tie went slack in Rosen's fist as Hickey's head flopped to his chest. "He said that you had things all wrong. He'd been acting as bait to snare a KGB colonel … and that you were going to blow it for him if he didn't get the file that you were taking to security."

Rosen released the tie and grasped Hickey's chin. He tilted it upward so that the teary eyes were level with his own. "And you *believed* that? You believed it without even asking me first?"

Hickey's eyes darted side to side, avoiding Rosen's. Tears and perspiration dripped down his tanned cheeks. Moisture tickled Rosen's upturned wrist as it dribbled off Hickey's twitching chin. "I wanted to believe it because I had no choice. I *had* to do what he told me."

If Rosen had not been mad enough to kill, he would have been astounded by Hickey's transformation. How could this cringing lump be the unflappable Mark Hickey that Rosen had known? Correction: *thought* he had known. Were his perceptions of all those who mattered in his life so distorted? Were those most important to him only tapestries woven from erroneously subjective recollections? Deep in his soul, Arnie Rosen shivered. Had he ever really known this man, Mark Hickey, in nearly twenty years … or anyone else, for that matter? Mercifully, rage washed over this deeper, blacker fear, sparing Rosen from the paralyzing implications of his terrifying riddle. Rosen's upper lip curled. "You son of a bitch!"

Hickey yanked away, dropping his head, uttering low sounds accompanied by little twitching movements.

At first, Rosen thought that Hickey was sobbing. Then the lawyer raised his head and Rosen saw that it was a sort of glazed laughter.

Before Rosen could lunge, Hickey cried out, "Because I'm not a son of a bitch. I'm a *daughter* of a bitch!" His head nodded and danced—a separate entity, unaccountable to his motionless body.

"What?" Rosen froze mid-stride.

"I'm gay. I'm gay," Hickey repeated, as if it were a revelation even to himself. "Somehow Van Damme found out, although I haven't had a relationship in years. He must have dug into my past when he learned that I knew you. I panicked. Promised to find out what I could that weekend. I wanted to believe that he was telling the truth and that I was doing the right thing. I never believed anything would happen to Barbara and the kids. I swear. I was sure that Van Damme was a good guy ..." Hickey watched Rosen's face screw up. "Yes, even though he blackmailed me. Sometimes people have to play rough to accomplish the right end. Hell, *I* do that as a lawyer." Hickey attempted to pull himself erect, then gave up, slumping more pronouncedly than before. "He made it sound as if you were just confused. You know, butting in where you shouldn't be." This time Mark Hickey *was* sobbing.

Rosen strode up to the heaving body. He was inured to his own shock and Hickey's misery. He scowled through a lock of hair that had dropped to his face and was sticking to the perspiration on the bridge of his nose. Rosen jabbed it aside as he spoke. "How in God's name could you spy on us? Your friends?"

Hickey sighed. Stared down. He was unable to meet Rosen's gaze as he gulped back his sobs. "You don't know how much I've been afraid, my whole life, of people knowing. *Me*—the big stud. It's always terrified and sickened me, and if some of my clients found out ..." A long sigh whistled out of Hickey's chest. "I'd be ruined. Corporations don't understand these things—"

"So instead you set up a friend? Get his family killed! Is that *easier* to live with than being gay?"

"You've got to believe me, Arnie, no matter what you do to me. I didn't know that anything like that would happen, not in my worst nightmares." Hickey struggled forward toward Rosen, like a child seeking a forgiving embrace. Rosen shoved him away. Hickey wheeled back, heading for the floor. Somehow, his flailing hands caught the edge of the bed. There was a muffled sloshing as he slumped down onto the water-filled mattress.

Rosen stood above the sniveling man. Screwing his lips together, he drew his fist back and planted himself on the balls of his feet. Hickey offered his red-eyed face up to Rosen, appearing to welcome the imminent blow. It never came. Rosen stood poised for a long moment, listening to Hickey's ragged breathing and soft sobs. Then he clenched his eyes shut, letting his fist dissolve as his arm dropped heavily to his side. He turned and walked away, fighting back the question that had been searing his mind since the matchbook. *One more chance,* he thought. *I'm giving you one more chance, old friend.* He was at the door when Hickey spoke.

"They'll be here soon, Arnie. You better get going." Rosen turned back. Hickey's face had a serenity that Rosen suspected hadn't been there for years. "I'd like to think that I was going to tell you about Van Damme's people coming … even without your having figured out what a miserable, cowardly shit I am." Hickey smiled sadly. "I guess now we'll never know."

Rosen could barely hear Hickey above the chorus of insects through the open window.

Hickey turned his palms upward in supplication. "Van Damme told me that I was an accomplice. That he would destroy me if—"

"I know, Mark." Rosen turned from his friend a second time. He cleared the doorway before turning back to say softly to the trembling figure on the bed, "You would have warned me, Mark." The look in Hickey's eyes justified Rosen's lie. He swallowed. "Come on with us, Mark. There isn't much of a future for any of us around here."

Hickey dropped his head, heaving a sigh that seemed unending. His big hands kneaded his thighs, making a barely audible rustling sound on the expensive fabric of his pants. "I think I'll stay. I make my money with my mouth. I should be able to delay them for a while." Hickey forced a laugh. "Come to think of it, how 'bout that gun of yours? I'm not feeling all that persuasive just now."

For an instant, Rosen recognized all the fine qualities that he identified with his friend. More important, he could see that Hickey was remembering them.

"Mark, you have to come …," Rosen began, but his friend's look stopped him. Hickey had come to terms with himself after so many years, and this was the price. "I'll get the Magnum. We'll tell the others that you'll follow us down in the second car." Rosen turned before Hickey could see the mist in his eyes. Gone. Gone. Now *everyone* was gone.

"Arnie." A soft whisper.

"Yeah?" Rosen said, without turning back.

"I am *so* sorry, and thanks."

"Yeah."

*   *   *

"I still don't understand why we had to go rushing off so fast. Weren't we all supposed to be leaving tomorrow?" The Lexus floated above the Delaware Turnpike like an airboat on the Everglades.

Rosen's insides churned as he held the pedal to a smooth seventy-five, but he talked confidently to Amos through the rearview mirror. He had worked out his lie ten miles back. "All I know is that Mark suddenly got very worried about his friends who owned the house getting involved. Said that they had three small children and what if they got hurt like … mine. How could I argue with that, Reggie?" They had mutually agreed by the time they left New Jersey that "Detective Amos" was too cumbersome. Rosen's confidence grew as the story took on a life of its own. He dispensed with the rearview and half turned toward Amos. "Hey, taking a motel room isn't going to kill us, is it? Hickey wanted to clean up and get a jump on things by making some calls tonight. We'll meet him tomorrow at five."

Amos's face was hard to read in the darkened back seat, but he did not pursue the conversation.

"I hope dot he iss dere," Otto intoned. "Ve need his help." His pudgy face, whitened like a full moon by a pair of approaching high beams, pivoted toward Rosen. "You don't zink dot he hass changed hiss mind about helping us? He vuss very strange ven ve left."

"No. He just had a lot on his mind. Don't worry. Hicker'll be there." Rosen's guilt at this new lie was immediately swallowed by black sorrow. Hickey would never be there … or anywhere … again. *My life keeps narrowing person by person,* thought Rosen. *What the hell am I fighting for? Who is left to fight for? C'mon. You just do it because … for all those people, Hickey included, who have been ripped out of your life through no fault of theirs and damn little fault of yours. That's why. Now shut up …* Rosen pressed the digital marvel of a car radio. *God, you should be able to land a plane with all those controls.* "Anyone mind?" he asked as a formality.

No response.

Voices, then music, then music, then a foreign language, snapping on and off in precise sequence as the scanner rolled along the stations. "—condemned the United States for harboring aggressive—" The non-discriminating scanner cut off the seemingly important news item without remorse. Rosen pressed back to the station.

"—commencement of Charles Van Damme's confirmation hearing tomorrow, for Director of the Central Intelligence Agency, also brought angry responses from President Boris Yeltsin of the Russian Republic. Like his counterpart in the Ukraine, Mr. Yeltsin has denounced Van Damme's allegation that elements within the Commonwealth are in the process of stealing American military secrets. President Yeltsin labeled it a ploy by the American government to renege on economic commitments made to him due to political pressures caused by the worsening US economy ..."

"My God," said Rosen.

"Yeah." Amos leaned his temple against Otto's headrest. "Haven't you heard this? It all started with Van Damme and that Amphora deal. Its been getting worse since he's been nominated as CIA director. Can't blame the Russians for being scared, knowing he's setting them up—"

"Please ... I want to hear."

"Yeltsin has joined with the presidents of the Ukraine and Belarus, the two other nuclear powers in the Commonwealth, in refusing to ship additional tactical or strategic nuclear weapons to dismantling points until, what they term 'The state of economic warfare initiated by the United States' ceases. This is a major blow to the Clendon administration's arms reduction program, which had set a target of one-third of the former Soviet Union's strategic nuclear arsenal being destroyed or immobilized by the end of the president's first term. For reaction from Washington, we take you to correspondent Les Afton. Les, what is the sentiment on Capitol Hill over President Yeltsin's announcement to halt disarmament?"

"Most of the congressmen whom I have talked to appear to be in shock from this major reversal to the peace process, Sam. Their reactions run the gamut from denial to outrage by the more conservative elements. However, some of Mr. Yeltsin's defenders are saying that he has no choice. With the growing wave of anti-American and anti-Democratic sentiment in his nation, he could be swept out of office by hard-liners like General Alexi Yermakov, of the three-and-a-half-million-member army, or the Soyuz faction of the former Communist Party. And on the other side of the political spectrum are the nationalists, headed by Anatoli Robichenko, who demanded restoration of the entire USSR by force. Yeltsin's only choice, say his friends on Capitol Hill, is to adopt a harder line against the United States in light of events of the past month."

"Les, is there any further word on this new espionage controversy between our country and Russia? And how is that impacting developments?"

"Well, needless to say, Sam, another intelligence scandal would escalate tensions even further. Both the military and intelligence communities here are keeping silent as to the nature of the weapon that has been allegedly stolen, but there have been rumors that it may be a new top secret satellite being developed in California. These are unconfirmed, though—"

"Yeah, right. We could damn well confirm—"

"Sh," Rosen hissed at Amos.

"... does Charles Van Damme, the proposed head of Central Intelligence, say?"

"Since he is involved in the current hearings, Mr. Van Damme has not been available for comment. However, Senator James Culcane, the heir apparent to the chairmanship of the Senate Foreign Relations Committee, stated today that Charles Van Damme's private assessment of this incident coincides with his own. The Senator believes that current intelligence policies have been too lax and that stricter procedures must be adopted for keeping track of the Russians."

"Les, there has been recent speculation that this appointment may be a stepping-stone for Charles Van Damme as it was for, let's say, George Bush. Is there any truth to that?"

"Well, Sam, there is no question that many officials here feel that Charles Van Damme had the right spin on the Russian situation long before his superiors and members of other agencies involved with national security caught on. In addition, he is a very charismatic figure with vast financial resources. The definite implication is that there may be bigger things in store for him in the future."

"You mean the Presidency?"

"Many insiders here see that as a possibility. The thinking is that he is tough enough to take the necessary measures to keep the former Soviet Union from ever reemerging. After all, no one wants to face a new Cold War. I'm not saying that everyone agrees, but as relations with Russia worsen, more and more people down here are mentioning a Van Damme candidacy."

"What the hell do you think of that?" mused Amos.

Rosen hardly heard him ... or newscaster Sam's dire reports of growing army defections to the Yermakov banner in unpronounceable provinces all over Russia. He was too numb to comprehend anything but the phrase roaring in his own ears: *President Charles Van Damme ... President Van Damme ... President Charles Van Damme ...*

CHAPTER **34**

Mark Hickey stared into a maple replica of an antique standing mirror. He had deliberately tilted it upward to reflect his face, haloed by the glow of the bedroom's multibulbed chandelier. The crickets competed fiercely with an army of boisterous katydids for dominance of the surrounding meadows. It was like having a working generator directly outside of his window, but Hickey hardly noticed.

His index finger and thumb kneaded and poked at emerging pockets of loose flesh around his cheeks and jaw. Now it was starting to show on the outside. How long until the internal decay oozed through every opening in his flesh so that the whole world could see him for what he was—and had been since those first horrible days of awareness during his first year of college—a queen. An ever-loving queen!

Hickey dropped the big, powerful hands that had let him down—or had he let *them* down?—against his thick thighs—which were also a lie—and studied his all-American hero—another lie—face. The nose was still perfectly straight, with a faint upturn at the tip. The cheekbones were still wide and prominent, like those of the most classic of Native Americans. The large eyes could still flash the fire of aggressive manhood. What a lie, all lies.

Hickey flopped back onto the bed, bobbing gently as the agitated water sloshed and gurgled about him. A waste. All his life he had been a waste. The classic all-American man who could not be a man. A homosexual who would not *let* himself be one. He had canceled himself out every day of his existence. What do you call that? Certainly not a *life*! What the hell had he been living all these years? A war. A goddamn war within himself, which he could never win. "The Hicker," Hickey mumbled aloud. "Yeah, right."

Hickey sunk his fingers deep into the undulating mass of water beneath him and shoved himself upright, working himself toward a perch on the bed's steady frame. His eyes locked upon a brass handle of the dresser for no particular reason except that it was comfortable to stare at. This was the last night of the war. No more Gettysburgs, or Koreas, or Vietnams, with his guts as the battleground. Not after tonight …

He pushed up and walked to the dresser. Arnie's Magnum lay next to an earring rack. The gentle collection of soft gold and glowing diamonds amplified the weapon's mechanical coldness.

Hickey grasped the Magnum and snapped it open. A sleek cartridge leered at him from the chamber. He closed it and strode into the kitchen, punching off the day-bright fluorescents, for no earthly reason, as he passed the switch. He sighed as he entered the living room, contemplating the indentations in the massive couch pillows. Flipping the Magnum upon one, he turned toward the liquor cabinet.

There was a quarter of a bottle of Dewar's left. *That should do it.* Hickey rinsed out a hefty glass and tipped the open bottle toward its center, savoring the tinkle of pouring liquid, holding his face close to sniff the aroma. He placed the empty bottle solidly down before returning to the couch.

Hickey sipped, letting the scotch permeate his mouth, honing in on every sensation. He finally swallowed, willing the hot liquid to descend slowly, feeling it coat his throat, attempting to savor its progress inch by inch.

Hickey studied the couch pillows. *Eggshell* he estimated, *Too bad.* He wished that they were darker, but the couch was where he wanted to be. He thought about looking for some plastic, but that sounded too damn tawdry.

Hickey picked a spot in the middle of the sectional and settled down. He scooped the Magnum toward him, then took a long sip and lay back, forcing his head into a cushion until its comfortable coarse material encircled his ears. He sipped again and studied the glass: about two sips left. Not a very long time…

*   *   *

They came up on the old farmhouse from the black meadow, grunting and cursing as they floundered through waves of matted grass, tripping on rodent holes camouflaged by the quarter moon's scanty light, exposed and vulnerable as the feverish insect chorus instantaneously silenced at their approach. They slapped at the persistent whine of unseen mosquitoes while ducking both real and imagined silhouettes of larger flying things.

By the time Craig and his team approached the rear door, they were bathed in perspiration and ready to shoot anything that moved. Nothing did. The house was remarkably quiet. No lights on the second floor and only the faint glow of distant illumination through the ground-floor window. The window itself was open about eight inches.

They listened. Nothing.

"Son of a bitch! Go around the front and see if there's any cars there," Craig hissed. One of the three clones peeled off from the group and vanished around the corner. Craig seethed. Not again. Not again, Rosen, you bastard!

James's shadow approached. "There's a car out front, a big Lincoln." Craig's teeth glowed in the moonlight. "All *riiight!*" He thought, *Now for you, Rosen.* He motioned them back a few yards from the window.

The ground was soft and yielding. Craig looked down. They stood on the front end of a twenty-by-forty vegetable garden. Sticks entwined with vines sprung up at odd angles, and farther back, Craig made out the leafy shapes of lettuces or cabbages. Something warm ignited in his chest. Some day he would tend acres of garden, nurturing the tiny green sprouts into the biggest tomatoes and finest greens anywhere around. Craig tensed. It wasn't for now, maybe not even for years. The fantasy shrunk back and back into a distant part of his mind until it was gone.

"Summers and Orduna, take the front." Craig was harsher than usual as he overcompensated for his sentimental lapse about the garden. "James and I'll go in the back. Two minutes. Count it off … *now.*"

Sommers and Orduna slipped away, only the slightest rustle of grass marking their progress. Soon they passed beyond hearing range.

*   *   *

"Now!" Craig pushed open the back door for James. Picking the lock had taken about thirteen seconds flat. That was Craig's style. Kicking doors open gave your opponent lots of time to grab for weapons or do other things that could hurt you. A nice quiet click of his little metal hook and Craig had it all his own way with whoever was in inside. He kind of hoped that the guys in front hadn't bothered to prepare like he had, because if they slammed the door down, any shooting would be at them, not him.

Bam! Just like that, he and James were rolling down the hall, poking each door open with their guns, squatting as they covered the rooms side to side, darting through the darkened kitchen as they worked their way closer and closer to the lighted part of the house. Hairs on Craig's neck rose as he anticipated the imminent combat: bullets and blood, his team having everything going for it; the other side outgunned, outmanned, and unprepared. Nice odds. And best of all, Rosen exploding as Craig's heavy bullets ripped into the bastard from different angles. Craig hoped Rosen stayed up until Craig could get off at least five shots, but his .38 Super would probably take Rosen out a lot sooner.

Lots of noise ahead. Those idiots were really working over the front door. Perfect. Now to come in from behind …

Craig blew into the living room, crouching, rolling, winding up behind a nice thick table with a perfect view of the area, just as the front door gave with a massive *pop*. His muzzle darted from one likely hiding place to the next: chair to chair, to desk, to table … finally the couch. James ducked in, diving for cover. The two at the door stood back-to-back, arms extended, sighting down on the room. Craig's eyes never left the couch. Two legs protruded from the part facing the big cabinet. There was no movement from the splayed feet, which were wedged under the chrome frame of a glass-topped coffee table. Craig studied the scene for an instant longer, then shrieked as he lunged for the couch.

*　　*　　*

Craig kept cursing and aiming at Hickey, but since the lawyer only had half a head, Craig was too well trained to fire. You never turned a suicide into a murder. Craig pointed the gun for a long while, saying, "Kuhhh … kuhhh … kuhhh" as he pretended to blast the body to shreds. Finally, he dropped to the floor, jamming his face into the couch next to Hickey's limp leg.

None of the others had the nerve to go over and see if he was actually crying.

*　　*　　*

A red fury engulfed Craig. It took all of his willpower not to push the Regal up and up until he and the car were careening as out of control as his rage.

James and the others exchanged glances, but no one spoke.

Craig had called Van Damme after he and the others had wiped the house down. There had been bored resignation in Van Damme's voice as he told Craig to come on back—that *he* would take care of things now.

Already moving me out of the picture, aren't you, you son of a bitch? thought Craig. He could just see Van Damme calling some new hotshot into his museum of an office. "I have this problem," Van Damme would tell the eager beaver—probably a guy with short hair, huge shoulders, and worshipful eyes. Craig couldn't figure out exactly what Van Damme's story would be, but he'd bet it would be un-fucking-believably great. A spellbinder. Van Damme would have the eager beaver ready to suck out every crapper at Langley, with a straw, within five minutes. Shit, hadn't the devilish bastard been able to do that to *him* any time he wanted? He was out. He was *out*, and some other little nobody—some Johnny-come-lately punk—was in. Well, no way! No way was someone else going to get the glory after all the crap he had done for that ungrateful bastard. He'd show Van Damme that he could still take care of business better than some snot-nosed punk! He would show him. No one was going to sell Ted Craig out *ever again*.

Not his dad. Not his coach. Not Van Damme. *No one*!

*   *   *

Craig was right. And wrong. Charles Van Damme did sit across from a bright-eyed, broad-shouldered young man with unfashionably short hair. But the youngster was FBI, not CIA. Van Damme leaned forward, reducing the distance and increasing the intimacy between himself and the other. "So you see, Bill … You don't mind if we get to first names, do you?"

The younger man agreed with an eager shake of his head. His wide-set brown eyes regarded Van Damme intently and he leaned closer as well, resting an elbow next to an intricate ivory depicting a group of saber-toothed tigers dragging down a lone mastodon.

Van Damme's eyes darted toward the sculpture. Once he had assured himself that the priceless piece was in no jeopardy of tumbling off his desk, Van Damme refocused on Bill Armstrong. "We have had an unfortunate history … your agency and mine … of competing rather than cooperating. I don't think that we can afford to do that anymore, considering the outside threats that face us."

Armstrong nodded vigorously.

"I think that it may be up to *us* to change things," Van Damme continued. "Now that the public is aware that that madman Yermakov, or one of the Soyuz-backed nutcases, may grab power any day, they want our agencies to be fully up to speed. If you and I capture Rosen and Gruhaber in a joint operation, then all of those old bromides about the FBI and CIA preferring to leave each other with egg on their faces will be laid to rest." Van Damme smiled. It wasn't his full rising-curtain smile; their conversation was too grave for that. Merely a slight confidence-building smile of mutual understanding.

*   *   *

William Masterson Armstrong acknowledged that he and Charles Van Damme were in accord with a tight-lipped smile of his own. *The man was right,* Armstrong thought. *Just as right as he had been about not trusting the Russians, while all the deadwood in the Bureau had said the Commies were through.* Oh, Armstrong knew about Charles Van Damme long before Van Damme became famous. Armstrong knew that Van Damme had been battling Savin and the national security people for years. Why, one afternoon last year, when Armstrong's boss spoke after Van Damme before the Security Council, he himself had heard some of them laughing about "Crazy Charlie." Well, no one was laughing at Charles Van Damme now. No, sir. Now they all knew just how dangerous the situation was over in Russia. How easily a new terror weapon like that Amphora could bring all their hopes for a Shirley Temple world down. It really frosted Armstrong: all those know-it-all idiots at the Bureau laughing at a man like this. People back home knew better. They weren't as sophisticated, maybe, but they sure knew right from wrong. Here in Washington, everyone covered up those moral judgments, which life demanded, with a veneer of cynicism. Nothing was really "good"; nothing really "bad"; everything was a little of both. Not true. The Communist way of life *was* bad. That's why it failed. And the "new Communism," or "Nationalism," or whatever else it would be called, would be just as bad. *My people in Iowa know it. Charles Van Damme knows it. And now he's making all the cynical idiots on top know it. And I'm going to help him. Mr. Van Damme is on the right side, and the Bureau should be too, darn it.*

CHAPTER 35

Rosen hunched over his double-decker Burger King. Rivulets of mustard dribbled from between the crumbly buns as he picked at it disgustedly. He hated mustard, hadn't paid attention when the listless attendant with the skewed hat had asked how he wanted it.

Otto nibbled his french fries like a squirrel storing up for winter. Amos, the skinniest, having already gnawed his two barbecued beefs down to their rumpled foils, perused the bright plastic menus posted on the wall beyond Rosen's head as if an encore were called for.

Although the hour was late, groups filtered in and out regularly through the electric double doors near their table. Rest stops on the Maryland Turnpike were miles apart. They were never empty.

A faded young mother, with two tiny kids in tow and a baby cradled against her nearly breastless chest, settled in at a nearby table. The two older children sagged in the positions that she had seated them. Her baby flopped against her neck as if it were drugged. Her eyes roved desperately until a dirty man with a bull neck and scrubby mustache sauntered over. She thrust the baby at him before he could seat himself and hurried off toward the restrooms. The man stared down at his child, gave it a look of displeasure that fluttered his mustache, and propped the little pink bundle on the chair next to him with grease-stained hands.

Rosen experienced a moment of intense hatred as he watched the reluctant father. He was tempted to walk over and scream into the man's sullen face that he had everything: a family—the only contribution that someone like him would ever make to the world—and that he should damn well cherish them every moment of his otherwise useless life. Rosen throttled down his rage. The human lump over there would never comprehend, even if he beat him to a pulp.

Rosen grasped his burger, staring at another pocket of mustard that erupted over his thumb. He wedged the disintegrating bun back into its plastic container without a bite. "We have to go after Van Damme as soon as possible. Tomorrow, at the Capitol. During the confirmation hearings."

Both heads across the table popped up as if their owners had received electrical jolts.

"Why? We need your friend Hickey's help first. He's the only one with the contacts that give us a chance of coming out of this alive." Amos's eyebrows arched upward. "I don't know about you, but I ain't in so much of a hurry that I can't wait a little while longer for *that* kind of help."

Otto nodded his head vigorously, "Umm" emitting from behind the fries protruding from his mouth.

Rosen let out a deep sigh. "Hickey isn't coming. More than likely, he and Van Damme's people are shooting at each other right now. Or … he's already dead."

Otto's teeth snapped shut, crunching the bottoms of his fries off onto his tray.

Amos's eyebrows descended into a nasty frown. "What're you talking about? He was supposed to take his car and follow—"

"I lied." Rosen shook his head slowly, talking down toward the table as if it were a third listener. "Mark had things to prove. He felt that the best way for him to help us was stopping them …" Rosen's right hand fluttered for a moment, then dropped into his lap "At least for a while."

"*What* things?" Amos's normally calm voice rasped as he battled his rage. "And how did both of *you* know that Van Damme's people were coming? That's why you got us out of there so fast, huh? Look at me. Who set us up?"

Rosen looked up. Dark fire danced in Amos's eyes. "It doesn't matter. Mark is making good for whatever he had to. More than you or I are." Rosen straightened. His blue eyes glowed with their own fervor. "We go on from here, just like he did."

"Vot iss diss." The whites of Otto's eyes threatened to engulf his pupils. "Vass *he* on der side, too?"

"No, Otto." Rosen reached out a hand, rested it momentarily on the other's forearm. "Believe me, he wasn't. He was only frightened—like all of us. Mark came through when he had to, like *we* will now." Rosen's lips curled upward into what he hoped was a convincing smile. He raised his voice up an octave for enthusiasm. "What do you think, Amos? Can you get us some help?"

Amos wasn't buying it. "Nah," he said in a sour tone. "All my contacts are cops … and any cop who has a chance at America's two most wanted"—he nodded toward the others—"would go for the collar first and ask questions later. What the hell am I talking about?" Forehead, cheeks, and chin pulled in toward his nose. "I've probably just worked my way up to the *third* most wanted."

Rosen rolled a snippet of the foil wrapper between his fingers until it emerged a shiny tube. He dropped it on the table and flicked one end with his nail, sending it spinning off. "Would it help us to get arrested?"

"Who knows?" Amos reached for one of Otto's french fries. If Otto noticed, he gave no indication. "Guys get killed in custody. Remember Jack Ruby? And Lee Harvey?"

Otto winced at the mention of each name.

Rosen shrugged, pursing his lips. "Then we just have to go for it. Tomorrow."

"Vy so vast? Ve haf to haf time to plan. Ve must not rush in foolizhly." The little man's back arched beneath his rigid neck.

Rosen spoke softly. "It wouldn't work, Otto. The longer that we're out of sight, the longer Van Damme has to find us. Each day that we wait works for him and against us. Right, Amos?"

"That's right, Otto. Van Damme has the manpower. If he gets time to mobilize his people, his odds of killing us get better than the Redskins not making the Super Bowl. We have our best chance right now."

"C'mon, Otto." Rosen forced a laugh. "Now that your cough is almost gone, who can stop us?"

"Yah. Thot iss very reazuring." Otto tried to smile back, but his facial skin was taught with tension.

"Good. Then we're agreed."

"I zuppoze zo … Yess."

"I think that the best place would be the Capitol." Rosen switched his attention to Amos, who kneaded the sides of his skull with stiff fingers. "He'll have a harder time stopping us there with all those witnesses."

Amos splayed his fingers, palms outward, in resignation. "You're right. If we make it in, we're okay. But will your proof hold up in front of those senators? You want to get before the intelligence committee, right?"

"Yes on both counts. I think we have enough to start with … and yes, where Van Damme's confirmation is." Rosen sucked at his orange soda.

His straw gurgled as the last of the liquid glided upward. "Once we're safe, I can reconstruct the rest of my proof. I just need the chance."

Amos flattened his palms against the table. "Then you're going to get the chance. Let's do it!" He pushed up from the littered little table. The others followed.

At the next table, the baby began to totter. The father was staring at a teenage girl in short shorts buying a taco. With a half cry, the little pink bundle skittered toward the chair's edge. Only a lunging grab by the returning mother kept her from plummeting to the floor. Staring at her husband with a mixture of hatred and resignation, the woman rocked her squalling child. Her husband stared at them briefly before digging ketchup-smeared fingers back into his french fries.

A group surrounded the newspaper machines near the row of glass doors. Coins thudded and metal doors squeaked as hand after hand grabbed for the remaining evening editions. Many of the purchasers engaged in conversation with those awaiting their turn. Fingers pointed at bold headlines, heads shook, voices rose. Rosen detoured around them, passing the group's outer fringe.

"See! These Commies ain't changed a bit. Look at this shit they're trying to pull." It was a youth in his early twenties, tall, in a white T-shirt that was badly yellowed. Heavy arm hair nearly obscured an anchor tattoo on his left forearm as he repeatedly punched the front page of his paper. A sprawl of jet-black hair swung across his eyes each time he thrust his poorly shaven jaw down at a dapper little man with a neat goatee. "This Yermakov guy is trying to get all them Russians pissed off at the United States so he can take over. You watch. Then he and his buddies, the KGB an' all them army guys go in an' *wham*, no more republics. Just one big mother of a Russia again with all its missiles pointing at us! Anybody but a schmuck could see that!"

Murmurs of affirmation chorused from many of those who had circled nearer the two. The young one surveyed his supporters, pressing his lips together and raising his paper as if it were a victory trophy.

"Yermakov is *saying* that our government is trying to discredit his movement by pretending that they are trying to steal our satellite, and he is probably right." The bearded man appeared undaunted by his opponent's superior support. "We only have the CIA's word for it that these mysterious plans of ours are not sitting in some safe at Langley while we blame the Russians. And I can tell you why … if you will have the courtesy to look at me."

The taller man stopped his posturing and rested his chin in the palm of his free hand as he goggled outrageously at his opponent.

Snickers from the crowd.

The smaller man smiled tolerantly as if to prove that he could not be reduced to his opponent's level. "Because Yermakov can give the Russian people back their pride, and we don't want that. We want them flat on their backs and dependent on us. Forever."

A few "yeahs" filtered back through the spectators.

"Guys like you always blame it on the CIA," the other sneered. "The Russians ain't trying to steal our satellite. Nah. The CIA really did it, even though the Russians have every motive in the world."

Loud muttering of support.

"Well, even if they are trying, why not? The CIA killed *their* people and stole *their* missile." The little man in the goatee was on tiptoe now.

"Yeah, well, what were we supposed to do, huh? Just pretend that we didn't know that they got that thing that could wipe out our whole country … an' our missiles couldn't stop it or nothing? That what you want?" The younger one's head came down to within inches of the other's. "An' anyway, what the hell were they doing with that Amphora thing when they're supposed to have changed and become our good buddies? Why didn't they just tell us about it or destroy it or something? Why were they hiding it?" The tendons in his neck twitched violently as his volume increased.

"Well, what are we doing with this secret weapon of ours if we're such peace lovers?" the little man shot back. His eyes were starting to show white around the sides, and a small trickle of spittle appeared on his lower lip.

"We weren't the losers. *That's* why!" The spectators really went for that one.

The taller one opened both palms and shrugged. "Hey, they lost—they gotta play ball with us." He sneered and raised his newspaper in a debate-ending gesture.

The little man waited until the hooting died down. "Well maybe they don't see it that way. Maybe they don't want our CIA to do whatever it wants while they just have to sit there and take it. Maybe Yermakov will—"

"Yeah. Well, maybe Van Damme will show Yermakov and the rest of those Russians that that's what you have to do when you're a fuckin' loser. Sit down an' shut up." It was not clear to Rosen whether the younger man's last comment was a directive to Yermakov and the Russians or to his opponent, but the older man chose it as an excuse for extricating himself from the argument. With a dismissive swipe of his hand, he hurried off toward the interior of the restaurant. The remaining combatant threw back his head, accepting the brief accolades of his recently discovered allies before their own worlds drew them away.

Rosen hurriedly pushed through the doors before the victorious debater, flushed with his newfound importance, could engage him.

Amos and Gruhaber stood waiting in the parking lot. Together they all walked to the car.

Chapter 36

The Senate Select Committee on Intelligence does not meet in a magnificent room adorned with the lavish murals of Constantino Brumidi, the Italian immigrant who devoted his life to beautifying the Capitol, like elaborate S-128, where appropriations convenes. Nor does the committee expose itself to press or public sensationalism, as is the wont of judiciary and foreign relations. Unlike its more flamboyant neighbors, intelligence meets in a small, plain room on the third floor of the Senate wing, with *very* private access. No one sets foot on the narrow stairway that leads to the committee room unless that person has high security clearance—or a damn good reason for being there.

Van Damme leaned back in his austere wooden chair and stared at the senators arrayed behind their plain wooden table. Three uncovered bulbs glared at him from a triangle-shaped fixture on the wall above the chairman's head.

Although it was only the second day, the hearing was bound to finish within a day or two more, at most. Van Damme was sure of it. The senators were already losing interest. No juicy scandal from his past, or during his tenure at the agency, had been unearthed by their staffs, so the liberal opposition had nothing to hang their hats on. Besides, he was an appointee of *their* Democratic President, which left them even more confused. As if those weren't reasons enough, no politician in his right mind was going to grandstand against Van Damme's determination to expand CIA intelligence activities. Not after the Amphora revelation and, now, the hysteria over the stolen US satellite plans.

No, Van Damme could see from the increasing vacuousness of their faces that the senators' thoughts had shifted from his credentials to their weekend social schedules. Even Culcane, who had come up to witness his progress, had wandered out of the stuffy room more than an hour ago.

Van Damme snuck a glance at his watch while half-listening to an inane question by the Junior Senator from Massachusetts. It was a rephrase of one that the man had already asked three times in the past two days. It was 11:17. Van Damme made a mental bet with himself that he would be approved no later than 5 p.m. the following afternoon.

*   *   *

Bill Armstrong's men had been deployed long before intelligence convened that day.

Four agents lounged against the walls of the rotunda, the capitol's circular central entry. Two stared up at the windowed dome, which, in the present light, appeared to float high above them. The other two studied detailed John Trumbull paintings of Washington progressing through the American Revolution. Except for slightly shorter hair than most, they were no different from the hundreds of other tourists echoing their way along the marble floors.

Two more huddled in the shallow alcoves along the Senate corridor.

A ninth peered down from between the columns of the smaller Senate Rotunda.

Armstrong kept in constant radio contact with them from his command post in the Old Senate Chamber. He stretched out behind a burnished wooden desk originally occupied by either a Southern slave owner, or Northern abolitionist, or a cattle baron from the West, who didn't give a damn—and stared possessively at the gold-inlayed trappings of his nation's history.

William Masterson Armstrong vowed to himself then that he would prevent anything from taking place today that would alter the destiny of his great land. He locked his strong fingers behind his curly-haired head and leaned back against his palms. His eyes traveled the expanse of the elegant half-dome ceiling high above. A cherubic smile of anticipation lit his face.

*   *   *

"C'mon, Otto. Let's move." Rosen turned back toward the perspiring little man who perched halfway up the Capitol steps, heaving for breath, looking for all the world like a slug trapped in the heat of the sun.

"Yess. I come." Otto began clumping methodically up the stairs, hauling one stubby leg, then the other, as if his shoes were concrete blocks. Amos darted nimbly back down, hefting Otto under the right shoulder.

Rosen's eyes swept the Capitol grounds as the two lurched toward him. Sunlight bounded off white stairs, white buildings, and white monuments. His eyes teared. He drew a sticky wrist across them, clearing his vision. He was dripping. The humidity would not allow his pores to release their fluids. His hair felt glued to his forehead.

Amos was having a hard time holding Otto and hiding his own gun at the same time. Although he palmed the weapon expertly, it darted out into the sunlight each time that Otto's momentum died and Amos had to propel him upward again. Finally, Amos let Otto rest against him while he re-holstered the weapon.

"Hurry," Rosen said as they approached the top. He spun, squinting into the darkened interior of the Senate Rotunda. His eyes acclimated as cool air washed over him. Where would they be? Mark Hickey hadn't known that Rosen was coming here; they had only decided on the turnpike after Hickey was more than likely dead. But had Van Damme figured anyway that they had no other choice but to come for him now? Why wouldn't he? The bastard had outthought Rosen every step of the way so far. Every single … So what? It was how you finished that counted, right? Who won in the end, right? Rosen stared into the ambling crowd. Were there guns trained on him right now?

Certainly not the gray-haired woman scrutinizing Abe Lincoln's bronze so minutely. Her busy little hands worked the shiny clasp of her black handbag, clicking it relentlessly as she circled the statue. Her thick orthopedic soles made sucking sounds against the floor.

Not the six little girls dressed in matching navy uniforms with snowy white blouses. They skipped happily behind their rapidly moving teacher, whose auburn hair stretched to the breaking point in a tight bun.

Not the turbaned group dutifully following their guide toward the House Wing.

Nor the fat man studying every brushstroke of *Washington Crossing the Delaware* while his well-tanned wife studied the butts of a nearby group of college boys.

But how about the three-piece-suit reading the paper next to *The Surrender of General Burgoyne*?

Or the stiff-looking youngster staring at the crowd from the Senate corridor?

Rosen wished now that he had taken Amos up on the .38 police special, which the detective had told him that he could arrange for him. At the time, Rosen had thought that explaining a weapon would be more trouble than benefit. Now, he wasn't so sure. Amos' credentials provided safe passage for his own .38.

"Over that way." Rosen nodded toward the Senate corridor as Amos tugged Otto over.

"Gif me just a minute." Otto's cough was deep and raspy. Perspiration glistened from every exposed portion of his pallid skin.

Rosen experienced deep concern for the little man. Whatever illness had taken hold of him in that cold basement in Germany had abated somewhat, but was still a cause for concern. Otto needed a hospital. Rosen looked at the little programer with fondness and respect. Otto Gruhaber was a courageous man. Rosen hoped that he could convince Otto of this when they had time—*if* they had any time left. He gestured with his head. "The Senate Intelligence Committee meets in a room up a set of stairs off that corridor. It's not open to the public, and it's usually guarded."

"Now you tell us." Amos rolled his eyes.

"I didn't want to discourage you."

"Oh, yeah," Amos grimaced. "Like we've got the luxury of giving up 'cause we're discouraged. *Right.*"

Rosen briefly raised his taught lips in a half smile, but he kept his eyes focused on each passing face. "Come on. You can be funny later." He slid through an oncoming group of Midwestern farmer types with pale eyes and leathered skin. Amos guided Otto around the group and followed.

*   *   *

"I told you." Craig leered at the three clones as they peered across the wide rotunda floor from the entrance to the corridor of the House of Representatives. "I knew the asshole would show up here, trying to screw up Mr. Van Damme's confirmation hearing." Craig shook his elongated head, snorting out of his elongated nose. "Just like I told you, *right?*" he snapped at James.

"Just like you told us," James replied dutifully. Contract money was good and he was damn well going to make a good impression, no matter what he thought of Craig personally. "You sure had him figured, Mr. Craig. You sure did."

Craig squinted hard at James, probing for any vestige of mockery in the granite-like face, but found none there. Hell, if James' face were ten thousand times bigger, the bastard could be added to Mount Rushmore. "Okay," he growled, "let's get them."

Each of them fingered the weapons hidden beneath their jackets. Ten minutes earlier in one of the large restrooms, they had been carefully unwrapped from the alloy cloth that rendered them undetectable to the simple metal detectors.

Craig and the three clones glided under the rotunda in tight formation. Sightseers in their path parted, as if the foursome's imminent violence created a force field as potent as the prow on an Arctic icebreaker.

*   *   *

Rosen's group passed beneath the small Senate Rotunda as Craig's people closed the gap. It was smooth and neat: guns jammed unobtrusively into their backs. Surely none of those enjoying the spectacular colors of the corridor's walls and ceilings had the slightest inkling that three men in their midst might die at any moment.

Craig appeared after the targets had been secured. His voice crackled with emotion as he brought his thick lips to Rosen's ear. "You're gonna die slow, Rosen." Then Craig had an inspiration. He stepped in front of Rosen, a big smile filling his horse-like face. "Not like your wife and kids." Rosen gave Craig a look that made Craig glad that he had a weapon; made him glad that he had the bastard just where he wanted him. Nothing was more satisfying than having the one you hated most hate you back even harder. Craig's testicles tingled. This was going to be great! He couldn't wait to get at Rosen—break him through constant pain before ending it. This was going to be better than sex with that little firecracker in secretarial. Craig's mouth was actually watering. *Shit,* he thought, *I really am a sick fucker, aren't I? Still, sick fuckers are entitled to their kicks too. Wasn't that like that bumper sticker a few years ago? Oh, yeah: "Even dirty old men need love."*

"We're going out the main exit ... so let's all turn around and walk real relaxed." Craig's eyes never left Rosen's.

"I'm a cop," Amos said, as calmly as if he were mentioning the fact to a next-door neighbor. "You know that the agency doesn't want you involved in killing *me*." His delicate hands moved gently toward his waist, but a jab from Orduna sent them back down against his thighs.

"Yeah? Well, we'll give that lots of consideration," Craig sneered through a curled upper lip. "C'mon … let's go."

"Fuck you!" Rosen smiled back at Craig. Sommers jabbed Rosen's kidney with his gun muzzle. Rosen winced but stood his ground.

Craig's face clouded in confusion. "*What?*" he said, louder than he had intended.

Otto groaned.

"Fuck yoooo-u!" Rosen mimed each vowel. "You think this is the movies, you stupid murdering asshole. You're going to kill us; you expect us to walk out nice and quiet so everything can be easy for you, like when you killed my five-year-old son?"

Craig's face unclouded. "Hey, Rosen, you're one clever son of a bitch, aren't you? You really got me, don't you, asshole? Orduna, is the cop packing?"

Orduna patted around Amos's waist and then moved his hand up the policeman's chest. The other two clones huddled in closer, expertly shielding his movements from passersby. "Yeah, he's packing a piece." Orduna moved in and groped under Amos's jacket. He handed the .38 to Craig, who quickly pocketed it.

"Well, now, Mr. Rosen." Craig shook his head in mock recrimination. "It actually looks like I have plenty of options. First, we can kill you right now and be out of here before anyone realizes what happened. Civilians, as you might know, do not react very quickly to sudden unexpected violence. If we call for someone to get a doctor, he'll be off in all directions looking for help. Some will even come over and hold your heads while we disappear. No one will remember our faces, believe me." Craig leered directly into Rosen's eyes. "Second, since you are very wanted criminals, we can just take you out for resisting arrest." Craig's smile broadened, revealing his slightly uneven row of very large teeth. "We're in hot pursuit, so we don't need to bring in the locals. As for you, cop"—he turned toward Amos—"how were we supposed to know you're not just one of their spy buddies?" His smile dropped away, revealing glistening black pupils that darted back to Rosen like a python on a mouse. "No more bullshit. You move or you die."

Arnie Rosen never found out what choice he would have made.

*　　*　　*

Young Wally Barnes had been peeping down from between two columns of the small Senate Rotunda for so long that his left cheek felt as if it was bonded to the cold stone surface. The early morning excitement of his first stakeout had waned as the hours dragged on. The monotony was only broken when he shifted his restless feet or whispered on the quarter hour to Agent Armstrong through the minute communications device fastened under his starched white collar.

For the first time, Wally questioned his choice of employer. Was Lisa right? His wife had been adamantly opposed to the Bureau. "You killed yourself to get an accounting degree. Killed me too since I've been supporting you for four years. It's why we don't have a baby yet, Wall. Now you want to take a llow-paying dangerous job with the FBI instead of going with a major accounting firm. How can you do this to us? You'd learn more in a year with Arthur Anderson than you ever will there," Lisa had said, eyes brimming. And she was right, of course. But he'd stood firm despite the arguments and the tears. Didn't know why. Just something he'd had to do.

Now he wondered. All he'd done for the past three months had been to go crazy researching the financial records of harmless nobodies. Now he was finding out that stakeouts were no better. Maybe he'd give it another six months and then tell Lisa that she was right. Wait … There was the medium-sized guy … *and the little one* … Who was the black guy? Wally Barnes tugged his cheek away from the column and prepared to talk to the device under his collar. *Whoa! Four more tough-looking characters just came up. Cripes, there are as many of them as of us!* "Agent Armstrong," he whispered a little too loudly.

Two elderly women frowned at the strange young man talking to himself, then hurried away.

"That you, Seven?" Armstrong's voice blasted into his ear.

"Yes, Sir."

"It would be easier if you identified yourself by your number when you report in."

"Yes, Sir. Number Seven reporting, Sir. I have located the suspects, and they are with five companions—"

"*Five!*" Barnes winced from Armstrong's volume. "Hold your position … and stay out of sight. I'll get everybody in. What is their exact position?"

"About fifteen feet past me, toward the Senate Chamber, Sir."

"Stay out of sight."

Armstrong's legs skidded off the historical desk as he hunched close to his miniature communicator. "Pike and Quinlan." Armstrong realized that in his excitement, he'd forgotten whose number was whose … Well, screw it. "Enter the corridor from the Senate side. Two targets and five suspects are converged near the Senate Rotunda … Morris, you, Akers, and Furriglio seal off the corridor from your side. Use extreme caution. I'll close in with Pike and Quinlan. Barnes, cover us from your position. *Go!*"

*   *   *

"Yermakov and the KGB and other right-wing elements are using the Indigo incident as a rallying cry to mobilize Russian sentiment against us. Even President Yeltsin and the presidents of the other republics are calling it an excuse, conjured up for our government by the CIA, to keep us from honoring our aid commitments during the present recession. In fact, they are so incensed that yesterday, as I'm sure you know, they issued a joint declaration refusing to collect or destroy any further tactical or strategic nuclear weapons until this issue is resolved. Don't you think you have been imprudent in breaking this news before the State Department could evaluate its effect on East-West relations?"

Van Damme stared back calmly at the Junior Senator from Massachusetts. It was the liberal youngster's last hurrah. The older committee members were glancing at their watches or doodling on scratch pads. God! Van Damme fought back a snicker. Old Harkins from Utah actually had a bony finger up his oversized nose, more involved in its contents than the current round of questions. And there was Senator Marion from Louisiana, Culcane's proxy on the committee: a Culcane look-alike, except that, impossible though it seemed, Marion was even fatter. *What does Marion remind me of sitting there behind the table,* thought Van Damme, despite himself. I've got it. The top half of a beach ball—don't laugh, damn it! The beach ball wore a contented smile. Marion, like everyone else in the room except the young Senator from Massachusetts, surely knew that Van Damme's confirmation was a foregone conclusion.

Van Damme smiled politely at Senator Chase. The young man was a handsome specimen of blue-blooded rearing: a product of Andover and Princeton, groomed for a career of public service since there were no financial constraints upon him. Their mutuality of backgrounds caused

Van Damme to identify with Chase, despite the contentious nature of his questions. Besides, it was already over. Chase just didn't know it.

"Senator, do you deny that the Russians still had Amphora on the boards? Our agency and the responsible officials with whom we consulted thought that it was in the public interest to reveal Amphora. Are we supposed to deny it now to appease the Commonwealth of Republics? And does not their theft of the Indigo satellite further prove their intent to recklessly endanger our population?"

"Mr. Van Damme, don't we still have weapons on our boards? What about this Indigo satellite that the republics are supposedly stealing? Or the nuclear submarines that we have just voted appropriations for? Their Amphora missile could have been in a winding-up stage or business as usual, just as we are guilty of. Why was it appropriate to use it to escalate international tensions? I believe that we need a statesman to head the Central Intelligence Agency, not a person who would enhance its importance at the expense of peaceful world relations."

Andover and Princeton and ending so many sentences with a preposition. Hmm, those schools must be slipping from his day. "Senator," Van Damme fluffed the edge of his moustache, his voice mild and pleasant, "we are in the business of gathering and disseminating intelligence to the proper sources. It is for the statesmen to utilize such information as they see fit. We are merely their servants in that regard. Would you have me, as the head of the Central Intelligence Agency, screen intelligence before sending it through the prescribed channels—"

"No, but ..." Chase fumbled with his notes. Beads of perspiration slithered down his smooth forehead, from under a glowing cloud of white-blond hair. "What about this Indigo situation? Was there sufficient proof to catapult this into a second international incident? Every Russian leader, even the hardest or their hard-liners, categorically deny any responsibility. The proof of your allegations is highly circumstantial according to my review. Are you shooting from the hip? If so, we cannot afford to have ..."

Van Damme practiced rib breathing while he awaited his turn to answer. Ironically, the young Senator was on the right track. But since no one else in the room believed him, he might as well be spitting into the wind. Oh well. Van Damme steepled his long fingers, resting his hands on the table like an attentive student. He had been young and idealistic himself once. Let the youngster have his fun. *If only that miserable fuck-up Craig gets here on time. I have psychologically pushed him to a point where*

Rosen's destruction should be the only meaningful objective in his life, so he should appear—uninvited—as I planned. Craig, what a disappointment you are. I really thought I could make something out of you. I don't like being wrong about people ...

"But, Senator ..." Van Damme turned his attention back to the bright-eyed lad who, from his strained voice and forward-thrusting posture, showed no signs of relenting.

*   *   *

"Fine," sneered Craig, "you're not moving?" His horse face pivoted from Rosen to Otto. "How about you? It's the only way you have a chance of living, believe me."

Otto's fleshy lips quivered and his eyes dropped away from Craig's, but his head shook an indistinct negative.

Craig shrugged at Amos. "Sorry, pal. Whatever you wanted, you've been outvoted. Put the first one in their spines," he snarled at the clones. "*Now!*"

"Mr. Craig."

"Goddammit! *What*, Orduna?"

"Someone's watching us from up there."

"*Where?*"

"That round thing up there."

Craig glanced up toward the rotunda. "You sure?"

"'Course I'm sure," Orduna responded petulantly.

"Two down at the end of the corridor too." Sommers's voice was tense. His face was blocked by Rosen's.

Craig stared bleakly past Rosen's head. "And two more down near the entrance. Fuck Van Damme. He's screwed this whole thing up!" Craig hissed out the last with such vehemence that his spittle caught Rosen's cheek. Rosen recoiled, but Craig didn't notice as his pale eyes darted high and low, sorting options. Tense facial muscles drove the blood from his pointy jaw.

*   *   *

In the next fifteen seconds, young Bill Armstrong made the greatest mistake of his life. He announced himself. He hadn't really planned to do it that way, considering that he was far closer than his colleagues to the seven men, but it was all those years of training. "We are the FBI. Drop your weapons!" was out of his mouth before he knew it. The consequences were both instantaneous and irreversible as two hissing bullets gouged fragments from the ancient doorway of the Old Senate Chamber, while a third gouged fragments from Armstrong's skull. He spun away from the entry as if in a dream, sprawling into the last row of bright mahogany desks. It was surprisingly painless, as Armstrong's ebbing logic told him that he must have badly damaged his face on the furniture's sharp edges.

*   *   *

Wally Barnes was ready to pee in his pants. He pressed his face tighter against the cold column, hoping that none of those animals beneath the rotunda had seen him. Agent Armstrong was dead, with the words barely out of his mouth. He had given them a chance, but those terrors from hell down there merely reacted; hadn't considered whether Armstrong was young, old, married, a father, a good man. Nothing! They shot him without a thought. Like moray eels, lashing out at anything passing too close without fear or consideration of the consequences. These were cold, deadly killers, and Wally Barnes suddenly wanted, more than anything, to be back doing boring research. *God, my adorable, smart, wonderful Lisa is right. God, I'll go straight to a big name accounting firm if I get out of this. God, this is real death ... God, it's not for me—get me out! Please.*

*   *   *

Akers screamed, "Those fuckers shot Armstrong! Those *fuckers!*"
"Get everyone back into the rotunda," Morris screeched at Furriglio. "Get them the hell out of this corridor!"
"Everyone back. Please!" The unflappable Furriglio not only managed a calm voice, but also a reassuring smile as he shooed reluctant bystanders back into the cavernous Main Rotunda. Furriglio even managed a grin as he handed a redheaded youngster, with ice cream smears circling his mouth, back to his parents after the kid tried to dodge around him to get a better view of the action.
"*Stop. FBI. Stay where you are and drop your weapons!*" Morris hollered, without conviction, as Furriglio returned. Both Furriglio and Akers took positions on either side of Morris, weapons extended.
The response Morris got was the screech of a ricocheting bullet.

"Son of a bitch!" screamed Akers. He grabbed his knee. Red oozed between his clenched fingers.

Morris fired wildly down the corridor. Their opposition under the small rotunda scattered, but no one went down.

Furriglio knelt beside Akers. He ripped a piece of the bleeding man's shirt, tightening it around the wound.

"God, can you believe that?" Akers's head bobbed mindlessly as he complained to Furriglio. "What a lucky shot! *What a goddamn lucky shot!*" Akers's head sagged. "Can you believe that?" he whimpered into his heaving chest.

* * *

"Shit, they're scattering. Now we'll have to root 'em out," Pike hissed. "Why the hell couldn't those idiots on the other side hold their fire until we got closer?"

"How are we supposed to get closer if they don't distract them, Agent Pike?" Quinlan did not like Pike. No one at the Bureau did, except that leper Gordorfer. Quinlan did like Morris. A lot. "It seems to me that Morris didn't have much choice, Pike. After all, they already shot Armstrong, Pike, so it looks like they don't want to talk. Doesn't it? So now that they're moving, why don't we move too? Okay, Pike?"

"Yeah, yeah, Quinlan."

Renewed gunfire crackled down the corridor. Forty feet ahead lay the Senate Conference Room. Pike and Quinlan sucked in air and sprinted toward its open doorway, firing as they hurtled forward.

* * *

His contract guys were scattering from pitifully inaccurate gunfire—those FBI assholes couldn't hit shit—running and diving like someone was firing howitzers at them. Craig couldn't believe it. "Hold it, for God's sake! Help me with these guys. They're gonna get away, you shmucks!"

The clones weren't listening. Orduna ran for a door to the left, with Sommers lumbering after him. James dodged right, leaping into the Old Senate Chamber.

"You chickenshit bastards!" screamed Craig. He raised his .38 Super, sighting on James, nearly blowing a hole in the man's broad back in that crazy second before he was able to get control of himself.

It was a costly second. As Craig spun back toward Rosen, he caught blurry movement from the corner of his eye. He swung the .38 toward Amos. *The cop is packing a second gun!* his mind shrilled out. *I knew the bastard could be packing more than one. Knew it. Orduna didn't even check his ankles. Sheeeet!*

Amos's bullet caught him in the right side. *Ahhhh, that fuckin' hurt!* Craig closed in on Amos before Amos could fire again, digging his gun into Amos's stomach, pumping one-two-three into Amos as he fought off Amos's gun hand with his own left hand, feeling Amos convulse with each muffled shot, feeling Amos's struggling stop, feeling Amos's breath whistle out along his neck as Amos died.

Craig thrust the dead cop off and snapped his .38 back toward Rosen. The sudden movement sent searing heat up his injured ribs, but Craig knew that he wouldn't die from one lousy bullet in his side—at least not until he'd shot Rosen's eyes out.

Craig was surprised to see how close Rosen had come to closing the gap between them. Surprised … and impressed. *Another second or two and Rosen would have had me,* he thought. *Can you beat that? Know-it-all Van Damme hadn't had a clue as to what he was getting into when he decided to go one-on-one with Rosen. If this bastard is an analyst, he's the goddamn Godzilla of analysts.* Craig raised the .38 a fraction higher so that it was level with Rosen's face.

"Nice try, but close only counts in horseshoes and hand grenades, right, Rosen?" Even in his pain, Craig was able to unleash a satisfying sneer.

*　*　*

Otto never recalled making a conscious decision to lunge at Craig. In fact, had he had time to think about it, he probably never would have done it. He was terrified of the big man with the huge gun, who swayed in front of Rosen in his blood-drenched shirt like a wounded bear, his eyes small and fiery red. No. He never would have tried to tackle Craig if he would have given himself time to think. But he hadn't. He just threw his arms forward in Craig's direction and let his feet stumble after him, tipping one way and then the other as he adjusted his course for the bloody center of Craig's shirt; clenching his eyes as he imagined the monster opening of Craig's gun shifting toward him; wincing as jagged bolts of pain shot from his shoulder into his spine when he contacted Craig's body, which was solid as tightly stacked bailing wire; freezing as Craig screeched; then thudding off of Craig and spinning dizzyingly along the smooth floor.

*   *   *

Craig reeled from the unexpected blow. He shifted the .38 reflexively toward the sprawling Otto, then snapped it back at Rosen. "No, you don't, Rosen … You don't get any closer. I'll kill that little tub of lard after I kill you." Craig blinked torrents of perspiration out of his eyes. *God, that little bastard hurt me*, he thought.

*   *   *

Morris finally put a shot where he wanted it. He watched in satisfaction as the big guy under the rotunda dropped his gun and clawed at his neck, staggering down to one knee, then both, then flopping face-first, his body slowly flattening along the floor.

I'd better get my ass over to the pistol range, Morris thought. Supervisor Enson's been telling me that all year. Eight shots and only one lousy hit. Jeez, that's pitiful. "Furriglio, how's Akers?"

"He'll be okay."

"Then let's move in on those two. I don't know what's going on, but it looked like the guy I got was gonna shoot Rosen down when the little one hit him. Shit, I sure hope the guy I shot wasn't a cop." Morris shook his rather flat face as Furriglio scrambled over. Then he bunched up his lips around his tongue and gave a typical Morris raspberry, spraying jets of saliva. "That would be some fine fuck-up, wouldn't it?"

Furriglio had to smile. Morris's facial gestures always amused him. Even now. "Don't worry about it, Benny. Those guys started shooting without even identifying themselves. Hell, they killed the boss. I don't think even DC cops would do that. I'll cover you. And Benny," Furriglio said with a wink, "great shooting."

Morris winced. "Thanks a lot, Furriglio … Thanks a lot." He turned and dove for cover behind the nearest recession in the corridor's sculptured wall.

*   *   *

Behind Morris and Furriglio, seven wide-eyed Senators popped their heads out of the entry to the L-shaped Senate cloakroom, which bordered the entrance to the Senate floor. The legislators had anticipated an early lunch, but the scene in the corridor altered their plans. As if one, the seven dove for the safety of the cloakroom's remotest wings. Jennings of Iowa was nominated to call Capitol security. The line was busy. His was the eighth call clogging their overloaded line.

*　　*　　*

Agent Akers did his best to warn the growing mob in the rotunda back, but he found it hard to be imposing sitting there on the floor hugging his smashed knee for dear life. "Keep back. Please! People are getting shot in there!" No good. The rubberneckers kept working their way forward toward the Senate corridor. Even if those at the front were inclined to heed his hoarse instructions, which Akers doubted, the curious mob behind continued to press them closer to the deadly fiasco. At his hearing for action unbecoming an FBI operative a month later, Akers, who had no recollection of the incident, listened open-mouthed as six civilian complainants testified that he had fired four shots over them and screamed, "The next asshole who takes one step farther gets shot!" Based upon his impaired physical condition at the time, Akers only received a reprimand.

*　　*　　*

Senate Minority Leader Marlin Cowens stood next to his marble fireplace, studying himself in the massive gold-leafed mirror that rested upon its mantel. His hair was meticulously parted, no errant whiskers marred his cheeks, and his blue-and-red striped tie was done in a perfectly symmetrical Windsor knot. Reflected above his head were the crystal tears of the oldest fixture in the Capitol: the chandelier that had lit this office when it had been the Supreme Court robing room a hundred years earlier. Cowens checked his yellowing teeth for signs of improvement—he'd been using a three-phase teeth-whitening system for the past month but damned if he could see a difference—and turned to make his Senate appearance. Cowens heard a gurgling sound from his anteroom. "Horace," he called to Horace Broomaster, his secretary of fifteen years. "*Horace!*"

A moment later, Horace plummeted through the entrance, followed by two huge men with guns. Horace hit Cowens's desk, full speed, sprawling over it with a severe *clunk*.

Cowens was no coward. Thirty years as a Republican in a Democratic Congress gave you big *cahones*. "What the hell is going on?"

"We are in—"

"How dare you break into my office like this? With guns." Cowens clearly had no intention of losing the initiative. It might be his and Horace's only chance. "Do you know where you are?"

"Yes," said a sheepish Sommers. "You're a senator—"

"Not *just* a senator. The Senate Minority Leader."

"Senate Minority Leader," echoed Sommers with suitable respect. "Yes, Sir, we're—"

"Now put those guns down immediately!"

"Do we waste him?" Sommers whispered to Orduna.

"*No!*" Orduna exclaimed. "Sir,"—Orduna's granite face contracted into a positively cherubic smile—"we are terribly sorry, but we have come under fire in the course of apprehending two internationally wanted suspects. We are temporarily commissioned by the CIA, but our supervising operative has been killed. We wish to put ourselves under your command." Orduna strode toward Cowens's desk. He lowered his Smith & Wesson, handle first, onto the bright mahogany just a foot away from Horace, who had gotten his hands under him and was struggling to push up.

Cowens's chest swelled. "And you?" He glared at Sommers.

Sommers brow contracted. He stared dumbly at Cowens, then at his own gun, which pointed halfway between Cowens and the thick tan carpet.

Then back at Cowens.

"Well?" said Cowens.

The side of Orduna's smile nearest to Sommers lifted. "Do it," he urged.

Sommers's Colt dropped to his side. He paused, shaking his head before reaching it toward Cowens.

"Take it, Horace," ordered the Senate minority leader.

Horace Broomaster reached for the weapon as if it were a giant scorpion.

Now, we'll see what's going on. Don't worry, gentlemen: you're under my protection." Cowens checked his reflection. Not even a hair out of place. Excellent—except for those damn yellow teeth. He reached for his phone.

*　*　*

Rosen stared down at Craig. Dead. Tears welled in the corners of Rosen's eyes. *Was it worth it, you inhuman son of a bitch? Was it worth it?*

He kicked at Craig's sightless face, raising a red smear on the unfeeling nose. His teeth ground together as he cocked his ankle for a devastating second blow.

Frantic hands shook his arm. A pleading voice poured into his right ear. "Rozan. Pleasss!" Otto's pupils dilated with terror.

His rational mind finally clamped down on his pointless rage, squeezing the numbing venom from his brain. Rosen scanned the corridor. There was a commotion at the rotunda entrance. Probably security. The Senate end was clear, but the FBI was somewhere between them … Who cared? Where was Van Damme? *That* was why they were here. Rosen studied Amos's sprawled body. The detective's dapper apparel was soaked and stained with his own blood. *Don't let all of them down now. All those who died so you could finish this, Arnie.* "Otto, we're going for that entry over there. There's a private stairway to intelligence. I appeared there once, and I'm sure that's it." He grasped Otto by the arm.

The little man was perspiring badly, and his eyes rolled in their red sockets.

"Listen," Rosen shrilled, "there are FBI over there, I think, and Van Damme's people there and there." He pointed jerkily at various doorways. "And security and the Secret Service will be swarming any second—"

"But—"

"Shut up and listen. Move while we talk." Rosen yanked Otto away from Craig and Amos toward the side of the corridor. The little man slipped and slid along the smooth floor in a parody of a comic movie character running on marbles, finally sprawling into an alcove beside the heavily breathing Rosen. "We have to get up there. Beg, cry, kill, but get up there and tell your story. Even if I don't make it, you keep going. You hear? The papers are here." Rosen slapped the side of his shirt. "So you find my body and take the envelope out and show them to the committee. You understand?"

Otto stared at Rosen. His lips worked, but nothing came out.

Rosen grabbed Otto's arms. They were gooey with perspiration. "Otto, you have to be able to do this. Can you?"

"Yesss, I cahn." It was the pleading in Rosen's eyes to which Otto responded. "I cahn. I vill."

Rosen stared into Otto's eyes. Resolution flickered on and off. It was the best that Rosen could expect under the circumstances. "All right. Let's go!"

*　　*　　*

Chief of Security Lester A. Crowley heaved his paunch through kids and old women alike as he penetrated the humming crowd at the entrance to Senate Corridor Two. Crowley disliked crowds like this. They were the same ones who slowed traffic to gawk at gory head-ons or encouraged potential suicides to leap from building ledges. They were why the TV news was filled with fatal fires and drug wars. Yep, he did not like crowds like this at all, so bumping the bloodthirsty bastards aside didn't bother Lester A. Crowley one bit. "Where're they at, Farber?" he hollered across to a man who was tightening a bloody cloth tourniquet around Agent Akers's knee.

"Down there, Chief." Farber kept the pressure on with his hands, nodding toward the inner reaches of the corridor. "Two in the conference room, two under control in the minority leader's office, and at least one in the Old Senate Chamber."

"Waddya mean, 'under control' in Cowens's office?" growled Crowley, elbowing aside a freckle-faced woman and her two freckle-faced youngsters as he forced his way toward Farber.

"Communications says Cowens called. He's got both their guns. They say they're with CIA, Chief."

"What!" Crowley shoved his heavy red face into Farber's. "That arrogant bastard Cowens will say anything to get attention. These effin' politicians." He swiped at the folds in his beet-red neck with a graying handkerchief.

Farber shrugged. His deft fingers began knotting the tourniquet. "That too tight?"

"Ssss o … kay," Akers mumbled, and passed out.

"Sorry, but it's gotta be pretty tight to do any good," Farber justified himself to the limp body.

Crowley shook his head impatiently. "Farber, who are the *others* supposed to be? The Mafia?"

Farber snapped his head up. "Sorry, Chief. No, but that's funny, Chief."

"Yeah, right," growled Crowley. He wanted one of his big Havanas right about now. Instead, he settled for a spicy little stick of Dentyne.

"This is almost as funny, Chief."

Damn Farber wasn't going to let go, thought Crowley.

"They yelled out 'FBI' before, only the Bureau has no record of an authorized operation here. And funnier yet—"

"Will you stop with the 'funny' already, Farber!" Crowley's complexion escalated to a higher level of redness.

"Sorry. Anyway, the CIA also denies having any operatives here."

"Son of a bitch!" Crowley rose back up. "These bastards really think they're cute. Well, I don't think they're cute a'tall! Not a'tall." By now, Crowley was surrounded by seven other security personnel. "C'mon. Let's show whoever these bastards are that they can't go fuckin' around in *my* Capitol—"

"I'll report you for that language. What kind of a policeman are you saying the F-word in front of my children?" The freckle-faced woman stood before Crowley, legs apart, hands on hips, bony jaw outthrust. The two little freckle-faces, each hugging one of her jean-clad legs, stared up with partially toothed mouths agape.

"Kiss mine, lady." Crowley drew his revolver as he brushed past her.

*   *   *

"We ought to take him, Pike. He's right next door." Quinlan hunched inside the heavy wooden door of the Senate Conference Room.

Pike wandered around near the bright marble fireplace at the opposite side. He came back reluctantly. "Why not the other two? Aren't they supposed to be the spies?"

Quinlan knew Pike loved to argue. If he had said, "Let's go after the two spies," Pike would have wanted to take the joker holed up next door. Quinlan spaced his words patiently. "Because he has the *gun*, Pike. If we go after them, maybe he goes after us."

"So why don't we stay here and wait him out?"

"Goddammit, Pike, because we're supposed to get something done here."

"All right." Pike's thick lips dipped into a full-scale pout. Traces of black stubble rippled as they moved. "All right. Let's just go, then. You first."

Quinlan turned toward the other. "Yeah, Pike. *Me first.*" His lips curled around the words. "You think I thought it would be any other way?"

"Yeah, yeah."

"Can you at least cover me?"

Pike's lips flapped upward in a half leer. "Sure, Quinlan, I can cover you."

Quinlan bolted.

Pike reached the entry in time to see his partner moving at a fast half crouch toward the Old Senate Chamber. Pike followed, his Safari .45 waist high. His mouth tasted like someone had washed his overalls in it. Fucking Quinlan. Suddenly, there was movement to his right. Hey, there were the two spies! *Looks like they're going for that doorway. Now there's a target worth going after. Fuck Quinlan,* Pike told himself. Those spies are what we're here for. Pike shoved off the wall and spread his legs, half stepping closer to Rosen and Otto as he locked his arms and aimed the .45.

*   *   *

James, leaderless now that Craig was dead, hunched behind a desk in the third row of the Old Senate Chamber. The adjustable front sight of his Smith & Wesson Classic Hunter blotted out a major portion of the cavernous room's marble doorway. James was excellent with the gun up to seventy yards. It would be like shooting fish in a barrel to hit anyone at this distance .

Quinlan hugged the outside wall next to the entry of the Old Senate Chamber. His breath wheezed harshly, not from the distance but from the tension of his run. "Okay, Pike?"

No answer.

Quinlan whipped his head around.

No Pike.

"Son of a bitch!" muttered Quinlan. *Oh, Pike, you bastard,* he thought. *Wait. Just wait until Morris and the others hear this. Even Gordorfer wouldn't be seen with Pike after this.* You never—*never*—bailed out on your partner. Out of the corner of his eye, Quinlan caught movement. There was Pike, the bastard, drawing a bead on the two who didn't have weapons. Big fucking hero Pike, while he had to take on the guy with the gun. *Pike, you son of a bitch!*

Quinlan drew a slow breath and peeked around the corner of the doorway. The room was magnificent with its marble columns, red velvet podium, and bright vaulted ceiling. The pair of size twelve soles facing him from the aisle beside the second row of desks was not magnificent. Armstrong's, he was sure. This shameful vestige of the vigorous man, who had trashed him in one-on-one hoops only two days before, cost Quinlan his concentration at the worst possible moment. Only a protective mechanism buried deep in his brain sent Quinlan hurtling to the ground as James's bullet chewed the marble above his head.

Quinlan hugged the carpeted floor, giving the chill in his spinal column a chance to drain. He peered past Armstrong's soles. The aisle rolled unobstructed down to the base of the strikingly red podium.

No one there.

He rolled behind a desk, hoisting himself up the stout wooden chair until he could see the room. *Where the hell was the guy?* Quinlan's stomach knotted as he sprawled beneath the desk. *Was he up on the old spectators' balcony, watching Quinlan's every move?* Quinlan's mind flashed back to his ant farm, so many years ago. There were the ants, thinking that they had all this privacy, and you were watching every damn thing they did from crapping to making love. Was that the spot that the guy had him in?

He hunched tighter under the desk. There was a pungent sweetness of freshly polished wood. On which side of the balcony would the guy be? Wait a minute. His man had run in through the main doorway … How could he have gotten up there? No way. There were no stairs to the viewers' gallery in the Old Senate any more than there were in the present Senate. Who wanted angry spectators coming down to the Senate floor? Nope … no way the guy could have gotten up there.

Quinlan took a long breath and slid out, knees first. His .357 Super Mag stuck to his moist palm. He was damp all over. The vein in the side of his temple was pulsing to some frenetic Latin beat. Quinlan's wide eyes narrowed as his fear metamorphosed to dark hatred: hatred for Pike for putting him in this position, hatred for the other man in the room. He slowly, quietly crawled toward the far end of his row of desks …

*   *   *

The FBI guy was lucky as shit—or damn good, thought James as his shot sent splinters of age-old marble raining toward the Senate Chamber floor. His coarse black eyebrows rose as he estimated the size of the chunk he'd taken out of the doorway, and then he stared at his gun in admiration. Wow, these new super loads that he had switched to could knock an elephant down! Now to put one in the FBI guy and get the hell out of here. There'd be lots of activity out there, lots of confusion, and James was very good at blending in, in spite of his size. All he had to do was get out that doorway before the security people pinned him in here, because once that happened, talking his way out of this would be a hell of a lot harder.

C'mon, you bastard, show your face. No one in the aisle but the dead guy. How 'bout some hair or something above the desk line? Nah. The guy was definitely being cute. Waiting him out, James slipped another load into the cylinder and gently clicked it shut. He couldn't afford to wait. He hadn't been doing contract work with the agency that long, but he knew enough to know that you didn't go running around Pennsylvania and DC shooting people up—*officially.* All the higher-ups would deny any knowledge of this fiasco. He'd taken the assignment because that's how you picked up points with them—doing the illicit shit—but don't expect them to bail you out if you got caught. That was the game; those were the rules. *You're on your own, so get your butt out of here fast, Jamesy.*

James's six-foot-four frame should have whacked out a few chairs or smacked a desk or two as he snaked his way down the row, but he negotiated each one without so much as a scrape. Sure, wobbling along on his stomach caused the rotator cuff in his right shoulder to scream in silent agony … and it sure wasn't doing his cartilage-less left knee any good, but he made it all the way to the right-hand aisle quickly and silently. At this rate, he could make it up the aisle and take the bastard from behind before he knew what hit him. James licked his lower lip in anticipation as he dragged his massive torso out into the aisle. Big mistake … The FBI guy was good, not lucky. There he was, two rows down, waiting …

James went for it anyway, fumbling the Super Mag into firing position. But it wasn't even close.

*   *   *

"Hold it right there!" Crowley and four others appeared on Pike's left. All had weapons, all of which were pointed at him.

"Hold it right there." *Wasn't that out of every bad cop story on TV?* Pike wondered. Great. He had two spies in his sights, and he was surrounded by the Keystone Cops. "I'm FBI," Pike called out of the corner of his mouth, trying his best not to let the spies out of his sight. The bigger spy was nearly to the doorway on the far side of the corridor. Pike adjusted the Safari a hair right and slightly down.

"Last chance to put that gun *down! Immediately!*" This came from his left.

"I'm FBI. Those two spies are getting away. Check my damn credentials, for God's sake!" Pike was torn between reaching into his jacket for the neat little black leather case with his Bureau ID and keeping that son of a bitch in front of him in his sights. He compromised, dropping his left hand and reaching toward his chest as he kept the .45 extended with his right hand. As Pike dug deeper into his jacket, his right arm inadvertently swung toward the closest and youngest member of Crowley's security force. Having been warned by his Chief, just thirty seconds ago, that these murdering intruders were posing as FBI and CIA, the young man felt perfectly justified in firing two bullets into Pike's lungs.

CHAPTER 37

Van Damme fought to repress a smile as one of the handpicked security team assigned to guard the highly secret Intelligence Committee meetings entered, approached the chairman, and whispered into his white-tufted ear. Obviously, there was a major emergency or the man never would have had the temerity to interrupt.

Within moments, the chairman's annoyed scowl had turned to shock. "Gentlemen, I am told that there is something in the nature of an actual gun battle going on directly below us. This gentlemen assures me that we are safe but that we should, under no circumstances, leave the committee room."

Leave it to the chairman to describe the situation as if he were writing a scene in a literary novel, thought Van Damme. Maybe that stood to reason. Hadn't he heard that old Fenton's firm did a lot of copyright law? Anyway, plan C was definitely working. He had hoped that A would do the trick—or at least B. But if not A or B, Van Damme congratulated himself for having had the foresight to devise plan C.

Plan A was simple: Rosen gets discouraged and goes into hiding; Craig, with an army at his disposal, eventually catches and kills him. Unfortunately, this Rosen was very hard to discourage.

Plan B was also simple: Craig kills Rosen outright at either Kennedy Airport or, failing that, in New York or, failing that, at the farmhouse in Pennsylvania. Unfortunately, from the reported gunfire downstairs, even that almanac's worth of locations hadn't been sufficient to prevent that idiot Craig from failing.

Ergo plan C: Go-getter Armstrong and his FBI people waylay Rosen, Gruhaber, and that busybody cop when Rosen decides that these hearings are his last chance to stop me. Then Craig and his people appear because Craig won't let it go, in spite of my orders. So the FBI shoots Craig, and Craig shoots the FBI— since neither knows the other is supposed to be here—and Capitol security shoots them both—since neither agency has notified the Chief of

Security about an operation here at the Capitol—and everyone shoots Rosen and Gruhaber and the cop … which is just what is happening downstairs this very minute.

Van Damme caressed his long chin. *Not bad, Charles. Everyone who knows about me will be gone. And if I have to explain why Rosen and the computer genius are here and not in Europe, that's easy enough. I'll say the same thing that I said to young Armstrong to get his help: either they were sent back to kill me by their Russian masters because I exposed the Russians' satellite scheme, or Rosen and Gruhaber came back out of revenge because the Russians panicked and refused to pay for the plans. Yes … I like that. It will prove how desperate the Russians are to stop me, which will make America want me more than ever. Hmmm, it would look even better if Rosen brought a gun … although in that fiasco, who'll know if he did or not? As for the cop … well, everyone knows that he was chasing Rosen, wasn't he? And now, unfortunately, he caught him—right during the biggest gun battle in Washington since the War of 1812.*

Van Damme snapped his thoughts back to those gathered in the cramped room. *Time to take charge here, Charles. Look at these fools. Old Harkins over there could be wetting his pants right about now. And Howard? My God, his nails are getting chewed below empty. How about my young persecutor, Chase? Why, he's crumpled the page with his final two hours of questions … What a shame. And fat Marion, Culcane's boy. Not so jolly now. He's checking that door as if he expects a scud missile to pop through. What a miserable bunch of cowards. No wonder our country has no direction … but soon I'll give these people direction—or have the voters plow them under.*

Van Damme rose, back erect, assuming his most regal posture.

"Gentlemen!" He thrust delicate fingers above the group.

Their nervous mumbling trailed off.

"Gentlemen."

Silence from the room.

Good, they were already learning to obey. "I am sure that we are perfectly safe, thanks to the dedication of that young gentleman." Van Damme gestured toward the security man who was standing at attention against the door. "And the others of his force."

The security man's neck flamed red from embarrassment, but he won the struggle to keep his eyes focused straight ahead.

"Mr. Chairman, I know that it is not for me to decide these things, but in light of whatever tragedy is transpiring downstairs, I am sure that this hearing is apt to be delayed. Now, I have been answering the committee's very astute questions for only a few days … and I am more than willing to spend whatever additional time is appropriate. However"—Van Damme bent forward at the waist, palms outward in supplication—"if you feel that I have truly satisfied your concerns, perhaps rather than delay the proceedings, you might consider a vote."

Van Damme stared unswervingly at young Chase, who stirred his papers but didn't look up.

"That way, if I am fortunate enough for you to honor me with your trust, I can immediately begin implementing a more efficient operational approach to our intelligence. There have been frightening developments within the former Soviet Republics, as you well know, and this is not a good time for the Central Intelligence Agency to be without a leader or a direction." Van Damme raised his mustache partially off his teeth in a slight smile calculated to soften the impact of his request.

Senator Fenton's white head was bobbing affirmatively even before Van Damme had settled back into his chair. "Gentlemen, I agree." Fenton's bushy white eyebrows arched, causing his unusually narrow forehead to nearly disappear beneath a massive shock of unruly white hair. "In light of the unusual circumstances, I feel that a vote would be appropriate. Are there any seconds?"

Affirmative grunts proliferated along the narrow table.

Only young Chase remained silent as he twisted his ballpoint between the thumb and first two fingers of his left hand.

"Does the *Junior* Senator from Massachusetts have an objection?" Fenton's voice rose an octave.

Chase's perfectly shaped lips compressed into a thin, pale line. "No, *Mr. Chairman.*" He was completely intent upon his spiraling pen.

Fenton leaned forward, squinting down the table at Chase, but the young Senator refused to look up. Fenton's forehead descended from under his snowy hairline, not stopping until it had crunched down upon the top of his nose. "Since the Junior Senator from Massachusetts has given us his kind permission, I propose that we vote."

*　　*　　*

Rosen sprawled through the doorway, hooking Otto's beefy neck in the crook of his elbow and yanking him along. He mashed his left shoulder on the sharp edge of a bottom stair but managed to squeeze his own chest protectively over Otto as a fusillade of bullets splintered the door and zinged off the walls. Rosen hunched, expecting mangled pieces of ricocheting metal to slice red hot into his brain. Otto squirmed beneath, burrowing even farther from the deadly storm. There was an acrid smell of urine as survival instincts superseded normal control, then a blessed moment of peace as the turbulence above their heads ceased abruptly.

Rosen yanked his head up against the tension in his shoulders and peered out of the partially opened door. Uniformed bodies were sprinting toward them, gun muzzles gaping like malignant eyes.

"Let's *move!*" He lugged Otto by the collar. They scrambled upward, the tips of the toes of their shoes *thunking* the stairs as they stumbled and skidded away from the pursuing footsteps. Salty perspiration dribbled between Rosen's lips.

Breath wheezed from Otto's heaving chest.

"Around that corner. C'mon!" Rosen gripped the rough-textured wall as they blundered around a bend in the stairs.

The wide-mouthed Magnums of four members of the Senate Intelligence Committee's permanent security force pointed down into their faces. "Turn around and move down the stairs with your hands way up," growled a narrow-hipped, broad-shouldered blond man with a face like a bulldog. "If your hands drop—*you* drop!"

Otto shuffled around to descend, coughing gently behind his clenched lips.

Rosen stared past the security people. There was a door ten feet behind them with light squeezing past its edges. It should be the intelligence committee … but was it? Had he made a mistake in the confusion downstairs, lost his bearings?

"*Move it!*" Bulldog's growl deepened. His gun rose slowly past Rosen's chest to the center of his forehead.

Rosen's pulse roared in his ears. *Go for it,* he thought. *Go for it now!* "Charles Van Damme is a fraud and a traitor!" he shrieked over the heads of the startled security men. "A traitor to the United States … and a murderer! He stole the Indigo satellite. I can prove it. Van Damme is a traitor!"

The security men shuffled their feet, poking their weapons at Rosen but clearly not certain what to do. They were obviously unwilling to shoot down a suspect whose hands were high and in plain view, just for screaming.

"Stop that … and turn around!" Bulldog finally reacted. He sounded more like an annoyed schoolteacher than a hardened law enforcement officer. Bulldog chomped on his lower lip as his embarrassed eyes darted right to left to gauge his compatriots' reactions. He felt slightly relieved that, at least, no one was laughing outright. "This is the *last time* I tell you!"

"Van Damme is a traitor! I have the proof. Let me show the committee. I have the proof!" Rosen had never yelled so loudly. His throat was constricting from the strain, his voice hoarsening, his volume plummeting. Could they even hear through that door, which appeared more solid and impenetrable by the second …?

*   *   *

"What on earth is going on out there? Are we under attack?" Chairman Fenton broke off formal recordation of the vote as the indistinct shouts outside of the door escalated in volume. "You said that we were safe here, son." He pointed a bony finger at the security man. "Are we, or are we not?" Fenton was proud of his commanding question—not quite so proud of the wavering of his voice as he asked it.

Marion, Harkins, and Howard seemed to be weighing the pros and cons of plunging under the committee table as opposed to diving for the windows.

Only Senator Chase seemed more curious than frightened. His young ears were surely better.

And clearly so were Charles Van Damme's. He rose, fighting back the panic as he realized that that miserable, un-killable, tenacious specter of a human being—the analyst—was right outside the door! For the first time since he was a helpless child, Charles Van Damme felt as if the inner portion of his skull were contracting over his brain, reducing it to spinning disorder. Was this how ordinary people tried to cope every day? It was impossible. The brain had to have space in which to perform. His brain couldn't be squeezed and pressured and be expected to function. He fought back the confines of his skull, giving his brain the room that it needed. Ideas commenced flowing. Much better. He strode toward the squirming senators.

"Senators, this room is surrounded by well-armed security people." Van Damme waved his hand at the door behind without looking. Thank goodness he had control of his voice. It was as smooth and resonant as if he were inviting this ridiculous group to his house for dinner, perish the thought. "Obviously they have caught whoever is doing that insane screeching, so I don't see what there is to worry about. Why don't we just—" He heard a soft scraping behind him.

"*No!*" Van Damme spun toward the door, which was being slowly opened by the security man in the room as he drew his weapon.

"A traitor as the Director of Central Intelligence!" rang through clearly. "Yes, guard," Fenton croaked from his seat at the center of the committee table. "Why are you doing such a foolish thing? You could be putting us in grave danger, young man."

The stocky security man was unfazed. "Sir, if I'm going to protect you, I have to know what's going on out there so I won't be taken by surprise." He spoke calmly, never removing his eyes from the narrow opening.

Chase's eyes narrowed with curiosity. He rose and approached the door.

"Senator, I think that it would be a lot safer to return to your seat!" Van Damme's voice crackled through the stale air. "And I think that the guard would be well advised to *shut that door* for the safety of everyone in this room."

Chase smiled back insolently. "Wasn't that your name I just heard mentioned, Mr. Van Damme? Why would that be?" He tiptoed to catch a glimpse over the guard's head, but the young man with the gun held him back, still without removing his face from the crack.

"Sorry, Senator, but you've gotta stay out of my way here!"

Van Damme thrust a long finger over those still in their seats. "Guard, *close that door*! You are endangering every one of these senators."

"Yes." Harkins's voice rose, high and frail, to join Van Damme's. "*Close that door!*"

Marion joined the strident chorus. "Close it fuh God's sake. Ah'll have yo job fuh this!" He pounded a handkerchief the size of a small dishtowel against his freckled forehead with each drawn-out vowel.

"Are the people who are yelling armed?" Chase asked the security man.

"I don't know, Sir, but their hands are up. They look completely subdued."

"Would it be safe to invite them in?"

"Senator Chase, have you lost your mind? Chairman Fenton's voice was approaching falsetto.

"No, Senator." Chase approached the crack in the door a second time. This time the security man allowed him to tiptoe for a peek. "The two men I see are completely under the control of four of our security people and"—the young legislator pulled away from the door to face Fenton—"they apparently have come here to testify against Mr. Van Damme, at great personal sacrifice." Chase's large eyes sparkled zealously. "I think that they should be given a chance to be heard."

Van Damme hurled his arms toward the ceiling. "This is insane!"

"This *is* insine," echoed Senator Marion.

"Absolutely," chimed in Harkins, who squeezed his flaccid cheeks with rigid fingers.

"Are we supposed to confirm this man when two people on the other side of this very door are calling him a traitor?" Chase aimed his index finger at the opening, which had enlarged considerably during the past few moments.

"Traitor and a murderer!" penetrated the committee room so distinctly now that even the most senior senators had no trouble making out the words.

Fenton glared at Chase, about to make a telling point about the Junior Senator's distorted concept of protocol, when he suddenly took a careful look at the bright and determined young face, possibly for the first time since the youngster had joined his committee. *Why did he insist on fighting it?* Fenton asked himself. *Youth was the way of the future. Hell, Jerry, you're no better than old Chairman Hartley, when you were cutting your eyeteeth on foreign relations. Are you that afraid of giving up the reins of this one last remaining responsibility, now that your boys are senior partners of Fenton, Fenton & Smith ... and Mary Lou is gone? God, I hadn't realized—until just now. It's time, Jerry ... Time to let go. But do it easy, little by little ... so it doesn't hurt so much. Start now with this young Senator Chase ... who is only standing up for what he thinks is right.* Senator Jerrold Fenton shrugged apologetically toward Van Damme before turning toward young Chase. "All right, Senator." *That was a good start, Jerry. You always rubbed in the "junior" before,* he thought, commending himself. "If the security people can assure our safety, we will invite these 'witnesses' of yours in."

Chase talked to the back of the security man's head. "Open the door."

The man darted his head away from the partially open door, seeking confirmation from the Chairman while keeping his weapon trained on the activity outside.

"Let them in, young man," Fenton told him.

The security man rose and swung the door open. He called out, "Bring them up."

"You sure, McKelvey?" Bulldog stared up at the man at the door. His pugnaciuos face furrowed with uncertainty.

"I'm sure. Are they clean?"

"Yeah. No guns or nothing."

"Then bring 'em up."

"You heard him. Let's get up there. And no more screaming."

Surrounded by the four brawny security men, Rosen and Otto were trotted upward. The clomp of heavy soles reverberated and re-reverberated in the narrow corridor, sounding to those in the committee room above as if an entire platoon were entering.

As they passed through the chamber doorway, McKelvey spun with military precision and faced the senators. "Here they are, *Sir,*" he reported .

Fenton looked embarrassed: unsure what came next. Howard and Harkins backed away, gawking at Rosen and Otto as if their clothes concealed armed hand grenades. Chase scrutinized Rosen unabashedly. Marion and two others stood behind the long table, casting sidelong looks at the captives as they whispered among themselves. Van Damme stood erect and motionless to the left of the table.

Marion and the other two stopped their nervous chatter.

The Select Committee on Intelligence were clearly contemplating Rosen and Otto in fearful silence …

Chase moved forward, snapping the common paralysis. "Is it true that you have information about our conferee, Mr. Charles Van Damme, or is this just some nonsense to postpone your arrest? Wasting our time is not going to help you with whatever you already are guilty of, believe me, my friends."

The man's patronizing approach annoyed Rosen, but he looked like their most likely ally in this room full of fossils. "We have plenty to tell you about that man." Rosen's glare crackled across the small room like an unleashed bolt of pure electrical current.

Its recipient, Charles Van Damme, stared back. A vague smile curled his precise mustache.

"Then could you start by telling us what you have to do with the shooting going on in the Senate Corridor?" asked Chase calmly. Confirming murmurs came from the other Senators.

Rosen licked his lips while nodding. "Yes, four of Charles Van Damme's operations goons followed us into the corridor and threatened to kill us if we wouldn't leave with them. Then a man came out of the Old Senate Chamber, saying that he was FBI and Van Damme's men should drop their guns, but Van Damme's men shot him, and then other people—I'm not sure who—started firing at us from both ends of the corridor. Craig, Van Damme's head man, killed the policeman who was with us, and then Craig got shot—"

"Whoa!" The young Senator threw up two elegantly tanned hands. "Were you involved in all of this mayhem? I mean were you shooting too, or are you just the proverbial 'innocent victims'?"

Rosen struggled with his composure. What he wanted to do was take this squash-playing, Aspen-vacationing son of a bitch and break his Ivy League face.

"Yes, Senator, we are," Rosen said as sweetly as his frayed nerves would allow. "Look, I am a member of the CIA—an analyst—so please stop treating me as if I'm the enemy when I'm trying—"

"Yes, he is—or I should *was*—an analyst." Van Damme's rich baritone washed over the group near the door. "He is Arnold Rosen: murderer, madman, and traitor. We have been chasing him since his recent escape … from a *mental institution*. He is quite dangerous, gentlemen, having killed not only his wife and young children but at least six of my men. He is also totally and absolutely insane."

Marion and his companions contemplated Rosen with bulging eyes, while Howard and Harkins distanced themselves by backing hand over hand down the committee table. Chairman Fenton cocked his regal white head, squinting as if trying to peer past Rosen's skin to the core of his killer's soul. Even Rosen's hardened guards stiffened. Two raised their weapons higher up along his chest, two others sliding in to pin his arms. McKelvey's gun rose toward Otto's face. Even Chase's tan peaked.

"This man with me is Otto Gruhaber, the one that Van Damme lied about. Van Damme says Otto's in Europe—right now—selling Indigo to the Russians."

In unison, all heads in the room turned back toward the Chief of the European Division, like spectators at a tennis match.

"Of course he's here," Van Damme sniffed as if the point were too obvious for rebuttal. He scrutinized each of the senators' faces and then sighed. "My agency has brought so much attention to Mr. Gruhaber's defection that even the Russians have decided that it is politically infeasible to grant him asylum. In short, we forced them to scrap their plans to steal the Indigo II satellite. Now that he and Rosen have been cheated of their treasonous payday, we thought that they might come after me for revenge."

Mass muttering enveloped the committee chamber.

Van Damme cut it short as he quickly resumed. "Another possibility, which we have considered, is that the Russians sent these two back to kill me in retribution for exposing their duplicity and depriving them of billions more in our aid."

More intense muttering from the floor.

Van Damme raised his arms like a messiah as he glided toward the nervous legislators. "Gentlemen, be calm. It doesn't matter what the exact reasons are for these two traitors to be here. We will find that out when we … or should I say when the Federal Bureau of Investigation interrogates them. The point is …" Van Damme used his pause to see if he had them. He had them. "The point is that your fine security force must confine them until the proper authorities can arrest them. Believe me, we are dealing with a traitor and a remorseless multiple killer, and I do not consider it wise for any of you to allow yourselves to be endangered for *another* instant."

"Yes, he's right. Get them out of here!" shrilled a shaking Harkins.

"Yuh, take 'em down ta sucu'ty raht now!" chimed in Marion from well behind the committee table.

Howard and the others chorused their agreement.

Only Chase remained silent, watching carefully.

McKelvey nodded to Bulldog.

"C'mon," growled Bulldog to the other three. "Let's get 'em downstairs." He nudged Rosen's ribs with his Magnum's muzzle.

"I have proof that Gruhaber and I were there when Van Damme stole the Amphora plans!" Rosen yelled above the senators' voices. "It's in my pocket."

"Get going *now*!" This time Bulldog jammed the gun into his ribs.

"It's the records of our arrest by German police, all documented, and it means Van Damme lied about Gruhaber's defection *because Gruhaber was with Van Damme in Berlin at the time—*"

A vicious dig from Bulldog's gun cut Rosen off.

"Look for yourselves." Rosen raised his right elbow, exposing the area where the packet lay under his shirt, risking another blow from Bulldog.

"Now I see the picture." Van Damme's baritone was tinged with ironic humor. "This is how the Russian Communists plan to attack me." He strode toward Rosen. "Keep a close eye on him," Van Damme warned the surrounding security men. He gripped Rosen's shirt, tugging it from out of his waist, snatching at the plastic packet and yanking it from its taped mooring along Rosen's ribs.

The senators winced, collectively, as the tape crackled free.

Van Damme opened the package slowly, elaborately, protracting the drama as he meticulously perused sheet after sheet, slipping each neatly back before retrieving the next, finally hoisting his tight lips in revelation. "Ingenious…. What devils they are."

The senators craned their necks, waiting and barely seeming to breathe. Even the security people seemed to have forgotten what they were about.

"These," Van Damme waved the packet victoriously above his head, "are records of the KGB *and* the former East German security forces: the BND. Despite what the media tells us about the antipathy between formerly conquered territories and the Russians, I can assure you gentlemen that many of the former secret police in those areas still remain loyal to their old Russian masters. So the KGB and its puppet police in Germany have obviously concocted a neat little scam, to use the vernacular, to sabotage my efforts on behalf of our country. And they are using these two traitors"—he thrust the packet toward Rosen and Otto—"*as their surrogates*. Now, is that clever?" Van Damme shot the hand cupping the document packet upward, like a TV game host soliciting applause.

With the exception of Chase, the senators chimed in with, "Can you believe that?" and "How dare they?" and "The Russians haven't changed."

"You security people, take them away," said Van Damme.

Rosen arched his head forward. "Gruhaber stayed at the same hotel in Berlin as Van Damme—*at the same time*—for God's sake!"

"He dit not let me yooss my real name," Otto blurted miserably.

"Oh. How convenient," laughed Van Damme. "No record of the traitors having been there … except for the word of a murderer." He skewered McKelvey with his glare. "I *told* you to take them."

"The hotel *staff* would recognize him—"

Rosen received another vicious jolt from Bulldog's gun. The security man's rough hand clamped down upon his neck, squeezing until Rosen's eyes teared, as he maneuvered Rosen toward the doorway.

"That makes sense," Chase said quietly.

"What you talhkin' 'bout, son?" Marion's fleshy face screwed up as if he had just smelled old fish.

Chase turned and said, "I said it makes sense, Senator. If this Gruhaber fellow was there, he certainly looks unique enough to be recognized by the staff."

Chase turned to Rosen and Bulldog. "Let go of his neck."

"This is not wise, Senator Chase. He is very dangerous—"

"Thank you for your concern, Mr. Van Damme." Sarcasm oozed from around the edges of Chase's reply. "But Mr. Rosen has made a very good point. What hotel would that be, Mr. Rosen?"

Rosen shook his head free of Bulldog's loosening grip. "The Kempinski. One of the biggest—"

"I'm familiar with the Bristol Hotel Kempinski, Mr. Rosen. A very large, very prestigious hotel … where the staff pays *very* close attention to its guests. I'm sure that there would be people there who would recall if Mr. …"

"Gruhaber."

Chase acknowled Otto's contribution. "Thank you. If Mr. Gruhaber was a guest there."

"But I vuss in disguise." Otto pointed a shaking finger. "He told me it vould make me zaver from the Rooshians aftervards …" Otto's voice dissolved into brutal coughing.

"Oh, this gets better and better." Van Damme paced before the group like a trial attorney summarizing to his jury. "First," Van Damme snapped up a rigid index finger, "we can't establish his existence at the hotel by his name, because he uses an alias." The next finger joined its mate. "Then we cannot have a visual identification because he wore a disguise. Really, how much of this nonsense are you distinguished gentlemen willing to tolerate—"

"Van Damme met with Colonel Nikolai Kharkov, one of Alexi Yermakov's fanatical followers. As pro-communist as you can get. And was able to get his hands on a top secret Russian weapon. How was he able to do that *without offering something important in return?*"

"This maniac is raving mad. He's immensely dangerous and very devious. *I warn you!*" Van Damme's voice escalated a good octave and his swanlike neck developed a noticeable flush. "I can't be responsible if he isn't put somewhere where he can't hurt—"

"He traded the Indigo plans for the Amphora Missile!" shrilled Rosen. "*That's* how he got it. Ask him … What else could he possibly have promised Kharkov that would make a fanatical Communist, high ranking in the KGB and committed to helping Yermakov seize power, bring the plans for Russia's most secret weapon?"

The eyes of the room turned toward Charles Van Damme.

"This is insulting nonsense. Gentlemen, how can you subject me to the insane accusations of these two criminals? These aren't the kinds of witnesses that a Senate conferee—recommended by your President—should listen to. This is a disservice to the entire confirmation process. I am here to serve my country ... but there are limits."

Marion, Harkins, and Howard joined in, decrying what Howard called "egregious breach of protocol." Fenton and Chase, however, continued to stare in silence.

"How *did* you acquire the Amphora missile from a man like Alexi Kharkov, Mr. Van Damme?" Senator Jerrold Fenton asked. "Our committee certainly is aware of where he stood politically. He was a vicious, remorseless Communist from the word go."

"I offered him money. Money overcomes all political credos, Senator. Senator, I will not subject myself to much more of this."

"That would take a hell of a lot of money, Senator," Rosen called out. "We could check CIA to see if any large amounts were authorized. That would all have to be cleared in advance—"

"I took it from personal funds," countered Van Damme. Tension lines drew down the corners of his lips and eyes.

"It should be easy enough to check your personal bank withdrawals for that period." Chase smiled helpfully. "And I really have to say, it's an honor to meet someone who uses his *personal* funds in the country's interest. We don't see many true patriots anymore, Mr. Van Damme.

"The opportunity came up, and I thought that it would take too long to go through the official requisition process. I planned to subsequently apply for reimbursement, but as you know, with Kharkov's death, that became unnecessary."

Chase nodded. "Then you can also show us the Kharkov payoff was returned to your account?"

Van Damme dug his narrow fingers into the gap between his tight starched collar and his neck, tugging the shirt away from his feverish skin. "Yes. *Yes*, Senator Chase. *Yes*, I will."

Chase approached Van Damme, his boyish face open, ingenuous. "By the way, what type of payment did Kharkov expect? Cash ... gold? In what form do they like their bribes over there so that the government can't trace them? Or was he going to have you put it in a Swiss account or the Caymans or some other place like that?"

"Yes, that's right, that's right. An account like that—"

"Then we can also get the identifying numbers of the account, can't we?" Chase was quite close to Van Damme now.

Van Damme stepped backward, staring vaguely over the looping blond wave of Chase's hair. "Uh, yes, Senator." He willed his eyes to engage those of the young man. "We can get all of this done *after* we attend to those two criminals. Isn't that the first order of business?" Van Damme's voice fluttered uncharacteristically upward, forcing him to lower it every few words. "By the way"—Van Damme's forehead curled down—"I understand that your mother was taken ill?"

"She's fine." Chase dismissed Van Damme's concern with a wave of his hand. Light twinkled from the dancing facets of a large diamond on his fourth finger. He looked at Fenton, who nodded encouragingly. "So you could tell us in what account you were told to put the money?"

"If I can remember, Senator Chase!"

All eyes went to Van Damme's, which were starting to smolder. Even Marion struggled out of his chair, resting his paunch against the table as he sought a closer look.

Van Damme blinked mightily and then comprehension dawned. "Excuse me for shouting, Senators ... and *particularly* Senator Chase. I have been under some degree of stress between these hearings and, as you will recall, because I believe that those two criminals"—Van Damme pointed at Rosen and Otto with his long index finger—"have come here to kill me. I would appreciate a recess, if the Senators would be so kind."

Fenton looked around the room. "Well, I suppose that we could do that, if there is anywhere we can safely go."

"Ask him why he didn't have time to go through channels for Kharkov's bribe," Rosen said. "Ask him whether he wasn't in contact with Kharkov long enough before their Berlin meeting to requisition that money ten times over!"

"Uhhh ..." Fenton looked toward Rosen, then to Chase, his watery eyes clouded by indecision.

Chase had no such problem. "How long before your Berlin meeting had you been in contact with Colonel Kharkov, Mr. Van Damme?"

"Not long. Not long enough—"

"I can reconstruct evidence from a file that he stole from me— *murdering my whole family to do it*—which proves that he was dealing with Kharkov for between one and two years before their final meeting." Rosen received a gratuitous jab from Bulldog for his effort.

"Stop hitting that man!" Fenton admonished the security guard.

"Well, Mr. Van Damme." Chase's blond eyebrows screwed down upon his sleek nose. "Which is it: did you start scheming with Colonel Kharkov long in advance of your meeting or not? If Mr. Rosen over there can reconstruct evidence to the effect that you had previous contacts with the Colonel, then that certainly raises questions about your veracity. And while I'm not familiar with the details of this terrible incident regarding Mr. Rosen's family, if these allegations are true, then perhaps your relationship with Mr. Rosen is more complicated than you would want us to believe."

"Yah, yah. He iss a very bad man. I cahn tell you." Otto's strident voice penetrated the room, although he himself was nowhere to be seen behind his much taller captors.

Startled, the senators all turned, craning their necks to locate the source of this harangue.

Van Damme took advantage of the diversion to slip behind Chase, fling his left arm around the young senator's throat, and place a compact Automag .22 against his temple. "Get away from that door … *everybody!*" Van Damme used Chase's body to press past the security people and their two captives.

Unwilling to concede, Bulldog planted his feet, pushing against Van Damme and his human shield, but McKelvey warned the big man off. "Can't have anyone hurt, Willis," McKelvey said in his usual unruffled tone. "We'll get this all resolved and everyone'll be just fine, right, Mr. Van Damme?"

"Don't play your stupid psychology with me. Just order this man out of my way."

"You heard him, Willis." There would be no reasoning with the nominee for CIA director today. In spite of the situation, McKelvey found his characterization of the tall man holding Senator Chase by the throat amusing. *Make that* former *nominee,* he corrected himself. Even in the brief second when McKelvey's attention had turned inward toward this personal insight, Van Damme and his prisoner were already through the doorway.

"I am closing this." Van Damme swung the door shut with his gun hand before snapping the slender automatic back against Chase's head. Before anyone could move, the heavy paneled door swung shut with an emphatic slam. "If you even *try* to open it, I will kill the Senator," he shrilled, backing himself and Chase down the curving staircase.

Chapter 38

Charles Van Damme forced Senator Dan Chase down the narrow stairway, hissing threats into his captive's ear each time Chase resisted.

His skull was clamping down on his brain again, so he couldn't think. He hadn't been able to think for the past five minutes inside that horrible, stifling little room, ever since this spoiled kid senator started siding with that miserable Rosen. He should have killed Rosen—put a bullet right between those spiteful eyes—but he'd had to get out of that awful room. That room wanted to crush him, like his skull wanted to crush his brain! Now he *had* to get into the open, out of this claustrophobic corridor, so its narrow walls wouldn't squeeze him to death. Then his skull would stop pushing in so he could remember his message. He *had* to tell the world his message, but he had to do it out in the open, where he could think.

The stairs skewed right. He looked back up at the door. It was still closed.

"You can't get anywhere."

"No more from you." Van Damme drew the crook of his elbow tighter around Chase's neck, eliciting a choking cough. "I have heard as much as I ever want to hear from you. Is that *clear*?" Van Damme dug the muzzle into Chase's temple, twisting it.

"Yesss!" Chase screamed.

The corridor was clean, sparkly, almost sterile. *Do they wipe these walls down after every committee meeting? Who cares, Charles? Who cares? Get focused. You need to focus. Your message. You have a message.*

* * *

The Senate corridor was chaotic. Security people hustled from doorway to doorway, covering each other with jutting revolvers as they cautiously peeked through. Two bodies lay neatly inside the doorway of the Old Senate Chamber. Their ankles overlapped its marble frame, creating a minor hazard for those dashing by. To Van Damme's left, squalling senators poked their heads from the cloakroom, while two men in handcuffs marched from the minority leader's office in the custody of a trio of grim-faced Secret Service types.

Bodies were everywhere. There was Craig, sprawled out like a slab of bloody meat, for God's sake.

Must be my nerves, thought Van Damme. *Why am I so upset by a dead body? I've seen more than I can count.*

Why was everyone stopping? Why the hell were they all turning and staring? This wasn't the way he had planned it. He was supposed to walk Chase out to the rotunda, lose himself in that loud crowd milling behind the security people at the corridor's entrance, and slip out of the Capitol unnoticed. *Unnoticed*—that was the operative word here. So why was everybody in the place *noticing* him? Van Damme's eyes dipped momentarily. He caught an indistinct image of his right hand.

My God—the gun! I left the gun out, right against this fool's head. Didn't tuck it against his ribs, hide it, anything; it's just there against his head like a big red flag! My brain—what's happened to my brain?

"This is Senator Chase. If anyone comes any closer, I will shoot him!" Van Damme screamed at the corridor's immobilized occupants. He spun Chase side to side, demonstrating the Massachusetts Senator's predicament.

A young man in a security uniform approached. He was quickly warned off by his red-faced superior. "I'm Crowley," the latter said, "Chief of Security. We won't do anything. We just want to talk—"

"I don't want to talk to you; I want to talk to *them*—the people over there." Van Damme spun Chase toward the teeming Main Rotunda.

"All right, Sir, you can do that. We'll take you over to talk to them. Just put down your gun."

"I'm not putting down my gun, and I'm not letting this man go until I talk to the people of the United States. *And I will not talk about it anymore.*" Van Damme glared like a deadly petulant child.

"Yes, Sir, whatever you say. Let's just make way for the man. C'mon, let 'im through!" Crowley snapped at stunned law enforcement people blocking Van Damme's path to the rotunda. Decisive as he might have sounded on the outside, Crowley's mind was racing. *No way I can let this madman get into that bunch in the rotunda, even though it's there own goddamn fault for hanging around, them and their nosy little brats, instead of getting the hell out of there like they were told. Not a'tall.*

*   *   *

"He's getting away. Are you all just going to stand here?" Rosen surveyed the members of the committee, realizing how ludicrous a question he had just posed. They'd stay here until their precious senatorial asses were safe, even if it took until Christmas. "At least let *me* try to stop him," Rosen implored Fenton. "He killed my family, for God's sake."

Jerrold Fenton studied his hands. He was unable to deny this young man's desperate need yet equally unwilling to sanction further violence. *Weren't committee chairmen supposed to make decisions?* Fenton wondered. *You really are too old, aren't you, Jerry? It's probably a good time to give up the reins.*

"I'm not waiting. You want to stop me, shoot me. I don't give a damn!" Rosen elbowed aside Bulldog's Magnum and grabbed for the door. A second security man, holding Rosen's arm, dropped like a rock as Rosen's elbow jammed his solar plexus. Before the others could react, the door flew open and Rosen was hurtling down the stairs.

Bulldog two-handed his weapon through the doorway, sliding his feet into a shooter's stance, lowering the big muzzle toward the center of Rosen's back.

Fenton watched the security man in horror. "*Don't!*" he screamed.

"Willis." McKelvey's voice jolted the other. Bulldog's body sagged. With a whoosh of breath, he reluctantly watched his massive revolver arc downward until it pointed toward the floor.

*   *   *

Relief flooded Rosen's tension-bunched muscles as he cleared the corner of the stairs. Any moment, he had expected one or more very large bullets to rip through him. He lunged into the corridor, completely unprepared for what he saw.

Those standing were as motionless as the twisted bodies on the marble floor. It was a tableau of desperate activity, caught in freeze-frame. Everyone was clearly mesmerized by the specter of Charles Van Damme manhandling a senator past the doorways of US history.

The drama's principal players shuffled into a cone of natural light under the Senate Rotunda. They continued toward its vast counterpart: the mighty dome at the Capitol's center.

As Rosen searched for an avenue of attack, a gleam from above attracted his eye—a gun thrust between the small rotunda's tobacco leaf–crested columns toward Van Damme's back. Abandoning caution, Arnie Rosen sprinted toward his adversary.

*　　*　　*

Agent Wally Barnes clutched a pillar for support as he watched the gaunt man and his captive weave through the chaos beneath him. His pulse pounded from his throat to his temples. Oh, God, how had he gotten himself into this? And what on earth was he supposed to do now? Wally watched in horror as the capitol security people stepped aside, no doubt to spare the young Senator. That was who the gunman said he was, although Wally had been unable to hear the rest of the exchange. No one was going to do anything. No one was going to stop him. Good God, now they were passing right below him. Could Wally just pretend he wasn't here? Could he possibly just *do* that? His brilliant wife, Lisa, would say yes: "Yes, Wall, that's *exactly* what I want you to do. I don't want to be the widow of an FBI hero; I want to be the *wife* of a live accountant!" But what should he do? More people could die if the gunman got to the crowds in the Main Rotunda, and Wally was a law enforcement officer, regardless of how much he regretted having become one.

Wally Barnes circled the rotunda on tiptoe, following the pair's progress through his Colt's sight. My God, he could actually see vestiges of white where the perp's hair tint had missed. He died his hair. By God, what a depressingly intimate thing to know about the person you were going to shoot. His philosophical diversion nearly permitted the duo to pass beyond his field of fire. It was now or never.

Wally held his breath and slowly began squeezing, when the elongated face of the Senator's captor registered in his brain. Wally had seen it two nights ago, framed by his own television screen. My God, he was about to shoot *Charles Van Damme*! "Mr. Van Damme!" exploded from young Wally's lips before he considered the ramifications of his impetuousness.

Startled by the clamor overhead, Van Damme pivoted and fired on sheer reflex.

The young man above gaped in astonishment, then stiffened, toppling behind the rotunda columns like a shooting gallery duck.

Unfortunately, Van Damme had used his other hand to prop the .22's grip, allowing that sneaky little bastard Chase to break for the crowd at the rotunda. *Going to lie to those people so that they won't listen to my message, aren't you, Mr. Communist Lover?* "Like hell you will," Van Damme answered himself aloud. He locked his Automag on the back of Chase's bright blond head.

*   *   *

Rosen launched himself through the air, smashing headfirst into the tall man's spine, colored spots dancing in his eyes as he sprawled on the painfully hard marble four feet past Van Damme's outstretched body. He dazedly watched Van Damme's undulating fingers grope for the .22. Shaking out the dizziness, Rosen scrambled for Van Damme, flinging himself at the Division Chief's outstretched hand—too late.

Amazingly, Charles Van Damme's fingers did not grasp the weapon, raising it and emptying it into his assailant's face, as Rosen expected. Instead, Van Damme's hands crept along the floor until his spaghetti-like arms extended toward the entrance to the Main Rotunda, his flattened palms making a soft sucking sound against the marble as he writhed forward.

Rosen swiped at Van Damme's head, rolled him onto his back, fists ineffectually tattooing the hated face until he could straddle Van Damme's narrow chest and really go to town. There was no resistance. Rosen pulled back a bloody fist from within an inch of his enemy's crimson face.

Charles Van Damme's long hands swam vainly toward the crowded rotunda. The whites of his eyes were unnaturally distended, while dribble bubbled along his bloody lips as he muttered breathlessly from under his disheveled mustache.

Despite himself, Rosen bent to listen, although his instinct was to go on hitting and punching Van Damme until there was nothing left to hit. But who was this imposter beneath him? How could this be the murdering manipulator of world events and future Presidential hopeful: Charles Lucien Van Damme? How could it be? Rosen dropped his ear to Van Damme's feverishly working mouth, trying to sort substance from babble.

"Message," whined the unanimous nominee for Director of Central Intelligence, with the pleading eyes of a hungry puppy. "My message … I must tell them." Van Damme's tremulous hands supplicated Rosen and the suddenly silent spectators ringed by firmly planted security people, only steps away. "Glasnost Conspiracy.… We must be vigilant.… Watch out.… Watch the Russians.… Watch …"

<h1 style="text-align:center">CHAPTER 39</h1>

Rain from a heavy front off the Atlantic, ponderously rumbling down the eastern states, pelted the exclusive homes of Wesley Heights.

Large droplets smacked the window behind Rosen's head with startling ferocity, but he rocked on, oblivious to their determined patter. He stared at his bed.

Barbara's cousin, Barry Samuels, had attended to the funeral arrangements. It was held at the Meyer-Levitz Memorial Chapel, under the auspices of Rabbi Irwin Cantor, during Rosen's absence. The house had also been set right by Barry, well before Rosen's return, indicating to Rosen that at least his closest remaining relatives hadn't condemned him. This knowledge made their reunion, although painful, at least possible.

Aside from Samuels, Rosen's only contact with people—except for checkout clerks and gas station cashiers—were his hospital visits to Otto. The little guy had responded so brilliantly to whatever new strain of "myosin" was in vogue at the moment that he was pronounced fit to travel back to California, and his computer, by week's end. Rosen had begged off a farewell dinner. There was nothing for him to celebrate, although he did concede to Otto an unspecified future reunion.

Rosen finally gave up trying to superimpose Barbara's, Ellie's, and Jonathon's outlines against his pillows. His imagination wasn't up to it. *How ironic,* he thought. They, Topper, Marquand, and Amos—yes, even Hickey—were collateral damage in a defunct cold war.

His imagination *was* up to conjuring his last image of Charles Van Damme.

Sometime during the strapping on of a straitjacket over his immobile torso, Van Damme's vitality returned vigorously. Kicking and lashing his stilt-like legs, Van Damme not only managed to catch the Chief of Capitol Security squarely in the groin but also immobilized two white-clad orderlies long enough to run—tottering like top-heavy daddy longlegs—toward the Central Rotunda. While six security people tugged him back, Van Damme loudly informed legions of rubberneckers that a certain group of Russian Communists would bury the United States, both economically and militarily, unless they were denied future aid. Such lucid oration from an apparent madman unnerved the crowd more than if Van Damme had showered them with profanities.

All at once, it had dawned on Rosen that in his own obsessively paranoid fashion, Charles Van Damme considered himself a patriot of the first order. As the Chief of European Division was trundled off, spitting and snapping at the straps that compressed his almost nonexistent shoulders, Rosen had involuntarily paraphrased a long-forgotten acting axiom he once read, not in justification of the monster but out of tragic recognition of one of life's atrocious ironies: "No villain perceives himself to be a villain."

EPILOGUE

Captain Uri Grigov hummed to himself as the spotless metro car rocked gently along its track. Before he knew it, the four-stop trip from the Kremlin to fashionable Lenin Hills was over. Grigov painfully negotiated the steps of a tidy but unobtrusive structure that was dwarfed by the surrounding halls of Moscow University. As he neared the top, Grigov studied the now-famous plaque that fronted its entry. There had been a television close-up of it during a New York anchorman's half-hour special inside this very building earlier in the year. Grigov paused to savor the scent of new-mown grass, alien to his own fume-infested neighborhood, before entering.

An efficient young woman with severely cropped hair, dressed in a form-hugging pantsuit, led him up a carpeted stairway. The undulation of her tightly enshrouded cheeks distracted Grigov from his perpetually throbbing leg.

"A moment, Captain." She knocked gently on a tall door at the rear of the second floor. After briefly darting her head in, she held the door open for Grigov. "He will see you now." She was gone before he could thank her.

Grigov gingerly swung the door wider.

"Come in, come in," resounded from the interior. The very important man rose. "This is no time to be shy, Captain. You have performed a great service to your country. Today is a day to be *proud!*" The important man gestured toward a velvet chair with armrests. Stacks of source books and periodicals nearly obscured an IBM computer on his overflowing desk. A wall-length bookcase towered behind, filled to capacity with reference material. The comfortable but not overly large room was paneled in wood of medium hue, which glowed warmly in soft lamplight along its perimeter. Glittering summer leaves trembled behind arched windows that stood taller than Grigov. There was a lingering aroma of apple-scented tobacco, although the captain could not see a pipe anywhere.

The important man resettled his stocky body behind his desk. He watched his visitor with a mildly amused look. Apparently, he was waiting for Grigov to open the conversation.

"Had it not been for your help in locating Colonel Kharkov, we would have been too late, Sir," Grigov croaked.

"Nonsense. You're being too modest." Although the other's lips dismissed Grigov's praise, his eyes accepted it as his due. "And my congratulations to your lieutenant … Putin?"

"Yes, Sir." Grigov was relieved to shift the conversation from himself. "He was the one who was essential in keeping Rosen and Gruhaber alive and feeding them the information you ordered so that they could destroy Charles Van Damme. I have already commended him, even though he still won't cut off that silly ponytail of his."

"I suppose if someone is as efficient as Putin, even the military can allow for an idiosyncrasy or two," the very important man observed, straight-faced.

Grigov's attempt at levity had gone unnoticed—he wouldn't try again. "I am recommending Putin for posting to the KG—ah, the Ministry of Information, for advance training at a higher pay scale."

"Certainly. Certainly. Whatever you think." The other rocked back, cupping his hands behind his head and smiling at the ceiling.

Grigov was embarrassed by such an intimate gesture from one so high, but the other seemed determined to reflect upon their victory, and it wasn't Grigov's place to say otherwise.

"Yes, things could not have gone better. That dinosaur Yermakov will be tried for exposing state military secrets to the Americans through his criminal henchman, Kharkov. In fact, his treasonous act has discredited *all* extremists, including those fanatic fascistic Nationalists."

"So we are assured of a moderate government, which keeps the Western Capitalists and the rich Japanese happily investing in developing our natural resources and our industries."

"*Exactly.*"

The Captain bit his lower lip. Had the very important man frowned? *Why don't you let him do the talking, Grigov, you idiot?* It was so hard to track the man's moods.

"And that CIA criminal Van Damme's diatribes against us have been discredited now that he is institutionalized for life. What a far better solution than killing him." The man behind the desk compacted his bushy eyebrows against the bridge of his nose as he chortled. "Martyrs make bad enemies; lunatics don't."

Buoyed by the other's enthusiasm, Grigov opened his mouth to speak. An impatient frown from across the desk deflated him. Grigov snapped his jaw closed, waiting.

"Having this Van Damme brought down by his own Government was brilliant, Uri Ivanovich."

Grigov experienced a thrill at a time in his life when thrills were less and less frequent. The other had applied the familiar use of his middle name. An honor indeed.

"The Americans would have been positive that we set him up if our evidence against him was made public in Germany—or here in Moscow. This way, he was undone by his own system." The important man seemed about to break into outright laughter as he rocked back to an upright position, placed his palms upon the desk, nodding his head in self-absorbed delight. "Our people are happy because the United States cleaned its own dirty laundry—and forgave us for Yermakov's intrigues against them. Anti-US sentiment here, like anti-Russian propaganda there, would be counterproductive to our purpose."

"Yes. It is all going wonderfully well for us, isn't it?" Grigov felt safe that this show of support was sufficiently innocuous not to be regarded as an interruption.

"Best of all, Uri Ivanovich, the American Congress is so guilty— Americans can't live without feeling guilty about something—that their Democrats and Republicans are fighting over who can give us the most money." He rose and walked to a full decanter in a hollow on his bookshelf. "Some excellent port?" he asked, already pouring two glasses. He handed Grigov's across his desk.

Grigov noted that for all the problems that the other had endured during the past year, his hand was steady as a rock.

The very important man raised his glass. Window light glinted from his eyes. "Isn't it ironic? This criminal, Van Damme, has actually speeded up our return to power by possibly five years."

Grigov hoisted his glass. "I am so pleased for you and the other comrades that your plan will prevail—"

"If only I didn't have to play the docile fool in the meantime." The important man's grip tightened on his glass. He quaffed its contents.

Grigov winced. The Captain had never tasted a wine more worthy of unhurried appreciation. Nor was he ever likely to again.

"Well, it may be too late for me, but the Party will rule again!" The great man's empty crystal glass thudded down upon the desk.

Grigov barely breathed.

"If only those fools had been patient. I went along with Schevardnadze's resignation, replaced moderate ministers with conservatives, proved that I was willing to crack down if reform got out of hand—*but still the thick-headed old guard had to threaten my government if I didn't go back to the old ways!*" He shook his head, idly fingering a pair of reading glasses next to the computer. "We couldn't. The Soviet Union could no longer afford to survive. So Yeltsin and the reformers gained the upper hand." There was a hiss of escaping breath as the important man's shoulders sagged. "Now we've *all* lost control." He aimlessly raised his glasses toward the light filtering in from between the leaves outside his windows. Tiny specks of dust, illumined by the rays, swirled in never-ending motion. The glasses descended back to their original location near the computer. "Oh, those fools."

Grigov's hands explored the contours of his lap.

"A toast, Captain!"

Grigov's head jerked upright. The very important man's glass, mysteriously full again, glinted above his round head. Grigov's flew to emulate it.

"To the American who brought down Charles Van Damme. He may be our Party's greatest hero in times to come."

Grigov watched in fascination as a beam of light from his upraised glass reflected directly on the continent-shaped red birthmark upon his host's forehead.

They waited a few moments in silence. Then the important man said, "It has been a pleasure seeing you again, Captain," as he placed his empty glass near a stack of papers, reached for his reading glasses, and began thumbing through the four-inch-high pile.

Grigov took his cue. The meeting was at an end. He drained the last of the port, placed his glass on his side of the desk, rose, and left without another word from the very important man. That was the way of it. With people like this, you were lucky if you had the spotlight for a few moments before you were forgotten in the pressing issues that constantly surrounded them like buzzing bees. Grigov felt no animosity toward the important man as he slipped unnoticed from his office and his life, until, if ever, he was needed again.

There before him stood the young woman in the suit. Had she been waiting the whole time or had his host somehow summoned her without Grigov noticing? He had no explanation. As they descended the stairs, the buzz of the fine port that he had just finished diminished the magnitude of the usual pain in his leg. At the door, she handed him a large tan envelope. "He thought that you might like this." As the young woman held open the door, Grigov noticed that her smooth hand had no rings of any kind. He laughed to himself. *Who am I kidding? Even if she were interested—which she wasn't—this old timer is through with the young ones. As his unfaithful ballerina ex-wife twirled in the back of Grigov's brain, he bid the young woman good-bye.*

*   *   *

There in the softly rocking metro, savoring the sweet aftertaste of port that he would likely never sample again, Grigov opened the flap of the envelope. When his fingers made contact with the extremely smooth surface of its contents, he smiled, nodding as he withdrew the eight-by-ten glossy. It would be carefully framed and hung in the most prominent place that he could find in his small office, probably over his head, behind his desk, for anyone entering to see. The very important man, posing next to his still-attractive wife, smiled at Grigov. Below, in dense black marker ink, flowing script read, "With thanks for superior service to your country. Always, Mikhail Gorbachov."

About the Author

After attending Cornell University of Pennsylvania School of Law, Bob Reich was appointed as an Assistant Attorney General for the State of New York, during his tenure he wrote and lobbied for the passage of the first consumer protection laws ever enacted there. He then journeyed to California as Region Counsel for a major corporation, specializing in taxation. He then became involved in real estate syndication and development. For the past twenty-plus years, his company has advised clients in more than ten states in financial and retirement planning from his offices in South Florida. He resides in Ft. Lauderdale with his wife Mary and cat Furgie.

After fifty years of intensive skiing, Bob now relaxes by working out, practicing self-defense, bicycle riding and building historical dioramas.

www.ingramcontent.com/pod-product-compliance
Lightning Source LLC
Chambersburg PA
CBHW060757210726
48292CB00013B/214